The Best
AMERICAN
SHORT
STORIES
1999

GUEST EDITORS OF
THE BEST AMERICAN SHORT STORIES

1978 TED SOLOTAROFF
1979 JOYCE CAROL OATES
1980 STANLEY ELKIN
1981 HORTENSE CALISHER
1982 JOHN GARDNER
1983 ANNE TYLER
1984 JOHN UPDIKE
1985 GAIL GODWIN
1986 RAYMOND CARVER
1987 ANN BEATTIE
1988 MARK HELPRIN
1989 MARGARET ATWOOD
1990 RICHARD FORD
1991 ALICE ADAMS
1992 ROBERT STONE
1993 LOUISE ERDRICH
1994 TOBIAS WOLFF
1995 JANE SMILEY
1996 JOHN EDGAR WIDEMAN
1997 E. ANNIE PROULX
1998 GARRISON KEILLOR
1999 AMY TAN

The Best
AMERICAN
SHORT
STORIES
1999

Selected from
U.S. and Canadian Magazines
by AMY TAN
with KATRINA KENISON

With an Introduction by Amy Tan

HOUGHTON MIFFLIN COMPANY
BOSTON · NEW YORK   1999

ISSN 0067-6233
ISBN 0-395-92683-1
ISBN 0-395-92684-X (pbk.)

Printed in the United States of America

QUM 10 9 8 7 6 5 4 3 2 1

Contents

Foreword

As I reread the stories Amy Tan has chosen to include in the
1999 edition of *The Best American Short Stories* — the last volume of
the twentieth century — I could not help but wonder what Edward
O'Brien, the creator of this eighty-five-year-old series, would have to
say about the evolution of his brainchild were he able to hold this
book, directly descended from the first, in his hands.

Could he have imagined, as he sifted through the 2200 short
stories published in periodicals in 1914 and selected 20 for his first
collection of "bests," that his successors would be performing much
the same task, in much the same way, nearly a century later? Perhaps, in his fondest dreams. What no editor, no matter how pre-
scient, could have foreseen in 1915, however, was the dramatic
upheavals — technological, medical, social, and personal — that
would transform early twentieth-century life into something altogether different by century's end. Thus, tales of farm labor, tuber-
culosis, sailing ships, Bible-thumping preachers, and séances — all
favorite themes in the early volumes — would be supplanted in the
years to come by stories of urban ennui, AIDS, Web surfing, New
Age gurus, and twelve-step groups. In the course of this series'
history, the icehouse became a Sub-Zero, the horse and buggy an
SUV, the letter from overseas an e-mail message. The details, the
stuff of daily life, have changed, and the stuff of fiction changed
with them.

Yet I suspect that O'Brien would still embrace *The Best American
Short Stories 1999*. Though the world as he knew it has largely
disappeared, the spirit in which he read stories and encouraged

writers to write them is the very spirit that informs this series today. Underlying his decision to launch an annual anthology of short stories was his conviction that the American short story would continue to develop as an essential literary genre in its own right. "The truth is," O'Brien asserted, "that the American short story cannot be reduced to a literary formula, and if we are to measure its progress at all, it must be with a growing reed. . . . During the past few years, slowly and naturally as the budding and growth of a plant, a new spirit in fiction has been making itself felt and spreading itself in many directions throughout the country."

From this vantage point, looking back over a century that has produced such masters as Ernest Hemingway, Flannery O'Connor, John Cheever, and Eudora Welty — and, more recently, Joyce Carol Oates, Alice Munro, Tobias Wolff, Cynthia Ozick, and Andre Dubus, to name only a few — I think it is safe to say that the growing reed is now indeed a tree, distinguished by deep roots, a vast canopy of branches, and abundant fruit. In other words, Edward O'Brien had it right when he peered into the future and foresaw the blossoming of this beloved, and quintessentially American, form. So perhaps he would not have been surprised either that by century's end, the short story's staunch defenders, readers and writers alike, would have succeeded in turning this series into a literary institution in its own right, attracting hundreds of thousands of devoted readers each year.

In all but one or two cases, the contributors to *The Best American Short Stories 1915* are long since forgotten. Any illusions about the permanence of literary reputation are swiftly quelled by a look at the contents page of that inaugural volume. Donn Byrne, Virgil Jordan, Merton Lyon, Newbold Noyes, Katharine Metcalf Roof, Elsie Singmaster — whatever became of you? And yet, reading these authors' works, I found much to appreciate; their voices still speak with some urgency to anyone with the time and inclination to listen. The magazines from which the first volume was compiled have long since folded up their tents too, though their names still exert a pull on the imagination: *The Midland, The Outlook, The Masses, Everybody's Magazine, The Fabulist.* . . . In our era of brand names and niche publishing, which has given rise to such ventures as *Fast Company, Vegetarian Times,* and *Cigar Aficionado,* one can't help but feel a certain nostalgia for the democratic inclusiveness of that earlier age. Imagine trying to launch *Everybody's Magazine* today!

Nonetheless, in a century during which so much else has changed, the guiding spirit behind this annual collection has remained remarkably consistent. "Here and there in quiet places, usually far from great cities, artists are laboring quietly for a literary ideal, and the leaven of their achievement is becoming more and more impressive every day," O'Brien wrote in his first introduction. "It is my faith and hope that this annual volume of mine may do something toward disengaging the honest good from the meretricious mass of writing with which it is mingled." Thus was set an editorial direction that has not been questioned or superseded to this day.

In this volume you will find stories that meet that standard, some by writers already acclaimed for their vision, others by writers just at the beginning of their careers. These twenty-one stories were chosen not because they are clearly of this time, but on the chance that they also might transcend it. After all, the strivings and concerns of the human spirit are not circumscribed by time or place. While art may serve to point up our differences, it also reaches across vast distances of time and space to remind us of our common humanity. What's more, it outlasts us. Perhaps at the next century's end, some yet-to-be-born editor will pull *this* volume off a shelf and wonder about the authors whose works are gathered here: Lorrie Moore, Junot Díaz, Annie Proulx, Rick Bass, Melissa Hardy. . . . But then, perhaps, that editor, casting about for an idea for an end-of-the-century foreword, will settle in to read a story or two and be surprised to discover that although the world is a very different place than it was way back in 1999, there is something about those old stories. They hold up.

From the moment Amy Tan and I exchanged our first e-mail messages early in 1998, I knew how fortunate we were that she had agreed to assume the guest editor's duties this year. We quickly formed a book group of two, via the Internet, and happily kept each other apprised of our reading and discoveries throughout the year. Her desire to do justice to the year's harvest of short fiction was immediately apparent, as was her willingness to take a stand in the line of guest editors whose tastes and predilections have shaped this series for the past twenty years. Like all the best critics and readers, Amy Tan combines a highly developed sense of what works with a genuine desire to give every story the benefit of the doubt. In practical terms, that meant that she devoted a great deal of her time to this process, considering each and every story fully, and on its own terms, before making a judgment. As she notes in her introduction, when you love a particular story, it seems a sacrilege to attempt to describe it, to say what it's "about." Better simply to put it into someone else's hands and say, "Please read it yourself." As I placed this year's stories in Amy Tan's hands, I knew that the writers of 1998 were fortunate indeed to have her in their corner. The readers of this volume will be equally well served.

The stories chosen for this anthology were originally published in magazines issued between January 1998 and January 1999. The qualifications for selection are (1) original publication in nationally distributed American or Canadian periodicals; (2) publication in English by writers who are American or Canadian, or who have made the United States or Canada their home; (3) original publication as short stories (excerpts of novels are not knowingly considered). A list of magazines consulted for this volume appears at the back of the book. Editors who wish their short fiction to be considered for next year's edition should send their publications to Katrina Kenison, c/o The Best American Short Stories, Houghton Mifflin Company, 222 Berkeley Street, Boston, MA 02116.

K.K.

Introduction

FORTY YEARS AGO, just before I turned seven, my father started reading to me from a volume of 365 stories with an equal number of pages.

The stories were supposed to be read in sequence, a tale a day, beginning with a sledding caper on a snowy January first. They concerned the ongoing activities of children who lived in lovely two-story homes on a block lined with trees whose changing leaves reflected the seasons. They each had a father and a mother as well as two sets of grandparents, and these older folk conveyed simple truths while taking cookies from a hot oven or fish from a cold stream. Each day the children had small adventures with baby animals, balloons, or bicycles. They enjoyed nice surprises, got into small troubles, and had fun problems that they could solve. They made thingamajigs out of mud and stone and paint, which wound up being the prettiest ashtray Mommy and Daddy had ever received. Within each of those five-hundred-word stories, the children learned a valuable lifelong lesson, which they promised never to forget.

By the middle of the book, I had learned to read well enough to finish a book in one day. And being impatient to learn what happened to the children in the rest of the year, I polished off the remaining stories in one sitting. On the last day of the year, the children went sledding again, completing the happy circle. Thus, I discovered that those children, between January first and December thirty-first, had not changed much.

I was glad, for that was the same year I accumulated many worries, which I numbered on my fingers. One was for the new home we had moved to, the fifth of more than a dozen I would occupy during my childhood. Two was for the dead rat crushed in a trap, which my father showed me, believing that this would assure me that the rat was no longer lurking in my bedroom. Three was my playmate, whom I saw lying in a coffin while my mother whispered, "This what happen when you don't listen to Mother." Four was for the operation I had, which made me think I had not listened to my mother. Five was for the ghost of my playmate who wanted me to come live with her. Six was for my mother telling me that when she was my age her mother had died, and the same sad fate might happen to me if I didn't appreciate her more. Eventually, I ran out of fingers.

That year, I believed that if I could make sense of my worries, I could make them stop. And when I couldn't, I would walk to the library. I went there often. I would choose my own books. And I would read and read, a story a day.

That girl from forty years ago has served as your guest editor for *The Best American Short Stories 1999*. I felt I should tell you about my earliest literary influences, because I'm aware that if you scan the table of contents, you might suspect that I have been reactionary in my choices. You may wonder if they are a vote against homogeneity, a vote for diversity in preordered proportions.

This collection holds no such political agenda. The stories I have chosen are simply those I loved above all others given to me for consideration. This is not to say that my literary judgment is without personal bias. I am a particular sort of reader, shaped by all kinds of influences — one of them being those bedtime stories of long ago, for I still do most of my reading in bed.

I also now realize that I dearly loved those stories. In fact, I regret that I finished them so quickly that my father no longer had to read them aloud to me each night, for what I loved most was listening to his voice. And what I love most in these twenty-one stories is the same thing. It is the voice of the storyteller.

At the beginning of 1998, the year these stories first appeared in magazines, I found myself in an airport lounge in Seoul, waiting for a connecting flight to Beijing. For reading material, I had brought with me *The Best American Short Stories 1992*, the volume whose guest editor was Robert Stone. I remember settling in with a cup of ginseng tea, then glancing up and seeing, with a shock of recognition, a woman who seemed like a younger version of me. She was Asian, I would guess even Chinese American, and she was with a husband who looked quite similar to mine in height and build and coloring. But more striking than these superficial similarities was what she held in her hands: the same teal-blue volume of *The Best American Short Stories.*

Did she notice me as well? She gave no indication that she did. Meanwhile, I had an urge to run up to her and ask all kinds of questions. Was she a writer? What story was she reading? Why had she picked this book to bring on a long flight to Asia?

But I remembered those times my mother used to embarrass me as a child, going up to strangers in public places just because they happened to look Chinese. So I stayed put, reading from my book, then wondering how she could not notice me, our similarity. After all, it wasn't as though we were reading the same blockbuster novel of the year. It wasn't a travel book on Asia. It wasn't even the most recent volume of *The Best American Short Stories.* So what was it about our lives, our tastes, our choices that had brought us to this literary meeting point in Seoul?

Shortly after I returned home, I was asked to serve as guest editor of *The Best American Short Stories 1999.* And from October 1998 until February 1999, I read stories, manna from heaven, or wherever it is that Katrina Kenison makes her home. And after I had made my selections and sat down to write this introduction, I thought about that woman at the airport. I wondered if she would one day read the stories in this volume and find compatibility with my choices. Or would she pose the hard-nosed literary question "Huh?"

That is the response I sometimes have after seeing certain movies or plays that others have raved about. In fact, my husband and I have friends we have long associated with a particular film, *Babette's Feast.* We recalled their saying it was subtle and unpretentious, artless in the way pure art should be. So we went to see it. Huh? We found it tedious, interminable. And so we avoided any future recommendations for movies by these same friends.

Babette's Feast had me thinking the other day that the same avoidance principles might apply to people who take on the role of literary arbiter for others — reviewers, critics, panels for prizes, and yes, even guest editors. Such people may have an eye for literary conventions and contrivances, allusions and innovations on the art.

But what are their tastes based on? What are their biases? Is part of it the common prejudice in the arts that anything that is popular is by default devoid of value? Do they tend to choose work that most resembles their own? Perhaps those critics who publicly declare "this is good and that is not" ought to present a list of more than just the titles of their most recently published works.

I, for one, would like a résumé of habits, a précis of personality. What movies would they watch twice? Do they make clever and snide remarks, but mostly about people who are doing better than they? When recounting conversations, do they imitate other people's voices? When sharing a meal with friends, do they offer to pick up the tab, split the bill evenly, or portion it out according to what they ordered and how little wine they drank? When a friend of theirs has suffered a terrible loss, do they immediately call or wait until things have settled down a bit? What are their most frequent complaints in life? What do they tend to exaggerate? What do they downplay? Do they think little dogs are adorable or appetizers for big dogs? And, of course, I would want to know the names of books they love and loathe and why.

In other words, if you ran into this person at a party, would you even like him or her? I am being only half facetious. I do think the answers would say something about a person's sensibility regarding life and human nature, and hence his or her sensibility regarding stories, beyond the surface of craft. I think the stories we love to read may very well have to do with our emotional obsessions, the circuitry between our brain and our heart, the questions we thought about as children that we still think about, whether they are about the endurance of love, the fears that unite us, the acceptance of irreversible decay, or the ties that bind that turn out to be illusory. In that context, I also think that if *Babette's Feast* was your all-time favorite film, then you might not like the stories I picked.

Anyway, for the woman at the airport, for our friends whose taste in movies serves as a reverse indicator, and for anyone now taking a flyer on my judgment, I want to reveal what kind of tastes I developed between the stories I read forty years ago and the stories I read this year.

As a worrisome child, I developed an osmotic imagination, and I loved fairy tales for their richness in the grotesque. I read them all:

Hans Christian Andersen, the Brothers Grimm, Aesop's Fables, Little Red Riding Hood — whatever was on the library shelf, a book a day, many of them devoured at bedtime, which my mother said is why I ruined my eyes and had to wear glasses at such a young age.

Because my father was a part-time Baptist minister, I also read Bible stories, which I thought were quite similar to fairy tales, for they too contained gory images, gut-clenching danger, magical places, and a sense that things are never as they first appear. By the end of these stories, much had always changed. Kingdoms and seas rose and fell. Humble creatures turned into handsome princes or prophets. Straw became gold, a crumb a thousand loaves. And a lot of bearded giants lost their heads.

I loved these stories because, along with the horrific, they contained limitless and amazing ways in which people, places, and circumstances changed. It gave me a sense of instability, distrust, and wonder that mirrored my own life. I remember a particular Halloween, being lost on a dark street, then finally seeing my mother, her red swing coat. I flew toward her, hugging the back of her coat, crying for joy because I was no longer lost, only to see a stranger's startled face looking down at me. As a child, I thought it was a kind of terrifying magic that my mother transformed into a woman with blond hair. She changed quickly in other ways as well. Sometimes she was happy with me, the next moment disappointed, wild with anger. And in her eyes, I too had changed, and she was ashamed beyond belief that I had strange, bad ingredients inside me that neither she or I had suspected were there until my awful behavior had leaked out like a stench. And I would wonder, who am I really? A fairy? An evil sprite? A good princess in the temporary form of a rotten Chinese girl?

With fairy tales, you could immerse your imagination like your big toe in a tub of hot water and retract it if it didn't agree with you. Part of the thrill was seeing what you could take, guessing what might happen, delighting if you were surprised, decrying if you were unfairly fooled. Kind creatures turned into genies. People who died, fell down holes, or became lost later might be transformed into happier beings. They could wind up in lands that nobody else knew existed. In stories, you could hide or escape.

Since my father was a minister and my mother a believer in bad fate, I used to wonder: What are the reasons that catastrophe happens? Is calamity a lesson, a curse, or a test? Is it a punishment for evil? Does it occur because of blind luck or blind revenge? Or does it simply happen for reasons we can never know or would not want to know? I was a child who rode a whirligig of questions and flew out in all directions.

Whatever the case, I was addicted to stories about the morbid: the beheadings, the stonings, the man who was three days dead and already stank when he came back to life. These were people with fates worse than mine. So far, at least. But just in case, I wanted to prepare for other dangers that might still await me.

Around this same time, I discovered a book at home that was also useful to me in this regard. It was a medical textbook my mother was studying so she could become a licensed vocational nurse. The textbook concerned medical anomalies. Inside were descriptions and photographs of people with acromegaly, elephantiasis, hirsutism, leprosy, and superfluous or missing appendages — all kinds of deformities that vied with *Ripley's Believe It or Not* for open-jawed disbelief.

I tried to imagine the lives of these people, how they felt, their thoughts as they stared back at me from the photographs. I imagined them before they had their disease. I imagined them cured. I imagined taking them to school and all the kids screaming in terror, while I alone remained calm, a true friend. I imagined them changing into genies, princes, and immortals. I imagined I might become just like them, now plagued and miserable, soon to be transformed into someone else. These people were my imaginary playmates. Their consciousness, I believed, was mine. And those notions, I think, were among the first stories I made up for myself.

Like many children, I read to be scared witless, to be less lonely, to believe in other possibilities. But we all become different readers in how we respond to books, why we need them, what we take from them. We become different in the questions that arise as we read, in the answers that we find, in the degree of satisfaction or unease we feel with those answers. We differ in what we begin to consider about the real world and the imaginary one. We differ in what we think we can know — or would want to know — and in how we continue to pursue that knowledge.

One story can be a different story in the hands of a different reader.

I believe that now, although in college I allowed myself to believe otherwise. Back then, I believed good taste was an opinion held by others — namely, the designated experts. I was an English major, and I remember that in my sophomore year I wrote a theme paper (as they were then called) on Hemingway's *The Sun Also Rises.* I thought the story was well written, but I did not like it much: the cynicism, the fact that by the end of the story the characters had not changed, which was the point, but one that I did not find interesting. I said so in my theme paper, and the following week my professor chose to read it aloud. He said it was remarkably different from the rest of the papers he had read in all his years of teaching. I blushed, thinking this was high praise. And then he started to read my sentences in a tone that became increasingly less benign. Soon his face was livid as he gasped after each of my paragraphs: "Who is *this* writer to criticize Hemingway, the greatest American writer of our century? *This* writer is an idiot! This novel deserves a better reader!" If *this* writer had had the means, she would have killed herself on the spot.

The following year, I was in another English class at another college, and the same novel was assigned. This time I wrote a theme paper that noted the brilliant characterization — how, despite the panorama of events and the opportunities afforded these characters, nothing much had changed in their lives, and how this so convincingly captured the realism of ennui. It represented the pervasive American sense of a lost generation whose lives, singly or together, held no hope or direction. My paper received high praise.

By the time I graduated, I was sick of reading literary fiction. My osmotic imagination had changed into one with filters, lint traps. I thought that literary tastes were an established norm that depended on knowing what others more expert than I thought was best.

For the next twelve years, I read an occasional novel. But I did not return to my habit of reading a story a day until 1985. By then I had become a successful but unhappy person, with work that was lucrative but meaningless. This was one of those moments that cause people to either join a religious cult, spend a lot of money on psychotherapy, or take up the less drastic and more economical practice of writing fiction.

Since I was a beginning writer, I believed that the short form was the easier one to tackle. It was the IRS approach to writing: use the short form if you have less to account for and the standard amount to withhold. Perusing a remainders table at my local bookstore, I picked up *The Best American Short Stories 1983*, the volume edited by Anne Tyler. Well, I was raised by a Chinese mother who taught me to aim high. This was the book for me, the best. With suggestions from my more literary-minded friends, I also began reading short story collections, and the ones I targeted first were by women — Flannery O'Connor, Eudora Welty, Lorrie Moore, Amy Hempel, Alice Adams, Jamaica Kincaid, Louise Erdrich, Jane Smiley, Mary Robison, Molly Giles, Alice Munro, Mary Hood, Ann Beattie. Of course, I also read fiction by men — John Updike, Gabriel García-Márquez, Donald Barthelme, Raymond Carver, Richard Ford, Ethan Canin, Lee Abbot, Tobias Wolff, Chekhov, Flaubert, and even Hemingway, whom I reread with new appreciation but mostly for his clean prose style. But I was particularly interested in fiction by women, because almost all the literary works I had read as an English major had been written by men, the one exception being those by Virginia Woolf. I discovered that stories by women included more stories about women, and I was startled to read, for the first time perhaps since *Jane Eyre*, voices that felt so intimate, that brought up questions, ambiguities, and contradictions common among us, yet I had not seen them expressed elsewhere.

Being a new writer, I was also intrigued by the craft of it, the art of the short story. I joined a writers' group. I think that is where I ceased being a typical reader. I started looking at the parts and not just the whole story, which is a terrible habit, in a way. It's like being Dr. Frankenstein, seeing how life can be created from previously inanimate parts. The Dr. Frankenstein in me would sometimes act as cosmetic surgeon, determining where the excess fat of the story was, how a little lift here, a tuck there could improve the whole. But what did I really know about the essence and bliss of the story? After all, hadn't another writer in the group criticized my work for its garrulity, its needless blather?

As a beginning writer and reader, I was still trying to figure out what qualified as a proper short story versus a prose poem, an anecdote, a character piece, a novella. I actually thought there were agreed-upon answers to questions like these: What is voice? What is story? Does voice determine story or vice versa? How should characters develop? What are the elements of a good ending? What are the virtues of short stories in general?

Along with these big abstract questions, I had pragmatic worries over craft. Why do so many writers these days use the present tense? Is it supposed to sound like dispassionate stage directions? What are the pros and cons of using first person, third person, or, for that matter, second person? Should the narrative follow a chronological sequence? Or is it more admired (that is, more intelligent-looking) to jump around, fracture it up a bit, so it resembles more realistically the way our poor memories actually work?

Then there was this: What is the existential meaning of the big white space between paragraphs? What is being said by not being said?

I truly thought that expert answers to these questions would help me become a better writer. I remember thinking that if someone could help me deconstruct the stories, figure out what works, I could then use those principles, tried and true and judged the best, to methodically write my own stories.

So I read piles and piles of short stories in those early years of learning to write. And I confess that with some stories I would arrive at the end with that same sense of epistemological wonder I have with depressing Swedish films: "Huh?" In other words, sometimes I just didn't get it. And this led me to believe that my former professor was right: I was missing some finer aesthetic sense. Perhaps I was too much of a realist and did not understand abstractions and fragments. Or perhaps the problem was that I was a romanticist, and certainly not a postmodernist, or whatever it was or was not that also made me unable to appreciate, say, a dollop of paint on a white canvas in a museum of modern art. Maybe I didn't get the stories because I was trying too hard to understand them. I was trying to analyze them instead of just reading them, experiencing them for all the many ways that art can appeal.

Of course, I did get some stories right away, too soon, too handily, with a herald of French horns and a boink on the head. They were weighted with epiphany, beginnings and endings that resonated too neatly or were boldfaced with the import of hindsight.

And with other stories, I noticed a trend of sorts — the ending that, like those bedtime stories of my childhood, showed that nothing much changed between the first page and the last. The stories concerned ordinary people doing ordinary things with just a bit of inner unease, and an omniscient narrator who provided the precise details that proved their lives were moving at glacial speed. They were a Chekhovian type of tale, except that they took place in more ordinary places and were about more mundane moments. Or perhaps they weren't Chekhovian after all, since Chekhov always included some casually observed detail at the end that made the whole story transcendent, whereas these stories sort of petered out, as if they had run out of energy. But wasn't that like life itself, or *The Sun Also Rises* — this realism of ennui? Maybe that was the effect the writers were going for. Either that or I just didn't get them.

Whatever the case, ennui was the arty way I ended one of the first short stories I wrote. I sent it off as an application to my first writers' workshop at the Squaw Valley Community of Writers. When my manuscript came up for critique, Elizabeth Tallent, my assigned leader, asked me in front of eleven other writers why my story ended with a bank of fog rolling over the coastal mountains as the narrator is headed for the airport. Naturally, I could not say to a *New Yorker* writer that the deadline for submission was May 15 and I had run out of time and ideas as well as interest. So I said the fog was a metaphor for confusion, which it was: mine.

I experienced more fog in my reading and writing. But by continuing to read and write, I gradually changed. It was not through deconstruction. It was through an awareness that each writer has a different consciousness, an attentiveness, inventiveness, and relationship to the world, both real and fictional. I discovered that the short story is a distillation of the personality of a whole world. The way a particular writer chooses to experience, edit, and express that is a matter of taste. And what I liked to read was not necessarily what I wanted to write. In fact, my reasons for writing had to do with what wasn't yet there.

I became a much better reader and, I think as a consequence, a better short story writer, or so I thought. In 1988, I completed my first work of fiction, *The Joy Luck Club,* which I wrote as a collection of short stories. When the book went out into the world, however, the reviewers called it a novel.

Last October, I was having an awful time writing my fourth novel when the first batch of forty stories, photocopies of tearsheets, arrived in the mail for my consideration. Naturally, I worried that my bad writing might affect my reading. Conversely, I worried that reading excellent stories would depress me and further undermine my writing. I worried that my fluctuating estrogen levels would impair the consistency of my judgment. I worried that I would overlook a masterpiece and that everyone, including my former professor, would gasp with rage: "Who is *this* writer to ignore our country's greatest writer?" I am still the same worrier I was as a child. I still try to sort out my worries, categorize them, organize them, find possible solutions to contain them or make them go away. And they still sit in my brain like a blood clot waiting to dissipate or explode.

I decided to set up a process that woud enable me to be as fair as possible. With a hundred and twenty stories to read over four months, that worked out to a story a day, quite doable and also the correct way to go about this, I thought. If I read too many stories at once, I might be comparing them one to the other for the wrong reasons. So I decided I would read one story each evening, while sitting in bed. To ensure that I was not susceptible to distractions, such as a ringing phone or my dogs barking at ghosts, I would wear headphones and listen to an environmental tape of rainfall. Per the series editor's recommendation, I would read the stories blind — that is, with the names of the writers and magazines blacked out. Using this method, I would keep an open ear. I would not be swayed by whether the writer was male or female, new or well established, or of a racial background that one could check on a marketing survey. Not that I would have such specious biases, but why worry that they might creep up unconsciously?

After a week, I worried about other biases. That by listening to rain, I was apt to choose only stories set in stormy weather, overlooking those with more sun-baked settings. That on days when my mind was cluttered with crisis, the stories I read were either better or worse than they really were.

At times, I also found myself trying to scratch beneath the surface and guess who the writer might be. I was a kid before Christmas, shaking the gifts to see if I could tell what was inside. I believed that certain writers' voices were as distinctive as fingerprints, and I had detected six of them (I was wrong in half the cases). And if I couldn't guess their names, I thought I could at least figure out their gender. But then I looked back at a pile of stories I had already read, and when I tried to discern what traits might be marked more male or female, I found that in most cases, my hunches were based only on whether the narrator was a man or a woman (and later this proved half the time to be a flawed way to guess).

So I broke nearly all the rules, or tried to. My proposed schedule to read a story a day? That lasted one day. Some rainy weekends I could not stop myself from reading five or six at a sitting. It was like eating a box of truffles. The next week I might go days without reading a single one, caught up in my own work.

But one rule I did abide by, and it was one I did not set for myself initially. I wound up reading each story from start to finish without interruption, so that I could sense its rhythm. For me, the rhythm is in the beats of the first sentence, in the way the story's pulse quickens or evens, lulls or leaps. And by the end, the story breathes and exhales with a certain tempo and force, as do I, depending on how I feel about the story. The act of reading has qualities similar to those of meditation, aerobic exercise, lovemaking. Disruptions can cause me to lose the story's focus or its essence, and at the very least its momentum. For that reason, I feel the short story is more akin to a poem than a novel in how it should be read. Its overall effect on me depends on my breathing along from beginning to end.

I kept this principle while reading in bed, on the plane, in doctors' waiting rooms, on long car rides in all those places where most people take time to read a short story in a magazine. But if I fell asleep before finishing a story, when I awoke I started that story from the beginning. If the nurse said the doctor was ready to see me before I was ready, I started the story again after my appointment. And in January, like fifty million other people suffering from holiday bloat, I joined a gym and took these stories along. There I discovered that this is where much of the magazine reading of America goes on in compressed blocks of time. If I did not finish a story within the twenty-five minutes I was programmed to be on the undulating machine, I kept pumping and sweating until I read the last word. Thus, between reading the first and the last story, I discovered that good fiction can change you in beneficial ways. I lost five pounds.

I also found that reading short stories helped my writing. It sprang me out of the doldrums, and I had the same fervor and compulsion toward writing that I had had when I started reading massive amounts of fiction back in 1985. By reading so many stories, so many voices, I unleashed what propelled me to write fiction in the first place: finding my own voice and telling my own story. As in conversation, one story begets another.

But what a curious experience, to read so many stories in a concentrated period of time, grabbing them in no particular order, for randomness in fiction can generate its own cosmic connections. A story about a dying parent would be followed by another story about a dying parent, a difficult mother by another difficult mother. Pizza Huts and Domino's Pizzas popped up in clusters like mushrooms after rain, as did references to the color cranberry and barking dogs, tourists in India and people falling under ice, reunions after sexual indiscretions and alcohol-addled sons. There were also many, many thoughts before dying. Bound together, they might be a codex on the collective unconscious. Or is that just a result of the kind of person I am? I tend to connect the dots and find patterns. The patterns, of course, could be meaningless. In any case, in reading the stories together, I was conscious that certain ones had similar images and circumstances, and some appealed to me much more than others.

In many of the hundred and twenty stories, I also found elements of fairy tales, the grotesque. Here is where an actual bias does come in. I was delighted to find these qualities, stunned that so many stories had them — not so much in the structure, but in the imagery: the underground worlds, a woman stumbling upon a much darker version of Snow White and the Seven Dwarfs, a secret place that no one else knows exists, ghosts in the attic, a tractor that talks. I saw a similar fairy tale quality in how characters transformed: the narrator discovers that others are not who they appear to be. The change occurs not through the wave of a wand, however, but through death or danger or despair.

There was one other worry I had as a reader. I looked at the stories I had placed in my pile of favorites. Many had an exotic flavor to them. Either the narrators were ethnic or the settings were outside America. I could imagine readers smugly nodding and saying, "Well, of course she would pick those, mm-hmm." I then looked at the larger pile of stories I had already decided to eliminate. Many of those had exotic settings and ethnic narrators as well.

And then I noticed there were a fair number of stories in both piles about hunters and cowboys and gritty-teethed people living in remote parts of North America. So what was it about me that would account for that? I guess I am the kind of reader who has less of a fondness for the ordinary. Maybe I'm still that kid who wants to see things I've never seen before. I like being startled by images I never could have conjured up myself.

By their nature, these were stories with distinctive voices, voices with interesting things to say. I imagine that was why certain magazine editors chose them in the first place. Having read a hundred and twenty stories, I know how quickly stories can blur into sameness and fall away from memory. The splendid ones are left standing. But in the end, only the vivid remain. Different does not always equal vivid, but the converse is certainly true.

For those hoping I might make some observations on the demographics of this collection and its significance to literary trends or diversity in American culture or the year 1998, I am sorry to disappoint. I don't think most literary fiction writers deliberately set out to write stories that are topical or representative. Great stories resist generalizations and categories. For me even to try to guess at how the subconsciouses of twenty-one writers followed certain patterns would be presumptuous, and I would likely be wrong. And think how embarrassing it would be if I ran into these writers at a literary seminar.

So I will leave it to the writers themselves to tell you what their intentions might have been, if they choose to reveal them.

So why do I think these stories are the best? What do they say about my tastes? Will they find harmony with yours, the woman in Seoul, my friends with the movie recommendations?

I love stories that have strong storytelling qualities. By this, I mean the kind of stories that have a narrative thread pulled taut by tensions, and this leads to some thought or emotion or clear-eyed perception. In each of these stories, when I reached the last page, I felt a change. I did not say, "Huh?" But the stories did not present their endings with the clang of gongs either. There is nothing preening or preachy about these stories. Rather, by the end, each story quietly but perceptibly lifted itself and me out of our skins. I'm not saying that every story was uplifting like a birthday balloon let go. The weightlessness was sometimes more akin to a bed of static, a sudden loss of gravity, a tiny aphid tumbled upward by wind. Sometimes this began to occur in the last few paragraphs. In certain instances, it was the last sentence. But always by the end I found myself suspended just a moment longer by a sense of wonder over the story's ability to make me feel what I felt. Every single story in this collection did that for me.

I am also an ardent admirer of prose style. That does not mean that I always want it to be as fancy as Humbert Humbert's, though *Lolita* does count as a favorite of mine for language. Whether seemingly simple or fancy, the prose I like is one in which everything is there for a reason — every word, every image, every bit of dialogue, is needed, adds, builds — and its dexterity is also, in a way, transparent. Yet it has a generosity to it. There's no skimpiness. That's the craft part of it for me. While the prose may seem offhand and effortless, it is imbued with a particular intelligence and purpose. That higher sense permeates the story, and only when you leave the story at the end do you realize how palpably it is still felt. All the stories here gave me that sensation.

What I look for most in a story, what I crave, what I found in these twenty-one, is a distinctive voice that tells a story only that voice can tell. The voice is not simply the language, the prose style, the imagery. It is that ineffable combination of life and lore that creates a triangulated relationship among the narrator, the reader, and the fictional world. It may have an intimacy or a distance, a certain degree of trustworthiness or edginess. The voice is this hour's guide to eternity and will immerse me in a particular consciousness, which observes some nuances of human nature and overlooks others. It is the keeper of forgiveness and condemnation. It will order perception and juxtapose events and rearrange time, then deliver me back to my consciousness slightly off-balance.

By the end of the story, what I've witnessed and experienced as a reader is so interesting, so intense, so transcendent that if someone were to ask me what the story is about, I would not be able to distill it into an easy answer. It would be a sacrilege for me to say it is about survival or hope or the endlessness of love. The whole story is what the story is about, and there is no shorthanding it. I can only say, Please read it yourself.

If this collection holds a common thread with regard to my tastes, it is what I think the best of fiction is by its nature and its virtues. It can enlarge us by helping us notice small details in life. It can remind us to distrust absolute truths, to dismiss clichés, to both desire and fear stillness, to see the world freshly from closer up or farther away, with a sense of mystery or acceptance, discontent or hope, all the while remembering that there are so many possibilities, and this is only one.

The best stories do change us. They help us live interesting lives.

AMY TAN

The Best
AMERICAN
SHORT
STORIES
1999

RICK BASS

The Hermit's Story

FROM THE PARIS REVIEW

AN ICE STORM, following seven days of snow; the vast fields and
drifts of snow turning to sheets of glazed ice that shine and shimmer blue in the moonlight, as if the color is being fabricated not by
the bending and absorption of light but by some chemical reaction
within the glossy ice; as if the source of all blueness lies somewhere
up here in the north — the core of it beneath one of those frozen
fields; as if blue is a thing that emerges, in some parts of the world,
from the soil itself, after the sun goes down.

Blue creeping up fissures and cracks from depths of several hundred feet; blue working its way up through the gleaming ribs of
Ann's buried dogs; blue trailing like smoke from the dogs' empty
eye sockets and nostrils — blue rising like smoke from chimneys
until it reaches the surface and spreads laterally and becomes en-
tombed, or trapped — but still alive, and smoky — within those
moonstruck fields of ice.

Blue like a scent trapped in the ice, waiting for some soft release,
some thawing, so that it can continue spreading.

It's Thanksgiving. Susan and I are over at Ann and Roger's house
for dinner. The storm has knocked out all the power down in town
— it's a clear, cold, starry night, and if you were to climb one of the
mountains on snowshoes and look forty miles south toward where
town lies, instead of seeing the usual small scatterings of light —
like fallen stars, stars sunken to the bottom of a lake, but still
glowing — you would see nothing but darkness — a bowl of silence
and darkness in balance for once with the mountains up here,
rather than opposing or complementing our darkness, our peace.

As it is, we do not climb up on snowshoes to look down at the dark town — the power lines dragged down by the clutches of ice — but can tell instead just by the way there is no faint glow over the mountains to the south that the power is out: that this Thanksgiving, life for those in town is the same as it always is for us in the mountains, and it is a good feeling, a familial one, coming on the holiday as it does — though doubtless too the townspeople are feeling less snug and cozy about it than we are.

We've got our lanterns and candles burning. A fire's going in the stove, as it will all winter long and into the spring. Ann's dogs are asleep in their straw nests, breathing in that same blue light that is being exhaled from the skeletons of their ancestors just beneath and all around them. There is the faint, good smell of cold-storage meat — slabs and slabs of it — coming from down in the basement, and we have just finished off an entire chocolate pie and three bottles of wine. Roger, who does not know how to read, is examining the empty bottles, trying to read some of the words on the labels. He recognizes the words *the* and *in* and *USA*. It may be that he will never learn to read — that he will be unable to — but we are in no rush, and — unlike his power lifting — he has all of his life in which to accomplish this. I for one believe that he will learn it.

Ann has a story for us. It's about one of the few clients she's ever had, a fellow named Gray Owl, up in Canada, who owned half a dozen speckled German shorthaired pointers and who hired Ann to train them all at once. It was twenty years ago, she says — her last good job.

She worked the dogs all summer and into the autumn, and finally had them ready for field trials. She took them back up to Gray Owl — way up in Saskatchewan — driving all day and night in her old truck, which was old even then, with dogs piled up on top of each other, sleeping and snoring: dogs on her lap, dogs on the seat, dogs on the floorboard. How strange it is to think that most of us can count on one hand the number of people we know who are doing what they most want to do for a living. They invariably have about them a kind of wildness and calmness both, possessing somewhat the grace of animals that are fitted intricately and polished into this world. An academic such as myself might refer to it as a kind of biological confidence. Certainly I think another word for it could be *peace.*

Ann was taking the dogs up there to show Gray Owl how to work them: how to take advantage of their newly found talents. She could be a sculptor or some other kind of artist, in that she speaks of her work as if the dogs are rough blocks of stone whose internal form exists already and is waiting only to be chiseled free and then released by her, beautiful, into the world.

Basically, in six months the dogs had been transformed from gangling, bouncing puppies into six raging geniuses, and she needed to show their owner how to control them, or rather, how to work with them. Which characteristics to nurture, which ones to discourage. With all dogs, Ann said, there was a tendency, upon their leaving her tutelage — unlike a work of art set in stone or paint — for a kind of chitinous encrustation to set in, a sort of oxidation, upon the dogs leaving her hands and being returned to someone less knowledgeable and passionate, less committed than she. It was as if there were a tendency in the world for the dogs' greatness to disappear back into the stone.

So she went up there to give both the dogs and Gray Owl a check-out session. She drove with the heater on and the window down; the cold Canadian air was invigorating, cleaner, farther north. She could smell the scent of the fir and spruce, and the damp alder and cottonwood leaves beneath the many feet of snow. We laughed at her when she said it, but she told us that up in Canada she could taste the fish in the streams as she drove alongside creeks and rivers.

She listened to the only radio station she could pick up as she drove, but it was a good one. She got to Gray Owl's around midnight. He had a little guest cabin but had not heated it for her, uncertain as to the day of her arrival, so she and the six dogs slept together on a cold mattress beneath mounds of elk hides: their last night together. She had brought a box of quail with which to work the dogs, and she built a small fire in the stove and set the box of quail next to it.

The quail muttered and cheeped all night and the stove popped and hissed and Ann and the dogs slept for twelve hours straight, as if submerged in another time, or as if everyone else in the world were submerged in time — encased in stone — and as if she and the dogs were pioneers, or survivors of some kind: upright and exploring the present, alive in the world, free of that strange chitin.

She spent a week up there, showing Gray Owl how his dogs worked. She said he scarcely recognized them afield, and that it took a few days just for him to get over his amazement. They worked the dogs both individually and, as Gray Owl came to understand and appreciate what Ann had crafted, in groups. They traveled across snowy hills on snowshoes, the sky the color of snow, so that often it was like moving through a dream, and except for the rasp of the snowshoes beneath them, and the pull of gravity, they might have believed they had ascended into some sky-place where all the world was snow.

They worked into the wind — north — whenever they could. Ann would carry birds in a pouch over her shoulder — much as a woman might carry a purse — and from time to time would fling a startled bird out into that dreary, icy snowscape — and the quail would fly off with great haste, a dark feathered buzz bomb disappearing quickly into the teeth of cold, and then Gray Owl and Ann and the dog, or dogs, would go find it, following it by scent only, as always.

Snot icicles would be hanging from the dogs' nostrils. They would always find the bird. The dog, or dogs, would point it, at which point Gray Owl or Ann would step forward and flush it — the beleaguered bird would leap into the sky again — and then once more they would push on after it, pursuing that bird toward the horizon as if driving it with a whip. Whenever the bird wheeled and flew downwind, they'd quarter away from it, then get a mile or so downwind from it and push it back north.

When the quail finally became too exhausted to fly, Ann would pick it up from beneath the dogs' noses as they held point staunchly, put the tired bird in her game bag and replace it with a fresh one, and off they'd go again. They carried their lunch in Gray Owl's day pack, as well as emergency supplies — a tent and some dry clothes — in case they should become lost, and around noon each day (they could rarely see the sun, only an eternal ice-white haze, so that they relied instead only on their rhythms within) they would stop and make a pot of tea on the sputtering little gas stove. Sometimes one or two of the quail would die from exposure, and they would cook that on the stove and eat it out there in the tundra, tossing the feathers up into the wind as if to launch one more flight and feeding the head, guts, and feet to the dogs.

Perhaps seen from above their tracks would have seemed aimless and wandering rather than with the purpose, the focus that was

burning hot in both their and the dogs' hearts — perhaps someone viewing the tracks could have discerned the pattern, or perhaps not — but it did not matter, for their tracks — the patterns,
direction, and tracing of them — were obscured by the drifting
snow, sometimes within minutes after they were laid down.

Toward the end of the week, Ann said, they were finally running
all six dogs at once, like a herd of silent wild horses through all that
snow, and as she would be going home the next day, there was no
need to conserve any of the birds she had brought, and she was
turning them loose several at a time: birds flying in all directions;
the dogs, as ever, tracking them to the ends of the earth.

It was almost a whiteout that last day, and it was hard to keep
track of all the dogs. Ann was sweating from the exertion as well as
the tension of trying to keep an eye on, and evaluate, each dog —
the sweat was freezing on her in places, so that it was as if she were
developing an ice skin. She jokingly told Gray Owl that next time
she was going to try to find a client who lived in Arizona, or even
South America. Gray Owl smiled and then told her that they were
lost, but no matter, the storm would clear in a day or two.

They knew it was getting near dusk — there was a faint dulling to
the sheer whiteness, a kind of increasing heaviness in the air, a new
density to the faint light around them — and the dogs slipped in
and out of sight, working just at the edges of their vision.

The temperature was dropping as the north wind increased —
"No question about which way south is; we'll turn around and walk
south for three hours, and if we don't find a road, we'll make
camp," Gray Owl said — and now the dogs were coming back with
frozen quail held gingerly in their mouths, for once the birds were
dead, they were allowed to retrieve them, though the dogs must
have been puzzled that there had been no shots. Ann said she fired
a few rounds of the cap pistol into the air to make the dogs think
she had hit those birds. Surely they believed she was a goddess.

They turned and headed south — Ann with a bag of frozen birds
over her shoulder, and the dogs, knowing that the hunt was over
now, all around them, once again like a team of horses in harness,
though wild and prancy.

After an hour of increasing discomfort — Ann's and Gray Owl's
hands and feet numb, and ice beginning to form on the dogs' paws,
so that the dogs were having to high-step — they came in day's last

light to the edge of a wide clearing: a terrain that was remarkable and soothing for its lack of hills. It was a frozen lake, which meant — said Gray Owl — they had drifted west (or perhaps east) by as much as ten miles.

Ann said that Gray Owl looked tired and old and guilty, as would any host who had caused his guest some unasked-for inconvenience. They knelt down and began massaging the dogs' paws and then lit the little stove and held each dog's foot, one at a time, over the tiny blue flame to help it thaw out.

Gray Owl walked out to the edge of the lake ice and kicked at it with his foot, hoping to find fresh water beneath for the dogs; if they ate too much snow, especially after working so hard, they'd get violent diarrhea and might then become too weak to continue home the next day, or the next, or whenever the storm quit.

Ann said she could barely see Gray Owl's outline through the swirling snow, even though he was less than twenty yards away. He kicked once at the sheet of ice, the vast plate of it, with his heel, then disappeared below the ice.

Ann wanted to believe that she had blinked and lost sight of him, or that a gust of snow had swept past and hidden him, but it had been too fast, too total: she knew that the lake had swallowed him. She was sorry for Gray Owl, she said, and worried for his dogs — afraid they would try to follow his scent down into the icy lake, and be lost as well — but what she was most upset about, she said — to be perfectly honest — was that Gray Owl had been wearing the little day pack with the tent and emergency rations. She had it in her mind to try to save Gray Owl, and to try to keep the dogs from going through the ice, but if he drowned, she was going to have to figure out how to try to get that day pack off of the drowned man and set up the wet tent in the blizzard on the snowy prairie and then crawl inside and survive. She would have to go into the water naked, so that when she came back out — if she came back out — she would have dry clothes to put on.

The dogs came galloping up, seeming as large as deer or elk in that dim landscape, against which there was nothing else to give them perspective, and Ann whoaed them right at the lake's edge, where they stopped immediately, as if they had suddenly been cast with a sheet of ice.

Ann knew they would stay there forever, or until she released them, and it troubled her to think that if she drowned, they too would die — that they would stand there motionless, as she had commanded them, for as long as they could, until at some point — days later, perhaps — they would lie down, trembling with exhaustion — they might lick at some snow, for moisture — but that then the snows would cover them, and still they would remain there, chins resting on their front paws, staring straight ahead and unseeing into the storm, wondering where the scent of her had gone.

Ann eased out onto the ice. She followed the tracks until she came to the jagged hole in the ice through which Gray Owl had plunged. She was almost half again lighter than he, but she could feel the ice crackling beneath her own feet. It sounded different too, in a way she could not place — it did not have the squeaky, percussive resonance of the lake-ice back home — and she wondered if Canadian ice froze differently or just sounded different.

She got down on all fours and crept closer to the hole. It was right at dusk. She peered down into the hole and dimly saw Gray Owl standing down there, waving his arms at her. He did not appear to be swimming. Slowly, she took one glove off and eased her bare hand down into the hole. She could find no water, and tentatively, she reached deeper.

Gray Owl's hand found hers and he pulled her down in. Ice broke as she fell, but he caught her in his arms. She could smell the wood smoke in his jacket from the alder he burned in his cabin. There was no water at all, and it was warm beneath the ice.

"This happens a lot more than people realize," he said. "It's not really a phenomenon; it's just what happens. A cold snap comes in October, freezes a skin of ice over the lake — it's got to be a shallow one, almost a marsh. Then a snowfall comes, insulating the ice. The lake drains in fall and winter — percolates down through the soil" — he stamped the spongy ground beneath them — "but the ice up top remains. And nobody ever knows any differently. People look out at the surface and think, *Aha, a frozen lake.*" Gray Owl laughed.

"Did you know it would be like this?" Ann asked.

"No," he said. "I was looking for water. I just got lucky."

Ann walked back to shore beneath the ice to fetch her stove and to release the dogs from their whoa command. The dry lake was only about eight feet deep, but it grew shallow quickly closer to shore, so that Ann had to crouch to keep from bumping her head

on the overhead ice, and then crawl; and then there was only space
to wriggle, and to emerge she had to break the ice above her by
bumping and then battering it with her head and elbows, like the
struggles of some embryonic hatchling; and when she stood up,
waist-deep amid sparkling shards of ice — it was nighttime now —
the dogs barked ferociously at her, but remained where she had
ordered them to stay, and she was surprised at how far off course
she was when she climbed out; she had traveled only twenty feet,
but already the dogs were twice that far away from her. She knew
humans had a poorly evolved, almost nonexistent sense of direction, but this error — over such a short distance — shocked her. It
was as if there were in us a thing — an impulse, a catalyst — that
denies our ever going straight to another thing. Like dogs working
left and right into the wind, she thought, before converging on the
scent.

Except that the dogs would not get lost, while she could easily
imagine herself and Gray Owl getting lost beneath the lake, walking
in circles forever, unable to find even the simplest of things: the
shore.

She gathered the stove and dogs. She was tempted to try to go
back in the way she had come out — it seemed so easy — but considered the consequences of getting lost in the other direction, and
instead followed her original tracks out to where Gray Owl had first
dropped through the ice. It was true night now, and the blizzard
was still blowing hard, plastering snow and ice around her face like
a mask. The dogs did not want to go down into the hole, so she
lowered them to Gray Owl and then climbed gratefully back down
into the warmth herself.

The air was a thing of its own — recognizable as air, and breath-
able, as such, but with a taste and odor, an essence, unlike any other
air they'd ever breathed. It had a different density to it, so that
smaller, shallower breaths were required; there was very much the
feeling that if they breathed in too much of the strange, dense air,
they would drown.

They wanted to explore the lake, and were thirsty, but it felt like a
victory simply to be warm — or rather, not cold — and they were so
exhausted that instead they made pallets out of the dead marsh
grass that rustled around their ankles, and they slept curled up on
the tiniest of hammocks, to keep from getting damp in the pockets
and puddles of dampness that still lingered here and there.

All eight of them slept as if in a nest, heads and arms draped across other ribs and hips, and it was, said Ann, the best and deepest sleep she'd ever had — the sleep of hounds, the sleep of childhood — and how long they slept, she never knew, for she wasn't sure, later, how much of their subsequent time they spent wandering beneath the lake, and then up on the prairie, homeward again — but when they awoke, it was still night, or night once more, and clearing, with bright stars visible through the porthole, their point of embarkation; and even from beneath the ice, in certain places where, for whatever reasons — temperature, oxygen content, wind scour — the ice was clear rather than glazed, they could see the spangling of stars, though more dimly; and strangely, rather than seeming to distance them from the stars, this phenomenon seemed to pull them closer, as if they were up in the stars, traveling the Milky Way, or as if the stars were embedded in the ice.

It was very cold outside — up above — and there was a steady stream, a current like a river, of the night's colder, heavier air plunging down through their porthole, as if trying to fill the empty lake with that frozen air — but there was also the hot muck of the earth's massive respirations breathing out warmth and being trapped and protected beneath that ice, so that there were warm currents doing battle with the lone cold current.

The result was that it was breezy down there, and the dogs' noses twitched in their sleep as the images brought by these scents painted themselves across their sleeping brains in the language we call dreams but which, for the dogs, and perhaps for us, was reality: the scent of an owl *real*, not a dream; the scent of bear, cattail, willow, loon, *real*, even though they were sleeping, and even though those things were not visible, only over the next horizon.

The ice was contracting, groaning and cracking and squeaking up tighter, shrinking beneath the great cold — a concussive, grinding sound, as if giants were walking across the ice above — and it was this sound that had awakened them. They snuggled in warmer among the rattly dried yellowing grasses and listened to the tremendous clashings, as if they were safe beneath the sea and were watching waves of starlight sweeping across their hiding place; or as if they were in some place, some position, where they could watch mountains being born.

After a while the moon came up and washed out the stars. The light was blue and silver and seemed, Ann said, to be like a living

thing. It filled the sheet of ice just above their heads with a shimmering cobalt light, which again rippled as if the ice were moving,
rather than the earth itself, with the moon tracking it — and like
deer drawn by gravity getting up in the night to feed for an hour or
so before settling back in, Gray Owl and Ann and the dogs rose
from their nests of straw and began to travel.

"You didn't — you know — *engage?*" Susan asks: a little mischie-
vously, and a little proprietary, perhaps.

Ann shakes her head. "It was too cold," she says. I sneak a glance
at Roger but cannot read his expression. Is he in love with her?
Does she own his heart?

"But you would have, if it hadn't been so cold, right?" Susan asks,
and Ann shrugs.

"He was an old man — in his fifties — and the dogs were around.
But yeah, there was something about it that made me think of . . .
those things," she says, careful and precise as ever.

"I would have done it anyway," Susan says. "Even if it was cold,
and even if he was a hundred."

"We walked a long way," Ann says, eager to change the subject.
"The air was damp down there, and whenever we'd get chilled,
we'd stop and make a little fire out of a bundle of dry cattails."
There were little pockets and puddles of swamp gas pooled here
and there, she said, and sometimes a spark from the cattails would
ignite one of those, and all around these little pockets of gas would
light up like when you toss gas on a fire — these little explosions of
brilliance, like flashbulbs, marsh pockets igniting like falling dominoes, or like children playing hopscotch — until a large-enough
flash-pocket was reached — sometimes thirty or forty yards away
from them, by this point — that the puff of flame would blow a
chimney-hole through the ice, venting the other pockets, and the
fires would crackle out, the scent of grass smoke sweet in their
lungs, and they could feel gusts of warmth from the little flickering
fires, and currents of the colder, heavier air sliding down through
the new vent-holes and pooling around their ankles. The moonlight would strafe down through those rents in the ice, and shards
of moon-ice would be glittering and spinning like diamond-motes
in those newly vented columns of moonlight; and they pushed on,
still lost, but so alive.

The mini-explosions were fun, but they frightened the dogs, and
so Ann and Gray Owl lit twisted bundles of cattails and used them

for torches to light their way, rather than building warming fires, though occasionally they would still pass through a pocket of methane and a stray ember would fall from their torches, and the whole chain of fire and light would begin again, culminating once more with a vent-hole being blown open and shards of glittering ice tumbling down into their lair . . .

What would it have looked like, seen from above — the orange blurrings of their wandering trail beneath the ice; and what would the sheet of lake-ice itself have looked like that night — throbbing with the ice-bound, subterranean blue and orange light of moon and fire? But again, there was no one to view the spectacle: only the travelers themselves, and they had no perspective, no vantage or loft from which to view or judge themselves. They were simply pushing on from one fire to the next, carrying their tiny torches. The beauty in front of them was enough.

They knew they were getting near a shore — the southern shore, they hoped, as they followed the glazed moon's lure above — when the dogs began to encounter shore birds that had somehow found their way beneath the ice through small fissures and rifts and were taking refuge in the cattails. Small winter birds — juncos, nuthatches, chickadees — skittered away from the smoky approach of their torches; only a few late-migrating (or winter-trapped) snipe held tight and steadfast, and the dogs began to race ahead of Gray Owl and Ann, working these familiar scents — blue and silver ghost-shadows of dog-muscle weaving ahead through slants of moonlight.

The dogs emitted the odor of adrenaline when they worked, Ann said — a scent like damp fresh-cut green hay — and with nowhere to vent, the odor was dense and thick around them, so that Ann wondered if it too might be flammable, like the methane — if in the dogs' passions they might literally immolate themselves.

They followed the dogs closely with their torches. The ceiling was low — about eight feet, as if in a regular room — so that the tips of their torches' flames seared the ice above them, leaving a drip behind them and transforming the milky, almost opaque cobalt and orange ice behind them, wherever they passed, into wandering ribbons of clear ice, translucent to the sky — a script of flame, or buried flame, ice-bound flame — and they hurried to keep up with the dogs.

Now the dogs had the snipe surrounded, as Ann told it, and one by one the dogs went on point, each dog freezing as it pointed to the birds' hiding places, and it was the strangest scene yet, Ann said, seeming surely underwater; and Gray Owl moved in to flush the birds, which launched themselves with vigor against the roof of the ice above, fluttering like bats; but the snipe were too small, not powerful enough to break through those frozen four inches of water (though they could fly four thousand miles to South America each year and then back to Canada six months later — is freedom a lateral component, or a vertical one?), and as Gray Owl kicked at the clumps of frost-bent cattails where the snipe were hiding and they burst into flight, only to hit their heads on the ice above them, they came tumbling back down, raining limp and unconscious back to their soft grassy nests.

The dogs began retrieving them, carrying them gingerly, delicately — not preferring the taste of snipe, which ate only earthworms — and Ann and Gray Owl gathered the tiny birds from the dogs, placed them in their pockets, and continued on to the shore, chasing that moon, the ceiling lowering to six feet, then four, then to a crawlspace, and after they had bashed their way out (with elbows, fists, and forearms) and stepped back out into the frigid air, they tucked the still-unconscious snipe into little crooks in branches, up against the trunks of trees and off the ground, out of harm's way, and passed on, south — as if late in their own migration — while the snipe rested, warm and terrified and heart-fluttering, but saved, for now, against the trunks of those trees.

Long after Ann and Gray Owl and the pack of dogs had passed through, the birds would awaken, their bright dark eyes luminous in the moonlight, and the first sight they would see would be the frozen marsh before them, with its chain of still-steaming vent-holes stretching back across all the way to the other shore. Perhaps these were birds that had been unable to migrate owing to injuries, or some genetic absence. Perhaps they had tried to migrate in the past but had found either their winter habitat destroyed or the path down there so fragmented and fraught with danger that it made more sense — to these few birds — to ignore the tuggings of the stars and seasons and instead to try to carve out new lives, new ways of being, even in such a stark and severe landscape: or rather, in a stark and severe period — knowing that lushness and bounty were still retained within that landscape. That it was only a phase; that better days would come. That in fact (the snipe knowing these things with their blood, ten-million-years-in-the-world), the austere times were the very thing, the very imbalance, that would summon the resurrection of that frozen richness within the soil — if indeed that richness, that magic, that hope, did still exist beneath the ice and snow. Spring would come like its own green fire, if only the injured ones could hold on.

And what would the snipe think or remember, upon reawakening and finding themselves still in that desolate position, desolate place and time, but still alive, and with hope?

Would it seem to them that a thing like grace had passed through, as they slept — that a slender winding river of it had passed through and rewarded them for their faith and endurance?

Believing, stubbornly, that that green land beneath them would blossom once more. Maybe not soon; but again.

If the snipe survived, they would be among the first to see it. Perhaps they believed that the pack of dogs, and Gray Owl's and Ann's advancing torches, had only been one of winter's dreams. Even with the proof — the scribings — of grace's passage before them — the vent-holes still steaming — perhaps they believed it was only one of winter's dreams.

It would be curious to tally how many times any or all of us reject, or fail to observe, moments of grace. Another way in which I think Susan and I differ from most of the anarchists and militia members up here is that we believe there is still green fire in the hearts of our citizens, beneath this long snowy winter — beneath the chitin of the insipid. That there is still something beneath the surface: that our souls and spirits are still of more worth, more value, than the glassine, latticed ice-structures visible only now at the surface of things. We still believe there's something down there beneath us, as a country. Not that we're better than other countries, by any means, but that we're luckier. That ribbons of grace are still passing through and around us — even now, and for whatever reasons, certainly unbeknownst to us, and certainly undeserved, unearned.

Gray Owl, Ann, and the dogs headed south for half a day until they reached the snow-scoured road on which they'd parked. The road looked different, Ann said, buried beneath snowdrifts, and they didn't know whether to turn east or west. The dogs chose west, and so Gray Owl and Ann followed them. Two hours later they were back at their truck, and that night they were back at Gray Owl's cabin; by the next night Ann was home again. She says that even now she still sometimes has dreams about being beneath the ice — about living beneath the ice — and that it seems to her as if she was down there for much longer than a day and a night; that instead she might have been gone for years.

It was twenty years ago, when it happened. Gray Owl has since died, and all those dogs are dead now too. She is the only one who still carries — in the flesh, at any rate — the memory of that passage.

Ann would never discuss such a thing, but I suspect that it, that one day and night, helped give her a model for what things were like for her dogs when they were hunting and when they went on point: how the world must have appeared to them when they were in that trance, that blue zone, where the odors of things wrote their images across the dogs' hot brainpans. A zone where sight, and the appearance of things — *surfaces* — disappeared, and where instead their essence — the heat molecules of scent — was revealed, illuminated, circumscribed, possessed.

I suspect that she holds that knowledge — the memory of that one day and night — especially since she is now the sole possessor — as tightly, and securely, as one might clench some bright small gem in one's fist: not a gem given to one by some favored or beloved individual but, even more valuable, some gem found while out on a walk — perhaps by happenstance, or perhaps by some unavoidable rhythm of fate — and hence containing great magic, great strength.

Such is the nature of the kinds of people living, scattered here and there, in this valley.

JUNOT DÍAZ

The Sun, the Moon, the Stars

FROM THE NEW YORKER

I'M NOT a bad guy. I know how that sounds — defensive, unscru-
pulous — but it's true. I'm like everybody else: weak, full of mistakes, but basically good. Magdalena disagrees. She considers me a
typical Dominican man: a *sucio,* an asshole. See, many months ago,
when Magda was still my girl, when I didn't have to be careful about
almost everything, I cheated on her with this chick who had tons of
eighties freestyle hair. Didn't tell Magda about it, either. You know
how it is. A smelly bone like that, better off buried in the back yard
of your life. Magda only found out because homegirl wrote her a
fucking *letter.* And the letter had *details.* Shit you wouldn't even tell
your boys drunk.

The thing is, that particular bit of stupidity had been over for
months. Me and Magda were on an upswing. We weren't as distant
as we'd been the winter I was cheating. The freeze was over. She was
coming over to my place and instead of us hanging with my knuck-
lehead boys — me smoking, her bored out of her skull — we were
seeing movies. Driving out to different places to eat. Even caught a
play at the Crossroads and I took her picture with some bigwig
black playwrights, pictures where she's smiling so much you'd think
her wide-ass mouth was going to unhinge. We were a couple again.
Visiting each other's family on the weekends. Eating breakfast at
diners hours before anybody else was up, rummaging through the
New Brunswick library together, the one Carnegie built with his
guilt money. A nice rhythm we had going. But then the Letter hits
like a *Star Trek* grenade and detonates everything, past, present,
future. Suddenly her folks want to kill me. It don't matter that I

helped them with their taxes two years running or that I mow their lawn. Her father, who used to treat me like his *hijo,* calls me an asshole on the phone, sounds like he's strangling himself with the cord. "You no deserve I speak to you in Spanish," he says. I see one of Magda's girlfriends at the Woodbridge Mall — Claribel, the *ecuatoriana* with the biology degree and the *chinita* eyes — and she treats me like I ate somebody's kid.

You don't even want to hear how it went down with Magda. Like a five-train collision. She threw Cassandra's letter at me — it missed and landed under a Volvo — and then she sat down on the curb and started hyperventilating. "Oh, God," she wailed. "Oh, my God."

This is when my boys claim they would have pulled a Total Fucking Denial. Cassandra who? I was too sick to my stomach even to try. I sat down next to her, grabbed her flailing arms, and said some dumb shit like "You have to listen to me, Magda. Or you won't understand."

Let me tell you something about Magda. She's a Bergenline original: short with big eyes and big hips and dark curly hair you could lose a hand in. Her father's a baker, her mother sells kids' clothes door to door. She's a forgiving soul. A Catholic. Dragged me into church every Sunday for Spanish mass, and when one of her relatives is sick, especially the ones in Cuba, she writes letters to some nuns in Pennsylvania, asks the sisters to pray for her family. She's the nerd every librarian in town knows, a teacher whose students fall in love with her. Always cutting shit out for me from the newspapers, Dominican shit. I see her like, what, every week, and she still sends me corny little notes in the mail: "So you won't forget me." You couldn't think of anybody worse to screw than Magda.

I won't bore you with the details. The begging, the crawling over glass, the crying. Let's just say that after two weeks of this, of my driving out to her house, sending her letters, and calling her at all hours of the night, we put it back together. Didn't mean I ever ate with her family again or that her girlfriends were celebrating. Those *cabronas,* they were like, *No, jamás,* never. Even Magda wasn't too hot on the rapprochement at first, but I had the momentum of the past on my side. When she asked me, "Why don't you leave me alone?" I told her the truth: "It's because I love you, *mami.*" I know this sounds like a load of doo-doo, but it's true: Magda's my heart. I didn't want her to leave me; I wasn't about to start looking for a girlfriend because I'd fucked up one lousy time.

Don't think it was a cakewalk, because it wasn't. Magda's stubborn; back when we first started dating, she said she wouldn't sleep with me until we'd been together at least a month, and homegirl stuck to it, no matter how hard I tried to get into her knickknacks. She's sensitive too. Takes to hurt the way water takes to paper. You can't imagine how many times she asked (especially after we finished fucking), "Were you ever going to tell me?" This and "Why?" were her favorite questions. My favorite answers were "Yes" and "It was a stupid mistake."

We even had some conversation about Cassandra — usually in the dark, when we couldn't see each other. Magda asked me if I'd loved Cassandra and I told her no, I didn't. "Do you still think about her?" "Nope." "Did you like fucking her?" "To be honest, baby, it was lousy." And for a while after we got back together everything was as fine as it could be.

But what was strange was that instead of shit improving between us, things got worse and worse. My Magda was turning into another Magda. Who didn't want to sleep over as much or scratch my back when I asked her to. Amazing how you notice the little things. Like how she never used to ask me to call back when she was on the line with somebody else. I always had priority. Not anymore. So of course I blamed all that shit on her girls, who I knew for a fact were still feeding her a bad line about me.

She wasn't the only one with counsel. My boys were like, "Fuck her, don't sweat that bitch," but every time I tried I couldn't pull it off. I was into Magda for real. I started working overtime on her, but nothing seemed to pan out. Every movie we went to, every night drive we took, every time she did sleep over seemed to confirm something negative about me. I felt like I was dying by degrees, but when I brought it up she told me that I was being paranoid.

About a month later, she started making the sort of changes that would have alarmed a paranoid nigger. Cuts her hair, buys better makeup, rocks new clothes, goes out dancing on Friday nights with her friends. When I ask her if we can chill, I'm no longer sure it's a done deal. A lot of the time she Bartlebys me, says, "No, I'd rather not." I ask her what the hell she thinks this is and she says, "That's what I'm trying to figure out."

I know what she's doing. Making me aware of my precarious position in her life. Like I'm not aware.

Then it was June. Hot white clouds stranded in the sky, cars being washed down with hoses, music allowed outside. Everybody getting ready for summer, even us. We'd planned a trip to Santo Domingo early in the year, an anniversary present, and had to decide whether we were still going or not. It had been on the horizon awhile, but I figured it was something that would resolve itself. When it didn't, I brought the tickets out and asked her, "How do you feel about it?"

"Like it's too much of a commitment."

"Could be worse. It's a vacation, for Christ's sake."

"I see it as pressure."

"Doesn't have to be pressure."

I don't know why I get stuck on it the way I do. Bringing it up every day, trying to get her to commit. Maybe I was getting tired of the situation we were in. Wanted to flex, wanted something to change. Or maybe I'd gotten this idea in my head that if she said, "Yes, we're going," then shit would be fine between us. If she said, "No, it's not for me," then at least I'd know that it was over.

Her girls, the sorest losers on the planet, advised her to take the trip and then never speak to me again. She, of course, told me this shit, because she couldn't stop herself from telling me everything she's thinking. "How do you feel about that suggestion?" I asked her.

She shrugged. "It's an idea."

Even my boys were like, "Nigger, sounds like you're wasting a whole lot of loot on some bullshit," but I really thought it would be good for us. Deep down, where my boys don't know me, I'm an optimist. I thought, Me and her on the Island. What couldn't this cure?

Let me confess: I love Santo Domingo. I love coming home to the guys in blazers trying to push little cups of Brugal into my hands. Love the plane landing, everybody clapping when the wheels kiss the runway. Love the fact that I'm the only nigger on board without a Cuban link or a flapjack of makeup on my face. Love the redhead woman on her way to meet the daughter she hasn't seen in eleven years. The gifts she holds on her lap, like the bones of a saint. "*M'ija* has *tetas* now," the woman whispers to her neighbor. "Last time I saw her, she could barely speak in sentences. Now she's a woman. *Imagínate.*" I love the bags my mother packs, shit for relatives and something for Magda, a gift. "You give this to her no matter what happens."

If this was another kind of story, I'd tell you about the sea. What it looks like after it's been forced into the sky through a blowhole. How when I'm driving in from the airport and see it like this, like shredded silver, I know I'm back for real. I'd tell you how many poor motherfuckers there are. More albinos, more cross-eyed niggers, more *tígueres* than you'll ever see. And the *mujeres* — *olvídate.* How you can't go five feet without running into one you wouldn't mind kicking it with. I'd tell you about the traffic: the entire history of late-twentieth-century automobiles swarming across every flat stretch of ground, a cosmology of battered cars, battered motorcycles, battered trucks, and battered buses, and an equal number of repair shops, run by any fool with a wrench. I'd tell you about the shanties and our no-running-water faucets and the sambos on the billboards and the fact that my family house comes equipped with an ever-reliable latrine. I'd tell you about my *abuelo* and his *campo* hands, how unhappy he is that I'm not sticking around, and I'd tell you about the street where I was born, Calle XXI, how it hasn't decided yet if it wants to be a slum or not and how it's been in this state of indecision for years.

But that would make it another kind of story, and I'm having enough trouble as it is with this one. You'll have to take my word for it. Santo Domingo is Santo Domingo. Let's pretend we all know what goes on there.

I must have been smoking dust, because I thought we were fine those first couple of days. Sure, staying locked up at my *abuelo*'s house bored Magda to tears, she even said so — "I'm bored, Yunior" — but I'd warned her about the obligatory Visit with Abuelo. I thought she wouldn't mind; she's normally mad cool with the *viejitos*. But she didn't say much to him. Just fidgeted in the heat and drank fifteen bottles of water. Point is, we were out of the capital and on a *guagua* to the interior before the second day had even begun. The landscapes were superfly — even though there was a drought on and the whole *campo*, even the houses, was covered in that red dust. There I was. Pointing out all the shit that had changed since the year before. The new Pizza Huts and Dunkin' Donuts and the little plastic bags of water the *tigueritos* were selling. Even kicked the historicals. This is where Trujillo and his Marine pals slaughtered the *gavilleros,* here's where the Jefe used to take his girls, here's where Balaguer sold his soul to the Devil. And Magda seemed to be enjoying herself. Nodded her head. Talked back a little. What can I tell you? I thought we were on a positive vibe.

I guess when I look back there were signs. First off, Magda's not quiet. She's a talker, a fucking *boca,* and we used to have this thing where I would lift my hand and say, "Time out," and she would have to be quiet for at least two minutes, just so I could process some of the information she'd been spouting. She'd be embarrassed and chastened, but not so embarrassed and chastened that when I said, "Okay, time's up," she didn't launch right into it again.

Maybe it was my good mood. It was like the first time in weeks that I felt relaxed, that I wasn't acting like something was about to give at any moment. It bothered me that she insisted on reporting to her girls every night — like they were expecting me to kill her or something — but, fuck it, I still thought we were doing better than anytime before.

We were in this crazy budget hotel near the university. I was standing outside staring out at the Septentrionales and the blacked-out city when I heard her crying. I thought it was something serious, found the flashlight, and fanned the light over her heat-swollen face. "Are you okay, *mami?*"

She shook her head. "I don't want to be here."

"What do you mean?"

"What don't you understand? I. Don't. Want. To. Be. Here."

This was not the Magda I knew. The Magda I knew was super-courteous. Knocked on a door before she opened it.

I almost shouted, "What is your fucking problem!" But I didn't. I ended up hugging and babying her and asking her what was wrong. She cried for a long time and then after a silence started talking. By then the lights had flickered back on. Turned out she didn't want to travel around like a hobo. "I thought we'd be on a beach," she said.

"We're going to be on a beach. The day after tomorrow."

"Can't we go now?"

What could I do? She was in her underwear, waiting for me to say something. So what jumped out of my mouth? "Baby, we'll do whatever you want." I called the hotel in La Romana, asked if we could come early, and the next morning I put us on an express *guagua* to the capital and then a second one to La Romana. I didn't say a fucking word to her and she didn't say nothing to me. She seemed tired and watched the world outside like maybe she was expecting it to speak to her.

By the middle of Day 3 of our All-Quisqueya Redemption Tour we were in an air-conditioned bungalow watching HBO. Exactly where I want to be when I'm in Santo Domingo. In a fucking resort. Magda was reading a book by a Trappist, in a better mood, I guess, and I was sitting on the edge of the bed, fingering my useless map.

I was thinking, For this I deserve something nice. Something physical. Me and Magda were pretty damn casual about sex, but since the breakup shit has gotten weird. First of all, it ain't regular like before. I'm lucky to score some once a week. I have to nudge her, start things up, or we won't fuck at all. And she plays like she doesn't want it, and sometimes she doesn't and then I have to cool it, but other times she does want it and I have to touch her pussy, which is my way of initiating things, of saying, "So, how about we kick it, *mami?*" And she'll turn her head, which is her way of saying, "I'm too proud to acquiesce openly to your animal desires, but if you continue to put your finger in me I won't stop you."

Today we started no problem, but then halfway through she said, "Wait, we shouldn't."

I wanted to know why.

She closed her eyes like she was embarrassed at herself. "Forget about it," she said, moving her hips under me. "Just forget about it."

I don't even want to tell you where we're at. We're in Casa de Campo. The Resort That Shame Forgot. The average asshole would love this place. It's the largest, wealthiest resort on the Island, which means it's a goddamn fortress, walled away from everybody else. *Guachimanes* and peacocks and ambitious topiaries everywhere. Advertises itself in the States as its own country, and it might as well be. Has its own airport, thirty-six holes of golf, beaches so white they ache to be trampled, and the only Island Dominicans you're guaranteed to see are either caked up or changing your sheets. Let's just say my *abuelo* has never been here, and neither has yours. This is where the Garcías and the Colóns come to relax after a long month of oppressing the masses, where the *tutumpotes* can trade tips with their colleagues from abroad. Chill here too long and you'll be sure to have your ghetto pass revoked, no questions asked.

We wake up bright and early for the buffet, get served by cheerful women in Aunt Jemima costumes. I shit you not: these sisters even have to wear hankies on their heads. Magda is scratching out a couple of cards to her family. I want to talk about the day before, but when I bring it up she puts down her pen. Jams on her shades.

"I feel like you're pressuring me."

"How am I pressuring you?" I ask.

We get into one of those no-fun twenty-minute arguments, which the waiters keep interrupting by bringing over more orange juice and *café*, the two things this island has plenty of.

"I just want some space to myself every now and then. Every time I'm with you I have this sense that you want something from me."

"Time to yourself," I say. "What does that mean?"

"Like maybe once a day, you do one thing, I do another."

"Like when? Now?"

"It doesn't have to be now." She looks exasperated. "Why don't we just go down to the beach?"

As we walk over to the courtesy golf cart, I say, "I feel like you rejected my whole country, Magda."

"Don't be ridiculous." She drops one hand in my lap. "I just wanted to relax. What's wrong with that?"

The sun is blazing and the blue of the ocean is an overload on the brain. Casa de Campo has got beaches the way the rest of the Island has got problems. These, though, have no merengue, no little kids, nobody trying to sell you *chicharrones,* and there's a massive melanin deficit in evidence. Every fifty feet there's at least one Eurofuck beached out on a towel like some scary pale monster that the sea's vomited up. They look like philosophy professors, like budget Foucaults, and too many of them are in the company of a dark-assed Dominican girl. I mean it, these girls can't be no more than sixteen, look *puro ingenio* to me. You can tell by their inability to communicate that these two didn't meet back in their Left Bank days.

Magda's rocking a dope Ochun-colored bikini that her girls helped her pick out so she could torture me, and I'm in these old ruined trunks that say "Sandy Hook Forever!" I'll admit it, with Magda half naked in public I'm feeling vulnerable and uneasy. I put my hand on her knee. "I just wish you'd say you love me."

"Yunior, please."

"Can you say you like me a lot?"

"Can you leave me alone? You're such a pestilence."

I let the sun stake me out to the sand. It's disheartening, me and Magda together. We don't look like a couple. When she smiles niggers ask her for her hand in marriage; when I smile folks check their wallets. Magda's been a star the whole time we've been here. You know how it is when you're on the Island and your girl's an octoroon. Brothers go apeshit. On buses, the machos were like, *"Tu sí eres bella, muchacha."* Every time I dip into the water for a swim, some Mediterranean Messenger of Love starts rapping to her. Of course, I'm not polite. "Why don't you beat it, *pancho*? We're on our honeymoon here." There's this one squid who's mad persistent, even sits down near us so he can impress her with the hair around his nipples, and instead of ignoring him she starts a conversation and it turns out he's Dominican too, from Quisqueya Heights, an assistant D.A. who loves his people. "Better I'm their prosecutor," he says. "At least I understand them." I'm thinking he sounds like the sort of nigger who in the old days used to lead bwana to the rest of us. After three minutes of him, I can't take it no more and say, "Magda, stop talking to that asshole."

The assistant D.A. startles. "I know you ain't talking to me," he says.

"Actually," I say, "I am."

"This is unbelievable." Magda gets to her feet and walks stiff-legged toward the water. She's got a half-moon of sand stuck to her butt. A total fucking heartbreak.

Homeboy's saying something else to me, but I'm not listening. I already know what she'll say when she sits back down. "Time for you to do your thing and me to do mine."

That night I loiter around the pool and the local bar, Club Cacique, Magda nowhere to be found. I meet a Dominicana from West New York. Fly, of course. *Trigueña*, with the most outrageous perm this side of Dyckman. Lucy is her name. She's hanging out with three of her teenage girl cousins. When she removes her robe to dive into the pool, I see a spiderweb of scars across her stomach. Tells me in Spanish, "I have family in La Romana, but I refuse to stay with them. No way. My uncle won't let any of us out of the house after dark. So I'd rather go broke and stay here than be locked in the prison."

I meet these two rich older dudes drinking cognac at the bar. Introduce themselves as the Vice President and Bárbaro, his body-guard. I must have the footprint of fresh disaster on my face. They listen to my troubles like they're a couple of capos and I'm talking murder. They commiserate. It's a thousand degrees out and the mosquitoes hum like they're about to inherit the earth, but both these cats are wearing expensive suits, and Bárbaro is even sporting a purple ascot. Once a soldier tried to saw open his neck and now he covers the scar. "I'm a modest man," he says.

I go off to phone the room. No Magda. I check with reception. No messages. I return to the bar and smile.

The Vice President is a young brother, in his late thirties, and pretty cool for a *chupabarrio*. He advises me to find another woman. Make her *bella* and *negra*. I think, Cassandra.

The Vice President waves his hand and shots of Barceló appear so fast you'd think it's science fiction.

"Jealousy is the best way to jump-start a relationship," the Vice President says. "I learned that when I was a student at Syracuse. Dance with another woman, dance merengue with her, and see if your *jeva*'s not roused to action."

"You mean roused to violence."

"She hit you?"

"When I first told her. She smacked me right across the chops."

"*Pero, hermano*, why'd you tell her?" Bárbaro wants to know. "Why didn't you just deny it?"

"*Compadre*, she received a letter. It had evidence."

The Vice President smiles fantastically and I can see why he's a vice president. Later, when I get home, I'll tell my mother about this whole mess, and she'll tell me what this brother was the vice president of.

"They only hit you," he says, "when they care."

"Amen," Bárbaro murmurs. "Amen."

All of Magda's friends say I cheated because I was Dominican, that all us Dominican men are dogs and can't be trusted. But it wasn't genetics; there were reasons. Causalities.

The truth is there ain't no relationship in the world that doesn't hit turbulence. Ours certainly did.

I was living in Brooklyn and she was with her folks in Jersey. We talked every day on the phone and on weekends we saw each other. Usually I went in. We were real Jersey, too: malls, the parents, movies, a lot of TV. After a year of us together, this was where we were at. Our relationship wasn't the sun, the moon, and the stars, but it wasn't bullshit, either. Especially not on Saturday mornings, over at my apartment, when she made us coffee *campo* style, straining it through the sock thing. Told her parents the night before she was staying over at Claribel's; they must have known where she was, but they never said shit. I'd sleep late and she'd read, scratching my back in slow arcs, and when I was ready to get up I would start kissing her until she would say, "God, Yunior, you're making me wet."

I wasn't unhappy and wasn't actively pursuing ass like some niggers. Sure, I checked out other females, even danced with them when I went out, but I wasn't keeping numbers or nothing.

Still, it's not like seeing somebody once a week doesn't cool shit out, because it does. Nothing you'd really notice until some new chick arrives at your job with a big chest and a smart mouth and she's like on you almost immediately, touching your pectorals, moaning about some *moreno* she's dating who's always treating her like shit, saying, "Black guys don't understand Spanish girls."

Cassandra. She organized the football pool and did crossword puzzles while she talked on the phone, and had a thing for denim skirts. We got into a habit of going to lunch and having the same conversation. I advised her to drop the *moreno*, she advised me to find a girlfriend who could fuck. First week of knowing her, I made the mistake of telling her that sex with Magda had never been topnotch.

"God, I feel sorry for you." Cassandra laughed. "At least Rupert gives me some Grade A dick."

The first night we did it — and it was good, too, she wasn't false advertising — I felt so lousy that I couldn't sleep, even though she was one of those sisters whose body fits next to you perfect. I was like, She knows, so I called Magda right from the bed and asked her if she was okay.

"You sound strange," she said.

I remember Cassandra pressing the hot cleft of her pussy against my leg and me saying, "I just miss you."

Another day, and the only thing Magda has said is "Give me the lotion." Tonight the resort is throwing a party. All guests are invited. Attire's formal, but I don't have the clothes or the energy to dress up. Magda, though, has both. She pulls on these supertight gold lamé pants and a matching halter that shows off her belly ring. Her hair is shiny and as dark as night and I can remember the first time I kissed those curls, asking her, "Where are the stars?" And she said, "They're a little lower, *papi.*"

We both end up in front of the mirror. I'm in slacks and a wrinkled guayabera. She's applying her lipstick; I've always believed that the universe invented the color red solely for Latinas.

"We look good," she says.

It's true. My optimism is starting to come back. I'm thinking, This is the night for reconciliation. I put my arms around her, but she drops her bomb without blinking a fucking eye: tonight, she says, she needs space.

My arms drop.

"I knew you'd be pissed," she says.

"You're a real bitch, you know that."

"I didn't want to come here. You made me."

"If you didn't want to come, why didn't you have the fucking guts to say so?"

And on and on and on, until finally I just say, "Fuck this," and head out. I feel unmoored and don't have a clue of what comes next. This is the endgame, and instead of pulling out all the stops, instead of *pongándome más chivo que un chivo,* I'm feeling sorry for myself, *como un parigüayo sin suerte.* I'm thinking, I'm not a bad guy.

Club Cacique is jammed. I'm looking for Lucy. I find the Vice President and Bárbaro instead. At the quiet end of the bar, they're drinking cognac and arguing about whether there are fifty-six Dominicans in the major leagues or fifty-seven. They clear out a space for me and clap me on the shoulder.

"This place is killing me," I say.

"How dramatic." The Vice President reaches into his suit for his keys. He's wearing those Italian leather shoes that look like braided slippers. "Are you inclined to ride with us?"

"Sure," I say. "Why the fuck not?"

"I wish to show you the birthplace of our nation."

Before we leave I check out the crowd. Lucy has arrived. She's alone at the edge of the bar in a fly black dress. Smiles excitedly, lifts her arm, and I can see the dark stubbled spot in her armpit. She's got sweat patches over her outfit, and mosquito bites on her beautiful arms. I think, I should stay, but my legs carry me right out of the club.

We pile in a diplomat's black BMW. I'm in the back seat with Bárbaro; the Vice President's up front driving. We leave Casa de Campo behind and the frenzy of La Romana, and soon everything starts smelling of processed cane. The roads are dark — I'm talking no fucking lights — and in our beams the bugs swarm like a biblical plague. We're passing the cognac around. I'm with a vice president, I figure what the fuck.

He's talking — about his time in upstate New York — but so is Bárbaro. The bodyguard's suit's rumpled and his hand shakes as he smokes his cigarettes. Some fucking bodyguard. He's telling me about his childhood in San Juan, near the border of Haiti. Liborio's country. "I wanted to be an engineer," he tells me. "I wanted to build schools and hospitals for the pueblo." I'm not really listening to him; I'm thinking about Magda, how I'll probably never taste her *chocha* again.

And then we're out of the car, stumbling up a slope, through bushes and *guineo* and bamboo, and the mosquitoes are chewing us up like we're the special of the day. Bárbaro's got a huge flash-light, a darkness obliterator. The Vice President's cursing, tram-pling through the underbrush, saying, "It's around here some-where. This is what I get for being in office so long." It's only then I notice that Bárbaro's holding a huge fucking machine gun and his hand ain't shaking no more. He isn't watching me or the Vice President — he's listening. I'm not scared, but this is getting a little too freaky for me.

"What kind of gun is that?" I ask, by way of conversation.

"A P-90."

"What the fuck is that?"

"Something old made new."

Great, I'm thinking, a philosopher.

"It's here," the Vice President says.

I creep over and see that he's standing over a hole in the ground. The earth is red. Bauxite. And the hole is blacker than any of us.

"This is the Cave of the Jagua," the Vice President announces in a deep, respectful voice. "The birthplace of the Tainos."

I raise my eyebrow. "I thought they were in South America."

"We're speaking mythically here."

Bárbaro points the light down the hole, but that doesn't improve anything.

"Would you like to see inside?" the Vice President asks me.

I must have said yes, because Bárbaro gives me the flashlight and the two of them grab me by my ankles and lower me into the hole. All my coins fly out of my pockets. *Bendiciones.* I don't see much, just some odd colors on the eroded walls, and the Vice President's calling down, "Isn't it beautiful?"

This is the perfect place for insight, for a person to become somebody better. The Vice President probably saw his future self hanging in this darkness, bulldozing the poor out of their shanties, and Bárbaro too — buying a concrete house for his mother, showing her how to work the air conditioner — but me, all I can manage is a memory of the first time me and Magda talked. Back at Rutgers. We were waiting for an E bus together on George Street and she was wearing purple. All sorts of purple.

And that's when I know it's over. As soon as you start thinking about the beginning, it's the end.

I cry, and when they pull me up the Vice President says, indignantly, "God, you don't have to be a pussy about it."

That must have been some serious Island voodoo: the ending I saw in the cave came true. The next day we went back to the United States. Five months later I got a letter from my ex-baby. I was dating someone new, but Magda's handwriting still blasted every molecule of air out of my lungs.

It turned out she was also going out with somebody else. A very nice guy she'd met. Dominican, like me.

But I'm getting ahead of myself. I need to finish by showing you what kind of fool I am.

When I returned to the bungalow that night, Magda was waiting up for me. Was packed, looked like she'd been bawling.

"I'm going home tomorrow," she said.

I sat down next to her. Took her hand. "This can work," I said. "All we have to do is try."

CHITRA DIVAKARUNI

Mrs. Dutta Writes a Letter

FROM THE ATLANTIC MONTHLY

WHEN THE ALARM goes off at 5:00 A.M., buzzing like a trapped wasp, Mrs. Dutta has been lying awake for quite a while. She still has difficulty sleeping on the Perma Rest mattress that Sagar and Shyamoli, her son and daughter-in-law, have bought specially for her, though she has had it now for two months. It is too American-soft, unlike the reassuring solid copra ticking she used at home. *But this is home now,* she reminds herself. She reaches hurriedly to turn off the alarm, but in the dark her fingers get confused among the knobs, and the electric clock falls with a thud to the floor. Its angry metallic call vibrates through the walls of her room, and she is sure it will wake everyone. She yanks frantically at the wire until she feels it give, and in the abrupt silence that follows she hears herself breathing, a sound harsh and uneven and full of guilt.

Mrs. Dutta knows, of course, that this ruckus is her own fault. She should just not set the alarm. She does not need to get up early here in California, in her son's house. But the habit, taught her by her mother-in-law when she was a bride of seventeen, *A good wife wakes before the rest of the household,* is one she finds impossible to break. How hard it was then to pull her unwilling body away from the sleep-warm clasp of her husband, Sagar's father, whom she had just learned to love; to stumble to the kitchen that smelled of stale garam masala and light the coal stove so that she could make morning tea for them all — her parents-in-law, her husband, his two younger brothers, and the widowed aunt who lived with them.

After dinner, when the family sits in front of the TV, she tries to tell her grandchildren about those days. "I was never good at starting that stove — the smoke stung my eyes, making me cough and cough. Breakfast was never ready on time, and my mother-in-law — oh, how she scolded me, until I was in tears. Every night I'd pray to Goddess Durga, please let me sleep late, just one morning!"

"Mmmm," Pradeep says, bent over a model plane.

"Oooh, how awful," Mrinalini says, wrinkling her nose politely before she turns back to a show filled with jokes that Mrs. Dutta does not understand.

"That's why you should sleep in now, Mother," Shyamoli says, smiling at her from the recliner where she sits looking through the *Wall Street Journal*. With her legs crossed so elegantly under the shimmery blue skirt she has changed into after work, and her unusually fair skin, she could pass for an American, thinks Mrs. Dutta, whose own skin is as brown as roasted cumin. The thought fills her with an uneasy pride.

From the floor where he leans against Shyamoli's knee, Sagar adds, "We want you to be comfortable, Ma. To rest. That's why we brought you to America."

In spite of his thinning hair and the gold-rimmed glasses that he has recently taken to wearing, Sagar's face seems to Mrs. Dutta still that of the boy she used to send off to primary school with his metal tiffin box. She remembers how he crawled into her bed on stormy monsoon nights, how when he was ill, no one else could make him drink his barley water. Her heart lightens in sudden gladness because she is really here, with him and his children in America. "Oh, Sagar," she says, smiling, "now you're talking like this! But did you give me a moment's rest while you were growing up?" And she launches into a description of childhood pranks that has him shaking his head indulgently while disembodied TV laughter echoes through the room.

But later he comes into her bedroom and says, a little shamefaced, "Mother, please don't get up so early in the morning. All that noise in the bathroom — it wakes us up, and Molli has such a long day at work . . ."

And she, turning a little so that he won't see her foolish eyes filling with tears, as though she were a teenage bride again and not a woman well over sixty, nods her head, *yes, yes.*

Waiting for the sounds of the stirring household to release her from the embrace of her Perma Rest mattress, Mrs. Dutta repeats the 108 holy names of God. *Om Keshavaya Namah, Om Narayanaya Namah, Om Madhavaya Namah.* But underneath she is thinking of the bleached-blue aerogram from Mrs. Basu that has been waiting unanswered on her bedside table all week, filled with news from home. Someone robbed the Sandhya jewelry store. The bandits had guns, but luckily no one was hurt. Mr. Joshi's daughter, that sweet-faced child, has run away with her singing teacher. Who would've thought it? Mrs. Barucha's daughter-in-law had one more baby girl. Yes, their fourth. You'd think they'd know better than to keep trying for a boy. Last Tuesday was Bangla Bandh, another labor strike, everything closed down, not even the buses running. But you can't really blame them, can you? After all, factory workers have to eat too. Mrs. Basu's tenants, whom she'd been trying to evict forever, finally moved out. Good riddance, but you should see the state of the flat.

At the very bottom Mrs. Basu wrote, *Are you happy in America?*

Mrs. Dutta knows that Mrs. Basu, who has been her closest friend since they both moved to Ghoshpara Lane as young brides, cannot be fobbed off with descriptions of Fisherman's Wharf and the Golden Gate Bridge, or even with anecdotes involving grandchildren. And so she has been putting off her reply, while in her heart family loyalty battles with insidious feelings of — but she turns from them quickly and will not name them even to herself.

Now Sagar is knocking on the children's doors — a curious custom, this, children being allowed to close their doors against their parents. With relief Mrs. Dutta gathers up her bathroom things. She has plenty of time. Their mother will have to rap again before Pradeep and Mrinalini open their doors and stumble out. Still, Mrs. Dutta is not one to waste the precious morning. She splashes cold water on her face and neck (she does not believe in pampering herself), scrapes the night's gumminess from her tongue with her metal tongue cleaner, and brushes vigorously, though the minty toothpaste does not leave her mouth feeling as clean as does the bittersweet neem stick she's been using all her life. She combs the knots out of her hair. Even at her age it is thicker and silkier than her daughter-in-law's permed curls. *Such vanity,* she scolds her reflection, *and you a grandmother and a widow besides.* Still, as she deftly fashions her hair into a neat coil, she remembers how her husband would always compare it to monsoon clouds.

She hears a sudden commotion outside.

"Pat! Minnie! What d'you mean you still haven't washed up? I'm late to work every morning nowadays because of you kids."

"But Mom, *she's* in there. She's been there forever . . ." Mrinalini says.

Pause. Then, "So go to the downstairs bathroom."

"But all our stuff is here," Pradeep says, and Mrinalini adds, "It's not fair. Why can't *she* go downstairs?"

A longer pause. Mrs. Dutta hopes that Shyamoli will not be too harsh with the girl. But a child who refers to elders in that disrespectful way ought to be punished. How many times did she slap Sagar for something far less, though he was her only one, the jewel of her eye, come to her after she had been married for seven years and everyone had given up hope? Whenever she lifted her hand to him, her heart was pierced through and through. Such is a mother's duty.

But Shyamoli only says, in a tired voice, "That's enough! Go put on your clothes, hurry!"

The grumblings recede. Footsteps clatter down the stairs. Inside the bathroom Mrs. Dutta bends over the sink, fists tight in the folds of her sari. Hard with the pounding in her head to think what she feels most — anger at the children for their rudeness, or at Shyamoli for letting them go unrebuked. Or is it shame she feels (but why?), this burning, acid and indigestible, that coats her throat in molten metal?

It is 9:00 A.M., and the house, after the flurry of departures, of frantic "I can't find my socks" and "Mom, he took my lunch money" and "I swear I'll leave you kids behind if you're not in the car in exactly one minute," has settled into its quiet daytime rhythms.

Busy in the kitchen, Mrs. Dutta has recovered her spirits. Holding on to grudges is too exhausting, and besides, the kitchen — sunlight spilling across its countertops while the refrigerator hums reassuringly in the background — is her favorite place.

Mrs. Dutta hums too as she fries potatoes for alu dum. Her voice is rusty and slightly off-key. In India she would never have ventured to sing, but with everyone gone the house is too quiet, all that silence pressing down on her like the heel of a giant hand, and the TV voices, with their strange foreign accents, are no help at all. As the potatoes turn golden-brown, she permits herself a moment of nostalgia for her Calcutta kitchen — the new gas stove she bought with the birthday money Sagar sent, the scoured-shiny brass pots stacked by the meat safe, the window with the lotus-pattern grille through which she could look down on white-uniformed children playing cricket after school. The mouthwatering smell of ginger and chili paste, ground fresh by Reba, the maid, and, in the evening, strong black Assam tea brewing in the kettle when Mrs. Basu came by to visit. In her mind she writes to Mrs. Basu: *Oh, Roma, I miss it all so much. Sometimes I feel that someone has reached in and torn out a handful of my chest.*

But only fools indulge in nostalgia, so Mrs. Dutta shakes her head clear of images and straightens up the kitchen. She pours the half-drunk glasses of milk down the sink, though Shyamoli has told her to save them in the refrigerator. But surely Shyamoli, a girl from a good Hindu family, doesn't expect her to put contaminated *jutha* things with the rest of the food. She washes the breakfast dishes by hand instead of letting them wait inside the dishwasher till night, breeding germs. With practiced fingers she throws an assortment of spices into the blender: coriander, cumin, cloves, black pepper, a few red chiles for vigor. No stale bottled curry powder for her. *At least the family's eating well since I arrived,* she writes in her mind. *Proper Indian food, puffed-up chapatis, fish curry in mustard sauce, and real pulao with raisins and cashews and ghee — the way you taught me, Roma — instead of Rice-a-roni.* She would like to add, *They love it,* but thinking of Shyamoli, she hesitates.

At first Shyamoli was happy enough to have someone take over the cooking. "It's wonderful to come home to a hot dinner," she'd say. Or "Mother, what crispy papads, and your fish curry is out of this world." But recently she has taken to picking at her food, and once or twice from the kitchen Mrs. Dutta has caught wisps of words, intensely whispered: "cholesterol," "all putting on weight," "she's spoiling you." And though Shyamoli always says no when the children ask if they can have burritos from the freezer instead, Mrs. Dutta suspects that she would really like to say yes.

The children. A heaviness pulls at Mrs. Dutta's entire body when she thinks of them. Like so much in this country, they have turned out to be — yes, she might as well admit it — a disappointment.

For this she blames, in part, the Olan Mills portrait. Perhaps it was foolish of her to set so much store by a photograph, especially one taken years ago. But it was such a charming scene — Mrinalini in a ruffled white dress with her arm around her brother, Pradeep chubby and dimpled in a suit and bow tie, a glorious autumn forest blazing red and yellow behind them. (Later Mrs. Dutta was saddened to learn that the forest was merely a backdrop in a studio in California, where real trees did not turn such colors.)

The picture had arrived, silver-framed and wrapped in a plastic sheet filled with bubbles, with a note from Shyamoli explaining that it was a Mother's Day gift. (A strange concept, a day set aside to honor mothers. Did the sahibs not honor their mothers the rest of the year, then?) For a week Mrs. Dutta could not decide where it should be hung. If she put it in the drawing room, visitors would be able to admire her grandchildren, but if she put it on the bedroom wall, she would be able to see the photo last thing before she fell asleep. She finally opted for the bedroom, and later, when she was too ill with pneumonia to leave her bed for a month, she was glad of it.

Mrs. Dutta was accustomed to living on her own. She had done it for three years after Sagar's father died, politely but stubbornly declining the offers of various relatives, well-meaning and otherwise, to come and stay with her. In this she surprised herself as well as others, who thought of her as a shy, sheltered woman, one who would surely fall apart without her husband to handle things for her. But she managed quite well. She missed Sagar's father, of course, especially in the evenings, when it had been his habit to read to her the more amusing parts of the newspaper while she rolled out chapatis. But once the grief receded, she found she enjoyed being mistress of her own life, as she confided to Mrs. Basu. She liked being able, for the first time ever, to lie in bed all evening and read a new novel of Shankar's straight through if she wanted, or to send out for hot eggplant pakoras on a rainy day without feeling guilty that she wasn't serving up a balanced meal.

When the pneumonia hit, everything changed.

Mrs. Dutta had been ill before, but those illnesses had been different. Even in bed she'd been at the center of the household, with Reba coming to find out what should be cooked, Sagar's father bringing her shirts with missing buttons, her mother-in-law, now old and tamed, complaining that the cook didn't brew her tea strong enough, and Sagar running in crying because he'd had a fight with the neighbor boy. But now she had no one to ask her querulously, *Just how long do you plan to remain sick?* No one waited in impatient exasperation for her to take on her duties again. No one's life was inconvenienced the least bit by her illness.

Therefore she had no reason to get well.

When this thought occurred to Mrs. Dutta, she was so frightened that her body grew numb. The walls of the room spun into blackness; the bed on which she lay, a vast four-poster she had shared with Sagar's father since their wedding, rocked like a dinghy caught in a storm; and a great hollow roaring reverberated inside her head. For a moment, unable to move or see, she thought, *I'm dead.* Then her vision, desperate and blurry, caught on the portrait. *My grandchildren.* With some difficulty she focused on the bright, oblivious sheen of their faces, the eyes so like Sagar's that for a moment heartsickness twisted inside her like a living thing. She drew a shudder of breath into her aching lungs, and the roaring seemed to recede. When the afternoon post brought another letter from Sagar — *Mother, you really should come and live with us. We worry about you all alone in India, especially when you're sick like this* — she wrote back the same day, with fingers that still shook a little, *You're right: my place is with you, with my grandchildren.*

But now that she is here on the other side of the world, she is wrenched by doubt. She knows the grandchildren love her — how can it be otherwise among family? And she loves them, she reminds herself, even though they have put away, somewhere in the back of a closet, the vellum-bound *Ramayana for Young Readers* that she carried all the way from India in her hand luggage. Even though their bodies twitch with impatience when she tries to tell them stories of her girlhood. Even though they offer the most transparent excuses when she asks them to sit with her while she chants the evening prayers. *They're flesh of my flesh, blood of my blood,* she reminds herself. But sometimes when she listens, from the other room, to them speaking on the phone, their American voices rising in excitement as they discuss a glittering, alien world of Power Rangers, Metallica, and Spirit Week at school, she almost cannot believe what she hears.

Stepping into the back yard with a bucket of newly washed clothes, Mrs. Dutta views the sky with some anxiety. The butter-gold sunlight

is gone, black-bellied clouds have taken over the horizon, and the
air feels still and heavy on her face, as before a Bengal storm. What
if her clothes don't dry by the time the others return home?

Washing clothes has been a problem for Mrs. Dutta ever since
she arrived in California.

"We can't, Mother," Shyamoli said with a sigh when Mrs. Dutta
asked Sagar to put up a clothesline for her in the back yard.
(Shyamoli sighed often nowadays. Perhaps it was an American
habit? Mrs. Dutta did not remember that the Indian Shyamoli, the
docile bride she'd mothered for a month before putting her on a
Pan Am flight to join her husband, pursed her lips in quite this way
to let out a breath at once patient and exasperated.) "It's just not
done, not in a nice neighborhood like this one. And being the only
Indian family on the street, we have to be extra careful. People here
sometimes —" She broke off with a shake of her head. "Why don't
you just keep your dirty clothes in the hamper I've put in your
room, and I'll wash them on Sunday along with everyone else's."

Afraid of causing another sigh, Mrs. Dutta agreed reluctantly.
She knew she should not store unclean clothes in the same room
where she kept the pictures of her gods. That would bring bad luck.
And the odor. Lying in bed at night she could smell it distinctly,
even though Shyamoli claimed that the hamper was airtight. The
sour, starchy old-woman smell embarrassed her.

She was more embarrassed when, on Sunday afternoons,
Shyamoli brought the laundry into the family room to fold. Mrs.
Dutta would bend intently over her knitting, face tingling with
shame, as her daughter-in-law nonchalantly shook out the wisps of
lace, magenta and sea-green and black, that were her panties, placing them next to a stack of Sagar's briefs. And when, right in front
of everyone, Shyamoli pulled out Mrs. Dutta's crumpled, baggy
bras from the heap, she wished the ground would open up and
swallow her, like the Sita of mythology.

Then one day Shyamoli set the clothes basket down in front of
Sagar.

"Can you do them today, Sagar?" (Mrs. Dutta, who had never,
through the forty-two years of her marriage, addressed Sagar's father by name, tried not to wince.) "I've *got* to get that sales report
into the computer by tonight."

Before Sagar could respond, Mrs. Dutta was out of her chair,
knitting needles dropping to the floor.

"No, no, no, clothes and all is no work for the man of the house. I'll do it." The thought of her son's hands searching through the basket and lifting up his wife's — and her own — underclothes filled her with horror.

"Mother!" Shyamoli said. "This is why Indian men are so useless around the house. Here in America we don't believe in men's work and women's work. Don't I work outside all day, just like Sagar? How'll I manage if he doesn't help me at home?"

"I'll help you instead," Mrs. Dutta ventured.

"You don't understand, do you, Mother?" Shyamoli said with a shaky smile. Then she went into the study.

Mrs. Dutta sat down in her chair and tried to understand. But after a while she gave up and whispered to Sagar that she wanted him to teach her how to run the washer and dryer.

"Why, Mother? Molli's quite happy to —"

"I've got to learn it . . ." Her voice was low and desperate as she rummaged through the tangled heap for her clothes.

Her son began to object and then shrugged. "Oh, very well. If it makes you happy."

But later, when she faced the machines alone, their cryptic symbols and rows of gleaming knobs terrified her. What if she pressed the wrong button and flooded the entire floor with soapsuds? What if she couldn't turn the machines off and they kept going, whirring maniacally, until they exploded? (This had happened on a TV show just the other day. Everyone else had laughed at the woman who jumped up and down, screaming hysterically, but Mrs. Dutta sat stiff-spined, gripping the armrests of her chair.) So she has taken to washing her clothes in the bathtub when she is alone. She never did such a chore before, but she remembers how the village washerwomen of her childhood would beat their saris clean against river rocks. And a curious satisfaction fills her as her clothes hit the porcelain with the same solid wet *thunk*.

My small victory, my secret.

This is why everything must be dried and put safely away before Shyamoli returns. Ignorance, as Mrs. Dutta knows well from years of managing a household, is a great promoter of harmony. So she keeps an eye on the menacing advance of the clouds as she hangs up her blouses and underwear, as she drapes her sari along the redwood fence that separates her son's property from the neighbor's, first wiping the fence clean with a dish towel she has secretly taken from the bottom drawer in the kitchen. But she isn't worried. Hasn't she managed every time, even after that freak hailstorm last month, when she had to use the iron from the laundry closet to press everything dry? The memory pleases her. In her mind she writes to Mrs. Basu: *I'm fitting in so well here, you'd never guess I came only two months back. I've found new ways of doing things, of solving problems creatively. You would be most proud if you saw me.*

When Mrs. Dutta decided to give up her home of forty-five years, her relatives showed far less surprise than she had expected. "Oh, we all knew you'd end up in America sooner or later," they said. She had been foolish to stay on alone so long after Sagar's father, may he find eternal peace, passed away. Good thing that boy of hers had come to his senses and called her to join him. Everyone knows a wife's place is with her husband, and a widow's is with her son.

Mrs. Dutta had nodded in meek agreement, ashamed to let anyone know that the night before she had awakened weeping.

"Well, now that you're going, what'll happen to all your things?" they asked.

Mrs. Dutta, still troubled over those traitorous tears, had offered up her household effects in propitiation. "Here, Didi, you take this cutwork bedspread. Mashima, for a long time I have meant for you to have these Corning Ware dishes; I know how much you admire them. And Boudi, this tape recorder that Sagar sent a year back is for you. Yes, yes, I'm quite sure. I can always tell Sagar to buy me another one when I get there."

Mrs. Basu, coming in just as a cousin made off triumphantly with a bone-china tea set, had protested. "Prameela, have you gone crazy? That tea set used to belong to your mother-in-law."

"But what'll I do with it in America? Shyamoli has her own set —"

A look that Mrs. Dutta couldn't read flitted across Mrs. Basu's face. "But do you want to drink from it for the rest of your life?"

"What do you mean?"

Mrs. Basu hesitated. Then she said, "What if you don't like it there?"

"How can I not like it, Roma?" Mrs. Dutta's voice was strident, even to her own ears. With an effort she controlled it and continued. "I'll miss my friends, I know — and you most of all. And the things we do together — evening tea, our walk around Rabindra

Sarobar Lake, Thursday night Bhagavad Gita class. But Sagar — they're my only family. And blood is blood, after all."

"I wonder," Mrs. Basu said drily, and Mrs. Dutta recalled that though both of Mrs. Basu's children lived just a day's journey away, they came to see her only on occasions when common decency dictated their presence. Perhaps they were tightfisted in money matters too. Perhaps that was why Mrs. Basu had started renting out her downstairs a few years earlier, even though, as anyone in Calcutta knew, tenants were more trouble than they were worth. Such filial neglect must be hard to take, though Mrs. Basu, loyal to her children as indeed a mother should be, never complained. In a way, Mrs. Dutta had been better off, with Sagar too far away for her to put his love to the test.

"At least don't give up the house," Mrs. Basu was saying. "You won't be able to find another place in case . . ."

"In case what?" Mrs. Dutta asked, her words like stone chips. She was surprised to find that she was angrier with Mrs. Basu than she'd ever been. Or was she afraid? *My son isn't like yours,* she'd been on the verge of spitting out. She took a deep breath and made herself smile, made herself remember that she might never see her friend again.

"Ah, Roma," she said, putting her arm around Mrs. Basu. "You think I'm such an old witch that my Sagar and my Shyamoli will be unable to live with me?"

Mrs. Dutta hums a popular Tagore song as she pulls her sari from the fence. It's been a good day, as good as it can be in a country where you might stare out the window for hours and not see one living soul. No vegetable vendors with enormous wicker baskets balanced on their heads, no knife sharpeners with their distinctive call — *scissors-knives-choppers, scissors-knives-choppers* — to bring the children running. No peasant women with colorful tattoos on their arms to sell you cookware in exchange for your old silk saris. Why, even the animals that frequented Ghoshpara Lane had personality — stray dogs that knew to line up outside the kitchen door just when the leftovers were likely to be thrown out; the goat that maneuvered its head through the garden grille, hoping to get at her dahlias; cows that planted themselves majestically in the center of the road, ignoring honking drivers. And right across the street was Mrs. Basu's two-story house, which Mrs. Dutta knew as well as her own. How many times had she walked up the stairs to that airy room, painted sea-green and filled with plants, where her friend would be waiting for her?

What took you so long today, Prameela? Your tea is cold already.

Wait till you hear what happened, Roma. Then you won't scold me for being late —

Stop it, you silly woman, Mrs. Dutta tells herself severely. *Every single one of your relatives would give an arm and a leg to be in your place, you know that. After lunch you're going to write a nice letter to Roma telling her exactly how delighted you are to be here.*

From where Mrs. Dutta stands, gathering up petticoats and blouses, she can look into the next yard. Not that there's much to see — just tidy grass and a few pale blue flowers whose name she doesn't know. Two wooden chairs sit under a tree, but Mrs. Dutta has never seen anyone using them. *What's the point of having such a big yard if you're not even going to sit in it?* she thinks. Calcutta pushes itself into her mind again, with its narrow, blackened flats where families of six and eight and ten squeeze themselves into two tiny rooms, and her heart fills with a sense of loss she knows to be illogical.

When she first arrived in Sagar's home, Mrs. Dutta wanted to go over and meet her next-door neighbors, maybe take them some of her special sweet rasogollahs, as she'd often done with Mrs. Basu. But Shyamoli said she shouldn't. Such things were not the custom in California, she explained earnestly. You didn't just drop in on people without calling ahead. Here everyone was busy; they didn't sit around chatting, drinking endless cups of sugar-tea. Why, they might even say something unpleasant to her.

"For what?" Mrs. Dutta had asked disbelievingly, and Shyamoli had said, "Because Americans don't like neighbors to" — here she used an English phrase — "invade their privacy." Mrs. Dutta, who didn't fully understand the word *privacy,* because there was no such term in Bengali, had gazed at her daughter-in-law in some bewilderment. But she understood enough not to ask again. In the following months, though, she often looked over the fence, hoping to make contact. People were people, whether in India or in America, and everyone appreciated a friendly face. When Shyamoli was as old as Mrs. Dutta, she would know that too.

Today, just as she is about to turn away, out of the corner of her eye Mrs. Dutta notices a movement. At one of the windows a woman is standing, her hair a sleek gold like that of the TV heroines whose exploits baffle Mrs. Dutta when she tunes in to an afternoon serial. She is smoking a cigarette, and a curl of gray rises lazily, elegantly, from her fingers. Mrs. Dutta is so happy to see another human being in the middle of her solitary day that she forgets how much she disapproves of smoking, especially in women. She lifts her hand in the gesture she has seen her grandchildren use to wave an eager hello.

The woman stares back at Mrs. Dutta. Her lips are a perfect painted red, and when she raises her cigarette to her mouth, its tip glows like an animal's eye. She does not wave back or smile. Perhaps she is not well? Mrs. Dutta feels sorry for her, alone in her illness in a silent house with only cigarettes for solace, and she wishes the etiquette of America did not prevent her from walking over with a word of cheer and a bowl of her fresh-cooked alu dum.

Mrs. Dutta rarely gets a chance to be alone with her son. In the morning he is in too much of a hurry even to drink the fragrant cardamom tea that she (remembering how as a child he would always beg for a sip from her cup) offers to make him. He doesn't return until dinnertime, and afterward he must help the children with their homework, read the paper, hear the details of Shyamoli's day, watch his favorite TV crime show in order to unwind, and take out the garbage. In between, for he is a solicitous son, he converses with Mrs. Dutta. In response to his questions she assures him that her arthritis is much better now; no, no, she's not growing bored being at home all the time; she has everything she needs — Shyamoli has been so kind. But perhaps he could pick up a few aerograms on his way back tomorrow? She obediently recites for him an edited list of her day's activities, and smiles when he praises her cooking. But when he says, "Oh, well, time to turn in, another working day tomorrow," she feels a vague pain, like hunger, in the region of her heart.

So it is with the delighted air of a child who has been offered an unexpected gift that she leaves her half-written letter to greet Sagar at the door today, a good hour before Shyamoli is due back. The children are busy in the family room doing homework and watching cartoons (mostly the latter, Mrs. Dutta suspects). But for once she doesn't mind, because they race in to give their father hurried hugs and then race back again. And she has him, her son, all to herself in a kitchen filled with the familiar, pungent odors of tamarind sauce and chopped coriander leaves.

"Khoka," she says, calling him by a childhood name she hasn't used in years, "I could fry you two-three hot-hot luchis, if you like." As she waits for his reply, she can feel, in the hollow of her throat, the rapid thud of her heart. And when he says yes, that would be very nice, she shuts her eyes tight and takes a deep breath, and it is as though merciful time has given her back her youth, that sweet, aching urgency of being needed again.

Mrs. Dutta is telling Sagar a story.

"When you were a child, how scared you were of injections! One time, when the government doctor came to give us compulsory typhoid shots, you locked yourself in the bathroom and refused to come out. Do you remember what your father finally did? He went into the garden and caught a lizard and threw it in the bathroom window, because you were even more scared of lizards than of shots. And in exactly one second you ran out screaming — right into the waiting doctor's arms."

Sagar laughs so hard that he almost upsets his tea (made with real sugar, because Mrs. Dutta knows it is better for her son than that chemical powder Shyamoli likes to use). There are tears in his eyes, and Mrs. Dutta, who had not dared to hope that he would find her story so amusing, feels gratified. When he takes off his glasses to wipe them, his face is oddly young, not like a father's at all, or even a husband's, and she has to suppress an impulse to put out her hand and rub away the indentations that the glasses have left on his nose.

"I'd totally forgotten," Sagar says. "How can you keep track of those old, old things?"

Because it is the lot of mothers to remember what no one else cares to, Mrs. Dutta thinks. *To tell those stories over and over, until they are lodged, perforce, in family lore. We are the keepers of the heart's dusty corners.*

But as she starts to say this, the front door creaks open, and she hears the faint click of Shyamoli's high heels. Mrs. Dutta rises, collecting the dirty dishes.

"Call me fifteen minutes before you're ready to eat, so that I can fry fresh luchis for everyone," she tells Sagar.

"You don't have to leave, Mother," he says.

Mrs. Dutta smiles her pleasure but doesn't stop. She knows that Shyamoli likes to be alone with her husband at this time, and today, in her happiness, she does not grudge her this.

"You think I've nothing to do, only sit and gossip with you?" she mock-scolds. "I want you to know I have a very important letter to finish."

Somewhere behind her she hears a thud — a briefcase falling over. This surprises her. Shyamoli is always careful with it, because it was a gift from Sagar when she was finally made a manager in her company.

"Hi!" Sagar calls, and when there's no answer, "Hey, Molli, you okay?"

Shyamoli comes into the room slowly, her hair disheveled as though she has been running her fingers through it. Hot color blotches her cheeks.

"What's the matter, Molli?" Sagar walks over to give her a kiss. "Bad day at work?" Mrs. Dutta, embarrassed as always by this display of marital affection, turns toward the window, but not before she sees Shyamoli move her face away.

"Leave me alone." Her voice is low, shaking. "Just leave me alone."

"But what is it?" Sagar says with concern.

"I don't want to talk about it right now." Shyamoli lowers herself into a kitchen chair and puts her face in her hands. Sagar stands in the middle of the room, looking helpless. He raises his hand and lets it fall, as though he wants to comfort his wife but is afraid of what she might do.

A protective anger for her son surges inside Mrs. Dutta, but she moves away silently. In her mind-letter she writes, *Women need to be strong, not react to every little thing like this. You and I, Roma, we had far worse to cry about, but we shed our tears invisibly. We were good wives and daughters-in-law, good mothers. Dutiful, uncomplaining. Never putting ourselves first.*

A sudden memory comes to her, one she hasn't thought of in years — a day when she scorched a special kheer dessert. Her mother-in-law had shouted at her, "Didn't your mother teach you anything, you useless girl?" As punishment she refused to let Mrs. Dutta go with Mrs. Basu to the cinema, even though *Sahib, Bibi aur Ghulam,* which all Calcutta was crazy about, was playing, and their tickets were bought already. Mrs. Dutta had wept the entire afternoon, but before Sagar's father came home, she washed her face carefully with cold water and applied *kajal* to her eyes so that he wouldn't know.

But everything is getting mixed up, and her own young, trying-not-to-cry face blurs into another — why, it's Shyamoli's — and a thought hits her so sharply in the chest that she has to hold on to her bedroom wall to keep from falling. *And what good did it do? The more we bent, the more people pushed us, until one day we'd forgotten that we could stand up straight. Maybe Shyamoli's the one with the right idea after all . . .*

Mrs. Dutta lowers herself heavily onto her bed, trying to erase such an insidious idea from her mind. Oh, this new country, where all the rules are upside down, it's confusing her. The space inside her skull feels stirred up, like a pond in which too many water buffaloes have been wading. Maybe things will settle down if she can focus on the letter to Roma.

Then she remembers that she has left the half-written aerogram on the kitchen table. She knows she should wait until after dinner, after her son and his wife have sorted things out. But a restlessness — or is it defiance? — has taken hold of her. She is sorry that Shyamoli is upset, but why should she have to waste her evening because of that? She'll go get her letter — it's no crime, is it? She'll march right in and pick it up, and even if Shyamoli stops in mid-sentence with another one of those sighs, she'll refuse to feel apologetic. Besides, by now they're probably in the family room, watching TV.

Really, Roma, she writes in her head, as she feels her way along the unlighted corridor, *the amount of TV they watch here is quite scandalous. The children too, sitting for hours in front of that box like they've been turned into painted dolls, and then talking back when I tell them to turn it off.* Of course she will never put such blasphemy into a real letter. Still, it makes her feel better to be able to say it, if only to herself.

In the family room the TV is on, but for once no one is paying it any attention. Shyamoli and Sagar sit on the sofa, conversing. From where she stands in the corridor, Mrs. Dutta cannot see them, but their shadows — enormous against the wall where the table lamp has cast them — seem to flicker and leap at her.

She is about to slip unseen into the kitchen when Shyamoli's rising voice arrests her. In its raw, shaking unhappiness it is so unlike her daughter-in-law's assured tones that Mrs. Dutta is no more able to move away from it than if she had heard the call of the *nishi*, the lost souls of the dead, the subject of so many of the tales on which she grew up.

"It's easy for you to say 'Calm down.' I'd like to see how calm *you'd* be if she came up to you and said, 'Kindly tell the old lady not to hang her clothes over the fence into my yard.' She said it twice, like I didn't understand English, like I was a savage. All these years I've been so careful not to give these Americans a chance to say something like this, and now —"

"Shhh, Shyamoli, I *said* I'd talk to Mother about it."

"You always say that, but you never *do* anything. You're too busy being the perfect son, tiptoeing around her feelings. But how about mine? Aren't I a person too?"

"Hush, Molli, the children . . ."

"Let them hear. I don't care anymore. Besides, they're not stupid. They already know what a hard time I've been having with her. You're the only one who refuses to see it."

In the passage Mrs. Dutta shrinks against the wall. She wants to move away, to hear nothing else, but her feet are formed of cement, impossible to lift, and Shyamoli's words pour into her ears like fire.

"I've explained over and over, and she still does what I've asked her not to — throwing away perfectly good food, leaving dishes to drip all over the countertops. Ordering my children to stop doing things I've given them permission to do. She's taken over the entire kitchen, cooking whatever she likes. You come in the door and the smell of grease is everywhere, in all our clothes even. I feel like this isn't my house anymore."

"Be patient, Molli. She's an old woman, after all."

"I know. That's why I tried so hard. I know having her here is important to you. But I can't do it any longer. I just can't. Some days I feel like taking the kids and leaving." Shyamoli's voice disappears into a sob.

A shadow stumbles across the wall to her, and then another. Behind the weatherman's nasal tones, announcing a week of sunny days, Mrs. Dutta can hear a high, frightened weeping. The children, she thinks. This must be the first time they've seen their mother cry.

"Don't talk like that, sweetheart." Sagar leans forward, his voice, too, anguished. All the shadows on the wall shiver and merge into a single dark silhouette.

Mrs. Dutta stares at that silhouette, the solidarity of it. Sagar and Shyamoli's murmurs are lost beneath the noise in her head, a dry humming — like thirsty birds, she thinks wonderingly. After a while she discovers that she has reached her room. In darkness she lowers herself onto her bed very gently, as though her body were made of the thinnest glass. Or perhaps ice — she is so cold. She sits for a long time with her eyes closed, while inside her head thoughts whirl faster and faster until they disappear in a gray dust storm.

When Pradeep finally comes to call her for dinner, Mrs. Dutta follows him to the kitchen, where she fries luchis for everyone, the perfect circles of dough puffing up crisp and golden as always. Sagar and Shyamoli have reached a truce of some kind: she gives him a small smile, and he puts out a casual hand to massage the back of her neck. Mrs. Dutta shows no embarrassment at this. She eats her dinner. She answers questions put to her. She laughs when someone makes a joke. If her face is stiff, as though she had been given a shot of Novocain, no one notices. When the table is cleared, she excuses herself, saying she has to finish her letter.

Now Mrs. Dutta sits on her bed, reading over what she wrote in the innocent afternoon.

Dear Roma,
Although I miss you, I know you will be pleased to hear how happy I am in America. There is much here that needs getting used to, but we are no strangers to adjusting, we old women. After all, haven't we been doing it all our lives?

Today I'm cooking one of Sagar's favorite dishes, alu dum. It gives me such pleasure to see my family gathered around the table, eating my food. The children are still a little shy of me, but I am hopeful that we'll soon be friends. And Shyamoli, so confident and successful — you should see her when she's all dressed for work. I can't believe she's the same timid bride I sent off to America just a few years ago. But Sagar, most of all, is the joy of my old age. . . .

With the edge of her sari Mrs. Dutta carefully wipes a tear that has fallen on the aerogram. She blows on the damp spot until it is completely dry, so the pen will not leave a telltale smudge. Even though Roma would not tell a soul, she cannot risk it. She can already hear them, the avid relatives in India who've been waiting for something just like this to happen. *That Dutta-ginni, so set in her ways, we knew she'd never get along with her daughter-in-law.* Or, worse, *Did you hear about poor Prameela? How her family treated her? Yes, even her son, can you imagine?*

This much surely she owes to Sagar.

And what does she owe herself, Mrs. Dutta, falling through black night with all the certainties she trusted in collapsed upon themselves like imploded stars, and only an image inside her eyelids for company? A silhouette — man, wife, children, joined on a wall — showing her how alone she is in this land of young people. And how unnecessary.

She is not sure how long she sits under the glare of the overhead light, how long her hands clench themselves in her lap. When she opens them, nail marks line the soft flesh of her palms, red hieroglyphs — her body's language, telling her what to do.

Dear Roma, Mrs. Dutta writes,

I cannot answer your question about whether I am happy, for I am no longer sure I know what happiness is. All I know is that it isn't what I thought it to be. It isn't about being needed. It isn't about being with family either. It has something to do with love, I still think that, but in a different way than I believed earlier, a way I don't have the words to explain. Perhaps we can figure it out together, two old women drinking cha in your downstairs flat (for I do hope you will rent it to me on my return) while around us gossip falls — but lightly, like summer rain, for that is all we will allow it to be. If I'm lucky — and perhaps, in spite of all that has happened, I am — the happiness will be in the figuring out.

Pausing to read over what she has written, Mrs. Dutta is surprised to discover this: now that she no longer cares whether tears blotch her letter, she feels no need to weep.

STEPHEN DOBYNS

Kansas

FROM THE CLACKAMAS LITERARY REVIEW

THE BOY hitchhiking on the back-country Kansas road was nineteen years old. He had been dropped there by a farmer in a Model
T Ford who had turned off to the north. Then he waited for three
hours. It was July and there were no clouds. The wheat fields were
flat and went straight to the horizon. The boy had two plums and
he ate them. A blue Plymouth coupe went by with a man and a
woman. They were laughing. The woman had blond hair and it was
all loose and blew from the window. They didn't even see the boy.
The strands of straw-colored hair seemed to be waving to him. Half
an hour later a farmer stopped in a Ford pickup covered with a
layer of dust. The boy clambered into the front seat. The farmer
took off again without glancing at him. A forty-five revolver lay next
to the farmer's buttocks on the seat. Seeing it, the boy felt something electric go off inside of him. The revolver was old and there
were rust spots on the barrel. Black electrician's tape was wrapped
around the handle.

"You seen a woman and a man go by here in a Plymouth coupe?"
asked the farmer. He pronounced it "koo-pay."

The boy said he had.

"How long ago?"

"About thirty minutes."

The farmer had light blue eyes and there was stubble on his chin.
Perhaps he was forty, but to the boy he looked old. His skin was
leather-colored from the sun. The farmer pressed his foot to the
floor and the pickup roared. It was a dirt road and the boy had to
hold his hands against the dashboard to keep from being bounced

around. It was hot and both windows were open. There was grit in the boy's eyes and on his tongue. He kept glancing sideways at the revolver.

"They friends of yours?" asked the boy.

The farmer didn't look at him. "That's my wife," he said. "I'm going to put a bullet in her head." He put a hand to the revolver to make sure it was still there. "The man too," he added.

The boy didn't say anything. He was hitchhiking back to summer school from Oklahoma. He was the middle of three boys and the only one who had left home. He had already spent a year at the University of Oklahoma and was spending the summer at Lawrence. And there were other places, farther places. The boy played the piano. He intended to go to those farther places.

"What did they do?" the boy asked at last.

"You just guess," said the farmer.

The pickup was going about fifty miles per hour. The boy was afraid of seeing the dust cloud from the Plymouth up ahead, but there was only straight road. Then he was afraid that the Plymouth might have pulled off someplace. He touched his tongue to his upper lip but it was just one dry thing against another. Getting into the pickup, the boy had had a clear idea of the direction of his life. He meant to go to New York City at the end of summer. He meant to play the piano in Carnegie Hall. The farmer and his forty-five seemed to stand between him and that future. They formed a wall that the boy was afraid to climb over.

"Do you have to kill them?" the boy asked. He didn't want to talk but he felt unable to remain silent.

The farmer had a red boil on the side of his neck and he kept touching it with two fingers. "When you have something wicked, what do you do?" asked the farmer.

The boy wanted to say he didn't know or he wanted to say he would call the police, but the farmer would have no patience with those answers. And the boy also wanted to say he would forgive the wickedness, but he was afraid of that answer as well. He was afraid of making the farmer angry and so he only shrugged.

"You stomp it out," said the farmer. "That's what you do — you stomp it out."

The boy stared straight ahead, searching for the dust cloud and hoping not to see it. The hot air seemed to bend in front of them.

The boy was so frightened of seeing the dust cloud that he was sure he saw it. A little puff of gray getting closer. The pickup went straight down the middle of the road. There was no other traffic. Even if there had been other cars, the boy felt certain that the farmer wouldn't have moved out of the way. The wheat on either side of the road was coated with layers of dust, making it a reddish color, the color of dried blood.

"What about the police?" asked the boy.

"It's my wife," said the farmer. "It's my problem."

The boy never did see the dust cloud. They reached Lawrence and the boy got out as soon as he could. His shirt was stuck to his back and he kept rubbing his palms on his dungarees. He thanked the farmer but the man didn't look at him, he just kept staring straight ahead.

"Don't tell the police," said the farmer. His hand rested lightly on the forty-five beside him on the seat.

"No," said the boy. "I promise." He slammed shut the dusty door of the pickup.

The boy didn't tell the police. For several days he didn't tell anyone at all. He looked at the newspapers twice a day for news of a killing, but he didn't find anything. More than the farmer's gun, he had been frightened by the strength of the farmer's resolve. It had been like a chunk of stone and compared to it the boy had felt as soft as a piece of white bread. The boy never knew what happened. Perhaps nothing had happened.

The summer wound to its conclusion. The boy went to New York. He never did play in Carnegie Hall. His piano playing never got good enough. The war came and went. He wasn't a boy any longer. He was a married man with two sons. The family moved to Michigan. The man was a teacher, then a minister. His own parents died. He told his sons the story about the farmer in the pickup. "What do you think happened?" they asked. Nobody knew. Perhaps the farmer caught up with them; perhaps he didn't. The man's sons went off to college and began their own lives. The man and his wife moved to New Hampshire. They grew old. Sixty years went between that summer in Kansas and the present. The man entered his last illness. He stayed at home but he couldn't get out of bed. His wife gave him shots of morphine. He began to have dreams even when he was awake. The visiting nurse was always chipper. "Feeling better today?" she would ask. He tried to be polite, but he had no illusions. He went from one shot a day to two, and then three. The doctor said, "Give him as many as he needs." His wife started to ask about the danger of addiction, then she said nothing.

The man hardly knew when he was asleep or awake. He hardly knew if one day had passed or many. He had oxygen. He didn't eat. The space between his eyes and the bedroom wall was always occupied with people of his invention, people of his past. He would lift his hand to wave them away, only to find his hand still lying motionless on the counterpane. Even music distracted him now. Always he was listening for something in the distance.

The boy was standing by the side of a dirt road. A Ford pickup stopped beside him and he got in. The farmer lifted a forty-five revolver. "I'm going to shoot my wife in the head."

"No," said the boy, "don't do it!"

The farmer drove fast. He had a red boil on the side of his neck and he kept touching it with two fingers. They found the Plymouth coupe pulled off into a hollow. There were shade trees and a brook. The farmer jammed down the brakes and the pickup slid sideways across the dirt. The man and woman were in the front seat of the Plymouth. Their clothes were half off. They jumped out of the car. The woman had big red breasts. The farmer jumped out with his forty-five. "No!" shouted the boy. The farmer shot the man in the head. His whole head exploded and he fell down in the dust. His head was just a broken thing on the ground. The woman covered her face and tried to cover her breasts as well. The farmer shot her as well. Bits of dust floated on the surface of her blood. "One last for me," said the farmer. He put the barrel of the gun in his mouth. "No, no!" cried the boy.

The boy was standing by the side of a dirt road. A Ford pickup stopped beside him and he got in. "I'm going to shoot my wife," said the farmer. He had a big revolver on the seat beside him.

"You can't," said the boy.

They talked all the way to Lawrence. The farmer was crying. "I've always been good to her," he said. He had a red boil on the side of his neck and he kept touching it.

"Give the gun to the police," said the boy.

"I'm afraid," said the farmer.

"You needn't be," said the boy. "The police won't hurt you."

They drove to the police station. The boy told the desk sergeant what had happened. The sergeant shook his head. He took the revolver away from the farmer. "We'll get her back, sir," he said. "Wife stealing's not permitted around here."

"I could have got in real trouble," said the farmer.

The boy was standing by the side of a dirt road. A pickup stopped beside him and he got in. The farmer said, "I'm going to kill my wife."

The boy was too frightened to say anything. He kept looking at the forty-five revolver. He was sure that he would be shot himself. He regretted not staying in Oklahoma, where he had friends and family. He couldn't imagine why he had moved away. The farmer drove straight to Lawrence. The boy was bounced all over the cab of the pickup but he didn't say anything. He was afraid that something would happen to his hands and he wouldn't be able to play the piano. It seemed to him that playing the piano was the only important thing in the entire world. The farmer had a red boil on the side of his neck and he kept touching it.

When they got to Lawrence, the boy jumped out of the pickup and ran. He saw a policeman and told him what had happened. An hour later he was getting a hamburger at a White Tower restaurant. He heard shooting. He ran out and saw the farmer's dusty pickup. There were police cars with their lights flashing. The boy pushed through the crowd. The farmer was hanging half out of the door of his pickup truck. There was blood all over the front of his workshirt. The forty-five revolver lay on the pavement. The policemen were clapping each other on the back. They had big grins. The boy began cracking his knuckles. They made snapping noises.

The boy was standing by the side of a dirt road. A pickup stopped beside him and he got in. The farmer pointed a forty-five revolver at his head. "Get in here," he said. They drove toward Lawrence. "I'm going to shoot my wife for wickedness," said the farmer.

"No," said the boy, "you must forgive her."

"I'm going to kill her," said the farmer, "and her fancy man besides."

The boy said, "You can't take the law into your own hands."

The farmer raised his forty-five revolver. "They're as good as dead." He had a red boil on the side of his neck.

The boy was a college student. It was the Depression. He wanted to go to New York and become a classical pianist. He had already been accepted by Juilliard. "Justice does not belong to you," said the boy.

"Wickedness must be punished," said the farmer.

They argued all the way to Lawrence. The boy stayed with the farmer. He could have jumped out of the pickup, but he didn't. The boy kept trying to convince him that he was wrong. The farmer drove to the train station.

The farmer's wife was in the waiting room with the man who had been driving the Plymouth coupe. She was very pretty, with blond hair and milky pink skin. She screamed when she saw the farmer. Her companion put his arms around her to protect her.

The boy hurried to stand between the woman and her husband. "Think of what you are doing," he said. "Think how you are throwing your life away." The first bullet struck him in the shoulder and whipped him around. He could see the woman open her mouth in a startled *Oh* of surprise. The second bullet caught him in the small of his back.

The man's family was with him in New Hampshire when he died: his wife and his two sons, neither of them young anymore. It was early evening in October at the very height of color. Even after sundown the maple trees seemed bright. The older son watched his father breathing. He kept twisting and trying to kick his feet. His face was very thin, his whole body was just a ridge under the middle of the sheet. He didn't talk anymore. He didn't want anyone to touch him. He seemed to be focusing his attention. He took a breath and they waited. He exhaled slowly. They continued to wait. He didn't breathe again. They waited several minutes. Then his wife removed the oxygen tubes from his nose, doing it quickly, as if afraid of doing something wrong.

The older son went back into the bedroom with the two men from the funeral home. They had a collapsible stretcher which they put next to the bed. They unrolled a dark blue body bag. They shifted the dead man onto the stretcher and wrestled him into the body bag, one at his feet, one at his head. The son stood in the doorway. The men from the funeral home muttered directions to each other. They were breathing heavily and their hair was mussed.

At last they got him into the body bag. The son watched closely as the zipper was drawn up and across his father's face. It was a large silver zipper and the son watched it being pulled across his father's forehead. All the days after that he kept seeing its glittering progress, a picture repeating itself in his mind.

NATHAN ENGLANDER

The Tumblers

FROM AMERICAN SHORT FICTION

WHO WOULD HAVE THOUGHT that a war of such proportions would bother to turn its fury against the fools of Chelm? Never before, not by smallpox or tax collectors, was the city intruded upon by the troubles of the outside world.

The Wise Men of Chelm had seen to this when the town council was first founded. They drew up a law on a length of parchment, signed it, stamped on their seal, and nailed it, with much fanfare, to a tree. Not a wind, not a whistle, not the shadow from a cloud floating outside city limits, was welcome in the place called Chelm.

These were simple people with simple beliefs, who simply wanted to be left to themselves. And they were for generations, no one going in and only stories coming out, as good stories somehow always do. Tales of the Wise Men's logic, most notably of Mendel's grandfather, Gronam the Ox, spread, as the war later would, to the far corners of the earth.

In the Fulton Street Fish Market the dockworkers laughed with Yiddish good humor upon hearing how Gronam had tried to drown a carp. At a dairy restaurant in Buenos Aires, a customer was overcome with hiccups as his waiter recounted the events of the great sour cream shortage, explaining how Gronam had declared that water was sour cream and sour cream water, single-handedly saving the Feast of Weeks from complete and total ruin.

How the stories escaped is no great mystery, for though outsiders were unwelcome, every few years someone would pass through. There had been, among the trespassers, one vagrant and one vamp, one troubadour lost in a blizzard and one horse trader on a mule. A Gypsy tinker with a friendly face stayed a week. He put new hinges on all the doors while his wife told fortunes to the superstitious in the shade of the square. Of course, the most famous visit of all was made by the circus troupe that planted a tent and put on for three days show after show. Aside from these few that came through the center of town, there was also, always, no matter what some say, a black market thriving on the outskirts of Chelm. For where else did the stores come up with their delicacies? Even the biggest deniers of its existence could be seen eating a banana now and then.

Gronam's logic was still employed when the invaders built the walls around a corner of the city, creating the Ghetto of Chelm. There were so many good things lacking and so many bad in abundance that the people of the ghetto renamed almost all that they had: they called their aches "mother's milk," and darkness became "freedom"; filth they referred to as "hope" — and felt for a while, looking at each other's hands and faces and soot-blackened clothes, fortunate. It was only death that they could not rename, for they had nothing to put in its place. This is when they became sad and felt their hunger and when some began to lose their faith in God. This is when the Mahmir Rebbe, the most pious of them all, sent Mendel outside the walls.

It was no great shock for Mendel, for the streets outside the cramped ghetto were the streets of their town, the homes their homes, even if others now lived in them. The black market was the same except that it had been made that much more clandestine and greedy by the war. Mendel was happy to find that his grandfather's wisdom had been adopted among the peasants with whom he dealt. Potatoes were treated as gold, and a sack of gold might as well have been potatoes. Mendel traded away riches' worth of the latter (now the former) for as much as he could conceal on his person of the former (now the latter). He took the whole business to be a positive sign, thinking that people were beginning to regain their good sense.

The successful transaction gave Mendel a touch of real confidence. Instead of sneaking back the way he came, he ventured past the front of the icehouse and ignored the first signs of a rising sun. He ran through the alley behind Cross-eyed Bilha's store and skirted around the town square, keeping on until he arrived at his house. It was insanity — or suicide — for him to be out there. All anyone would need was a glimpse of him to know — less than that even, their senses had become so sharp. And what of the fate of the potatoes? They surely wouldn't make it to the ghetto if Mendel were caught and strung up from the declaration tree with a sign that said SMUGGLER hung around his neck. Those precious potatoes that filled his pockets and lined his long underwear from ankles to elbows would all go to waste, softening up and sprouting eyes. But Mendel needed to see his front gate and strip of lawn and the shingles he had painted himself only two summers before. It was then that the shutters flew open on his very own bedroom window. Mendel turned and ran with all his might, having seen no more of the new resident than a fog of breath. On the next street he found a sewer grate and, with considerable force, yanked it free. A rooster crowed and Mendel heard it at first as a call for help and a siren and the screeching of a bullet. Lowering himself underground and replacing the grate, he heard the rooster's call again and understood what it was — nature functioning as it should. He took it to be another positive sign.

Raising himself from the sewer, Mendel was unsure on which side of the wall he had emerged. The Ghetto of Chelm was alive with hustle and bustle. Were it not for the ragged appearance of each individual Jew, the crowd could have belonged to any cosmopolitan street.

"What is this? Has the circus returned to Chelm? Have they restocked all the sweetshops with licorice?" Mendel addressed the orphan Yocheved, grabbing hold of her arm and cradling in his palm a tiny potato, which she snatched away. She looked up at him, her eyes wet from the wind.

"We are all going to live on a farm and must hurry not to miss the train."

"A farm, you say." He pulled at his beard and bent until his face was even with the child's. "With milking cows?"

"And ducks," said Yocheved before running away.

"Roasted? Or glazed in the style of the Chinese?" he called after her, though she had already disappeared into the crowd, vanishing with the finesse that all the remaining ghetto children had acquired. He had never tasted glazed duck, only knew that there was somewhere in existence such a thing. As he wove through the scrambling ghettoites Mendel fantasized about such a meal, wondered if it was like biting into a caramel-coated apple or as tender and dark as the crust of yolk-basted bread. His stomach churned at the thought of it as he rushed off to find the Rebbe.

The decree was elementary: only essential items were to be taken on the trains. Most packed their meager stores of food, some clothing, and a photograph or two. Here and there a diamond ring found its way into a hunk of bread or a string of pearls rolled itself into a pair of wool socks.

For the Hasidim of Chelm, interpreting such a request was far from simple. As in any other town where Hasidim live, two distinct groups had formed. In Chelm they were called the Students of the Mekyl and the Mahmir Hasidim. The Students of the Mekyl were a relaxed bunch, taking their worship lightly while keeping within the letter of the law. Due to the ease of observance and the Epicurean way in which they relished in the Lord, they were a very popular group, numbering into the thousands.

The Mahmir Hasidim, on the other hand, were extremely strict. If a fast was to last one day, they would cease eating the day before and starve themselves a day later, guarding against the possibility that in setting their lunar calendars they had been fooled by the phases of the moon. As with the fasts went every requirement in Jewish law. Doubling was not enough, so they tripled, often passing out before pouring the twelfth glass of wine required of the Passover seders. Such zealousness takes much dedication. And considering the adjusted length of the holidays — upward of three weeks at a shot — not any small time commitment either. The Mahmir Hasidim, including children, numbered less than twenty on the day the ghetto was dissolved.

Initially circulating as rumor, the edict sparked mass confusion. The inhabitants of the ghetto tried to make logical decisions based on whispers and the skeptical clucking of tongues. Heads of households rubbed their temples and squeezed shut their eyes, struggling to apply their common sense to a situation anything but common.

To ease the terror spreading among his followers, the leader of the Mekyls was forced to make a decree of his own. Hoisted atop a boxcar, balancing on the sawed-off and lovingly sanded broomstick that had replaced his mahogany cane, he defined "essential items" as everything one would need to stock a summer home. In response to a query called out from the crowd of his followers, he announced that the summer home was to be considered unfurnished. He bellowed the last word and slammed down the broomstick for emphasis, sending an echo through the empty belly of the car below.

Off went the Mekyls to gather bedsteads and bureaus, hammocks and lawn chairs — all that a family might need in relocation. The rabbi of the Mahmir Hasidim, in his infinite strictness (and in response to the shameful indulgence of the Mekyls), understood "essential" to exclude anything other than one's long underwear, for all else was excess adornment.

"Even our ritual fringes?" asked Feitel, astonished.

"Even the hair of one's beard," said the Rebbe, considering the grave nature of their predicament. This sent a shudder through his followers, all except Mendel, who was busy distributing potatoes amid the humble gathering. No one ate. They were waiting for the Rebbe to make the blessing. But the Rebbe refused his share. "Better to give it to a Mekyl who is not so used to doing without."

They all, as if by reflex, stuck out their hands so Mendel should take back theirs too. "Eat, eat!" said the Rebbe. "You eat yours and give me the pleasure of watching." He smiled at his followers. "Such loyal students even Rebbe Akiva, blessed be his memory, would've been honored to have."

The Mahmirim rushed back to their cramped flats, the men shedding their gabardines and ritual fringes, the women folding their frocks and slipping them into drawers. Feitel, his hand shaking, the tears streaming down his face, began to cut at his beard, bit by bit, inch by inch. "Why not in one shot?" his wife, Zahava, asked. "Get it over with." But he couldn't. So he trimmed at his beard like a barber, as if putting on finishing touches that never seemed right. Zahava paced the floor, stepping through the clumps of hair and the long dusty rectangles of sunshine that, relentless, could not be kept from the ghetto. For the first time in her married life Zahava left her kerchief at home, needlessly locking the door behind her.

They returned to the makeshift station to find the Students of the Mekyl lugging mattresses and dishes and suitcases so full they leaked sleeves and collars from every seam. One little girl brought along her pet dog, its mangy condition made no less shocking by the fact that it looked healthier than its mistress. The Mahmirim turned their faces away from this laxity of definition. An earthly edict, even one coming from their abusers, should be translated strictly lest the invaders think that Jews were not pious in their observance.

The Mahmir Rebbe ordered his followers away from that mass of heathens in case — God forbid — one of the Mahmirim, shivering in long underwear and with naked scalp, should be mistaken for a member of that court. They trudged off in their scanty dress, the women feeling no shame, since the call for such immodesty had come from their teacher's mouth.

Not even the last car of the train was far enough away for the Rebbe. "Come," he said, pushing through the crowd toward the tunnel that was and was not Chelm.

Though there was a track and a tunnel, and a makeshift station newly constructed by the enemy, none of it was actually part of town. Gronam had seen to this himself when the railroad first laid track along the edge of the woods. He had sworn that the train itself would not pass through any part of Chelm (swore, he thought, safely — sure it wasn't an issue). Checking over maps and deeds and squabbling over whether to pace the distances off heel-toe or toe-heel, the Wise Men discovered that the hill through which the workers were tunneling was very much part of Chelm. They panicked, argued, screamed themselves hoarse in a marathon meeting. It was almost midnight when Gronam came up with a plan.

Tapping on doors, whispering into sleep-clogged ears, the Wise Men roused every able body from bed, and together they sneaked down to the site armed with chisels and kitchen knives, screwdrivers and hoes. It was the only time any of them had been, though only by a few feet, outside of Chelm. Taking up bricks destined for tunnel walls, they waited for Gronam's signal. He *hoo-hoo*ed like an owl and they set to work, etching a longitudinal line around each one. Before dawn, before the workers returned to find the bricks stacked as they were at quitting time the day before and a fine snow of dust around the site, Gronam made a declaration. The top half of every brick was to be considered theirs, and the bottom half, everything below the line, belonged to the railroad. In this way, when the train entered the tunnel, it would not actually pass through Chelm. They reveled in Gronam's wisdom, having kept the railroad out of town and also made its residents richer in the bargain — for they were now the proud owners of so many top halves of bricks which they hadn't had before.

Mendel recalled that morning. He had stood in his nightshirt in the street outside his parents' home and watched his grandfather — the massive Gronam — being carried back to the square on the shoulders of neighbors and friends. Simple times, he thought. Even the greatest of challenges, the battle against the railroad, all seemed so simple now.

The memory left him lightheaded (so grueling was the journey from that morning as a child back to the one that, like a trap, bit into their lives with iron teeth). He stumbled forward into the wedge of Mahmirim, nearly knocking little Yocheved to the ground. He steadied himself and then the girl as they moved slowly forward, forging their way across the current of Jews that swirled, rushed, and finally broke against the hard floors of the cattle cars.

Mendel did not understand how the Rebbe planned to reach the tunnel alive, though he believed they would succeed. The darkness had been getting closer for so long, it seemed only just that it should finally envelop them, pull them into its vacuum — the tunnel ready to swallow them up like so many coins dropped into a pocket.

And that is how it felt to Mendel, like they were falling away from an open hand, plunging, as they broke away from the crowd.

In the moment that two guards passed the entrance to the tunnel in opposite directions, their shepherds straining on their leashes, in the moment when the sniper on the top of the train had his attention turned the other way, in the moment before Mendel followed the Rebbe into the tunnel, Yocheved spotted her uncle Misha and froze. Mendel did not bump into her again, though he would, until his death, wish he had.

Yocheved watched her uncle being shoved, brutalized, beaten into a boxcar, her sweet uncle who would carve her treats out of marzipan: flowers, and fruits, and peacocks whose feathers melted on her tongue.

"Come along, Yocheved," the Rebbe called from the tunnel, without breaking stride. But the darkness was so uninviting, and there was Uncle Misha — a car length away — who always had for her a gift.

Her attention was drawn to the sound of a healthy bark, an angry bark, not the type that might have come from the sickly Jewish dog, which had already been put down. It was the bark of a dog that drags its master. Yocheved turned to see the beast bolting along the perimeter of the crowd.

Before the dog could reach her and tear the clothes from her skin and the skin from her bones, the sniper on the train put a single bullet through her neck. The bullet left a ruby hole that resembled a charm an immodest girl might wear. Yocheved touched a finger to her throat and turned her gaze toward the sky, wondering from where such a strange gift had come.

Only Mendel looked back at the sound of the shot; the others had learned the lessons of Sodom.

The Mahmirim followed the tracks around a bend where they found, waiting for them, a passenger train. Maybe a second train waited outside every ghetto so that Mahmirim should not have to ride with Mekylim. The cars were old, a patchwork of relics from the last century. The locomotive in the distance looked too small for the job. Far better still, Mendel felt, than the freight wagons and the chaos they had left on the other side of the tunnel. Mendel was sure that the conductor waited for the next train at the next ghetto to move on with its load. There had never been enough travel or commerce to warrant another track and suddenly there was traffic, so rich was the land with Jews.

"Nu?" the Rebbe said to Mendel. "You are the tallest. Go have a look."

At each car, Mendel placed his foot on the metal step and pulled himself up with the bar bolted alongside. His hands were huge, befitting his lineage. Gronam's own were said to have been as broad as a shovel's head. Mendel's — somewhat smaller — had always been soft, ungainly but unnoticed. The ghetto changed that. It turned them hard and menacing. There was a moment as he grabbed hold of the bar when the Mahmirim wondered if Mendel would rise up to meet the window or pull the train over on their heads.

Leaning right, peering in, Mendel announced his findings.

"Full," he said. "Full." Then, "Full, again." Pressed together as one, the Rebbe and his followers moved forward after each response.

On the fourth attempt the car was empty and Mendel pushed open the door. The Mahmirim hurried aboard, still oblivious to their good fortune and completely unaware that it was a gentile train.

On any other transport the Mahmirim wouldn't have gotten even that far. But this happened to be a train of showmen, entertainers waiting for clear passage to a most important engagement. These were worldly people traveling about during wartime. Very little in the way of oddities could shock them — something in which they took great pride. And, of course, as Mendel would later find out, there had been until most recently the Romanian and his bear. Because of him — and the bear — those dozing in the last few cars, those who saw the flash of Mendel's head and the pack of identically clad fools stumbling behind, were actually tickled at the sight. Another lesson in fate for Mendel. The difference between the sniper's bullet and survival fell somewhere between a little girl's daydream and a fondness for bears.

The Romanian had been saddled with a runtish secondhand bear that would not dance or step up on a ball or growl with fake ferociousness. Useless from a life of posing with children in front of a slack-shuttered camera, the bear refused to do anything but sit. From this the Romanian concocted a routine. He would dress the bear as a wounded soldier and lug his furry comrade around the stage, setting off firecrackers and spouting political satire. It brought audiences to hysterics. A prize act! From this he came up with others: the fireman, the side-splitting Siamese twins, and — for the benefit of the entertainers themselves — the bride. When the train was chugging slowly up a hill, the Romanian would dress the bear in bridal gown and veil. He'd get off the front car cradling his bride and pretend they'd just missed their honeymoon train to the mountains. The entertainers howled with joy as he ran alongside the tracks, crying out for a conductor and tripping over a giant tin pocket watch tied to his waist and dragging behind. A funny man, that Romanian. And strong. A very strong man it takes to run with a bear.

When the Mahmirim appeared at the back of the train, all who saw them remembered their friend. How they all missed his antics after he was taken away. And how the bear had moped. Like a real person. Yes, it would be good to have a new group of wiseacres. And they turned in their seats, laughing out loud at these shaved-headed fools, these clowns without makeup — no, not clowns, acrobats. They could only be acrobats in such bland and colorless attire — and so skinny, too. Just the right builds for it. Lithe for the high wire.

In this way, the Mahmirim successfully boarded the train.

They busied themselves with choosing compartments, seeing that Raizel the widow had space to prop up her feet, separating the women from the men, trying to favor husbands and wives and to keep the youngest, Shraga, a boy of eleven, with his mother. In deference to King Saul's having numbered the people with lambs, the Rebbe, as is the fashion, counted his followers with a verse of Psalms, one word for each person, knowing already that he would fall short without Yocheved. This is the curse that had befallen them. Always one less word.

Mendel, who had once been a Mekyl but overcome by the wisdom of the Mahmirim had joined their small tribe, still hadn't lost his taste for excessive drink. He found his way to the bar car — well stocked for wartime — without even a pocket, let alone a zloty, with which he might come by some refreshment. Scratching at the wool of his long underwear, he stared at the bottles, listening as they rocked one against the other, tinkling lightly like chimes. He was especially taken with a leaded crystal decanter. Its smooth single-malt contents rode up and down its inner walls, caressing the glass and teasing Mendel in a way that he considered cruel.

Dismissing the peril to which he was exposing the others, Mendel sought out a benefactor who might sport him a drink. It was in this way — in which only God can turn a selfish act into a miracle — that Mendel initially saved all of their lives.

An expert on the French horn complimented Mendel on the rustic simplicity of his costume and invited him to join her in a drink. It was this tippler who alerted Mendel to the fact that the Mahmirim were assumed to be acrobats. Talking freely, and intermittently cursing the scheduling delays caused by the endless transports, she told him of the final destinations of those nuisance-causing trains.

"This," she said, "was told to me by Günter the Magnificent —
who was never that magnificent, considering that Druckenmüller
always outclassed him with both the doves and the rings." She
paused and ordered two brandies. Mendel put his hand out to
touch her arm, stopping short of contact.

"If you wouldn't mind, if it's not too presumptuous." He pointed
to the decanter, blushing, remembering the Rebbe's lectures on
gluttony.

"Fine choice, fine choice. My pleasure." She knocked an empty
snifter against the deep polished brown of the table (a color so rich
it seemed as if the brandy had seeped through her glass and dis-
tilled into the table's surface). Not since the confiscation of the
Mekyl Rebbe's cane had Mendel seen such opulence. "Barman, a
scotch as well. Your finest." The barman served three drinks and
the musician poured the extra brandy into her glass. She drank
without a word. Mendel toasted her silently and, after the blessing,
sipped at his scotch, his first in so very long. He let its smoky flavor
rise up and fill his head, hoping that if he drank slowly enough, if
he let the scotch rest on his tongue long enough and roll gradually
enough down his throat, then maybe he could cure his palate like
the oak slats of a cask. Maybe then he could keep the warmth and
the comfort with him for however much longer God might deem
that they should survive.

"Anyway, Günter came to us directly from a performance for the
highest of the high, where his beautiful assistant Leine had been
told in the powder room by the wife of an official of unmatched
feats of magic being performed with the trains. They go away full —
packed so tightly that babies are stuffed in over the heads of the
passengers when there's no room for another full grown — and
come back empty, as if never before used."

"And the Jews?" asked Mendel. "What trick is performed with the
Jews?"

"Sleight of hand," she said, splashing the table with her drink and
waving her fingers by way of demonstration. "A classic illusion. First
they are here, and then they are gone.

"According to the wife of the official, those who witness it faint
dead away, overcome by the grand scale of the illusion. For a moment the magician stands, a field of Jews at his feet, then nothing."
She paused for dramatic effect, not unaccustomed to life in the

theater. "The train sits empty. The magician stands alone on the platform. Nothing remains but the traditional puff of smoke. This trick he performs, puff after puff, twenty-four hours a day.

"After Günter heard, he forgot all about Druckenmüller and his doves and became obsessed with what Leine had told him. He would sit at the bar and attempt the same thing with rabbits, turning his ratty bunnies into colored bursts of smoke, some pink, some purple, occasionally plain gray. He swore he wouldn't give up until he had perfected his magic. Though he knew, you could tell, that it would never match the magnitude of a trainload of Jews. I told him myself when he asked my opinion. Günter, I said, it takes more than nimble fingers to achieve the extraordinary." With that Mendel felt a hand on his knee.

Pausing only to finish his drink, Mendel ran back to the car full of Mahmirim and relayed to the Rebbe the tales of horror he had heard. Mendel was the Rebbe's favorite. Maybe not always so strict in his service of the Lord, Mendel was full of His spirit; this the Rebbe could see. For that reason he ignored the prohibition against gossip and took into consideration his student's most unbelievable report.

"It can't be, Mendele!" said the Rebbe.

"Their cruelty knows no bounds," cried Raizel the widow.

The Rebbe sat in silence for some minutes, considering the events of the last years and the mystery of all those who had disappeared before them. He decided that what Mendel told them must be so.

"I'm afraid," he said, "that the gossip Mendel repeats is true. Due to its importance, in this instance there can be no sin in repeating such idle talk." The Rebbe glanced at the passing scenery and pulled at the air where once had been his beard. "No other choice," he said. "A solitary option. Only one thing for us to do . . ." The followers of the Mahmir Rebbe hung on his words.

"We must tumble."

Mendel had been to the circus as a boy. During the three-day engagement, Mendel had sneaked into the tent for every performance, hiding under the bowed pine benches and peering out through the space beneath all the legs too short to reach the hay-strewn ground.

Though he did not remember a single routine or feat of daring, he did recall, in addition to the sparkling of some scandalously placed sequins, the secret to convincing the other performers that they were indeed acrobats. The secret was nothing more than an exclamation. It was, simply, a "Hup!" Knowing this, the Mahmirim lined the corridor and began to practice.

"You must clap your hands once in a while as well," Mendel told them. The Rebbe was already nearing old age and therefore clapped and hupped far more than he jumped.

Who knew that Raizel the widow had double-jointed arms, or that Shmuel Berel could scurry about upside down on hands and feet, mocking the movements of a crab? Falling from a luggage rack from which he had tried to suspend himself, Mendel, on his back, began to laugh. The others shared the release and laughed along with him. In their car near the end of the train, there was real and heartfelt delight. They were giddy with the chance God had granted them. They laughed as the uncondemned might, as free people in free countries do.

The Rebbe interrupted this laughter. "Even in the most foreign situation we must adhere to the laws," he said. Therefore, as in the laws of singing, no woman was to tumble unless accompanied by another woman, and no man was to catch a woman — though husbands were given a dispensation to catch their airborne wives.

Not even an hour had gone by before it was obvious what state they were in: weak with hunger and sickness, never having asked of their bodies such rigors before — all this on top of their near-total ignorance of acrobatics and the shaking of the train. At the least, they would need further direction. A tip or two on which to build.

Pained by the sight of it, the Rebbe called a stop to their futile flailing about.

"Mendel," he said, "back to your drunks and gossips. Bring us the secrets to this act. As is, not even a blind man would be tricked by the sounds of such graceless footfalls."

"Me!" Mendel said, with the mock surprise of Moses, as if there were some other among them fit to do the job.

"Yes, you," the Rebbe said, shooing him away. "Hurry off."

Mendel did not move.

He looked at the Mahmirim as he thought the others might. He saw that it was only by God's will that they had gotten that far. A

ward of the insane or of consumptives would have been a far better
misperception in which to entangle this group of uniformly clad
souls. Their acceptances as acrobats was a stretch, a first-glance
guess, a benefit of the doubt granted by circumstance and only as
valuable as their debut would prove. It was an absurd undertaking.
But then again, Mendel thought, no more unbelievable than the
reality from which they'd escaped, no more unfathomable than the
magic of disappearing Jews. If the good people of Chelm could
believe that water was sour cream, if the peasant who woke up that
first morning in Mendel's bed and put on Mendel's slippers and
padded over to the window could believe, upon throwing back the
shutters, that the view he saw had always been his own, then why not
pass as acrobats and tumble across the earth until they found a
place where they were welcome?

"What am I to bring back?" Mendel said.

"The secrets," answered the Rebbe, an edge in his voice, no time
left for hedging or making things clear. "There are secrets behind
everything that God creates."

"And a needle and thread," said Raizel the widow. "And a pair of
scissors. And anything, too."

"Anything?" Mendel said.

"Yes, anything," Raizel said. "Bits of paper or string. Anything
that a needle can prick or thread can hold."

Mendel raised his eyebrows at the request. The widow talked as if
he were heading off to Cross-eyed Bilha's general store.

"They will have," she said. "They are entertainers — forever losing buttons and splitting seams." She clucked her tongue at Mendel, who still had his eyebrows raised. "These costumes, as is, will
surely never do."

It was the horn gleaming on the table next to the slumped form of
its player that first caught Mendel's attention. He rushed over and
sat down next to her. He stared out the window at the forest rushing by. He tried to make out secluded worlds cloaked by the trees.
Little Yocheved's farm must be out there somewhere, a lone homestead hidden like Eden in the woods. It would be on the other side
of a broad and rushing river where the dogs would lose scent of a
Jewish trail.

Mendel knocked on the table to rouse the musician and looked
up to find gazes focused upon him from around the bar. The

observers did not appear unfriendly, only curious, travel weary, interested — Mendel assumed — in a new face who already knew a woman so well.

"You?" she said, lifting her head and smiling. "My knight in bed-clothes has returned." The others went back to their drinks as she scanned the room in half consciousness. "Barman," she called. "A drink for my knight." She rested her head on the crook of her arm and slid the horn over so she could see Mendel with an uninter-rupted view. "You were in my dream," she said. "You and Günter. I mustn't tell such stories anymore, they haunt me so."

"I've torn my costume," Mendel said, "the only one I have. And in a most embarrassing place."

Shielded by the table, she walked her fingers up Mendel's leg.

"I can't imagine where," she said, attempting a flutter of alcohol-deadened lids.

"Thread," Mendel said, "and a needle. You wouldn't happen to have —"

"Of course," she said. She tried to push herself up. "In my com-partment, come along. I'll sew you up there."

"No," he said. "You go, I'll stay here — and if you could, if you wouldn't mind making an introduction, I'm in desperate need of advice."

"After I sew you," she said. She curled her lip into a pout, accen-tuating an odd mark left by years of playing. "It's only two cars away."

"You go," Mendel said. "And then we'll talk. And maybe later tonight I'll come by and you can reinforce the seams." Mendel winked.

The horn player purred and went off, stumbling against the rhythm of the train so that she actually appeared balanced. Mendel spied the open horn case under the table. Rummaging through it, he found a flowered cotton rag, damp with saliva. Looking about, nonchalant, he tucked it into his sleeve.

"It's called a Full Twisting Voltas," Mendel said, trying to approxi-mate the move as he had understood it. Aware that as much as had been lost during a half-demonstration in a smoke-filled bar car, twice that was again lost in his return to the Mahmirim, and another twice that lost again in his body's awkward translation of the move.

Shmuel Berel, intent and driven, attempted the move first, prov-
ing — as he would throughout the afternoon — to be almost completely useless when it came to anything where timing was involved.
Under protest, for he wanted to do his share, Shmuel was told to
scuttle about the stage continuously during the performance doing
his upside-down backward walk. Coordination proved to be a problem for Raizel the widow and Shraga's mother, and — not surprisingly — for the Rebbe as well. For them Mendel returned again to
the bar car in search of simpler, less challenging moves. For Shraga,
a live wire and a natural performer, he inquired about some more
complicated combinations on which to work.

Mendel paused between cars, pondering the rush of track and tie
and the choices it raised. How would it be if he were to jump off and
roll, in faulty acrobatic form, down an embankment and into a
stretch of field? What if he were to start himself off on another
tributary of the nightmare, to seek out a scheme as random and
hopeless as the one of which he was a part; and what of the wheels
and the possibility of lowering himself underneath, thrusting himself into some new hell that would at least guarantee a comfort in its
permanence — how much easier to face an eternity without wonder? Over and over again, Mendel chose neither, feeling the rush of
wind and moving on into the next car, passing and excusing, smiling his way along, his senses sharpened like a nesting bird's, eagle-
eyed and watching for scraps of cotton or lost ribbon, anything to
bring back to Raizel and her needle.

Two men, forever at the same window and smoking a ransom's
worth of cigars, had come to recognize Mendel and begun to make
friendly jokes at his expense. The pair particularly relished the
additions to his costume. "The Ragdoll Review," one would say. And
the other, rotating the cigar, puff, puff, puffing away at it like a
locomotive himself, would yank it from his mouth and say, "How
many of you are there, each adorned with one more scrap?"

As many as the cars, Mendel thought, and the trains, and the
lengths of track. As many as have been taken and wait at the stations
and right now move toward another place. As plentiful as the drops
of rain that puddle the world over, except in Chelm, where they
gather in the gutters into torrents of sour cream.

Each time Mendel returned to the Mahmirim, he found the car
seemingly empty. At most he'd catch a rustling of curtains, or find

Raizel smiling sheepishly — too slow to seal herself into a compartment before his entrance. It reminded him of the center of town
when strangers stumbled through. All the townspeople would disappear, including Cross-eyed Bilha, who also ran the inn. (The inn
was a brainchild of the Wise Men — for whether or not strangers
were welcome, no one should be able to say that Chelm was so
provincial as to lack accommodations.) Eventually, out of curiosity
or terror, a resident who could stand the suspense no longer would
venture a look outside. The circus, prepared for a three-day ex-
travaganza, whip and chair already in the ring and tigers poised on
overturned tubs, had sat three times three days until one of the
Wise Men first dared peer into the tent.

"Open up," Mendel called. "It gets dark, and there's work to be
done." Compartment doors opened and Mendel told everyone to
remain in their seats. "Just Shraga," he said, "and Feitel and Zahava.
We are going to break the routine down into sections, and each will
learn his own part."

"No," the Rebbe said. "There isn't time. What if we should arrive
in an hour, before all have learned what it is they are to do?"

"There is time," Mendel said. "The train barely moves now. Up
front they get off and walk alongside, only to climb on a few lengths
back. We will have the whole of tomorrow morning and up until
noon. The horn player told me — we are headed to an evening
performance."

"It sounds like they are maybe trying to make a fool of you,"
Feitel said. "As if maybe they know."

"Do they know?" Zahava asked.

"What is it they know?" Little Shraga came out of his compartment, frightened.

"No one knows," Mendel said. "If they knew, it would be over and
done with — of that you can be sure. As for practicing, there is
great wisdom in the sections. They will allow you to rest, Rebbe, and
Raizel to sew." Mendel smiled at Raizel as she fastened a cork to
Feitel's chest. Feitel chewed on a bit of thread to keep away the
Angel of Death, for only the dead wear their garments while they
are sewn. "It is called choreography, Rebbe. It is the way such things
are done."

That understood, they worked on the choreography in the aisle
that ran the length of the car. Those watching sat in their compartments with the doors slid open and tried to pick up the moves from

the quick flicker of a body in motion passing before them. It was like learning how to dance by thumbing through a flip book, page by page.

While some worked on cartwheels and somersaults, rolling in a line first one way and then the other, Shraga, reckless and with more room in which to move his spindly body, actually showed a great deal of promise. So much that the Rebbe said, "In another world, my son, who knows what might have become of you?"

The Mahmirim worked until they could work no more. That night they rolled in their sleep while the engineer up front tugged his whistle in greeting to the engines pulling the doomed the other way.

Shraga was the first to rise, an hour before dawn. He woke each of the others with a gentle touch on the shoulder. Each one, snapping awake, looked around for a moment, agitated and confused.

They began to practice right off, doing the best they could in the darkness. The Rebbe interrupted as the sky began to lighten. "Come up from there," the Rebbe said to Raizel. She was on the floor tearing bits of upholstery from under the seats, from where the craftsmen had cinched the corners. These she would sew into a moon over Zahava's heart. "Come along," the Rebbe said. Mendel, who was fiddling with a spoon Raizel had fastened to a sleeve and advising Shraga on the length of his leap, came with the others to crowd around the Rebbe's compartment.

"More than one kind of dedication is required if we are to survive this ordeal." The Rebbe looked out the window as he spoke.

They separated the men from the women and began to say their morning prayers. It was not a matter of disregarding the true peril to which it exposed them but an instance in which the danger was not considered. They called out to the heavens in full voices. When they had finished there was a pause, a moment of silence. It was as if they were waiting for an answer from the Lord.

The train stopped.

Feitel was in the air when it did. He landed with a momentum greater than the train's and rolled pell-mell into the hardness of a wall.

"I've broken my back," he said. The others ignored him. There wasn't the urgency of truth in his voice. And outside the windows there were tracks upon tracks and platform after platform and the first uncountable stories of a building, higher, surely, than the Tower of Babel was ever meant to be.

By the time Feitel got to his feet, the performers had already begun to pour out onto the platform, lugging trunks and valises, garment bags and makeup cases with rounded edges and silver clasps.

The door to the car slammed open and a head and shoulders popped in. On the face was a thin mustache that, like a rain gutter, diverted the sweat away from pale lips. And how the sweat ran; in that very first moment the face reddened noticeably and new beads of perspiration drove on the last.

"Who are you?" the man asked. "What might this ragtag bunch perform?"

Mendel stepped forward.

"We are the tumblers."

"Have you tumbled off the garbage heap?"

Feitel felt the ridiculousness of his costume and put his hand over the five-pointed star of champagne corks fastened to his chest.

"No matter," the man said. "How much prep time do you need?"

"Prep?" Mendel said.

"I've no patience for this. We're three hours late already. They'll have my head, not yours." A hand plunged through the door. The man looked at the watch on the wrist and wiped the sweat from his brow as best he could. The hand appeared an odd match, as if this intruder were constructed of loose parts. His face reddened further and he puffed out his cheeks. "Prep time," he said. "Trampolines, pommel horses, trapezes. What needs to be set up?"

"Nothing," Mendel said.

"As plain as you look, eh? Fine. Then, good." He appeared to calm slightly — ever so slightly. "Then you're on first. Now get down there and help the others lug their chattel to the theater."

The Mahmirim rushed out the door, Mendel's mouth opening wide as he followed the rest of the building into the sky. He let out a whistle and then continued to gape. It was beautiful and menacing. The whole place was menacing, for every wonder was in some way marred, every thing of beauty stained gray with war. To try to escape from it, to schedule galas and dress for balls, was farcical even for the enemy. The gray mood was all-pervading. The performers hurried along with their preshow expressions, looking dyspeptic. Impostors, one and all. Their stage smiles, Mendel knew, would sparkle.

Raizel the widow led a monkey on a leash. The monkey held a banana, the first any had seen in years. The widow would pick up her pace and then stop suddenly. The monkey did the same. Her crooked fingers were bunched into a single claw, ready to snatch the prize away at first chance. Mendel stood behind her, a trunk on his head, watching Raizel try to trick a banana from a monkey. He was surprised, as always, to witness a new degradation, to find another display of wretchedness original enough to bring tears to his eyes. He took a deep breath and ignored his sense of injustice, a rich man's emotion, a feeling Mendel had given up on experiencing horrors and horrors before.

It was only a short time until they reached their destination, a building as wide as the train was long. The interior promised to be grand. But the Mahmirim didn't get to see any of the trompe l'oeil or gold leaf that adorned the lobby. They were ushered backstage through double doors.

As the procession filed in, the mood of the entertainers transformed. There was a newfound energy, a heightened professionalism. Even the drinkers from the bar car and the tired smokers Mendel had shuffled past in the passageways moved with a sudden precision. Mendel took note of it as a juggler grabbed the monkey and began, with detached brutality, to force the animal into trousers. He noted it as the aging dancers hid their heads behind the lids of mirrored cases, only to look up again, having created an illusion of youth that from any seat in the house would go unchallenged. Mendel went cold with terror, watching, trying to isolate what in these innocuous preparations was so disturbing.

As the stage manager hurried by, his shirt transparent with perspiration, his arms full of tin swords, and screaming "Shnell" at anyone whose idle gaze he caught, Mendel figured out to what his great terror was due. It was the efficiency displayed by each and every one, the crack hop-to-it-ness, the discipline and order. He had seen it from the start, from the day the intruders marched into town and, finding the square empty, began kicking down doors, from the instant meticulousness demanded that a war of such massive scope make time to seek out a happily isolated dot-on-the-map hamlet-called-city where resided the fools of Chelm. It was this efficiency, Mendel knew, that would catch up with them.

"It's like we are in the bowels of the earth," Raizel said, motioning to the catwalk and the sandbags and the endless ropes and pegs.

"Which one to pull for rain?" Feitel said. "And which for a good harvest?"

"And which for redemption?" the Rebbe said, his tone forlorn and as close as he came to despair.

"You did a wonderful job," Mendel said. He, against all they had been taught, put a hand to Raizel's cheek. "The costumes are most imaginative." He knocked his elbows together, and the spoons clinked like a dull chime.

"A wonder with a needle and thread. It's true." This from Zahava in a breastplate of cigarette boxes and with pipe cleaners sewn to her knees.

The widow slipped an arm around Zahava's waist — always such a trim girl, even before — and pulled her close as she used to do Sabbath mornings on the way out of the shtibl. Raizel squeezed her as tightly as she could, and Zahava, more gently, squeezed back. Both held their eyes closed. It was obvious that they were together in another place, back outside the shtibl when the dogwoods were in bloom, both in new dresses, modest and lovely.

Mendel and the Rebbe and Feitel, all the Mahmirim who could not join in the embrace or the escape to better times, looked away. It was too much to bear unopaqued by any of the usual defenses. They raised their eyes as Zahava planted a kiss on the old woman's head, a kiss so sincere that Mendel tried to cut the gravity by half.

"You know," he said, "never has so much been made of the accidental boarding of a second-class train."

His observation, a poor joke, did not get a single smile. It only set the Mahmirim to looking about once again, desperate for a place on which to rest their gazes.

It may have come from a leaky pipe, a hole in the roof, or off the chin of the stage manager darting about, but most likely it was a tear abandoned by an anonymous eye. It hit the floor, a single drop, immediately to the right of the Rebbe.

"What is this?" the Rebbe said. "I won't have it. Not for a minute!"

Mendel and the others put on expressions as if they did not know to what he referred, as if they did not sense the somberness and the defeat rising up around them.

"Come, come," said the Rebbe. "We are on first, and Shraga has not yet perfected his Full Twisting Voltas." He tapped out a four beat with his foot. "Hup," he said. "From the top," he said, exhausting all of the vocabulary that he had learned.

They made a space for themselves and ran through the routine, the Rebbe not letting them rest for a moment and Mendel loving him with all his heart.

The manager came for them at five minutes to curtain. It was then, from the wings, that they got to see it all. The red carpets and festooned gold braids, the chandelier and frescoed ceiling — full of heroes and maidens and celestial rays — hemmed in by elaborate moldings. And the moldings themselves were bedecked with rosy-cheeked cherubim carved from wood. There was also the audience — the women in gowns and hair piled high, the men in their uniforms, pinned heavy with medals for efficiency and bravery and strength. An important audience, just the kind to make a nervous man sweat. There was also a box up and off to the left; in it sat a leader and his escort, a man of great power, on whom, Mendel could tell, a part of everyone was focused. The chandelier was turned down and the stage lights came up and the manager whispered "Go" so that Shraga stepped out onto the stage. The others followed. It was as plain as that. They followed because there was nothing else to do.

For a moment, then two, then three, they all stood at the back of the stage, blinded. Raizel put a hand up to her eyes. There was a cough and then a chuckle. The echo had not yet come to rest when the Rebbe called out:

"To your marks!"

Lifting their heads, straightening their postures, they spread out across the hard floor.

"Hup," cried the Rebbe, and the routine commenced. Shraga cartwheeled and flipped. The widow Raizel jumped once and then stood off to the side with her double-jointed arms turned inside out. Mendel, glorious Mendel, actually executed a springing Half Hanlon and, with Shmuel Berel's assistance (his only real task), ended in a Soaring Angel. Feitel, off his mark, missed his wife as she came toward him in a leap. Zahava landed on her ankle, which let out a crisp, clear crack. She did not whimper, quickly standing up. Though it was obvious even from the balcony that her foot was not on right. There was, after a gasp from the audience, silence. Then, from above, from off to the left, a voice was heard. Mendel knew from which box it came. He knew it was the most polished, the most straight and tall, a maker of magic, to be sure. Of course, this is conjecture, for how could he see?

"Look," said the voice. "They are as clumsy as Jews." There was a pause, and then singular and boisterous laughter. The laughter echoed and was picked up by the audience, who laughed back with lesser glee, not wanting to overstep their bounds. Mendel looked to the Rebbe, and the Rebbe shrugged. Young Shraga, a natural survivor, took a hop-step as if to continue. Zahava moved toward the widow Raizel and rested a hand on her shoulder.

"More," called the voice. "The farce can't have already come to its end. More!" it said. Another voice, that of a woman, came from the same place and barely carried to the stage.

"Yes, keep on," it said. "More of the Jewish ballet." The fatuous laugh that followed, as with the other, was picked up by the audience and the cavernous echo, so that it seemed even the wooden cherubim laughed from above.

The Rebbe took a deep breath and began to tap with his foot.

Mendel waved him off and stepped forward, moving downstage, the spotlight harsh and unforgiving against his skin. He reached out past the footlights into the dark, his hands cracked and bloodless, gnarled and intrusive.

Mendel turned his palms upward, benighted.

But there were no snipers, as there are for hands that reach out of the ghettos; no dogs, as for hands that reach out from the cracks in boxcar floors; no angels waiting, as they always do, for hands that reach out from chimneys into ash-clouded skies.

TIM GAUTREAUX

The Piano Tuner

FROM HARPER'S MAGAZINE

THE PHONE RANG Monday morning while the piano tuner was
shaving, and he nicked himself. The strange lady was on the line,
the one who hardly ever left her big house stuck back in the cane
fields south of town. The piano tuner told her he'd come out, and
then he wiped the receiver free of shaving cream and blood. Back
at the lavatory he went after his white whiskers, remembering that
she was a fairly good-looking woman, quite a bit younger than he
was, in her mid-thirties. She also had a little money, and the piano
tuner, whose name was Claude, wondered why she didn't try to lose
some of it at the Indian casino or at least spend a bit cheering
herself up with a bowl of gumbo at Babineaux's Café. He knew that
all she did was sit in a 150-year-old house and practice pop tunes on
a moth-eaten George Steck upright.

Claude gathered his tuning kit, drank coffee with his wife, then
headed out into the country in his little white van. He made a
dozen turns and got on the clamshell road that ran by Michelle
Placervent's unpainted house, a squared-off antique thing set high
up on crumbling brick pillars. Behind the house were gray wood
outbuildings, and behind those the sugar cane grew taller than a
man and spread for miles, level as a giant's lawn.

As he pulled his tool kit out of the van, Claude recalled that
Michelle was the end of the line for the Placervents, Creole plant-
ers who always had just enough money and influence to make
themselves disliked in a poor community. Her mother had died ten
years before, after Michelle had graduated with a music degree and
come home to take care of her. He looked up on the balcony,

stopping a moment to remember her father, a pale, overweight man with oiled hair who would sit in a rocker and yell after cars speeding in the dusty road, as though he could control the world with a mean word.

The piano tuner remembered that Mr. Placervent began to step up his drinking after his wife died, and Michelle had to tend him like a baby until he dropped dead in the yard yelling at a postman about receiving too many advertisements from Kmart. From that point on it was just her, the black housekeeper, the home place, and a thousand acres the bank managed for her. Then the house-keeper died.

It had been a year since she had called him for a tuning. He stopped under a crape myrtle growing by the porch, noticing that the yard hadn't been cut in a month and the spears of grass were turning to seed. The porch was sagging into a long frown, and the twelve steps that led to it bounced like a trampoline as he went up. He knocked and Michelle turned the knob and backed away, wav-ing him in with a faint hand motion and a small smile, the way Placervents had been doing for two hundred years to people not as good as they were, but Claude didn't hold it against her because he knew how she had been raised. Michelle reminded him of one of those pastries inside the display case down at Dufresne's Bakery — pretty, but when you tried to handle them they fell apart, and your fingers went through to the goo inside. She was bouncing on the balls of her feet, as if she expected she might float off at any minute. He saw that she'd put on a few pounds and wasn't carrying her shoulders well but also that there was still a kind of graceful and old-timey shape to her hips and breasts. Her hair was dark and curly, and her eyes were the brown of worn sharps on an old up-right. A man could take an interest in her as long as he didn't look in those eyes, the piano tuner thought. He glanced around the house and saw that it was falling apart.

"I'm glad you could come so soon," she said. "C above middle C is stuck." She pointed to an ornate, walnut-cased vertigrand, and he remembered its rusty harp and dull, hymning soundboard. It would take three hours to get it pulled back up to pitch. He saw an antique plush chair, faded, with the imprint of her seat in its velvet, and knew that was where she would sit until he was finished. Claude usually talked while he did regulations, so he chatted as he unscrewed the fall board, pulled off the front, and flopped back the lid. After a little while he found an oval pill wedged between two keys and fished it out with a string mute. When she saw what it was, she blushed.

"This one of yours?" he asked, putting it on a side table.

Her eyes followed his hand. "You remember Chlotilde?"

He nodded. "She sure could cook, I heard."

"She called it a happy pill. She told me that if things got too much for me to handle, I could take it." She glanced up as though she'd told a secret by accident, and her eyes grew round. "I never took it, because it's the only one."

Claude stole a look at her where she sat in front of the buckled plaster wall and its yellowed photographs of dead Placervents. It occurred to him that Michelle had never done anything, never worked except at maintaining her helpless mother and snarling old man. He remembered seeing her in town, always in stores, sometimes looking half dead and pale, sometimes talking a mile a minute as she bought food, medicines for the aged, adult diapers, coming in quick, going out the same way, enveloped in a cloud of jasmine perfume.

"You know," he said, "you could probably go to a doctor and get another pill or two."

She waved him off with two fingers. "I can't stand to go to doctors. Their waiting rooms make me want to pass out."

"There," he said, running a trill on the freed ivory. "One problem solved already."

"It's good to get rid of at least one," she said, folding her hands in her lap and leaning forward from the waist.

"What problems you having, Michelle?" He put a tuning hammer onto a pin and struck a fork for A. His electronic tuner was being repaired at the factory, so he'd gone back to listening, setting temperament by ear.

"Why, none at all," she said, too brightly and breathlessly. Claude thought she spoke like an actress in a 1940s movie, an artificial flower like Loretta Young who couldn't fish a pill from between two piano keys to save her soul.

He struck the fork and laid the butt on the upturned lid and tuned A 440, then the A below that, and set perfect reference notes in between, tuning by fifths and flatting strings until the sounds in the steel strings matched the sounds in his head. He then tuned by octaves from the reference notes, and this took over an hour. Michelle sat there with her pale hands in her lap as though she had bought a ticket to watch. The piano's hammers were hard, so he gave them a quick grind with his Moto-tool, then massaged the dampers, which were starting to buzz when they fell against the strings. He went over the tuning pins again. "I don't know if this job will hold perfect pitch, Michelle, but if a note or two falls back, give me a call and I'll swing by."

She nodded. "Whenever you're out this way you can stop in. If something's wrong with the piano, I'll be glad to pay to get it fixed." She smiled a little too widely, like someone desperate to have company, which the tuner guessed she was. He sat down to play a little tune he tested instruments with but stopped after half a minute.

What the tuner remembered is that he'd never heard Michelle play. Judging from the wear on the hammers, she must have practiced all the time, so he asked her. She stood, fluffed her skirt, and walked over with a goosey step. Claude expected that she might wring the notes out more or less in time, the way most players do, but after about ten measures of "As Time Goes By," he could hear that she had a great natural touch, old George laying the hammers against the strings like big felt teardrops and making note-words that belled out into the room. The piano tuner was moved by what she was doing with his work. Next, she surprised him by playing something that sounded like Mozart. Claude had hung around kiddy recitals enough to know a little about classical music, though he'd seldom heard it out here in the cane fields. He watched her long fingers roll and dart.

When she began a slow, fingertippy introduction to "Stardust," he had to sit down. He'd heard the song played by everybody and their pet dogs, but her touch was something else, like Nat King Cole's voice made from piano notes, echoey and dusty. She used the old bass sustain pedal to milk the overtones out of the new tuning job, and Claude closed his eyes and saw the notes floating slowly around the room.

The piano tuner was the kind of person who hated for anything to go to waste and thought the saddest thing in the world was a fine instrument that nobody ever touched, so it made him uneasy that someone who could play like this lived alone and depressed in an antique nightmare of a house ten miles from the nearest ear that knew what the hell her fingers were doing. When she finished, he asked her how she spent her time.

She folded her music and glanced at him out of the corner of her eye. "Since my father's gone, there's not much to do," she said, turning on the bench to face him. "Sometimes the different people who lease the land come by to talk. I have television." She motioned to a floor-cabinet model topped by an elaborate set of rabbit ears.

"Lord, why don't you get a satellite dish?"

She turned over a hand in her lap. "I really don't watch anything. It just keeps me company when I can't sleep at night." She gave him kind of a goofy, apologetic smile.

He began to set his tuning forks in their felt pockets. "As good as you play, you ought to get a decent piano."

The corners of her little mouth came down a bit. "I tried to get Lagneau's Music to bring out a new upright, but they said the old steps wouldn't hold a piano and moving crew." She placed an up-turned hand on George's yellowed teeth. "They told me they'd never get this big thing off the porch. We're seven feet above the ground here."

"You can't take it out the back?"

"The steps are worse there. Rotted through." She let the fall board drop over the ivories with a bang. "If I could get a new instrument, I'd push this out of the back door and let it fall into the yard for the scrap man." She passed a hand quickly above her dark hair as though waving off a wasp.

He looked up at the rain-splotched plaster. "You ever thought about moving?"

"Every day. I can't afford to. And anyway, the house, I guess it's like family."

Claude picked up a screwdriver. "You ought to get out more. A woman your age needs . . ." He started to say that she needed a boyfriend, but then he looked around at the dry-rotted curtains, the twelve-foot ceilings lined with dusty plaster molding, and then back at her trembly shoulders, realizing that she was so out of touch and rusty at life that the only man she should see was a psychiatrist, so then he said, "a job," just because he had to finish the sentence.

"Oh," she said, as though on the edge of crying.

"Hey, it's not so bad. I work every day, and I'm too busy to get blue."

She looked at his little box of mutes and felts. "I can't think of a thing I know how to do," she said.

At supper, Claude's wife was home from her little hole-in-the-wall insurance office, and he asked if she knew Michelle Placervent.

"We don't carry her," she said, going after a plate of red beans and rice and reading a pamphlet on term life.

"That's not what I asked you."

She looked up and the light caught in her bottle-brown hair. "Is she still living out in that little haunted castle?"

"Yeah. The whole place shakes just when you walk through it."

"Why'd they build it on such tall piers? Did the water get that high before they built the levees?"

"Beats me. You ever hear anything about her?" He handed her the hot sauce and watched her think.

"I heard she was depressed as hell, I can tell you that. Boney LeBlanc said she had a panic attack in his restaurant and had to leave just as the waitress brought her shrimp étouffée." Evette shook her head. "And Boney makes dynamite étouffée."

"She can play the hell out of a piano," he said.

"Seems like I heard that." Evette turned the page of her pamphlet. "Sings too."

"She needs to get a job."

"Well, she knows how to drive a tractor."

"What?"

"I heard her father forced her to learn when she was just a kid. I don't know why. Maybe he was mad she wasn't born a boy." Evette took a long drink of iced tea. "I heard if a field hand left a tractor by the gate and a rain was coming up, he'd send Michelle out to bring it under the shed. Wouldn't even let her change out of her dress, just made her climb up on the greasy thing and go."

"Damn, I wouldn't have thought she could operate a doorbell," Claude said.

His wife cut her eyes over to him. "It might surprise you what some people can do," she told him.

Two weeks later Claude was sitting in his recliner, his mind empty, a football game playing in it, when the phone rang. It was Michelle Placervent, and her voice struck his ear like the plea of a drowning sailor. She was crying into the receiver about how three notes on her keyboard had soured and another key was stuck. The more she explained what was wrong with her piano, the more she cried, until she began to weep, Claude thought, as if her whole family had died in a plane crash, aunts and cousins and canaries.

"Michelle," he interrupted, "it's only a piano. Next time I'm out your way, I'll check it. Maybe Monday sometime?"

"No," she cried. "I need someone to come out now."

He hung up and went to find his wife. Evette was at the sink peeling onions, and he told her about Michelle. She banged a piece of onion skin off her knife. "You better go fix her piano," she said. "If that's what needs fixing." She looked up at the piano tuner's gray hair as though she might be wondering if Michelle Placervent found him attractive.

"You want to come for the ride?" he asked.

She shook her head and kissed him on the chin. "I've got to finish supper. When Chad gets home from football practice, he'll be starving." She picked up another onion and cut off the green shoots, her eyes flicking up at him. "If she's real sick, call Dr. Meltier."

Claude drove out there as quickly as he could, sorry he'd ever tuned the worn-out piano in the first place. Giving a good musician a fine tuning is always a risk, because when the first string starts to vibrate, he gets dissatisfied and calls up, as if one little note that's just a bit off ruins the whole song.

She was dressed in faded stretch jeans and a green sweatshirt, and her hair was unbrushed and oily. The house was as uncombed as she was. Claude looked at her trembly fingers and her wild eyes, then asked if she had any relatives or friends in town. "Everybody is dead or moved far away," she told him, her eyes streaming and her face red and sticky. So he went into the kitchen to make her some hot tea. The cabinets looked as though someone had thrown the pots into them from across the room. The stove was a first-genera-tion gas range that should have been in a museum, and it was listing, the floor sagging under it. The icebox was full of TV din-ners, and the pantry showed a few cans of Vienna sausage and beanie-weenies. Claude realized that he would be depressed him-self if that was all he had to eat.

When he brought the tea she was in a wing chair, leaning to one side, her shoulders rounded in. He sat on the bench and carefully checked the keyboard by unisons and fifths, and found nothing out of pitch, no stuck key. At that moment, he knew that when he turned around he had two choices: to say there's nothing wrong, get in his van, and go on with his life, or to deal with her. He inspected the alligatored finish on the George Steck's case for a long time, examined the sharps for lateral play. Even while he was turning on the satiny bench, he didn't know what he was going to say. Then he saw her eyes, big with dread of something like a diagnosis. Claude felt as though he were slipping off into quicksand when he opened his mouth.

"Michelle, who's your doctor?"

Her eyes went to the dark, wax-caked floor. "I'm not going."

"You got to. Look at yourself. You're sadder'n a blind man at a strip show."

"I just need a little time to adjust. My father's been gone only six months." She put a hand on her forehead and hid her eyes from him.

"You need a little something, all right, but it ain't time. You got too *much* time on your hands." Then he told her what her doctor could do for her. That her depression was just a chemical thing. She could be straightened up with some medicine, he told her. He said many things off the top of his head, and he convinced her to make an appointment with Dr. Meltier. He talked with her a long time in her cold living room. When a thunderbolt lit up the yard and a storm blew in from the west, he helped her put out pots to catch leaks. He held her hand at the door and got her calm so she wouldn't call him out of his warm bed in a few hours to tell him that her piano'd gone up in pitch or was playing itself.

A month or so passed, and Claude was cutting grass when suddenly he saw Michelle's old black Lincoln charge up the drive, and she got out smiling too widely, wearing a navy cotton dress that was baggy and wrinkled. He asked her to come in for coffee, and he listened to her talk and talk. The doctor had given her some medications to test for a couple of months, and her eyes were bright. In fact, her eyes showed so much happiness they scared him. She asked if he could help her find a job playing the piano.

"When you're ready, I'll help." For years Claude had tuned pianos for places that used lounge pianists, and he knew all the managers.

She put four spoons of sugar in her coffee with steady hands.

"I'm ready right this minute," she said. "I've got to make my music go to work for me."

The piano tuner laughed at that, thinking the poor thing was so cheery and upbeat he should call Sid Fontenot, who managed the lounge in that big new motel over in Lafayette. "Sid's always trying out pianists," he told her. "I'll give him a call for you."

When he got off the phone, she asked, "How do you play in a lounge?" and Claude tried to keep his face from screwing up.

"There's nothing to it," he said, sitting down with her and frowning into his coffee cup. "You must know a thousand show tunes and ballads."

She nodded. "Okay. I play requests. I play what they ask me to." She adjusted a thin watchband, and then looked him in the eye.

Claude got up and put their cups in the sink. "Sid asked me if you can sing. You don't have to, but he said it would help. You get a lot of requests for old stuff in a classy motel lounge."

"I was good in voice," she said, clasping her hands until they went white. And then he thought he saw a weakening of the mood flash through her eyes, a little electrical thrill of fright. "How do I dress?"

He lathered up a dishcloth and looked at her hair, which was short, coffee-brown. He regarded the white skin on her face, the crow's-feet, the dryness. "Why don't you go to Sears and buy a black dress and some fake pearls. Get a little makeup while you're at it. You'll be the best-looking thing in the lounge. Sid says he'll try you tomorrow night in the bar at nine o'clock. It's the big new motel on the interstate."

Claude's wife had often told him that he invented reality by saying it, and he was thinking this as he talked to the medicated, hermitlike woman seated in his kitchen. He was also thinking that the last place on earth he would want to be was in the piano bar of a Lafayette motel at nine at night. And, naturally, the next question to come out from between Michelle Placervent's straight teeth was "Can't you please come with me this first time?"

Claude took a breath and said, "I'd be glad to," and again she clasped her hands like an organ grinder's monkey. He wondered what she was taking and how much of it.

He almost convinced Evette to go along with them, but Chad came down with the flu and she stayed home to nurse. She made her husband wear a sport coat, but he refused to put on a tie. "You want to look good for your date," she told him with a smirk.

He turned red in the face and went out on the porch to wait in the night air.

Michelle picked him up, and he had to admit that she looked blue-blood sharp. He imagined she must have bought a girdle along with her velvety black dress. On the way to Lafayette, the Lincoln drifted above the narrow, flat highway through the sugar cane, and Claude got her to talk about herself. She told him that she had been engaged twice, but old man Placervent was so nasty to the young men he just ran them off. Her grandfather had wanted to tear the old house down "from bats to termites" and build a new place, but her father wouldn't hear of it. She said he'd worn the building like a badge, some proof that he was better than anyone else. "The only proof," Michelle said. "And now I'm trapped in it." The piano tuner didn't know what to say, other than she could look forward to hurricane season, but he kept his mouth closed.

The lounge was a long room, glass walls on one side and a long bar with a smiling lady bartender on the other. He introduced Michelle to Sid, a bright-looking man, savvy, dressed in an expensive suit. Sid smiled at her and pointed out the piano, and the next thing Claude knew, Michelle was seated behind a rebuilt satin-black Steinway playing "Put on a Happy Face," her high-heeled foot holding down the soft pedal. The room began to fill after a while with local oilmen and their glitzy women, plus the usual salesmen sprawling at the tables, and even a couple of cowboys who lit like dragonflies at the bar. A slim, tipsy woman in tight white jeans and spike heels approached the piano and made a request, putting a bill into a glass on the lid. Michelle stared at the money for a moment and started "Yesterday," playing for six minutes.

Claude sat at a tiny table next to the window overlooking the swimming pool and ordered a German beer. He'd never done anything like this and felt out of place. When he did visit a bar, it was the kind of place with Cajun music on the jukebox and a gallon jar of pigs' feet on the counter. Michelle finished the tune and looked over at him, and he gave her the okay sign. She smiled and sailed into another, then tickled off a half dozen more over the next forty-five minutes. At one point, she walked over to Claude's table and asked how she was doing. He could see, even in the dim light, that her eyes were too intense, the way a person's eyes get when he's having too much fun.

The piano tuner wanted to say, "Lighten up on the arpeggios. Slow your tempo." But she was floating before him as fragile as a soap bubble, so he gave her the thumbs-up. "Perfect. Sid says you can have a hundred dollars for four hours, plus tips."

"Money," she squealed, bouncing back to the piano and starting "The Pennsylvania Polka," playing with a lot of sustain pedal. A brace of oilmen looked over briefly, but most people just leaned closer to talk or patted their feet. Claude signaled her to quiet it down a bit.

For an hour and a half, he watched as Michelle played and grinned at people coming to her tip glass. She sang one song through the microphone over her keyboard and drew a moderate wave of applause. She was a good-looking woman, but she had never learned how to move around people, and Claude got the feeling that folks who studied her close up thought she was a little silly. He sat there wishing there was a regulating button on the back of her head that he could give just a quarter turn.

Eventually the piano tuner became drowsy and hungry in the dim light of the lounge, so he walked across the lobby to the restaurant and treated himself to a deluxe burger basket and another cold bottle of beer. He sat there next to the plant box full of plastic flowers and worried about Michelle and whether he'd done the right thing by turning a Creole queen into a motel lounge pianist.

As soon as he left the restaurant, he could tell something was not exactly right. A young couple walked out of the lounge with quick steps, and then he heard the music. Hungarian Rhapsody No. 2. Sid appeared at the lounge entrance and waved him over. "Michelle's really smoking our Steinway," he said, putting his mouth to the piano tuner's ear. "You know, this crowd thinks classical music is something like Floyd Cramer's Greatest Hits." Claude looked into the room, where customers seemed to bend under the shower of notes like cows hiding from a thunderstorm. Some of the loud salesmen had stopped selling mud pumps and chemicals to listen, and the drunk cowboys, who had picked up two women, were trying to jitterbug.

Sid put a hand on Claude's shoulder. "What's going on? She's got to know that's not the right music for this place."

"I'll talk to her."

Sid glanced over his shoulder. "She's smiling a lot. Is she on something?" He knew musicians.

"Depression medicine."

He sniffed. "Well, I guess that music'll drive you off the deep end."

After the big rumbling finale, the cowboys let out a rebel yell, but no one applauded, and Claude walked over and put his hand on her back, bending down. "That was good, Michelle." What was he supposed to say to her? he thought.

She looked up at him and her eyes were wet, her skin flushed and sweating. "You don't fool me. I know what you're thinking. But I couldn't help it. I just got this surge of anger and had to let it out."

"What are you mad at?" He saw that her shoulders were trembling.

She didn't say anything at first, and then she looked up at him. "I've been sitting here thinking that I would have to play piano five nights a week for twenty-three years to pay for the renovation of my house." She straightened up and looked over the long piano at the bartender, who had both hands on the bar, watching her. "What am I doing here?" She ran a palm down her soft throat. "I'm a Placervent."

Claude pushed her microphone aside. "Your medications are maybe a little out of adjustment," he said in a low voice, wishing he were anyplace on earth other than where he was. He looked over at Sid, then told her, "You ought to finish this set."

"Why? I can survive without the money. I mean, I appreciate you getting me this job, but I think I'm ready to go home." She seemed out of control, but she didn't move.

He was sure his face showed that he was getting upset himself. She stared down at the keys until, finally, one of the cowboys, really just a French farm boy from down in Cameron Parish, wearing a loud shirt and a Wal-Mart hat, came up and put a five in her tip glass. "Hey lady, can you play any Patsy Cline?"

An injured little smile came to her lips. She straightened her back and started to say something to him, but instead she looked at Claude, at his embarrassed and hopeful face. Her mouth closed in a line, and her right hand went down and began picking out the intro. Then, to his amazement, she started to sing, and people looked up as though Patsy Cline had come back, but without her country accent, and the whole room got quiet to listen. "Crazy," Michelle sang, soft as midnight fog outside a bedroom window, "crazy for feeling so lonely."

He didn't see her for a long time. At Sid's, someone spilled a highball into the Steinway, and when Claude was over there straightening it out, the manager told him she was still playing on weekends, and off and on at the Sheraton, and a little at the country club for the oil-company parties. He said that she had gotten her dosage pretty straightened out and she played well, except toward the end of the night when she would start singing blues numbers and laughing out loud between the verses as though she were telling jokes in her head. Laughing very loud. The piano tuner wondered if she would ever get on an even keel.

In the middle of December she called him to come tune a new console she'd bought. She'd finally gotten a carpenter to put knee braces under the front steps so that Lagneau's Music could bring a piano into the house. They'd told her they didn't want George as a trade-in, though, and that they wouldn't take the big verti-grand down into the yard for a million dollars. It was built like a wooden warship, with seven five-by-five back braces, and it weighed nearly eight hundred pounds. When Claude got there, the entry was open, the dark giant of a piano at the head of the long hall that led to the back porch. As he stepped in, he saw the new piano in the parlor, a cheap, ugly, blond-wood model. He couldn't believe she'd chosen it. Michelle appeared at the far end of the hall looking wild-eyed, her hair falling in loose, dangly ringlets. She was wearing rust-smudged tan slacks under a yellow rain slicker and was lugging the end of a half-inch cable in her cotton gardening gloves.

"Claude," she said, shaking her head. "You wouldn't believe the trouble I've had this morning. I had Lagneau's crew push the old piano into the hall, but the rollers on the bottom locked up. Just look what they did to the floor." She swept a hand, low. The floors were so covered with two-hundred-year-old divots brimming with cloudy wax that he couldn't spot much new damage. "They managed to get it up on this old braided rug, and I figured I could tow it off the back porch and let it fall into the yard."

He looked in her eyes to see what was going on. "You gonna skid this thing down the hardwood on this rug? We can't just push it ourselves?"

"Give it a try."

He leaned on it, but the piano didn't budge. "I see what you mean." He looked down the hall to the open rear door. "You think it'll slide onto the porch and fall through the back steps?"

"They have to be replaced anyway. Mr. Arcement said he would cart away the mess next week." She ran the cable under the keyboard and around the back through the handholds, completing a loop and setting the hook. When she passed by the piano tuner he smelled gasoline in her clothes, and he walked to the back door to see what she'd hooked the cable to. Idling away in the yard was a John Deere 720, a big two-cylinder tractor running on propane.

"God almighty, Michelle, that tractor's the size of a locomotive."

"It's the only one out in the barn that would start," she said, dropping the cable's slack into the yard.

He looked out at the rust-roofed outbuildings, their gray cypress darkening in the drizzle. She began picking her way down the porous steps, which didn't look as if they'd support his weight, so he went out the front door and walked around to the back. He found Michelle standing on the right axle housing of the tractor, facing backward, looking into the hall at the piano. The machine's exhausts were thudding like a bass drum. He remembered that a John Deere has a long clutch level instead of a foot pedal, and she was easing this out to take up slack in the cable. A tire rolled up on the septic-tank lid, and the front end veered sharply. Claude didn't know exactly what she was trying to do, but he offered to help.

"I've planned this through. You just stay on the ground and watch." She sat in the seat, found reverse gear, backed the tractor closer to the house, snugged the steering wheel with a rubber tie-down so it wouldn't wander again, then eased forward in lowest gear until the cable was taut. With the slack out of the line, she put the lever all the way forward, and the machine began to crawl. Claude walked way out in the yard, stood on tiptoe, and saw George skidding down the hall, wandering from side to side but looking as though it would indeed bump out of the house and onto the back porch. About three feet from the door, the piano rolled off the rug and started to turn broadside to the entryway. Michelle stopped the tractor and yelled something. He couldn't understand it over the engine noise, but she might have been asking him to go inside and straighten the piano. She stepped out onto the axle again, leaned forward to jump to the ground, and the piano tuner held his breath because there was something wrong with the way she was getting off. Her rain slicker caught on the long lever and he heard the clutch pop as it engaged. Michelle fell on her stomach, the big tractor moving above her. Claude ran over, and when she came out from under the draw bar he grabbed her arm to get her up. Meanwhile, the tractor had pulled the piano's soundboard flat against the entryway to the house, where it jammed for about half a second. The tractor gasped as its governor opened up and dumped gas in its engine, and *chak-chak*, the exhausts exploded, the big tires squatted and bit into the lawn, and the piano came out with the back wall of the entire house, three rows of brick piers collapsing like stacks of dominoes, the kitchen, rear bedroom, and back porch disintegrating in a tornado of plaster dust and cracking, wailing boards. A musical waterfall of slate shingles rattled down from the roof, the whole house trembled, nearly every windowpane tinkled out, and just when Claude and Michelle thought things had stopped collapsing, the hall fell in all the way to the front door, which swung closed with a bang.

The tractor kept puttering away toward the north at around four miles an hour, and the piano tuner wondered if he should run after it. Michelle began to make a whining noise deep down in her throat. She hung on to him and started to swing as if she'd pass out. He couldn't think of a word to say, and they were staring at the wreck of the house as though considering putting it back together with airplane glue when a big yellow jet of gas flamed up about where the stove would be in all the rubble.

"A fire," she said breathlessly, tears welling up in her eyes.

"Where's the closest neighbor?" he asked, feeling at least now he could do something.

"The Arcements'. About a mile off." Her voice was tiny and broken as she pointed a thin white arm to the east, so he gathered her up and walked her to the front, putting her in his van and tearing out down the blacktop toward the nearest working telephone.

By the time the Grand Crapaud Volunteer Fire Department got out to Michelle Placervent's place, the house was one big orange star, burning so hot it made little smoke. The firemen ran up to the fence but lost heart right there. They began spraying the camellias at roadside and the live oaks farther in. Claude had rescued Michelle's Lincoln before the paint blistered off, and she sat in it on the side of the road, looking like a World War II refugee he had seen on the History Channel. Minos LeBlanc, the fire chief, talked to her for a while and asked if she had insurance.

She nodded. "The only good thing the house had was insurance." She put her face in her hands then, and Claude and Minos looked away, expecting the crying to come. But it didn't. She asked for a cup of water, and the piano tuner watched her wash down a pill. After a while she locked her Lincoln and asked him to take her into town. "I have an acquaintance I can stay with, but she won't come home from work until five-thirty."

She ran her eyes up a bare chimney rising out of the great fire. "All these years and only one person who'll put me up."

"Come on home and eat supper with us," he said.

"No." She looked down at her dirty slacks. "I wouldn't want your wife to see me like this." She seemed almost frightened and looked around him at the firemen.

"Don't worry about that. She'd be glad to loan you some clothes to get you through the night." He placed himself between her and the fire.

She ran her white fingers through her curls and nodded. "All right." But she watched him out of the corner of her eye all the way into town, as though she didn't trust him to take her to the right place. About a block before Claude turned down his street, she let out a giggle, and he figured her chemicals were starting to take effect. Evette showed her the phone and she called several people, then came into the living room, where Claude was watching TV. "I can go to my friend Miriam's after six-thirty," she said, settling slowly into the sofa, her head toward the television.

"I'll take you over right after we eat." He shook his head and looked at the rust and mud on her knees. "Gosh, I'm sorry for you."

She kept watching the screen. "Look at me. I'm homeless." But she was not frowning.

After a while, the six o'clock local news came on channel 10, and the fifth story was about a large green tractor that had just come out of a cane field at the edge of Billeaudville, dragging the muddy hulk of a piano on a long cable. The announcer explained how the tractor plowed through a woman's yard and proceeded up Lamonica Street toward downtown, where it climbed a curb and began to struggle up the steps of St. Martin's Catholic Church, until Rosalie Landry, a member of the Ladies' Altar Society who was sweeping out the vestibule, stopped the machine by knocking off the tractor's sparkplug wires with the handle of her broom. As of five-thirty, Vermilion Parish sheriff's deputies did not know where the tractor had come from or who owned it and the battered piano.

Claude stood straight up. "I can't believe it didn't stall out somewhere. Billeaudville's four miles from your house."

Michelle began to laugh, quietly at first, her shoulders jiggling as she tried to hold it in. Then she opened her mouth and let out a big, sailing laugh, and kept it going, soaring up into shrieks and gales, some kind of tears rolling on her face. Evette came to the door holding a big spoon, looked at her husband, and shook her head. He reached over and grabbed Michelle's arm.

"Are you all right?"

She tried to talk between seizures of laughter. "Can't you see?" she keened. "It escaped." On the television a priest was shaking his head at the steaming tractor. She started laughing again, and this time Claude could see halfway down her throat.

A year later, he was called out for four tunings in Lafayette on one day. September was like that for him, with the start of school and piano lessons. On top of it all, Sid called him to fish a bottle of bar nuts out of the lounge piano. He got there late, and Sid bought him supper in the restaurant before he started work.

The manager wore his usual dark gray silk suit, and his black hair was combed straight back. "Your friend," he said, as if the word *friend* held a particularly rich meaning for them, "is still working here, you know."

"Yeah, I was over at her apartment last month tuning a new console for her." Claude shoveled up pieces of hamburger steak.

"You know, there's even some strange folks that come in as regulars just to hear her."

Claude looked up at him. "She's a good musician, a nice woman," he said between chews.

Sid took another slow drink, setting the glass down carefully.

"She looks nice," he said, emphasizing the word *looks*. The piano tuner recognized that this was how Sid talked, not explaining, just using his voice to hint at things. The manager leaned in to him. "But sometimes she starts talking right in the middle of a song. Strange things." He looked at his watch. "She's starting early tonight, for a convention crowd, a bunch of four-eyed English teachers."

"What time?"

"About eight." He took a drink and looked at the piano tuner. "Every night, I hold my breath."

That evening the room was cool and polished. A new little dance floor had been laid down next to the piano, and Michelle showed up wearing round, metal-frame glasses and a black velvet dress. The piano was turned broadside to the room so that everyone could watch her hands. She started playing immediately, a nice old fox trot Claude had forgotten the name of. Then she played a hymn, then a ragtime number. He sat there, enjoying the bell quality of his own tuning job. Between songs, she spotted him, and her eyes ballooned; she threw her long arms up and yelled into the microphone, "Hey, everybody, I see Claude from Grand Crapaud, the best piano tuner in the business. Let's give Claude a round of applause." A spatter of clapping came from the bar. Claude gave her a worried glance, and she made herself calm, put her hands in her lap, and waited for the applause to stop. Then she set a heavy book of music on the rack. Her fingers uncurled into their ivory arches, and she began a slow Scott Joplin number with a hidden tango beat, playing it so that the sad notes bloomed like flowers. Claude remembered the title — "Solace."

"Did you know," she asked the room over her microphone during the music, "that Scott Joplin played piano in a whorehouse for a little while?" Claude looked out at all the assembled English teachers, at the glint of eyeglasses and name tags and upturned, surprised faces. He understood that Michelle could never adjust to being an entertainer. But at least she was brave. "Yes," she continued, "they say he died crazy with syphilis, on April Fool's Day, 1917." She nodded toward the thick music book, all rags, marches, and waltzes. "One penicillin shot might have bought us another hundred melodies," she told the room. "That's kind of funny and sad at the same time, isn't it?"

She pulled back from the microphone, polishing the troubling notes. Claude listened and felt the hair rise on his arms. When she finished he waved at her, then got up and walked toward the lobby, where he stood for a moment watching the ordinary people. He heard her start up a show tune, and he turned and looked back into the lounge as three couples rose in unison to dance.

MELISSA HARDY

The Uncharted Heart

FROM THE ONTARIO REVIEW

OF COURSE HE KNEW its coordinates, its longitude and latitude, where it lay in relation to other geographical features: east of Frederick House River and west of Prosser Lake, north of Gowanmarsh and south of Little Lake. It was not three miles from the Buskegau, although that river didn't feed it. Nor had it any other tributaries. It lay where the retreating ice had torn a hole in the Shield and the rain had filled it, the little round blue lake stranded in bush that had been called no name for so long, only The Lake. . . . No, he knew exactly where The Lake was, had known it all along, even though he had not included it on the original survey of 1910 or on later ones or, for that matter, on his famous map or its first revision. He had known of its existence, its whereabouts for more than a decade but told no one.

Years later the old geologist lay in the oncology ward of the Toronto General Hospital, stretched out on his cantilevered bed like a man on a rack, each of his bones aching like a separate sore tooth. Cancer had driven the marrow from them, spread in its place. His bones glowed like embers. McQuat had just started him on morphine, dripped through the IV tube into the popped blue vein of his skeletal left hand. McQuat was his doctor. The drug distanced him from the pain, threw a shimmering, transparent veil up through which he observed himself dying in a darkened room; he noted the pain, even acknowledged that it was his, without actually participating in it. He felt light, blown, like a burst milkweed pod toward the end of autumn, which teeters on its stalk, tugged by breezes. Soon the stalk would break and the geologist would tumble, end over end, across the meadow toward the river.

In the midst of all this floating, he suddenly remembered that he had a secret. How surprising! Not that he had ever really forgotten. The morphine had distracted him, borne him up in soft arms and, beating its big angel wings, spirited him to a lofty vantage point from which he might look down on his past from a different angle. And there it is, he marveled. A blue lake under a sky filled with clouds. A beautiful woman. An incurable sweetness like an illness that soothingly debilitates. A point not charted on a map until it was all over.

The knowledge of this thing he had done long ago had burned in him for six decades like a slow ground fire that gives off no smoke but only consumes what lies beneath it. Slowly. Inexorably. And now it had come to this: his death. The key question in his mind now was, had it really happened or had he made it up?

His tongue stirred in his mouth, as sluggish and thick-blooded as a wintering snake. "Marguerite!" he managed.

Margie Macoun Dawkins glanced sharply up from the old issue of *Chatelaine* which she was struggling to read by the light that seeped through the door from the corridor — one-pot suppers and makeovers for tired bathrooms.

"What is it, Dad?" she asked.

She was a soft, spongy, middle-aged woman with pale, freckled skin. The freckles were the same color as her hair — taffy — and her eyes behind the pink glasses flecked with gold were that bright blue that is sometimes described as china blue.

"So you're here then!" he exclaimed in a hoarse whisper. "My little Marguerite! And here I was wondering if I had made you up."

"I've been here since nine this morning, Dad," she replied wearily, and a little sharply too. "I'm here every morning by nine." Her father's prolonged illness had poked her life full of holes, not that she had had much of one since the divorce; through these holes what small store of love and patience she still possessed had slowly seeped away. Who would have thought it would have taken him so long to die? Of course, she corrected herself, it's that I hate watching him suffer. I would have preferred for him to die with dignity than this way, a hollow husk pumped full of drugs. Rising, she crossed to the bed, bent forward and touched the loose bag of bones that was his hand, grazed his bumpy forehead with her lips. "So . . . how are you feeling?" she asked more tenderly.

"Like a bird!" the geologist trilled.

Convinced that they could subordinate large-scale physical geography to human needs by applying the principles of geometry to it and driven by a terrible urge to do so, the Victorians had already produced a rough map of New Ontario during the latter part of Queen Victoria's reign. However, since silver had been discovered in Cobalt in 1903 and gold in the Porcupine six years later, the government commissioned more precise maps of the region, to facilitate claim-staking and the consequent collection of fees. Therefore, in 1910, the Bureau of Mines, which formed part of the Department of Crown Lands, dispatched a number of geologists north to survey the region collectively.

One of those geologists was George Dewey Macoun. He was twenty-six years old at the time, a graduate of Queen's University in Kingston. He had apprenticed for two years with the renowned Toronto firm of Deville, King and Klotz before signing on with the Bureau of Mines. George was tall and lanky, heavy-boned, a little stooped, and possessed of a long, gaunt face that ran to exaggerated hollows, pits, and protuberances. Sun and windburn had already begun to toughen his skin, which, because of years of fieldwork, was tanned all year round. His eyes stared clear and hazel out of their pronounced sockets. Once he had endeavored to grow a set of gingery muttonchop whiskers (his hair, already thinning at the crown, was the dull dun color of a mouse). When his master, Surveyor General Edoard Deville, remarked of these whiskers in passing, "It appears, Mr. Macoun, that you may have developed mange," George promptly shaved them off. It was to be his only attempt at self-adornment, although he was quite partial to the surveyors' quasi-military uniform of khaki, kerchief, and Stetson hat.

George was engaged to marry Miss Frieda Eckert, a somewhat sturdy young lady of eighteen, the daughter of one of his natural science professors at Kingston. Frieda was big, pallid, and given to both bouts of tremendous enthusiasm and terrific sloughs of despond — at these times, a kind of bleak melancholy would descend over her parents' tranquil household like a low-pressure weather system blown in from off the Great Lakes, oppressive and menacing. Frieda's looks were as changeable as her moods: her milk-white skin would be clear as a field of fresh snow one moment; at the slightest provocation, however, she would break out in stupendous hives. She also tended toward random puffiness and was exceptionally susceptible to pinkeye.

The marriage was scheduled in the autumn of 1910, by which time it was hoped that Frieda would have passed her Royal Conservatory exams, a goal that thus far had eluded her due to an apparently inherent inability to beat time.

According to the directive he received from the Bureau of Mines, George was to follow mining-claim lines north of the Porcupine and advised not only to survey the terrain but also to report with reference to means of access, topography, wildlife, and vegetation.

George took the Canadian Pacific to Mattagami, a little settlement about seventy miles west of Sudbury, purchased a cottonwood canoe, and paddled it down the Spanish to the Mattagami River and down the Mattagami to Porcupine Lake. This lake formed the center from which the gold camp, which extended over several small settlements, radiated. He was to set up headquarters at the new town of Golden City on the northeast shore of the lake, as it boasted both a post and a telegraph office.

He took with him a small tent, rope, twine, wire, an ax, brush hooks, a spade, a grindstone, a whetstone, a scythe, packstraps, survey pickets, chain-pins, a standard Gunter's Chain one hundred links, or sixty-six feet, long, scribing irons and an instrument box containing a Dollard's sextant with a ten-inch radius, an artificial horizon, a thermometer, a solar compass accurate within two minutes, a micrometer, and two aneroid barometers. George's telescope, or "brasses," as surveyors named this instrument, was a small, portable astronomical transit that he could mount on a tree stump. In a battered leather portfolio he carried compiled mathematical tables, a half a dozen blank journals, two pens, a box of pencils, and a supply of black ink. He also carried a duffle bag, with a change of uniform, and, neatly folded and tucked away in its own case, the Union Jack and the red-and-white pennant of the Geological Survey. These he was instructed to fly so that anyone encountering him in the bush might recognize that he was a government surveyor working in an official capacity.

"Suspected claim-jumpers have been known to meet with mischief in the wild, unruly north," his supervisor had advised him. "Even to disappear entirely."

Golden City was little more than a main street dug out of thick, fecund mud and haphazardly lined with shanties in various states of construction or disrepair. In addition to the post and telegraph office (housed in the trading post), there were a couple of outhouses (one for hire), a saddler's, a structure that resembled a woodpile but was in fact a public house, and a two-story log rooming house run by Mrs. Flowers.

Mrs. Flowers was a bulky woman of indeterminate middle age who wore a fringed buckskin coat and wellingtons all year round. She rented out eight rooms to prospectors and others trafficking in the bush. Sometimes she grubstaked them. George, however, earned $45 a month, and so paid the full board of sixty cents a day. "It would cost you less if you shared a bed," Mrs. Flowers advised him. " 'Course, then there's lice to worry about."

Mrs. Flowers kept a cow called Betty, famous for her omnivorous nature.

"Once," Mrs. Flowers told George, "she ate a whole pile of socks I was fixing to darn. Another time she ate a Bible."

In anticipation of future settlement and to facilitate the surveyance of a large tract of heavily timbered terrain, a grid had been laid over the area in order to parse it up in discrete chunks or townships, which were then named after various men in the bureau and their friends: Blackstock, Childerhose, Wark, Zavitz. Eighty in all. The term *township* was somewhat misleading in that there were, in fact, no towns. This was because there were, in fact, no people. Outside of the little settlements of Golden City, Pottsville, South Porcupine, and Aura Lake and the occasional trapper working his lines in isolation or the Ojibwa fishing camp made up of two or three families and pitched by a lake, the entire country was untrammeled, unexplored bush.

George's experience bore this out. Since leaving Golden City early one morning two weeks before to survey the northernmost townships of Moberly, Thorburn, Reid, Carnegie, Prosser, Tully, and Little, he had seen a mother bear and her cubs, a whole score of deer, a fox, martens, a colony of beavers, three wolves ravening what looked to be a caribou . . . but no human beings.

Then he saw her.

But first he saw the moose.

It was just before sunrise and he was paddling down a snaking green river called the Buskegau, heading east toward Frederick House Lake. The tops of the trees were bathed in mist the color of goose down. The air was thick, soft, and cool. It was very quiet; the birds had not yet begun to sing; he could hear the river run.

Suddenly he heard a crashing sound in the bush — branches snapping, vegetation crushed underfoot. Moments later, a massive bull moose lumbered out of the forest and stood winking at him from the bank, a distance of some fifteen feet. Its big, bony face looked forlorn, its hide moth-eaten and patchy.

George had never observed a moose at such close proximity. Quickly he maneuvered the canoe into some bulrushes along the opposite bank and, laying his paddle across his lap, leaned forward eagerly to watch the huge beast.

The moose observed all this activity on the geologist's part with a sorrowful and somewhat puzzled expression, then waggled its un-wieldy antlers. The gesture did not appear hostile so much as an attempt on the part of the animal to shake off a ridiculous oversized party hat that had somehow become affixed to its head. Moose shed their antlers after the fall rut, George knew. He wondered if they itched.

After the moose was done shaking its antlers, it delicately picked its way to the water's edge and, stretching out its neck, began to munch on the yellow water lilies that grew there with its big square herbivore teeth, its lips fumbling about the coarse stalks. Through-out all this, its gaze remained riveted on George.

Carefully, so as not to startle the animal, George extracted a notebook and pencil from the breast pocket of his khaki jacket and set it on his knee. "First moose I've seen up close," he wrote in his precise hand. Then he glanced to either side of him. "Wild plum on river's bank," he continued, "in full bloom." A red-winged black-bird dropped down on a bulrush a few feet from where the canoe drifted and began to scream her territory at George. *Mine! Mine!* Overhead a black crow crackled a raucous alarm. *Macoun! Macoun!*, as if the invader were a known entity whose terrible arrival had long been anticipated. "Just before dawn. Birds waking up. Crow. Red-winged blackbird," George concluded, closing the notebook and setting it on his knee. His chin resting on his hand, he regarded the moose. The moose regarded him back, munching water lilies. In this way ten minutes passed, then twenty. George's eyes drifted shut; his head dropped to one side; he slumped forward. The slight current rocked the canoe idly like a weary mother tips a cradle, back and forth, back and forth.

Strata . . . Data . . . Strata . . . Data . . . The words alternated in his mind: one, then the other. Like the tick-tocking of Frieda's metronome. He was trying to come up with a rhyme for *strata* that wasn't *data*. How about *matter* or *evolutionary ladder?* George had written poetry since his undergraduate days at Kingston, employing geological metaphors for the most part, as these were the terms and concepts with which he was most familiar. Once he had read several verses of a dandy one on synclinal folds and anticlinal hollows out loud to Frieda. It was more or less a love sonnet. His fiancée had responded by looking stunned — not the response he had hoped for. Later she explained that she had been thinking of something else.

A gauzy mist swirled around the reeds, trailed disembodied cloud fingers over the dark green water, bathed his face in coolness. Suddenly there was the sound of branches snapping and vegetation being crunched underfoot. Startled, George opened his eyes. The moose had finished its meal and was clambering up the bank and into the bush, its big head lolling from side to side, its tail twitching.

"What?" George sputtered, half starting from his seat. His action sent the notebook flying. He dove for it, catching it just before it pitched over the side into the river and jerking it up over his head, for the moment he had lunged, he had felt the canoe tip. A second later it rolled over, tumbling George into the waist-high water.

A gasp of muffled laughter.

George froze, still holding the notebook aloft; then slowly he twisted around and looked back over his shoulder in the direction from which the sound had come. Half hidden in the shadow of the wild plums, he could just make out a slender form, a girl perhaps, or a small woman, clothed in something white, a shift of some kind that ended mid-calf. "Hello?" he ventured.

The figure retreated a step and half turned, as if to run away.

"Wait!" said George. "Don't go. Please. You needn't be afraid of me." He replaced the notebook in his breast pocket and buttoned it closed. "My journal," he explained. "Can't lose that! Very important. I'm a geologist, you see. We take a lot of notes. Oh, I say! Maybe you're French. A lot of Frenchmen in these parts. *Bonjour, mademoiselle! Comment allez-vous?"*

She turned toward him. *"Bonjour,"* she replied in a small voice, scarcely audible.

"Well, then!" George beamed. "That's dandy! The only problem is I don't speak French. Not apart from *bonjour* and *au revoir,* that is. I speak German. German is the language of science, and I . . . well, I'm a scientist, you see."

She said nothing, only looked at him with big round eyes of some indescribable color.

"I know I'm talking an awful lot, but it's been two weeks since I've seen another human being. . . . Oh! Don't be frightened now," he cautioned her, "but I'm wet, you see. How do you say it? *Humide?* I'm just going to right this canoe and come ashore so I can dry off." He flipped the canoe over and pushed it up onto the riverbank. Then he plucked the oilskin bag that held his instruments from the river's weedy bottom and clambered ashore. As if there were some requisite distance that must be maintained between them, she retreated a few steps backward into the bush as he came forward. "Thank goodness for oilskin," he said, setting the bag on the ground and opening it. "Lucky for me most of my gear is at base camp." He hunkered down and, removing his instruments from the bag, set them on the grass to dry.

"What are these?" She took a tentative step forward, pushing a bough of plum out of the way as she did and leaning forward to get a better look at the implements.

"You speak English!" he exclaimed.

"Papa was English; Maman . . . she spoke French," she answered softly. "But these shiny things . . . How do you call them? They are very pretty."

"Well, this is what's called a Dollard sextant." George showed her the sextant. "And this is an artificial horizon. I'm doing a survey, you see."

She stared at him quizzically for a moment, then cocked her head to one side. "What?" she asked.

"A geological survey for the Bureau of Mines."

She frowned, as though still confused.

"For making a map," he continued.

"Oh," she said. "And what is a . . . how do you call it?"

"A map. It's a sort of picture of a place," George explained. "This country around here. Of the rivers and the lakes and how far it is from one place to the other."

"Ah!" she exclaimed.

"But where do you live?" George asked.

"Over there," she replied. Turning, she pointed in a southeasterly direction.

"Far?" George asked.

"Not far," she replied. "On the lake."

"What lake?" George reached for his notebook.

"The lake," she answered.

"I mean . . . what is it called? This lake?"

"The lake," she articulated carefully, as though he might be hard of hearing. "But I must go now."

"No!" cried George. "I mean, can't you wait a minute?"

"No," she said. *"Au revoir, monsieur!"*

She turned on her heel then and, pushing the plum boughs out of her way, darted into the forest. For a moment he could discern a glint of her white dress as she moved between the trees, then nothing. She was gone.

George sat down heavily on the bank and stared hard at the river. As long as she had been standing opposite him, it had been all he could do not to stare at her or, for that matter, to speak coherently; yet now, moments after she had gone, he found that he could not recall a single feature of her face or aspect of her figure — how young or old she might be, what the color of her hair was, whether her complexion was pale or swarthy. Nothing save that she had been dressed in white and was the most beautiful woman he had ever seen . . . if, indeed, he had seen her and she was not some hallucination born of his extended isolation or an angel tumbled into this remote northern place by some celestial accident.

Starting to his feet and taking up his instruments, he began to determine his coordinates. How many degrees north and west. The place where first he had seen her.

July 17, 1910

Dearest Frieda,

I can't imagine that you would like this godforsaken place. It is very rough and fraught with all sorts of dangers. Just yesterday I came upon a hole in which one hundred garter snakes lay tangled in one wriggling

mass as big as a beach ball — a repulsive sight which I'm sure would
have made you scream and faint — and the blackflies are now in full
season. I cannot begin to describe the horror of the blackfly. Every inch
of my body that is not covered by clothing is slavered with fly dope; a
more evil smell I can't imagine, and still the demons crawl and bite!
Well, I know how much you hate snakes and flies. It's no place for
women, that's for sure, so don't even think about coming, as you suggested in your last letter. In fact, the only woman I have met so far up
here is Mrs. Flowers, who runs the rooming house, and she smokes
cigars.

I am glad to hear that the Schubert is going well, but please don't
trouble yourself so much on account of the meter. If you would only
relax a little, the ringing in your ears might abate and then you could
hear the metronome more clearly.

Fondest regards,
George

Telling himself that he must double-check his earlier coordinates,
George made his way back to the Buskegau in late July — he had
made his calculations at dawn, after all, without reference to any
celestial body. In order to arrive at a more accurate reading, he
must first determine his astronomic meridian, which in turn meant
that he must observe the elongation of Polaris. This could only be
done at night, when the star was visible. Accordingly, he set up a
station in a little clearing downstream of the grove of wild plums in
which he had first encountered the woman or sprite — he was not
entirely convinced that he had not imagined their conversation.
The spot boasted a stump on which to set up his transit and a
stretch of flat, dry ground carpeted with fragrant jack pine needles
on which to pitch his tent. He struck camp and settled down to wait
for nightfall.

At a quarter past eight, just as he was transcribing the last of the
day's field notes into his journal, he heard a labored, dragging
sound such as a predator, perhaps a wolf, might make dragging
prey to its lair. Standing carefully, so as to make no sound, he
reached for his rifle. Just as his fingers closed around the stock of
the gun, he saw a lone figure standing in the shadows. It was the
woman. She was wearing a man's plaid shirt and denim overalls
much too large for her. Her hair hung loose and tangled around
her face. She was breathing heavily, as if from some great exertion.
George could see her chest rise and fall beneath the plaid shirt. He

could just make out a travois of some kind that she was dragging. It was loaded down with bundles whose shape was difficult to determine in the half-light of dusk.

"Hello!" he exclaimed. "Well, golly! So you're real after all!" He leaned the rifle against a jack pine.

She swallowed and glanced uncertainly at him. "Is it you then?" she asked, her voice subdued, strangely ragged. She seemed dazed, unsteady on her feet. Her hands rose to her face, clawed the hair away from her eyes. "You came back, then." He could see that her face was smudged with what looked like soot from a fire and streaked from . . . what? From tears?

"Come to check my coordinates," he explained, suddenly solicitous. "But what is that you're dragging? It looks pretty heavy. Maybe I could help you." He pointed. "My canoe is right over there."

She glanced at the travois's contents and then back at him. Her eyes were large and gray, like glass, empty of expression. "My children," she said flatly. "My children are in the travois."

"Children!" George exclaimed, surprised. He had not reckoned on her having children. She scarcely looked old enough, or at any rate, he could not tell how old she looked. "Well," he stammered. "Children! How many?"

"Two," she replied. "There are two."

"A boy and a girl?" George asked.

She nodded, then bowed her head and half turned away, covering her face with her hands.

"What? What is it?" George demanded. Striding over to her, he took her by the shoulder.

"Dead!" she cried. "They are dead!"

"What?" He fell back a step.

"They are dead," she repeated. Then, her words coming in a rush, "They died last night. Both of them. First the boy, then the girl. Pamphile died night before last. Pamphile was my husband. I buried him yesterday. Tonight I bury them. There is a good burying place . . . up there." She pointed to a spar of high ground upriver — it was about sixty feet distant and visible from the clearing. "I could not drag Pamphile so far, but they are little . . . not so heavy as Pamphile. I buried him near the shed. All night long the wolves came . . . the ravens. I did not want to hear them come for my children too."

George dropped to his haunches and peered into the travois.

Two oblong bundles, each about three feet long, wrapped in faded pink flannelette. He reached out one hand to touch the bundle nearest him — felt a density that leaked cold through the worn cloth, as if the flannelette encased stones. A shovel, still clumped with damp earth, presumably from her last excavation, was lashed to the poles with Gillings twine. "What . . . what happened?" he whispered.

"Spots, fever," she explained. "Their eyes rolled back into their heads. Later I realized that they were dead. Gone. That they did not breathe. I don't know what the illness is. . . . If it has a name. All three of them. . . . Two days was all it took." She stumbled forward as if she might fall, then caught herself, swaying. In the dim light she looked pale, ghastly, as though the blood had been drained from her. There were mauve circles smudged under her eyes, the color of a bruise — these were almost too large for her heart-shaped face and the transparent gray color of moonstones. George's eyes caught on them like a drifting leaf will catch on a twig and hung there for a moment, pierced, pinioned.

Then he realized with a start, the woman couldn't have slept for the past thirty-six hours. She must be exhausted, barely able to stand. He rose quickly from the travois and, stepping forward, took her forearm in one hand and her shoulder in the other. "Here," he said gently, urgently, his lips close to her ear as he steadied her with his hands. "You're not to worry now. I will help you."

"Yes," the woman agreed, clinging to him. "Yes, please. That would be good. You are very kind."

Releasing her, he stepped out in front of the travois and, grasping the two poles behind him, started to drag the sledge up the little rise. It was heavy — much heavier than he would have thought possible, given the age of the children, which he reckoned by the length of the bundles to be no more than four or five years. The woman stumbled along behind him, reaching out now and again to catch at the back of his belt to steady herself. He had no idea how she could have dragged such a heavy object any distance at all — the top of her head barely reached his collarbone, and she appeared very slight beneath what he thought must be her husband's clothes.

When they reached the top of the rise, he set the travois down, untied the twine that held the shovel in place, and dug two shallow graves in the rocky soil. Then he excused himself and returned to his campsite for his oil lamp, for the sun had set and it had grown quite dark while he was digging. When he returned, the two pink bundles lay tucked into the earth as if in two narrow beds. The woman knelt, arranging the flannelette as though the shrouds were bedclothes, tucking the fabric in here and smoothing it there.

"You should have waited," George protested. "I would have done that for you."

"I am putting them to bed for the last time," she said. "These are my children. I will have no more. *Padre, filie, et spiritu sancti.*" She leaned over the little bodies, making the sign of the cross over each. "*Padre, filie, et spiritu sancti.*" Then she stood, brushing the soil from her knees. "Quickly," she told George. "We must cover them up."

George shoveled earth over the flannel bundles and, at the woman's insistence and with her frenzied help, collected big stones and heaped them upon the graves.

"I cannot bear to find their bones strewn about," she explained as she crouched, fitting the stones more tightly into place. "Once my father found an old woman's head that an animal had torn from her body and dragged away. He threw it deep into the bush, only to have it turn up in a different place. It was a terrible-looking thing, its eyes gouged out, the flesh laid bare and half eaten off the bone. Stinking. The third time he found it, he was going to throw it in the lake, but Mother said no, we must fish in that lake, and so he buried it instead."

When they had finished, George offered to pack up his gear and tent and take the woman anywhere she wished to go. "Perhaps you'll want to be with your family," he suggested.

She shook her head. "My family is dead. I have no family," she said.

"You won't want to be alone," he advised her. "I'll take you down to Golden City and put you up at Mrs. Flowers's. I'll pay for your room and board . . . until you can get yourself settled."

She shook her head again. "No," she said. "I live by the lake. I have always lived by the lake. Why should I leave?"

"Well, then," said George, not knowing what to do — for surely chivalry demanded that he take some action to assure her safety and well-being. "I'll take you home. I'll camp outside your door. Make sure you are all right. Just for tonight."

"No need. I have lived alone before. After Papa died. Before Pamphile. I can do so again." She held out her hand to him and he took it eagerly. Her slender fingers were cool; her hand felt boneless.

"At least tell me your name," George urged her.

"Marguerite," she replied. "My parents called me Marguerite."

"And I'm George. George Macoun."

"Thank you for helping me bury my children, George Macoun. You have been very kind." She withdrew her hand from his grasp and, turning, bent down to pick up the shovel.

"No, let me do that," George insisted.

"It is not necessary," she said, and picking up the shovel, she swung it over her shoulder.

"What about the sledge?" he asked.

"Some poles lashed together. . . . I do not want it," she said. "Goodbye, George Macoun!" She started off into the thick forest.

"Marguerite, wait! You're going the wrong way!" George cried. "My camp is that way. West!"

"I'm taking a shortcut," she called over her shoulder, continuing to make her way through the bush, not looking back.

"No! Really! I insist!" cried George, starting after her. "I'll make you some tea! Wait up!"

"Don't follow me, George Macoun!" she called. "I will be all right."

"But Marguerite! What about wolves? What about bears?"

"Why should wolves or bears bother me?"

He could no longer see her; then the forest swallowed even the sound of her footfalls.

August 3, 1910

Dear Frieda,

After several weeks in the region of Evelyn, I have come east again to the Tully township and the green, meandering Buskegau. It seems that my efforts to survey this little part of the world are doomed to frustration and failure, for the journal in which I had recorded my field notes for that region tumbled out of my packsack and into picturesque Ice Chest Lake of an evening as I was lazily paddling across its cool and tranquil waters. I fished about for twenty minutes and finally managed to dredge it up from the weedy bottom with my brush hook; it was, of course, a soggy and illegible wreck.

So it seems I will be an additional few weeks in the north. I am so very sorry, my dearest, but expect that you and your mother can continue to plan the wedding with the same energy and aplomb in my absence as you have all along. After all, what need for the humble George but to exist . . . and to be at the altar of St. Andrews at 11 AM sharp on October 4, of course! In the meantime, I'm sure you would agree that it would not do to disappoint the Bureau of Mines which (rumors have it) will be increasing my salary to a princely $50 a month if all goes well here in the Porcupine Country.

Yours with the greatest of affection,
George

Three days later George was tracking Marguerite south of his base camp when a thunderstorm blew up, driven from the southwest by strong, hot winds. It was going on to five o'clock in the afternoon when it arrived in the form of slanting rain, followed by big chunks of hail and thunderbolts so loud it sounded as though the granite Shield beneath his feet were being split in two by a giant sledgehammer. The ground shook. The air was charged with electricity. George's instruments began to spark and buzz as though they had come to sudden, distraught life. The hair on his head and neck stood on end. He could feel the hairs tugging at their follicles. A jagged bolt of lightning struck a jack pine not twenty feet from where he had sought shelter under a felled tree. There was an acrid smell of frying pine sap and sulfur. The jack pine sizzled like a sparkler, then burst into hot orange flame.

It was then that he saw her, a dark figure silhouetted against the burning jack pine, her head and shoulders covered by a blanket as she moved toward him through the thick brush. "Here," she cried, extending her arm to offer him shelter under the blanket. "My house is nearby."

He scrambled to his feet, stooped to go under the blanket. "But how did you know I was here?" he asked.

"You've been here for days," she replied. "Do you think I haven't known?"

She led him down a rooty path to a trapper's rough cabin huddled in a grove of tall birches beside a small lake, round as a cauldron. The storm lashed the lake; its waters churned and boiled. Through the hard, driving rain the sentinel birches wavered like pale, elongated ghosts guarding the pile of moss-chinked logs; their papery leaves fluttered lightly, like the wings of a hundred little birds. Shoving open the heavy, sticking door, she pushed him inside, tossed the wet blanket over a chair back, and, moving to a battered table, bent over to light the coal oil lamp.

The wick caught the flame and held it; a moment later, a portion of the room ballooned into a soft pool of yellow light. George blinked to adjust his vision, then looked around him. The peeled log walls had been hewn and recently whitewashed. One corner was completely taken up with a large iron bedstead on which a feather tick lay; this was covered with a faded patchwork quilt. In the other corner squatted an oval tin stove, dented and shiny. The floor was made up of uneven planks cut from silvery white pine and strewn here and there with rag rugs in muted blues and greens. A chipped blue vase on the table beside the lamp held a spray of magenta heather. He inhaled deeply. The cabin smelled of resin, faintly of woodsmoke and of something else besides, a composite of odors — lavender, chamomile, witch hazel, and borage.

Marguerite pulled out a rickety three-legged stool for him, handed him a dry Hudson Bay blanket to wrap himself in, and set the kettle on the stove for tea, which she gave to him in a blue granite-chip mug. It was not ordinary tea but some tisane decocted from bark or a root tasting faintly of licorice. "I have no English tea," she explained. "It is all gone. Sometimes Pamphile would buy it from the trader when he sold his furs. Roses. Twining. Not me. I have never been to town."

"Would you like to go?" George asked.

"Oh, no!" replied Marguerite, shuddering.

Gingerly George sipped the hot, strong fluid and watched her towel her hair dry. He could not tell what color that hair was even now, by the light of the coal oil lamp . . . or even its length. Like her eyes, it seemed almost colorless, the shade of grayish dun that woodsmoke is, or haze, and it not so much fell from her head as emanated from it, like a mist at dawn that clings to the body of the river that begets it.

The cloth of her wet shift clung here and there to her slender body as she lifted her arms and turned a little this way and that to accomplish the toweling. George looked at her hungrily, then, realizing what he was doing, averted his glance. You are a gentleman, George Macoun, he reminded himself, an alumnus of Queen's

University and engaged to be married in but a few months' time to . . . Who was he marrying? Frantically he poked around in his brain until, a moment later, he had uprooted the name: Frieda! Yes, of course! He was marrying Frieda Eckert.

Frieda?

"What is the matter, George?" Marguerite asked. "You look so strange."

George swallowed. "You said you had been watching me."

Marguerite shrugged. "Yes," she replied.

"Why?" George asked.

The woman tossed the towel over the back of a chair and pushed her damp hair from her face. She did not answer for a moment. Then she said, "In the winter there are Pamphile's trap lines to work, but in the summer there's not much to do." She pointed to a fishing pole that leaned against the door. "Now and then I fish. There are sauger in the lake, and walleye. Do you like to fish, George Macoun?"

But George would not be diverted. "Why did you keep yourself hidden, Marguerite?" he asked. "Did you think I wouldn't want to see you? I . . . I wanted to see you. Very much. Well, what I mean is, I was worried about you. Concerned, I mean."

"Concerned?" she repeated.

"A woman alone . . . a pretty one . . ." George faltered. Surely the concept of female helplessness was too obvious to require an explanation!

"Oh! But I was alone for many years after Papa died," she reassured him. "Five or six at least. Let's see. Maman turned to dust when I was just gone eight and Papa a few years later. . . . He died of gangrene. His right leg. All the way to the groin. In the end, I had to shoot him. Later Pamphile —"

George spat a mouthful of tea into his lap. "What?" he blurted out.

"Pardon?" she inquired, blinking at him.

"You shot" — George sputtered — "your father?"

"He was suffering," she said softly. "You wouldn't believe the screaming . . . or the stench, to be quite honest! So you see, you needn't be concerned for me, George. I am good at taking care of myself."

George wiped his mouth with the back of his hand and mopped

at his lap with a frayed corner of the scratchy blanket. "I suppose," he admitted ruefully. He was trying to imagine Frieda, whom a metronome could reduce to tears and shrieks, taking aim at a howling, reeking Dr. Eckert with the professor's pearl-handled der-ringer — Dr. Eckert kept just such a gun in his desk drawer. "In case a thief bent upon stealing my prize butterfly collection should break into my office," the professor had explained. George found the image a difficult one to conjure.

"Anyway," Marguerite continued, "I was curious to see if you could find me. I am hard to find, it seems."

"Very hard," George agreed.

"So I found you instead. Because, in truth, you were not so hard to find, and besides, it was enough that you should have looked for me in the first place."

George's heart snagged on her words as if on a thorn, and hung from them, beating like a wounded thing that struggles and can-not tear itself free. Blood roared in his ears, making it difficult for him to hear, to think. "Enough for what?" he managed to whisper. "What are we talking about?"

"I am supposed to stay right here," Marguerite explained. "By the lake. I am not supposed to go across the river or to go beyond the grove of birches to the west or the vale of the jack pines to the east. I may go no farther south than an hour's walk."

"What do you mean, 'not supposed to,' 'can't go'?" George asked. "Of course you can go!"

"No," insisted Marguerite firmly. "I cannot. I am different from you, George. Different from Papa and Pamphile too. I am like my mother. Papa tried to take her across the river when she was ill with fever. She told him not to move her, but he wouldn't listen. Then she became feverish and no longer understood what was being said to her. It was January and very cold. Papa wrapped her up in his warmest furs and laid her in the toboggan. He hitched up the dogs, calling to me to wait and to stay inside no matter what. Later that night he returned. No sooner had they crossed the ice on the river than Maman had shivered away into a handful of white dust that the wind blew everywhere. Papa said he had never seen anything like it. She simply disintegrated. She always told him that some-thing terrible would happen were she to leave the lake — that was what her own mother had told her — but she was never sure what that thing was. After that, Papa made sure I understood that I could never leave. And I made sure Pamphile knew it. You see, Papa found Maman here at the lake the way her papa had found her maman. Just as Pamphile found me . . . just as you found me. As far as I know, that is the way it always has been."

"But it's a fairy story you've just told me," George objected. "Surely you can't believe it. For one thing, the French came into this country at the very earliest two hundred years ago. That's hardly forever."

Marguerite shrugged. "I don't know. Perhaps we were not French."

George stared at her, at her creamy, pale skin, her haze of color-less hair, her transparent eyes. "What do you mean, not French?" he whispered.

She did not answer. Instead she tugged the mug of tea from his hands and set it on the table. He stood, as if she had drawn him to his feet by taking away the cup, and turned as if to leave. For surely he must leave and quickly, he told himself. His thinking was all muddled, and there was . . .

Marguerite caught him by the sleeve of his shirt. "Don't go!" she pleaded, her voice low, as warm as fur.

There was someone called Frieda . . .

Reluctantly, inexorably, George turned to Marguerite and, as he did, found himself hurled off his feet and spun into a wild vortex in which there was no sound, no footing to be found, but only hands and twining arms and hair as soft as mist and warm mouths.

George stayed at the little lake in the woods for a fortnight. Then he returned to Mrs. Flowers in Golden City in preparation for his journey to Kingston. The morning before he was to portage out, however, he wrote his fiancée another letter.

August 21, 1910

Darling Frieda,

The most ridiculous news imaginable! I begin to think my expedition to this place has been cursed by those Greek and Roman gods which so oft find their way into our stimulating literary discussions. No sooner had I completed my field notes for the Tully township and journeyed to Gold-en City in joyful and expectant anticipation of returning to you, my beloved, than my journal was eaten by Mrs. Flowers's ridiculous cow! The greedy creature left only the spine! That means that I must return yet again to the bush as I cannot show my face at the bureau without the information I was sent to collect. Would you mind dreadfully if we were to postpone the wedding just one week? I shall endeavor to fulfill my task as quickly as possible, God and weather permitting — not to mention voracious ruminants! — so that I may return to you and put an end to this long separation.

Sincerely,
Your adoring George

For by this time George had learned to lie.

After posting the letter, George went out back of the rooming house to Mrs. Flowers's cowshed and held his journal for Old Betty to eat.

George Dewey Macoun returned to Kingston from northern Ontario in the late fall of 1910 and married Frieda Eckert on October 22 of that year. Several months later, the new Mrs. Macoun failed her Royal Conservatory exams for the third time. By then, however, she was carrying the first of their four children and was too overwhelmed by nausea to do more than take to her bed. There she lay moaning, with a damp towel folded over her pale and tremendous forehead and a bucket strategically placed by the head of her bed.

George was not on hand when the second George Macoun, his namesake, was born. He had gone north again for the purpose of performing more precise observations regarding longitude. He explained the process to Frieda once. Something to do with exact local time and when the moon crosses the meridian of the observation plane — whatever that meant! To tell the truth, Frieda had only been half listening to her husband, who could be quite pedantic when he started in on his stream gauging and his catchment delineation.

"Such an odd, dusty duck! Just like Father with his bugs!" laughed Frieda.

When George went north, he always stayed at Mrs. Flowers's. At least that was the address to which Frieda posted her bright, chatty letters, full of news about herself and their children. Often he didn't reply to those letters for weeks. But he was often in the field and only returned to town for supplies or to file reports.

After years of exacting and meticulous fieldwork, George produced an admirable rendering of the 1,239 square miles that would later become incorporated as the City of Timmins, the largest municipality, in terms of landmass, in all of Canada. He mapped its streams, its rivers, its many little and big lakes and all the islands in them. There was one lake, however, that he failed to include on his map.

Shortly before the birth of his fourth child, George Macoun went north again. Because there had been problems with the printer regarding the second edition of his map, he had been unable to leave southern Ontario for more than six months. He had never been away from the Porcupine so long, not since he had first begun going north more than a decade earlier.

"The ministry wants me to suggest some potential reservoir sites," he explained to Frieda. "I'll need to establish some benchmarks."

When he arrived at the little cabin by the uncharted lake, all was still. The cabin had a derelict quality, as though it had been abandoned for a season. The roof sagged and the logs were dark with rot, while the woodpile on the porch was tumbled, sticks here and there as though an animal had been rooting through them. The foundation of the cabin was still banked with clay; Marguerite always removed the clay after the thaw to let the logs breathe, and here it was well into June.

George's heart squeezed into a tight fist. "Marguerite!" he called hoarsely.

There was no reply.

The cabin door was ajar. Flinging it open, George glanced quickly about the dusky room. It looked as it always did — the chairs and table and bed in their accustomed places, the rag rugs placed just so. However, it smelled different. Empty. He stepped into the room, his heart turning over heavily in his chest like a punctured tire. She had left him a note on the table, one corner of it weighted down by the coal oil lamp.

Dear George,
You have been gone so long. Months and months. I expected you before the thaw, yet that has long since passed. So I have decided to go looking for you. I think perhaps you are right and I will not turn to dust if I cross the river. We shall see. . . .
                                                                    Marguerite

That night George pitched his tent beside the lake and watched the loons run maniacally along the surface of the water to gain the necessary speed for flight. Year after year they returned to this point on a map that did not exist on paper but was nevertheless etched deep into their hearts. Loons mate for life, Marguerite had told him.

Behind him the cabin burned. There was no wind that night. The fire burned straight up. He could feel its heat spread across his back like the palm of a big hand. Now and then there was a loud crack as a jack pine cone, pried open by the heat, burst, scattering its seeds.

Before he had poured coal oil over the cabin's contents and, taking a match from the tin box he kept in his kit, ignited it, George had climbed up to the ridge where he and Marguerite had buried her children so many years before and, one at a time, removed the rocks that still covered the shallow graves. In truth, he had long wondered if he had not buried rocks or some other thing that night, for the little bodies had seemed too heavy, too stone cold for children, and there was much about Marguerite he did not understand. The pink flannelette that had served the little bodies as shrouds had long since rotted into the soil, leaving it tinged with faint color. In each grave he found not stones or bones but this: an elongated heap of snow-white dust stretched into the shape of a child.

George asked Frieda if he could name their fourth child. Frieda found this mildly peculiar. "He showed absolutely no interest in naming the first three," she told her euchre club. "It was all up to me. Well, you know George. Nose in his notes if he's not in the field. But the name he chose! My dears! Outlandish! French, you know. Marguerite. I call her Margie, of course, but no nicknames for George. He always calls her by her full name. And how he dotes on that child, when, truth be told, he never paid one bit of attention to little George or Donald or Evelyn. The first thing he did after she was born was name a lake in northern Ontario after her. A little glacial lake he had only just discovered: Lake Marguerite. How Evelyn carried on. Whining and weeping. Where's my lake, Daddy? she wanted to know, and rightly so, if you ask me. And then, to top it all off, he buys all the land around the lake and builds a cottage

and a boathouse and that's why I have to miss Edna's Dominion
Day tea, because every summer without fail the whole Macoun
family has to train up to Lake Marguerite and catch sauger and
walleye and be eaten alive by those appalling flies!"

"Marguerite!" gasped George, clutching at his daughter's plump
hand. The hospital room was dark and shadowy, scarcely there at
all. A millimeter above the white, glowing bed, the old geologist
floated, not quite in contact with the sheets, suspended. "So you're
still here, my dearest! Not gone? Not turned to dust?"

"Not yet, Daddy," Margie replied wanly. "Soon."

"I've been having the strangest dreams!" George told her. "I . . . I
found you in the bush and you were young and beautiful, but so
strange. And there were two children and a cabin. I never saw the
children. For years I —"

"Shhh!" Margie advised him, withdrawing her cool, fleshy hand
from his feverish one and laying it on his steaming forehead instead. "Try and rest, Dad. They've got you on a morphine drip. It's
no wonder your dreams are strange."

The 5:22

FROM STORY

FOR MORE THAN A YEAR Walter Mason and the woman with one ear nodded to each other at 5:22 P.M., or thereabouts, when the Western Local pulled into Lincoln station. As he descended the steep metal steps clutching his briefcase, she would be standing near last in the small line of passengers waiting on the wooden platform to board. If it were lightly raining or snowing, she might hold a newspaper over her head. Sometimes she turned her face to the sky and opened her mouth a little, as if thirsty. In heavy rain she held a small yellow umbrella while the others waited under the eaves of the nearby shops. She always carried an overstuffed white shopping bag, but nothing ever protruded from the top to hint at what was inside.

Her complexion was dark, perhaps Mediterranean or Middle Eastern. But she dressed as any American woman might, in a blouse and skirt, or pants and a sweater. Invariably, though, she wore a colorful scarf around her head, wrapped delicately, it seemed to Walter, as one would a bouquet or live thing.

The scarf covered, of course, the missing right ear, as Walter assumed it was meant to do. He would never have known of the deformity if a gust of wind one afternoon had not whipped the scarf suddenly free of her head. She dropped her purse and shopping bag and fumbled to secure the fine silk under her chin. Then she looked up and saw his rude stare. It was awful of him, he knew that, and he averted his eyes. What had possessed him to gaze at her for those few seconds that the crimson scarf fluttered in the wind, revealing the thick, slashing scars of an ear that wasn't there anymore?

*

When the woman didn't appear on the platform the following Monday, Walter didn't think much of it. She had missed other days over the last year — he could recall two for sure. But both were during snowstorms, it occurred to him as he crossed the rutted dirt parking lot, not on unusually warm spring days such as this. He opened the door of his Saab to let the day's hot air exhale from the car. Then it came to him: perhaps she had not appeared today because he had noticed her missing ear. It charmed Walter to think of this woman's being so shy. He was shy himself. He hadn't married, even though he was forty-seven and interested — that in itself would demonstrate a lagging sense of forwardness. He did cheerfully submit to the blind dates arranged for him through the unstinting efforts of the married women at the institute. But they remained one-time affairs — or rather more precisely, one-time intersections of two people looking for something other than what they found.

What was he looking for? A certain sweetness of temperament was uppermost on his list, a flexible mind (though not one incapable of holding a firm opinion), and perhaps a sense of mankind's insignificance in the totality of the universe. The ability to apply order to the world would also be handy in a wife. These attributes, which he obligingly scrawled down as an aid to the matchmakers in his department, apparently were no help at all. They wanted to know what he desired in height and weight, profession, previous marital status, and postmarital attachments, such as children. He supposed it was curious that he never thought in those terms, but there it was. He didn't care about shape, occupation, or legal connections, just as he hoped a woman wouldn't care that he was unfit in the athletic sense of the word, underemployed for the number of degrees appended to his name, and suspiciously unattached for all of his adult years. He didn't try to camouflage the gray in his hair or wear the kind of tailored suits that would slim down the excesses of his appetite. Though he was not overly proud of his condition, he was at least comfortable with it. But if he had only one ear, he wondered, what would he do, without a scarf to hide the terrible secret?

When the woman didn't appear on Tuesday, Walter concluded with some certainty that she had begun a week's vacation. Each succeeding day that the train arrived at 5:22 and she was not there only stiffened his reasoning. On Thursday, cold rain draped the region, and Walter found himself lamenting that the woman's time off might be spoiled by inclement weather. Perhaps she was a reader and would be happy enough within doors. When he leafed through the *New York Times Book Review* that Sunday, he imagined her vacation reading list, perhaps a book on exotic foods, such as *Bengali Cooking,* or an intimate collection of short stories, such as *Women in Their Beds.* For a lingering moment, Walter pictured her as the woman on the cover of that book, with her long black hair languishing on the pillow and one breast peeking above the sheet.

It was with some sense of anticipation on the following Monday that Walter rose from his usual seat and hurried along the aisle even before the train began its slow braking into Lincoln. He reached the heavy sliding door just as Mel, the conductor, opened it from the other side and called out, "Next stop, Lincoln. That's Lincoln, next stop."

Walter squeezed past him so he would have a good view out of the open car. "Where's the fire?" Mel asked.

"Oh, no fire, Mel," Walter answered with a little shrug. "I'm just . . . expecting someone."

Mel winked at him, which made Walter feel a bit odd. The train crept past the crossing signal on Concord Road, and he leaned out of the car to scan the small group waiting to get on. The woman with one ear was not among them.

"Mind your step," Mel said as Walter made his way down to the platform, and these words reassured him, as always, that his welfare was being looked after. He walked slowly across the parking lot, glancing over his shoulder to make sure the woman didn't come running late from one of the station stores. In a few moments, the train took off without her.

Why was he so disappointed? It wasn't a sexual attraction, Walter decided, unless one so subtle that he couldn't discern it. Frankly, he didn't find her particularly attractive. He supposed that in another age she would have been considered a handsome woman. But he disliked handsome women — the blocky faces, the large eyes, the broad cheekbones. To another man, he supposed, she might be considered mysterious, and thereby interesting. But Walter disliked mystery. The simple question "What if?" could lead to so many disturbing places.

He was obviously not attracted to this woman sexually, and the evidence was perfectly clear: he had never spoken to her. Surely if he were propelled by a secret fuel of desire he would have managed some small step on the route to intimacy — a brief hello, a smile, perhaps even "Have a good day." No, not that insulting phrase. Who was he to be using the imperative with this woman? "I *hope* you have a very nice day" — that would be perfectly appropriate. And yet, there were only so many words one could say in passing. She might not hear all of them. She might misconstrue. Better not to risk conversation at the station, but rather simply stay on board one day in a seat precisely halfway down the car — her customary spot — where the rows turned from facing backward to facing forward. She would slide into the wide seat without even realizing he was there.

As the second week of the woman's absence stretched on, Walter became worried. His concentration, normally among his strongest attributes at work, failed him several times. At one point, a fellow researcher had the temerity to tap him on the shoulder and ask, "Daydreaming, Walter?" "No," he had replied courteously, "I was thinking." Thinking he certainly was, about why a person would take vacation time at the end of March, of all months, known as mud season in these parts. There were other possibilities, of course. She might have fled to some warm-weather island. Perhaps the woman with one ear had simply returned to wherever she had come from, or moved on to someplace new. Perhaps she would never again take the 5:22.

By Thursday Walter had decided to make inquiries, starting with Mel. The conductor knew something about each of his passengers, and it was his habit to share the news, discreetly, up and down the car. For example, with a nod of his head and a few well-chosen words, Mel let it be known to the single women in the car that James, the investment adviser, had just landed a big promotion and was available. On the other hand, Kelly — the young woman with the sad brown eyes — was definitely "not looking and might never be again." She had recently lost her boyfriend of three years as well as her beloved Honda Civic, events that left her crying some days and required Mel to start carrying tissues.

Walter had overheard himself being referred to in a respectful tone as "the professor . . . MIT — never married." That wasn't strictly true. He had been hired as a senior researcher to conduct experiments in machine vision, his specialty. It suited Walter to labor among just a few other engineers and their support staff. It suited him even more to retreat each evening to his apartment in the suburbs, where he could work uninterrupted on his book of odd designs. He was near finishing his collection of Impossible Objects, such as a teapot with the spout and handle on the same side. It amused him to imagine things that could never work. Often he listened to his shortwave, and the crackling sound of far-off voices seemed to him as if coming from a large immigrant family living on the other side of the thin walls. Sometimes, usually before one of his arranged dates, he imagined a woman in his apartment, a wife. What would she be doing right now, he wondered, what would she do there?

When Walter, with money in hand, looked up from his seat to ask Mel about the missing woman, he was shocked to see another conductor. "Where to?" the man asked. Mel never talked in such a clipped expression. He always asked, "And where would you be heading?" or "Where can I take you today?"

Walter handed over his three dollars to Edward, as the man's badge read, and said brusquely, "Lincoln."

"Lincoln it is."

"Where's Mel," Walter asked as he peered over the seats, "working up front?"

"Mel? Don't know him."

"He's been the conductor on this line for years."

Edward handed over the ticket. "Well, that explains it then. I've only been the conductor for a day."

"You mean you've replaced Mel?"

Edward shook his head. "I can't say that exactly, not knowing anything about Mel. I guess he was before my time."

Your time? Walter thought. You've only worked this train for one day. You haven't had a "time" yet. Edward moved through the train. Every few rows Walter heard him say, "Where to?"

There were others besides Mel to ask about the woman with one ear. Several people regularly waited with her at the station to board. Perhaps she had spoken to them.

Walter spent the twenty-minute ride to Lincoln plotting what he would say in the brief seconds as he got off and the others got on.

"Excuse me," he might begin, "I just wanted to ask — do you happen to know anything about the woman with . . ." He certainly couldn't mention the ear. ". . . the woman in the colorful scarves who used to get on here each day?" Walter practiced his question at different speeds and emphases as the train slowed into Lincoln. As he moved down the aisle toward the door, he noticed that no one else was getting off with him, and no one was waiting to get on either. The Western Local left quickly.

Because March 28 was Good Friday, Walter had no opportunity to continue his inquiry until the following Monday. On that day, he boarded in Cambridge as always, took his seat at the back of the car, and waited for the conductor. This time he would be forceful in inquiring about Mel. Then in Lincoln he would stop in the shops by the station to ask about the woman. Surely she had made some small purchases there — a newspaper or mints, perhaps even medicine at the pharmacy. She would be remembered.

Edward approached, humming. "Where to?" he asked, with not a hint of recognition in his eyes.

"Lincoln," Walter said with a trace in his voice of *You should know that by now. Mel knew the second day.*

"Don't stop at Lincoln," Edward said.

The words and tone confused Walter. Was the conductor offering advice — *Do not stop at Lincoln* — or some new information? "What do you mean?" Walter asked. "The five o'clock out of Cambridge always stops in Lincoln."

"I wouldn't know about always," Edward said. "I only know about today. Today this train doesn't stop at Lincoln — the engineer told me himself. Now where else do you want to go?"

"I don't want to go anywhere else. I live in Lincoln. I've been getting off there for two years."

"I can see your problem," Edward said. "That's why people should always ask when they get on where the train's stopping. Saves a lot of this kind of trouble."

The train pulled into Waverly station, and Edward hurried to attend to the doors. When he returned he said, "Where to?"

Was it some kind of game this strange conductor was playing? Walter wondered. But Edward didn't appear to be a man capable of sustaining a joke this long. He did appear to be a man capable of stupidity, and so Walter said, "I'll prove the train stops in Lincoln. Let me see a schedule."

Edward checked inside his lapel pocket, but his hand came back empty. "Sorry, all out."

Walter had reached that point his mother had customarily referred to as "her wit's end." He had no wit left, at least to deal with Edward. Walter stood up to appeal to the familiar faces of the Western Local. There were more people than he had ever seen in this car before, but he recognized none of them. Walter sank in his seat. "Just let me off at the next stop — that's still Concord, isn't it?"

"Of course it is," Edward said, taking the three dollars. "That will be another fifty cents."

Walter exited from the train at Concord and stood alone on the platform. His Saab was a couple of miles back in Lincoln. There was no cab in sight. A few cars were going by, but he couldn't imagine standing with his thumb out while dressed in a tie and jacket. He would walk. And since the shortest route between stations was undoubtedly the rail line, he would go by the tracks.

He felt a bit adventuresome as he set out. The dwindling daylight did not bother him. He had never been afraid of the dark. He started off briskly, walking between the rails and stretching his stride to land on every other wooden plank. After a while he broke the monotony by balancing on one rail, and he surprised himself by how far he could do it. He looked back frequently, even though he knew he would hear a train coming well before he would need to step aside. At one point he knelt and pressed his ear to the cold rail to sense the vibration of an approaching train, but he felt nothing.

The woman gone, Mel gone, the Lincoln stop gone — what else might disappear from his life? Walter descended the long stairway to the platform in Cambridge on Tuesday. Perhaps the train itself wouldn't show up today. Then tomorrow, the whole station would vanish. He laughed at these fanciful ideas. They were more appropriate for some giddy science fiction story, not the real life of a mechanical engineer.

The train approached on time. Walter climbed aboard behind a half-dozen strangers. The car was quite full of commuters already. Walter scanned the aisle and finally spotted a vacant seat midway

down the car, where the rows turned from facing forward to backward. As he slid into the wide seat, the train pulled away.

"Where can I take you today, my friend?"

Walter practically jumped at the voice. He turned around, and
there was Mel at the end of the car punching out tickets. Walter
called to him, but the conductor was busy and did not look up. The
train sped on from one station to another, and Mel slowly worked
his way closer. When he reached Walter he said, "Hey, Professor,
how's your book coming?"

"Mel," Walter stammered, "where have you been?"

The old conductor leaned against the seat for a moment. "Oh,
just a little safety retraining course they put us through every few
years. You know, a train crashes out west and they rush everybody
into emergency classes. Why, what did you think?"

"I don't know. You were just suddenly gone."

"That's how the railroad works, they don't give anybody notice."
Mel slipped his punch over the green ticket. "Lincoln, I presume."

"Lincoln?" Walter said. "No, I came in from Concord this morning. You don't stop in Lincoln anymore. Didn't they tell you?"

Mel laughed and pulled a paper from his lapel pocket. "Here's
the new supply of schedules — just came out today." His big forefinger worked down the row of times and stopped at 5:22. "There it
is," he said, "Lincoln."

"But yesterday the train didn't stop there — Edward made me go
to Concord."

Mel nodded as if not overly surprised. "We had to drop Lincoln
on the earlier run at 4:50 to gain some time going to Springfield.
The engineer subbing yesterday must have gotten the stops confused."

The explanation pleased Walter. Edward had been wrong. "Well,
today I'll have to go to Concord, where my car is."

"Did you ever notice," Mel said as he processed the ticket, "how
people always return to where they come from? Wouldn't it be a
more interesting world if people sometimes ended up far away
from where they set out?"

Walter shook his head to dismiss the crazy thought. But why did
each day have to be a perfect circle? Why couldn't a person take a
sidetrack, go a little way, and then come back, if need be?

As the train neared Lincoln, a few people got up, and Walter wondered how they knew it would stop there today when he did not. He watched them crossing the parking lot to their cars. As the train moved on, he sensed a person sitting down at the edge of his seat. When he looked over, he saw the woman with one ear.

"I am sorry to intrude," she said, "but the train is so full today."

"No, it's fine, there's plenty of room," he said, drawing himself closer to the window so she would not be frightened. Walter breathed the intoxicating scent of some delicate perfume. He felt the vinyl seat shift under him as she settled into her place. He said, "It's nice to see you again."

She nodded pleasantly and fixed her large shopping bag on the floor between them. The top fell open and he could see a white uniform inside, the kind a nurse might wear. Then her thin hand reached to the knot beneath her chin and began loosening the bright orange scarf. What could she be doing? Walter looked away so as not to stare at the scar. But as he gazed into the train window he saw the reflection of the silk fall from her head. She folded the scarf neatly on her lap.

He turned to her. There on the right side of her head was a perfectly formed little pink ear. It was smoothly curved at the top and delicately lobed at the bottom. The ear seemed magical to him, as if sewn on by miniature hands.

She tucked a few errant strands of her short black hair behind the ear. He smiled at this gesture, wishing that he had something new and wonderful about himself to show her. She smiled back at him. "Wasn't that your stop?"

He was pleased that she had noticed. He looked through the bleary window at the lights of Lincoln station receding quickly. "No," he said, "I'm going farther today."

Islands

FROM PLOUGHSHARES

1

WE GOT UP at dawn, ignored the yolky sun, loaded our navy-blue Austin with suitcases, and then drove straight to the coast, stopping only on the verge of Sarajevo, so I could pee. I sang communist songs the entire journey: songs about mournful mothers looking through graves for their dead sons; songs about the revolution, steaming and steely, like a locomotive; songs about striking miners burying their dead comrades. By the time we got to the coast, I had almost lost my voice.

2

We waited for the ship on a long stone pier, which burned the soles of my feet as soon as I took off my sandals. The air was sweltering, saturated with sea ozone, exhaustion, and the smell of coconut sun lotion, coming from the German tourists, already red and shellacked, lined up for a photo at the end of the pier. We saw the thin stocking of smoke on the horizon-thread, then the ship itself, getting bigger, slightly slanted sideways, like a child's drawing. I had a round straw hat with all the seven dwarfs painted on it. It threw a short, dappled shadow over my face. I had to raise my head to look at the grownups. Otherwise I would look at their gnarled knees, the spreading sweat stains on their shirts and sagging wrinkles of fat on their thighs. One of the Germans, an old, bony man, got down on his knees and then puked over the pier edge. The vomit hit the surface and then dispersed in different directions, like children running away to hide from the seeker. Under the wave-throbbing ocher and maroon island of vomit, a school of aluminum fish gathered and nibbled it peevishly.

3

The ship was decrepit, with peeling steel stairs and thin leaves of rust that could cut your fingers on the handrails. The staircase wound upward like a twisted towel. "Welcome," said an unshaven man in a T-shirt picturing a boat with a smoke-snake wobbling on the waves and, above it, the sun with a U-smile and the umlaut of eyes. We sat on the upper board and the ship leapt over humble waves, panting and belching. We passed a line of little islands akin to car wrecks by the road, and I would ask my parents, "Is this Mljet?" and they would say, "No." From behind one of the islands, shaven by a wild fire, a gust of waylaying wind attacked us, snatched the straw hat off my head, and tossed it into the sea. I watched the hat teetering away, my hair pressed against my skull like a helmet, and I understood that I would never, ever see it again. I wished to go back in time and hold on to my hat before the surreptitious whirl-wind hit me in the face again. The ship sped away from the hat, and the hat was transformed into a distant beige stain on the snot-green sea. I began crying and sobbed myself to sleep. When I woke up, the ship was docked and the island was Mljet.

4

Uncle Julius impressed a stern, moist kiss on my cheek — the cor-ner of his mouth touched the corner of my mouth, leaving a dot of spit above my lip. But his lips were soft, like slugs, as if there was nothing behind to support them. As we walked away from the pier, he told us that he forgot his teeth at home, and then, so as to prove that he was telling us the truth, he grinned at me, showing me his pink gums with cinnabar scars. He reeked of pine cologne, but a whiff redolent of rot and decay escaped his insides and penetrated the cologne cloud. I hid my face in my mother's skirt. I heard his snorting chuckle. "Can we please go back home!" I cried.

5

We walked up a sinuous road exuding heat. Uncle Julius's sandals
clattered in a tranquilizing rhythm and I felt sleepy. There was a
dense, verdureless thicket alongside the road. Uncle Julius told us
that there used to be so many poisonous snakes on Mljet that
people used to walk in tall rubber boots all the time, even at home,
and snakebites were as common as mosquito bites. Everybody used
to know how to slice off the bitten piece of flesh in a split second,
before the venom could spread. Snakes killed chickens and dogs.
Once, he said, a snake was attracted by the scent of milk, so it curled
up on a sleeping baby. And then someone heard of the mongoose, how it kills snakes with joy, and they sent a man to Africa
and he brought a brood of mongooses and they let them loose on
the island. There were so many snakes that it was like a paradise
for them. You could walk for miles and hear nothing but the hissing of snakes and the shrieks of mongooses and the bustle and
rustle in the thicket. But then mongooses killed all the snakes
and bred so much that the island became too small for them.
Chickens started disappearing, cats also, there were rumors of
rabid mongooses, and some even talked about monster mongooses
that were the result of paradisiacal inbreeding. Now they were trying to figure out how to get rid of mongooses. "So that's how it
is," he said, "it's all one pest after another, like revolutions. Life
is nothing if not a succession of evils," he said, and then stopped
and took a pebble out of his left sandal. He showed the puny
gray pebble to us, as if holding unquestionable evidence that he
was right.

6

He opened the gate and we walked through a small, orderly garden
with stout tomato stalks like sentries alongside the path. His wife
stood in the courtyard, her face like a loaf of bread with a small
tubby potato in the middle, arms akimbo, her calves full of bruises
and blood vessels on the verge of bursting, ankles swollen. She was
barefoot; her big toes were crooked, taking a sudden turn, as if
backing away in disgust from each other. She enveloped my head
with her palms, twisted my head upward, and then put her mouth

over my mouth, leaving a thick layer of warm saliva, which I hastily wiped off with my shoulder. Aunt Lyudmila was her name.

7

I clambered, dragging a bag full of plastic beach toys, after my sprightly parents, up a concrete staircase on the side of the house, with sharp stair edges and pots of unconcerned flowers, like servants with candles, on the banister side.

8

The room was fragrant with lavender, mosquito-spray poison, and clean, freshly ironed bedsheets. There was an aerial picture of a winding island (Mljet, it said in the lower right corner) and a picture of Comrade Tito, smiling, black-and-white, on the opposite wall. Below the window, the floor was dotted with mosquitoes — with a large green-glittering fly or a bee here and there, still stricken by the surprise. When I moved toward them, the wisp caused by my motion made them ripple away from me, as if retreating, wary of another surprise.

9

I lay on the bed, listening to the billowing-curtain flaps, looking at the picture of Mljet. There were two oblong lakes, touching each other, at the top end of the picture-island, and on one of those lakes there was an island.

10

I woke up and the night was rife with the cicada hum, perpetual, as if it were the hum of the island engine. They were all sitting outside, around the table underneath the shroud of vine twisting up the lattice. There was a long-necked carafe, full of black wine, in the center of the table, like an axis. Uncle Julius was talking and they all laughed. He would bulge his eyes, lean forward, he would thrust his fist forward, then open it, and the hand would have the index finger pointed at the space between my mother and his wife, and then the hand would retract back into the fist, but the finger would reappear, tapping its tip against the table, as if telegraphing a message. He would then stop talking and withdraw back into the starting position, and he would just watch them as they were laughing.

11

Uncle Julius spoke: "We brought beekeeping to Bosnia. Before the Ukrainians came, the natives kept their bees in mud-and-straw hives, and when they wanted the honey they would just kill them all with sulfur. My grandfather had fifty beehives three years after coming to Bosnia. Before he died, he was sick for a long time. And the day he died, he asked to be taken to the bees and they took him there. He sat by the hives for hours, and wept and wept, and wept out a sea of tears, and then they put him back into his bed and an hour later he died."

"What did he die of?" Aunt Lyudmila asked.

"Dysentery. People used to die of that all the time. They'd just shit themselves to death."

12

I went down the stairs and declared my thirst. Aunt Lyudmila walked over to the dark corner on my right-hand side, turned on the light ablaze, and there was a concrete box with a large square wooden lid. She took off the lid and grabbed a tin cup and shoved her arm into the square. I went to the water tank (for that's what it really was) and peeked over. I saw a white slug, as big as my father's thumb, on the opposite wall. I could not tell whether it was moving upward or it was just frozen by our sudden presence. The dew on its back twinkled, it looked like a severed tongue. I glanced at Aunt Lyudmila, but she didn't seem to have noticed anything. She offered me the cup, but I shook my head and refused to drink the water, which, besides, appeared turbid.

So they brought me a slice of cold watermelon and I drowsily masticated it. "Look at yourself," Uncle Julius said. "You don't want to drink the water! What would you do if you were so thirsty that you were nearly crazy and having one thought only — water, water! — and there's no water? How old are you?" "Nine," my mother said.

13

Uncle Julius told us that when he was in the Arkhangelsk camp, Stalin and his parliament devised a law that said if you were repeatedly late for school or missed several days with no excuse, you would get six months to three years in a camp. So suddenly, in 1943, the camp was full of children only a little bit older than me — twelve, fifteen years old. They didn't know what to do in the camp, so the criminals took the nicest looking to their quarters and fed them and, you know (no, I didn't), abused them. So they were there. They died like flies, because it was cold, and they lost their warm clothing, they didn't know how to preserve or protect the scarce food and water they were allotted. Only the ones that had protectors were able to survive. And there was a boy named Vanyka: gaunt, about twelve, blond, blue eyes. He survived by filching food from the weaker ones, by lending himself to different protectors and bribing guards. Once — I think he drank some vodka with the criminals — he started shouting: "Thank you, Vozhd, for my happy childhood!" From the top of his lungs: "Thank you, Stalin, for my happy childhood!" And they beat him with gun butts and took him away.

14

"Don't torture the boy with these stories. He won't be able to sleep ever again."

"No, let him hear, he should know."

15

Then they sent Uncle Julius to a different camp, and then to another one, and he didn't even know how much time or how many camps he passed through, and he found himself in Siberia. One spring his job was to dig big graves in the thawing ground, take the dead to the grave on a large cart, and then stuff them into the grave. Fifty per grave was the prescribed amount. Sometimes he had to stamp on the top of the graveload to get more space and meet the plan. He had big, big boots. One day they told him that there was a dead man in solitary confinement, so he pushed his cart there and put the corpse on the cart, and as he was pushing, the corpse moaned, "Let me die! Let me die!" I was so scared I almost died, I fell down, and he kept moaning, "Let me die! I don't want to live!" So I pushed the cart behind the barrack and I leaned over him. He was emaciated and had no teeth and one of his ears was missing, but he had blue, blue eyes. It was Vanyka! He looked much older, oh my God! So I gave him a piece of bread that I had saved for the bad days and told him that I remembered him and this is what he told me.

16

They took him away and mauled him for days and did all sorts of things to him. Then they moved him to another camp and he had problems there all the time, because he would speak out again, despite his better judgment. He knew how to steal from the weaker and there were still men who liked him. He won acclaim when he killed a marked person, some Jew, after losing a card game. He killed more. He did bad, bad things and learned how to survive, but he could never keep his snout shut. So they sent him to the island where they kept the worst of the worst. The nearest guard was on the shore fifty kilometers away. They let the inmates rob and kill each other like mad dogs. Once a month the guards would come in, leave the food, and count the corpses and graves and go back to their barracks by the sea. So one day Vanyka and two others killed some other inmates, took their food and clothes, and set out on foot toward the shore. It was a very, very cold winter — pines would crack like matches every day — so they thought they could walk over the frozen strait, if they avoided the guards. But they got lost and ran out of food, and Vanyka and one of the other two agreed by exchanging glances to kill the third one. And they did and they ate his flesh, and they walked and walked and walked. Then Vanyka killed the other one and ate him. But the guards with dogs tracked him down and caught him and he ended up in solitary confinement here and he didn't know how long he had been there. All he wanted was to die and he'd smash his head against the walls and he'd try to choke himself with his tongue. He refused to eat, but they'd force him, if only to make him live longer and suffer more. "Let me die!" he cried and cried.

17

Uncle Julius was reticent and no one dared to say anything. But I asked, "So what happened to him?"

"He was killed," he said, making a motion with his hand, as if thrusting me aside, out of his sight.

18

I woke up and didn't know where I was or who I was, but then I saw the photo of Mljet and I recognized it. I got up, out of my nonbeing, and stepped into the inchoate day. It was purblindingly bright, but I could hear the din of the distant beach: bashful whisper of waves, echoes of sourceless music, warbling of boat motors, shrieks of children, syncopated splashing of oars. Bees levitated over the staircase flowers and I passed them cautiously. There was breakfast on the table in the netlike shadow of the vines: a plate with smoldering, soggy eggs, a cup with a stream of steam rushing upward, and seven slices of bread, on a mirroring steel tray, leaning on each other like fallen dominoes. There was no one around, apart from shadows stretching on the courtyard stone pavement. I sat down and stirred my white coffee. There was a dead bee in the whirl and it kept revolving on its back, slower and slower, until it came to a reluctant stop.

19

After breakfast we would go down a dirt path resembling a long burrow in the shrub. I'd carry my blue-and-white Nivea inflatable ball and sometimes I would inadvertently drop it and it would bounce ahead of us in slow motion. I'd hear bustle in the thicket — a snake, perhaps. But then there would be more bustle and I'd imagine a mongoose killing the snake, the whole bloody battle, the writhing snake entangled with the mongoose trying to bite off its head, just the way I saw on TV, on *Survival.* I'd wait for my parents, for I didn't know what sort of feeling a fierce mongoose would have toward a curious boy — would it perhaps want to bite his head off?

20

We'd get to the gravel beach near the dam dividing the two lakes. I'd have to sit on the towel for a while before I would be allowed to swim. On the left, there would usually be an old man, his skin puckered here and there, a spy novel over his face, white hair meekly bristling on his chest, his belly nearly imperceptibly ascending and descending, with a large metallic-green fly on the brim of his navel. On our right, two symmetrical old men, with straw hats, in baggy trunks, would play chess in serene silence, with their doughy breasts overlooking the board. There were three children a little farther away. They would sit on the towel, gathered around a woman, probably their mother, who would distribute tomatoes and slices of bread with a layer of sallow spread on them. The children would all simultaneously bite into their slices and their tomatoes and then chew vigorously. The tomato slime would drip down their chins, they would be seemingly unperturbed, but when they were done eating, the mother would wipe their recalcitrant faces with a stained white rag.

21

Finally my parents would tell me I could swim and I'd totter over the painful gravel and enter the shallows. I would see throbbing jellyfish floating by. The rocks at the bottom were covered with slimy, slippery lichen. I'd hesitantly dive and the shock of coldness would make me feel present in my own body — I'd be clearly aware of my ends, I'd be aware that my skin was the border between the world and me. Then I'd stand up, the quivering lake up to my nipples, and I'd wave to my parents and they'd shout, "Five more minutes!"

22

Sometimes I'd see fish in pellucid water, gliding along the bottom. Once I saw a school of fish that looked like miniature swordfish, with silver bellies and pointed needle noses. They were all moving as one and then they stopped before me, and hundreds of little

wide-open eyes stared at me in dreadful surprise. Then I blinked
and they flitted away.

23

We walked up the path as the sun was setting. Everything attained a
brazen shade, and now and then there would be a thin gilded
beam, which managed to break through the shrub and olive trees
like a spear sticking out of the ground. Cicadas were revving and
the warmth of the ground enhanced the fragrance of dry pine
needles on the path. I entered the stretch of the path that had been
in the shadow of the tall pines for a while, and the sudden coolness
made me conscious of how hot my shoulders felt. I pressed my
thumb firmly against my shoulder, and when I lifted it, a pallid blot
appeared, then it slowly shrank, back into the ruddiness.

24

There was a man holding a German shepherd on a leash, much of
which was coiled around his hand. The shepherd was attempting to
jump at a mongoose backed against a short ruin of a stone wall. As
the dog's jaw snapped a breath away from the mongoose's snout,
the man would pull the dog back. The mongoose's hair bristled
up, and it grinned to show its teeth, appearing dangerous, but I
knew it was just madly scared. The eyes had a red glow, akin to the
glow that people who glanced at the flashbulb have on bad color
photos. The dog was growling and barking and I saw the pink-and-
brown gums and the bloodthirsty saliva running down the sides of
the jaw. Then the man let the dog go and there was, for just a
moment, hissing and wheezing, growling and shrieking. The man
pulled the dog back and the mongoose lay on its back, showing its
teeth in a useless scowl, the paws spread, as if showing it was harmless now, and the eyes were wide open, the irises stretched to the
edge of the pupils, flabbergasted. There was a hole in its chest —
the dog seemed to have bitten off a part of it — and I saw the heart,
like a tiny tomato, pulsating, as if hiccuping, slower and slower,
with slightly longer moments between the throbs, and it simply
stopped.

25

We walked through the dusk. My sandals were full of pine needles and I would have to stop to take them out. Thousands of fireflies floated in the shrubs, lighting and vanishing, as if they were hidden fairy photographers with flashbulbs, taking our snapshots. "Are you hungry?" my mother asked.

26

We would sit under the cloak of vines with a rotund jar of limpid honey and a plate of pickles. Uncle Julius would dip a pickle into the honey and several bees would peel themselves off the jar and hover above the table. I would dip my finger and try to get it to my lips before the thinning thread of honey would drip on my naked thighs, but I would never make it.

Sometimes, around lunchtime, Uncle Julius would take me to his apiary. He would put on a white overall and a white hat with a veil falling down on his chest, so he looked like a bride. He would light a torn rag and order me to hold it, so as to repel the bees. He would tell me to be absolutely silent and not to move and not to blink. I'd peek from behind his back, my hand with the smoldering rag protruding. He would take the lid off a beehive carefully, as if he were afraid of awakening the island, and the buzz would rise like a cloud of dust and hover around us. He would scrape off the wax between the frames and then take them out one by one and show them to me. I'd see the molasses of bees fidgeting. "They work all the time," he'd whisper. "They never stop." I'd be frightened by the possibility of being stung, even though he told me that the bees would not attack me if I pretended not to exist. The fear would swell, and the more I'd think about it, the more unbearable the unease would be. Eventually I'd break down and run back to the house, get on the stairs, from where I'd see him, remote, immobile apart from the slow, wise motions of his apt hands. I'd watch him as if he were projected on a screen of olive trees and isles of beehives, then he'd turn to me and I could discern a peculiar, tranquil smile behind the veil.

27

Mother and Father were sitting at the stern, with their feet in tepid bilgewater, Uncle Julius was rowing, and I was sitting at the prow, my feet dangling overboard. The surface of the lake would ascend with an inconspicuous wave and my feet would delve into the coolness of menthol-green water. With the adagio of oars, creaking and splashing, we glissaded toward the lake island. There was a dun-colored stone building with small drawn-in windows, and an array of crooked olive trees in front of it. Uncle Julius steered the scow toward a puny, desolate pier. I slipped stepping out, but Uncle Julius grabbed my hand and I hung for a moment over the throbbing lake with a sodden loaf of bread and an ardently smiling woman on a magazine page stuck to the surface, like an ice floe.

28

"These lakes," Uncle Julius said, "used to be a pirate haven in the sixteenth century. They'd hoard the loot and bring hostages here and kill them and torture them — in this very building — if they didn't get the ransom. They say that this place is still haunted by the ghosts of three children they hung on meat hooks because their parents didn't pay the ransom. Then this was a nunnery and some people used to believe that even the nuns were not nuns but witches. Then it was a German prison. And now, mind you, it's a hotel, but there are hardly any tourists ever."

29

We walked into the sonorous chill of a large stone-walled hall. There was a reception desk, but nobody behind it, and a smiling Tito picture over the numbered cubbyhole shelf. Then we walked through a long tunnel and then through a low door, so everyone but me had to bow their heads, then we were in a cubicle-like windowless room ("This used to be a nun cell," Uncle Julius whispered), then we entered the eatery (they had to bend their knees and bow their heads, as if genuflecting, again) with long wooden tables and on them two parallel rows of plates and utensils. We sat there waiting for the waiter. There was a popsicle-yellow lizard, as

big as a new pencil, on the stone wall behind Uncle Julius's back. It
looked at us with an unblinking marble eye, apparently perplexed,
and then it scurried upward, toward an obscure window.

30

This was what Uncle Julius told us:

"When I was a young student in Moscow, in the thirties, I saw
the oldest man in the world. I was in a biology class, it was in a
gigantic amphitheater, hundreds of rows, thousands of students.
They brought in an old man who couldn't walk, so two comrades
carried him and he had his arms over their shoulders. His feet were
dangling between them, but he was all curled up like a baby. They
said he was a hundred and fifty-eight years old and from somewhere in the Caucasus. They put him sideways on the desk and he
started crying like a baby, so they gave him a stuffed toy — a cat, I
think, but I can't be certain, because I was sitting all the way up in
one of the last aisles. I was looking at him as if through the wrong
end of a telescope. And the teacher told us that the old man cried
all the time, ate only liquid foods, and couldn't bear being separated from his favorite toy. The teacher said that he slept a lot,
didn't know his name, and had no memories. He could say only a
couple of words, like *water, poo-poo,* and such. I figured out then that
life is a circle, you get back right where you started if you get to be a
hundred and fifty-eight years old. It's like a dog chasing its own tail
— all is for naught. We live and live, and in the end we're just like
this boy" — he pointed at me — "knowing nothing, remembering
nothing. You might as well stop living now, my son. You might just
as well stop, for nothing will change."

31

When I woke up, after a night of unsettling dreams, the suitcases
were agape and my parents were packing them with wrinkled underwear and shirts. Uncle Julius came up with a jar of honey as big
as my head and gave it to my father. He looked at the photo of Mljet
and then put the tip of his finger at the point in the upper right
corner near the twin lakes, which looked like gazing eyes. "We are
here," he said.

32

The sun had not risen yet from behind the hill, so there were no shadows and everything looked muffled, as if under a sheet of fine gauze. We walked down the narrow road and the asphalt was cold and moist. We passed a man carrying a cluster of dead fish, with the hooks in their carmine gills. He said "Good morning!" and smiled.

We waited at the pier. A shabby boat, with paint falling off and *Pirate* written in pale letters on the bow, was heading, coughing, toward the open sea. A man with an anchor tattooed on his right arm was standing at the rudder. He had a torn red-and-black flannel shirt, black soccer shorts, and no shoes — his feet were bloated and filthy. He was looking straight ahead toward the ferry that was coming into the harbor. The ferry slowed down to the point of hesitant floating, and then it dropped down its entrance door, like a castle bridge, with a harsh peal. It was a different ship from the ship we had come on, but the same man with the hobbling-boat shirt said "Welcome!" again, and smiled, as if recognizing us.

We passed the same islands. They were like heavy molded loaves of bread dropped behind a gigantic ship. On one of the islands, and we passed it close by, there was a herd of goats. They looked at us, mildly confounded, and then, one by one, lost interest and returned to grazing. A man with a camera, probably a German tourist, took a picture of the goats and then gave the camera to his speckle-faced, blue-eyed son. The boy pointed the camera toward the sun, but the man jokingly admonished him, turning him and the camera toward us, while we grinned at him, helpless.

33

It took us only four hours to get home from the coast and I slept all the time, oblivious to the heat, until we reached Sarajevo. When we got home, the shriveled plants and flowers were in the midst of the setting-sun orange spill. All the plants had withered, because the neighbor who was supposed to water them died of a sudden heart attack. The cat, having not been fed for more than a week, was emaciated and nearly mad with hunger. I would call her, but she wouldn't come to me, she would just look at me with irreversible hatred.

PAM HOUSTON

The Best Girlfriend
You Never Had

FROM OTHER VOICES

A PERFECT DAY in the city always starts like this: my friend Leo
picks me up and we go to a breakfast place called Rick and Ann's
where they make red flannel hash out of beets and bacon, and then
we cross the Bay Bridge to the gardens of the Palace of the Fine Arts
to sit in the wet grass and read poems out loud and talk about love.

The fountains are thick with black swans imported from Siberia,
and if it is a fine day and a weekend there will be wedding parties,
almost entirely Asian. The grooms wear smart gray pinstripe suits
and the women are in beaded gowns so beautiful they make your
teeth hurt just to look at them.

The roman towers of the palace façade rise above us, more yellow
than orange in the strengthening midday light. Leo has told me
how the towers were built for the 1939 San Francisco World's Fair
out of plaster and papier-mâché, and even though times were hard
the city raised the money to keep them, to cast them in concrete so
they would never go away.

Leo is an architect, and his relationship to all the most beautiful
buildings in this city is astonishing given his age, only five years
older than I. I make my living as a photographer; since art school
I've been doing magazine work and living from grant to grant.

The house Leo built for himself is like a fairy tale, all towers and
angles, and the last wild peacock in Berkeley lives on his street. I live
in the Oakland hills in a tiny house on a street so windy you can't
drive more than ten miles per hour. I rented it because the ad said

this: "Small house in the trees with a garden and a fireplace. Dogs welcome, of course." I am dogless for the moment, but it's not my natural condition. You never know when I might get overwhelmed by a desire to go to the pound.

It's a warm blue Saturday in November, and there are five Asian weddings under way at the Palace of the Fine Arts. The wedding parties' outfits do not match but are complementary, as if they have been ordered especially, one for each arch of the golden façade.

Leo reads me a poem about a salt marsh at dawn while I set up my old Leica. I always get the best stuff when nobody's paying me to shoot. Like the time I caught a bride waltzing with one of the caterers behind the hedgerow, his chef's cap bent to touch the top of her veil.

Then I read Leo a poem about longing in Syracuse. This is how we have always spoken to each other, Leo and I, and it would be the most romantic thing this century except that Leo is in love with Guinevere.

Guinevere is a Buddhist weaver who lives in a clapboard house on Belvedere Island. She makes cloth on a loom she brought back from Tibet. Although her tapestries and wall hangings have made her a small fortune, she refuses to use the air conditioner in her Audi, even when she's driving across the Sacramento Valley. Air conditioning, she says, is just one of the things she does not allow herself.

That Guinevere seems not to know Leo is alive causes him no particular disappointment, and that she forgets — each time she meets him — that she has met him several times before only adds to what he calls her charming basket of imperfections. The only Buddha I could love, he says, is one who is capable of forgetfulness and sin.

Guinevere is in love with a man in New York City who told her in a letter that the only thing better than three thousand miles between him and the object of his desire would be if she had a terminal illness. "I could really get behind a relationship with a woman who had only six months to live" was what he wrote. She showed me the words as if to make sure they existed, though something in her tone made me think she was proud.

The only person I know of who's in love with Leo (besides me, a little) is a gay man named Raphael who falls in love with one straight man after another and then buys each one a whole new collection of CDs. They come, Leo says, as if from the Columbia House Record Club, once a month like clockwork, in a plain cardboard wrapper, no return address and no name. They are by artists most people have never heard of, like Cassandra Wilson and Boris Grebeshnikov; there are Andean folksongs and hip-hop and beat.

Across the swan-bearing lake a wedding has just reached its completion. The groom is managing to look utterly solemn and completely delirious with joy at the same time. Leo and I watch the kiss, and I snap the shutter just as the kiss ends and the wedding party bursts into applause.

"Sucker," Leo says.

"Oh, right," I say. "Like you wouldn't trade your life for his right this minute."

"I don't know anything about his life," Leo says.

"You know he remembered to do all the things you forgot."

"I think I prefer it," Leo says, "when you reserve that particular lecture for yourself." He points back across the lake, where the bride has just leaped into her maid of honor's arms, and I snap the shutter again. "Or for one of your commitment-phobic boyfriends," Leo adds.

"I guess the truth is, I can't blame them," I say. "I mean, if I saw me coming down the street with all my stuff hanging out, I'm not so sure I'd pick myself up and go trailing after."

"Of course you would," Leo says. "And it's because you would, and because the chance of that happening is so slim, and because you hold out hope anyway that it might . . . that's what makes you a great photographer."

"Greatness is nice," I tell him. "I want contact. I want someone's warm breath on my face." I say it as if it's a dare, which we both know it isn't. The flower girl across the lake is throwing handfuls of rose petals straight up in the air.

I came to this city near the ocean over a year ago because I recently spent a long time under the dark naked water of the Colorado River and I took it as a sign that the river wanted me away. I had taken so many pictures by then of the chaos of heaved-up rock and petrified sand and endless sky that I'd lost my balance and fallen into them. I couldn't keep separate anymore what was the land and what was me.

There was a man there named Josh who didn't want nearly

enough from me, and a woman called Thea who wanted way too much, and I was sandwiched between them, one of those weaker rock layers like limestone that disappears under pressure or turns into something shapeless like oil.

I thought there might be an order to the city: straight lines, shiny surfaces, and right angles that would give myself back to me, take my work somewhere different, maybe to a safer place. Solitude was a straight line too, and I believed it was what I wanted, so I packed whatever I could get into my pickup, left behind everything I couldn't carry, including two pairs of skis, a whole darkroom full of photo equipment, and the mountains I'd sworn again and again I couldn't live without.

I pointed myself west down the endless two lanes of Highway 50 — *The Loneliest Road in America* say the signs that rise out of the desert on either side of it — all the way across Utah and Nevada to this white shining city on the bay.

I got drunk on the city at first, the way some people do on vodka, the way it lays itself out as if in a nest of madroñas and eucalyptus, the way it sparkles brighter even than the sparkling water that surrounds it, the way the Golden Gate reaches out of it, like fingers, toward the wild wide ocean that lies beyond.

I loved the smell of fresh blueberry muffins at the Oakland Grill down on Third and Franklin, the train whistle sounding right outside the front door, and tattooed men of all colors unloading crates of cauliflower, broccoli, and peas.

Those first weeks I'd walk the streets for hours, shooting more film in a day than I could afford in a week, all those lives in such dangerous and unnatural proximity, all those stories my camera could tell.

I'd walk even the nastiest part, the blood pumping through my veins as hard as when I first saw the Rocky Mountains so many years ago. One night in the Tenderloin I rounded a corner and met a guy in a wheelchair head on, who aimed himself at me and covered me with urine. Baptized, I said to my horrified friends the next day, anointed with the nectar of the city gods.

Right off the bat I met a man named Gordon, and we'd drive down to the Oakland docks in the evening and look out at the twenty-story hydraulic boat lifts, which I said looked like a battalion of Doberman pinschers protecting the harbor from anyone who might invade. Gordon's real name was Salvador, and he came from poor people, strawberry pickers in the Central Valley, two of his brothers stillborn from Malathion poisoning. He left the valley and moved to the city when he was too young by law to drive the truck he stole from his father's field boss.

He left it double-parked in front of the Castro Theater, talked a family in the Mission into trading work for floor space, changed his name to Gordon, changed his age from fifteen to twenty, and applied for a grant to study South American literature at San Francisco State.

He had his Ph.D. before he turned twenty, a tenure-track teaching job at Berkeley by twenty-one. When he won his first teaching award, his mother was in the audience; when their eyes met, she nodded her approval, but when he looked for her afterward, she was nowhere to be found.

"Can you believe it?" he said when he told the story, his voice such a mixture of pride and disappointment that I didn't know which was more unbelievable, that she had come or that she had gone.

"If one more woman I used to date turns into a lesbian," Leo says, "I'm moving to Minneapolis."

The wedding receptions are well under way, and laughter bubbles toward us across the lagoon.

"It's possible to take that as a compliment," I say, "if you want to bend your mind that way."

"I don't," he says.

"Maybe it's just a choice a woman makes," I say, "when she feels she has exhausted all her other options."

"Oh yeah, like you start out being a person," Leo says, "and then you decide to become a car."

"Sometimes I think it's either that or Alaska," I say. "The odds there, better than ten to one."

I remember a bumper sticker I saw once in Haines, Alaska, near the place where the ferries depart for the lower forty-eight: *Baby*, it said, *when you leave here you'll be ugly again.*

"In Alaska," I say, "I've actually had men fall at my feet."

"I bet a few men have fallen at your feet down here," he says, and I try to look him in the eye to see how he means it, but he keeps them fixed on the poetry book.

He says, "Aren't I the best girlfriend you never had?"

The last woman Leo called the love of his life only let him see her twice a week for three years. She was a cardiologist who lived in the Marina who said she spent all day with broken hearts and she had no intention of filling her time off with her own. At the start of the fourth year, Leo asked her to raise the number of dates to three times a week, and she immediately broke things off.

Leo went up on the bridge after that. This was before they put the phones in, the ones that go straight to the counselors. It was a sunny day and the tide was going out, making whitecaps as far as he could see into the Pacific. After a while he came down, not because he felt better but because of the way the numbers fell out. There had been 250 so far that year. Had the number been 4 or 199 or even 274, he says he might have done it, but he wasn't willing to go down officially with a number as meaningless as 251.

A woman sitting on the grass near us starts telling Leo how much he looks like her business partner, but there's an edge to her voice I can't identify, an insistence that means she's in love with the guy, or she's crazy, or she's just murdered him this morning and she has come to the Palace of the Fine Arts to await her impending arrest.

"The great thing about Californians," Leo says when the woman has finally gotten up to leave, "is that they think it's perfectly okay to exhibit all their neuroses in public as long as they apologize for them first."

Leo grew up like I did on the East Coast, eating Birdseye frozen vegetables and Swanson's deep-dish meat pies on TV trays next to our parents and their third martinis, watching *What's My Line?* and *To Tell the Truth* on television, and talking about anything on earth except what was wrong.

"Is there anyone you could fall in love with besides Guinevere?" I ask Leo, after he's read a poem about tarantulas and digger wasps.

"There's a pretty woman at work," he says. "She calls herself the Diva."

"Leo," I say, "write this down. I think it's a good policy to avoid any woman who uses an article in her name."

There are policemen at the palace grounds today handing out information about how we can protect ourselves from an epidemic of carjackings that has been taking place in the city for the last five months. The crime begins, the flyer tells us, with the criminal bumping the victim's car from behind. When the victim gets out of the car to exchange information, the criminal hits her — and it's generally a woman — over the head with a heavy object, leaves her on the sidewalk, steals her car, and drives away.

The flyer says we are supposed to keep our windows rolled up when the other driver approaches, keep the doors locked, and say through the glass, *"I'm afraid. I'm not getting out. Please follow me to the nearest convenience store."* It says under no circumstances should we ever let the criminal drive us to crime scene number two.

"You couldn't do it, could you?" Leo asks, and slaps my arm like a wise guy.

"What do you think they mean," I say, "by crime scene number two?"

"You're evading the question because you know the answer too well," he says. "You're the only person I know who'd get your throat slit sooner than admit you're afraid."

"You know," I say to Leo, to change the subject, "you don't act much like a person who wants kids more than anything."

"Yeah, and you don't act like a person who wants to be married with swans."

"I'd do it," I say. "Right now. Step into that wedding dress, no questions asked."

"Lucy," Leo says, "seriously, do you have any idea how many steps there are between you and that wedding dress?"

"No," I say. "Tell me."

"Fifty-five," he says. "At least fifty-five."

Before Gordon I had always dated the strong silent types, I think, so I could invent anything I wanted to go on in their heads. Gordon and I talked about words and the kind of pictures you could make so that you didn't need them, and I thought what I always thought in the first ten minutes: that after years and years of wild pitches, I'd for once in my life thrown a strike.

It took me less than half a baseball season to discover my oversight: Gordon had a jealous streak as vicious as a heat-seeking missile, and he could make a problem out of a paper bag. We were asked to leave two restaurants in one week alone, and it got to the point, fast, where if the waitperson wasn't female, I'd ask if we could go somewhere else or have another table.

Car mechanics, piano tuners, dry cleaners, toll takers — in Gordon's mind they were all out to bed me, and I was out to make them want to. A honey pot, he'd called me once, and he said he and all other men in the Bay Area were a love-crazed swarm of bees.

When I told Guinevere how I'd fallen for Gordon, she said, "You only get a few chances to feel your life all the way through. Before — you know — you become unwilling."

I told her the things I was afraid to tell Leo: how the look on Gordon's face turned from passion to anger, how he yelled at me in a store so loud one time that the manager slipped me a note that said he would pray for me, how each night I would stand in the street while he revved up his engine and scream *Please, Gordon, please, Gordon, don't drive away.*

"At one time in my life I had breast implants just to please a man," she said. "Now I won't even take off my bracelets before bed."

Guinevere keeps a bowl of cards on her breakfast table between the sugar and the coffee. They are called angel cards and she bought them at the New Age store. Each card has a word printed on it, *sisterhood* or *creativity* or *romance,* and there's a tiny angel with her body in a position that is supposed to illustrate the word.

That morning I picked *balance,* with a little angel perched in the center of a teeter-totter, and when Guinevere reached in for her own word she sighed in disgust. Without looking at the word again, without showing it to me, she put the card in the trash can and reached to pick another.

I went to the trash can and found it. The word was *surrender,* and the angel was looking upward, with her arms outstretched.

"I hate that," she said, her mouth slightly twisted. "Last week I had to throw away *submit.*"

Guinevere brought me a cookie and a big box of Kleenex. She said that choices can't be good or bad. There is only the event and the lessons learned from it. She corrected my pronunciation gently and constantly: the *Bu* in *Buddha,* she said, is like the *pu* in *pudding* and not like the *boo* in *ghost.*

When I was twenty-five years old, I took home to my parents a boy named Jeffrey I thought I wanted to marry. He was everything I believed my father wanted. He had an MBA from Harvard. He had patches on the elbows of his sportcoats. He played golf on a course that only allowed men.

We spent the weekend drinking the wine and eating the pâté Jeffrey's mother had sent him from her *fermette* in the southwest of France. Jeffrey let my father show him decades' worth of tennis trophies. He played the piano while my mother sang her old torch songs.

I waited until I had a minute alone with my father. "Papa," I said — it was what I always called him — "how do you like Jeffrey?"

"Lucille," he said, "I haven't ever liked any of your boyfriends, and I don't expect I ever will. So why don't you save us both the embarrassment and not ask again?"

After that I went back to dating mechanics and river guides. My mother kept Jeffrey's picture on the mantel till she died.

The first time I was mugged in the city, I'd been to the late show all alone at the Castro Theatre. It's one of those magnificent old moviehouses with a huge marquee that lights up the sky like a carnival, a ceiling that looks like it belongs in a Spanish cathedral, heavy red velvet curtains laced with threads that sparkle gold, and a real live piano player who disappears into the floor when the previews begin.

I liked to linger there after the movie finished, watch the credits and the artificial stars in the ceiling. That Tuesday I was the last person to step out of the theater into a chilly and deserted night.

I had one foot off the curb when the man approached me, a little too close for comfort even then.

"Do you have any change you can spare?" he said.

The truth was, I didn't. I had scraped the bottom of my purse to put together enough quarters, nickels, and dimes to get into the movie, and the guy behind the glass had let me in thirty-three cents short.

I said I was sorry and headed for the parking lot. I knew he was behind me, but I didn't turn around. I should have gotten my keys out before I left the theater, I thought. Shouldn't have stayed to see every credit roll.

About ten steps from my car I felt a firm jab in the middle of my rib cage.

"I bet you'd feel differently," the man said, "if I had a gun in my hand."

"I might feel differently," I said, whirling around with more force than I intended, "but I still wouldn't have any money."

He flinched, changed the angle of his body, just slightly back and away. And when he did, when his eyes dropped from mine to his hand holding whatever it was in his jacket pocket, I was reminded of a time I almost walked into a female grizzly with a nearly grown cub. How we had stood there posturing, how she had glanced down at her cub just that way, giving me the opportunity to let her know she didn't need to kill me. We could both go on our way.

"Look," I said. "I've had a really emotional day, okay?" As I talked, I dug into my purse and grabbed my set of keys, a kind of weapon in their own right. "And I think you ought to just let me get in the car and go home."

While he considered this, I took the last steps to my car and got in. I didn't look in the rearview mirror until I was on the freeway.

By mid-afternoon Leo and I have seen one too many happy couples get married, and we drive over the Golden Gate to Tiburon to a restaurant called Guymos where we drink margaritas made with Patrón tequila and eat ceviche appetizers and look out on Angel Island and the city — whitest of all from this perspective, rising like a mirage out of the blue-green bay.

We watch the ferry dock, unload the suburbanites, then load them up again for the twice-hourly trip to the city. We are jealous of their starched shirts and brown loafers, how their clothes seem a testament to the balance in their lives.

The fog rolls over and down the lanyard side of Mount Tamalpais, and the city moves in and out of it, glistening like Galilee one moment, then gray and dreamy like a ghost of itself the next, and then gone, like a thought bubble, like somebody's good idea.

"Last night," I say, "I was walking alone down Telegraph Avenue. I was in a mood, you know. Gordon and I had a fight about John Lennon."

"Was he for or against?" Leo says.

"Against," I say, "but it doesn't matter. Anyway, I was scowling, maybe crying a little, moving along pretty fast, and I step over this homeless guy with his crutches and his little can and he says, 'I don't even *want* any money from you, I'd just like *you* to smile.'"

"So did you?" Leo says.

"I did," I say. "I not only smiled, but I laughed too, and then I went back and gave him all the money in my wallet, which was only eighteen dollars, but still. I told him to be sure and use that line again."

"I love you," Leo says, and takes both of my hands in his. "I mean, in the good way."

When I was four years old and with my parents in Palm Beach, Florida, I pulled a seven-hundred-pound cement urn off its pedestal and onto my legs, crushing both femurs. All the other urns on Worth Avenue had shrubs in them trimmed into the shapes of animals, and this one, from my three-foot point of view, appeared to be empty.

When they asked me why I had tried to pull myself up and into the urn, I said I thought it had fish inside it and I wanted to see them, though whether I had imagined actual fish or just tiny shrubs carved into the shape of fish, I can't any longer say.

The urn was empty, of course, and waiting to be repaired, which is why it toppled over onto me. My father rolled it off with some of that superhuman strength you always hear about and picked me up — I was screaming bloody murder — and held me until the ambulance came.

The next six weeks were the best of my childhood. I was hospitalized the entire time, surrounded by doctors who brought me presents, nurses who read me stories, candy stripers who came to my room and played games.

My parents, when they came to visit, were always happy to see me and usually sober.

I spent the remaining years of my childhood fantasizing about illnesses and accidents that I hoped would send me to the hospital again.

One day last month Gordon asked me to go backpacking at Point Reyes National Seashore, to prove to me, he said, that he could take an interest in my life. I hadn't slept outside one single night since I came to the city, he said, and I must miss the feel of hard ground underneath me, must miss the smell of my tent in the rain.

Gordon borrowed a backpack, got the permit, freed the weekend, studied the maps. I was teaching a darkroom workshop in Corte Madeira on Saturday. Gordon would pick me up at four when the workshop ended; we'd have just enough time to drive up the coast to Point Reyes Station and walk for an hour into the first camp. A long second day would take us to the beach, the point with the lighthouse, and back to the car with no time again to spare before dark.

I had learned by then how to spot trouble coming, and that morning I waited in the car with Gordon while first one man, way too young for me, and then another, way too old, entered the warehouse where my workshop was going to be held.

I got out of the car without seeing the surfer, tall and blond and a little breathtaking, portfolio under the arm that usually held the board. I kept my eyes away from his, but his handshake found me anyway. When he held the big door open, I went on through. I could hear the screech of tires behind me through what felt like a ton of metal.

That Gordon was there when the workshop ended at 4:02 surprised me a little. Then I got in the Pathfinder and saw only one backpack. He drove up the coast to Point Reyes without speaking. Stinson, Bolinas, Dogtown, and Olema. The white herons in Tomales Bay had their heads tucked under their arms.

He stopped at the trailhead, got out, threw my pack into the dune grass, opened my door, and tried with his eyes to pry me from my seat.

"I guess this means you're not coming with me," I said, imagining how we could do it with one pack, tenacious in my hope that the day could be saved.

What you're thinking right now is why didn't I do it, get out of that car without making eye contact, swing my pack on my back, and head off down the trail? And when I tell you what I did do, which was to crawl all the way to the back of the Pathfinder, holding on to the cargo net as if a tornado were coming, and let go with one ear-splitting, head-pounding scream after another till Gordon got back in the car, till we got back down the coast, back on the 580, back over the bridge, and back to Gordon's apartment, till he told me if I was quiet, he'd let me stay, you would wonder how a person, even if she had done it, could ever in a million years admit to such a thing.

Then I could tell you about the sixteen totaled cars in my first fifteen winters. The Christmas Eve my father and I rolled a Plymouth Fury from meridian to guardrail and back four full times with nine complete revolutions, how they had to cut us out with chainsaws, how my father, limber from the Seagram's, got away unhurt. I could tell you about the neighbor girl who stole me away one time at the sound of my parents shouting, how she refused to give me back to them even when the police came with a warrant, how her ten-year-old hand must have looked holding my three-year-old one, how in the end it became a funny story that both sets of parents loved to tell. I could duplicate for you the hollow sound an empty bottle makes when it hits Formica and the stove is left on and the pan's started smoking and there's a button that says off but no way to reach.

I could tell you the lie I told myself with Gordon. That anybody is better than nobody. And you will know exactly why I stayed in the back of that Pathfinder, unless you are lucky, and then you will not.

"Did I ever tell you about the time I got mugged?" Leo asks me, and we both know he has but it's his favorite story.

"I'd like it," I say, "if you'd tell it again."

Before Leo built his house on the street with the peacocks, he lived in the city between North Beach and the piers. He got mugged one night, stepping out of his car fumbling for his house keys; the man had a gun and sneaked up from behind.

What Leo had in his wallet was thirteen dollars, and when he offered the money he thought the man would kill him on the spot.

"You got a cash card," the man said. "Let's find a machine."

"Hey," I say when he gets to this part, "that means you went to crime scene number two."

The part I hate most is how he took Leo's glasses. He said he would drive, but as it turned out he didn't know stick shifts, and the clutch burned and smoked all the way up Nob Hill.

"My name's Bill," the man said, and Leo thought since they were getting so friendly, he'd offer to work the clutch and the gearshift to save what was left of his car. It wasn't until Leo got close to him, straddling the gearbox and balanced against Bill's shoulder, that he smelled the blood under Bill's jacket and knew that he'd been shot.

They drove like that to the Marina Safeway, Bill's eyes on the road and his hands on the steering wheel, Leo working the clutch and the shifter according to feel.

At the cash machine Leo looked for help but couldn't get anyone's eyes to meet his, with Bill and his gun pressed so close to his side.

They all think we're a couple, he thought, and laughter bubbled up inside him. He told Bill a lie about a hundred-dollar ATM limit, pushed the buttons, handed over the money.

They drove back to Leo's that same Siamese way, and when they got there Bill thanked Leo, shook his hand, asked one more favor before he took off.

"I'm going to give you a phone number," Bill said. "My girlfriend in Sacramento. I want you to call her and tell her I made it all right."

"Sure," Leo said, folding the paper.

"I want you to swear to God."

"Sure," Leo said, "I'll call her."

Bill put the end of the gun around Leo's belly button. "Say it, motherfucker, say, 'I swear to God.'"

"I swear to God," Leo said, and Bill walked away.

Back in his apartment, Leo turned on Letterman. When the shaking stopped, he called the police.

"Not much we can do about it," the woman at the end of the line told him. "We could come dust your car for fingerprints, but it would make a hell of a mess."

Two hours later Leo looked in a phone book and called a Catholic priest.

"No," the priest said, "you don't have to call her. You swore to God under extreme circumstances, brought down upon you by a godless man."

"I don't think that's the right answer," I had said when I first heard the story, and I say it again, on cue, today. The first time we had talked about the nature of godlessness, and how if a situation requires swearing to God, it is by definition extreme.

But today I am thinking not of Bill or even of Leo's dilemma, but of the girlfriend in Sacramento, her lover shot, bleeding, and hijacking architects and still remembering to think of her.

And I wonder what it was about her that made her stay with a man who ran from the law for a living, and if he made it home to her that night, if she stood near him in the kitchen dressing his wounds. I wonder how she saw herself, as what part of the story, and how much she had invested in how it would end.

"I'm so deeply afraid," Gordon had said on the docks our first night together, "that I am nothing but weak and worthless. So I take the people close to me and try to break them, so they become as weak and worthless as me."

I want to know the reason I could hear and didn't hear what he was saying, the reason that I thought the story could end differently for me.

Things ended between Gordon and me in a bar in Jack London Square one night when we were watching the 49ers play the Broncos. It was Joe Montana's last year in San Francisco; rumors of the Kansas City acquisition had already begun.

It was a close game late in the season; the Broncos had done what they were famous for in those days, jumped out to a twenty-point lead and then lost it incrementally as the quarters went by.

The game came right down to the two-minute warning, Elway and Montana trading scoring drives so elegant it was as if they had shaken hands on it before the game. A minute twenty-seven left, ball on the Niners' twenty-two: Joe Montana had plenty of time and one last chance to shine.

"Don't tell me you're a Bronco fan," a guy on the other side of me, a late arrival, said.

"It's a tough job," I said, not taking my eyes off the TV set. For about the hundredth time that evening the camera was off the action and on a tearful, worried, or ecstatic Jennifer Montana, one lovely and protective hand around each of her two beautiful blond little girls.

"Geez," I said, when the camera came back to the action several seconds too late, "you'd think Joe Montana was the only football player in America who had a wife."

The guy next to me laughed a short choppy laugh. Joe took his team seventy-eight yards in seven plays for the win.

On the way to his Pathfinder, Gordon said, "That's what I hate about you sports fans. You create a hero like Joe Montana just so you have somebody to knock down."

"I don't have anything against Joe Montana," I said. "I think he throws the ball like an angel. I simply prefer watching him to watching his wife."

"I saw who you preferred watching," Gordon said as we arrived at the car and he slammed inside.

"Gordon," I said, "I don't even know what that man looked like."

The moon was fat and full over the parts of Oakland no one

dares to go to late at night, and I knew as I looked for a face in it that it didn't matter a bit what I said.

Gordon liked to drive the meanest streets when he was feeling meanest, and he was ranting about my shaking my tail feathers and keeping my pants zipped, and all I could think to do was remind him I was wearing a skirt.

He squealed the brakes at the end of my driveway, and I got out and moved toward the dark entryway.

"Aren't you going to invite me in?" he asked. And I thought about the months full of nights just like this one when I asked his forgiveness, when I begged him to stay.

"I want you to make your own decision," I said over my shoulder, and he threw the car in second, gunned the engine, and screeched away.

First came the messages taped to my door, the words cut out from ten different typefaces, held down with so many layers of tape they had the texture of decoupage. Then came the slit tires, the Karo Syrup in my gas tank, my box set of Dylan's *Biography* in a puddle at the foot of my drive. One day I opened an envelope from a magazine I'd shot for to find my paycheck ripped into a hundred pieces and then put back in the envelope, back in the box.

Leo and I trade margaritas for late-afternoon lattes, and still the fog won't lift all the way.

"What I imagine," I say, "is coming home one night and Gordon emerging from between the sidewalk and the shadows, a Magnum .357 in his hand, and my last thought being, 'Well, you should have figured that this was the next logical thing.'"

"I don't know why you need to be so tough about it," Leo says. "Can't you let the police or somebody know?"

I say, "This is not a good city to be dogless in."

Leo puts his arm around me; I can tell by the way he does it he thinks he has to.

"Do you wish sometimes," I say, "that you could just disappear like that city?"

"I can," Leo says. "I do. What I wish more is that when I wanted to, I could stay."

The ferry docks again in front of us, and we sit quietly until the whistles are finished and the boat has once again taken off.

"Are you ever afraid," I say to Leo, "that there are so many things you need swirling around inside you that they will just overtake you, smother you, suffocate you till you die?"

"I don't think so," Leo says.

"I don't mean sex," I say, "or even love exactly — just all that want that won't let go of you, that even if you changed everything right now it's too late already to ever be full."

Leo keeps his eyes fixed on the city, which is back out again, the Coit Tower reaching and leaning slightly like a stack of pepperoni pizza pies.

"Until only a few years ago, I used to break into a stranger's house every six months like clockwork," he says. "Is that something like what you mean?"

"Exactly," I say. A band of fog sweeps down, faster than the others, and takes away the city, even the site of Leo's mugging, even the apartment where Gordon now stays.

When I was eighteen years old, I met my parents in Phoenix, Arizona, to watch Penn State play USC in the Fiesta Bowl. I'd driven from Ohio, they'd flown from Pennsylvania, and the three of us — for the first time ever — shared my car.

My father wanted me to drive them through the wealthy suburbs, places with names like Carefree and Cave Creek. He'd been drinking earlier in the day than usual, they both had, and he got it into his head that he wanted to see the world's highest fountain shoot three hundred gallons of water per minute into the parched and evaporative desert air.

We were halfway through Cave Creek, almost to the fountain, when the cop pulled me over.

"I'm sorry to bother you," he said, "but I've been tailing you for four or five minutes, and I have to tell you, I really don't know where to start."

The cop's nameplate said Martin "Mad Dog" Jenkins. My father let out a sigh that hung in the car like a fog.

"Well, first," Officer Jenkins said, "I clocked you going 43 in a 25. Then you rolled through not one but two stop signs without coming to a safe and complete stop, and you made a right-hand turn into the center lane."

"Jesus Christ," my father said.

"You've got one taillight out," Officer Jenkins said, "and either your turn signals are burned out too, or you are electing not to use them."

"Are you hearing this?" my father said to the air.

"May I see your license and registration?"

"I left my license in Ohio," I said.

The car was silent.

"Give me a minute, then," Officer Jenkins said, "and I'll call it in."

"What I don't know," my father said, "is how a person with so little sense of responsibility gets a driver's license in this country to begin with." He flicked the air vent open and closed, open and closed. "I mean, you gotta wonder if she should even be let out of the house in the morning."

"Why don't you just say it, Robert," my mother said. "Say what you mean. Say *Daughter, I hate you.*" Her voice started shaking. "Everybody sees it. Everybody knows it. Why don't you say it out loud?"

"Ms. O'Rourke?" Officer Jenkins was back at the window.

"Let's hear it," my mother went on. *"Officer, I hate my daughter."*

The cop's eyes flicked for a moment into the back seat.

"According to the information I received, Ms. O'Rourke," Officer Jenkins said, "you are required to wear corrective lenses."

"That's right," I said.

"And you are wearing contacts now?" There was something like hope in his voice.

"No, sir."

"She can't even lie?" my father asked. "About one little thing?"

"Okay now, on three," my mother said. *"Daughter, I wish you had never been born."*

"Ms. O'Rourke," Officer Jenkins said, "I'm just going to give you a warning today." My father bit off the end of a laugh.

"Thank you very much," I said.

"I hate to say this, Ms. O'Rourke," the cop said, "but there's nothing I could do to you that's going to feel like punishment." He held out his hand for me to shake. "You drive safely now," he said, and he was gone.

When the Fiesta Bowl was over, my parents and I drove back up to Carefree to attend a New Year's Eve party given by a gay man my mother knew who belonged to the wine club called the Royal Order of the Grape. My father wasn't happy about it, but he was silent. I just wanted to watch the ball come down on TV like I had every year of my childhood with the babysitter, but the men at the party were showing home movie after home movie of the club's indoctrination ceremony, while every so often two or three partygoers would get taken to the cellar to look at the bottles and taste.

When my father tried to light a cigarette, he got whisked outside faster than I had ever seen him move. I was too young to be taken to the cellar, too old to be doted on, so after another half-hour of being ignored I went outside to join my father.

The lights of Phoenix sparkled every color below us in the dark.

"Lucille," he said, "when you get to be my age, don't ever spend New Year's Eve in a house where they won't let you smoke."

"Okay," I said.

"Your mother," he said, as he always did.

"I know," I said, even though I didn't.

"We just don't get love right, this family, but . . ." He paused, and the sky above Phoenix exploded into color, umbrellas of red and green and yellow. I'd never seen fireworks before, from the top.

"Come in, come in, for the New Year's toast!" Our host was calling us from the door. I wanted more than anything for my father to finish his sentence, but he stabbed out his cigarette, got up, and walked inside. I've finished it for him a hundred times, but never to my satisfaction.

We pay the bill and Leo informs me that he has the temporary use of a twenty-seven-foot sailboat in Sausalito that belongs to a man he hardly knows. The fog has lifted enough for us to see the place where the sun should be, and it's brighter yet out by the Golden Gate, and we take the little boat out and aim for the brightness, the way a real couple might on a Saturday afternoon.

It's a squirrelly boat, designed to make fast moves in a light wind, and Leo gives me the tiller two hundred yards before we pass under the dark shadow of the bridge. I am just getting the feel of it when Leo looks over his shoulder and says, "It appears we are in a race," and I look too, and there is a boat bearing down on us, twice our size, ten times, Leo tells me, our boat's value.

"Maybe you should take it then," I say.

"You're doing fine," he says. "Just set your mind on what's out there and run for it."

At first all I can think about is Leo sitting up on top of the bridge running numbers in his head, and a story Gordon told me where two guys meet up there on the walkway and find out they are both survivors of a previous jump.

Then I let my mind roll out past the cliffs and the breakers, past the Marin headlands and all the navigation buoys, out to some place where the swells swallow up the coastline and Hawaii is the only thing between me and forever, and what are the odds of hitting it if I just head for the horizon and never change my course?

I can hear the big boat's bow breaking right behind us, and I set my mind even harder on a universe with nothing in it except deep blue water.

"You scared him," Leo says. "He's coming about."

The big boat turns away from us, back toward the harbor, just as the giant shadow of the bridge crosses our bow. Leo jumps up and gives me an America's Cup hug. Above us the great orange span of the thing is trembling, just slightly, in the wind.

We sail on out to the edge of the headlands, where the swells get big enough to make us both a little sick and it's finally Leo who takes the tiller from my hand and turns the boat around. It's sunny as Bermuda out here, and I'm still so high from the boat race that I can tell myself there's really nothing to be afraid of. Like sometimes when you go to a movie and you get so lost in the story that when you're walking out of the theater you can't remember anything at all about your own life.

You might forget, for example, that you live in a city where people have so many choices they throw words away, or so few they will bleed in your car for a hundred dollars. You might forget eleven or maybe twelve of the sixteen-in-a-row totaled cars. You might forget that you never expected to be alone at thirty-two or that a crazy man might be waiting for you with a gun when you get home tonight or that all the people you know — without exception — have their hearts all wrapped around someone who won't ever love them back.

"I'm scared," I say to Leo, and this time his eyes come to meet mine. The fog is sitting in the center of the bay as if it's over a big pot of soup and we're about to enter it.

"I can't help you," Leo says, and squints his eyes against the mist in the air.

When I was two years old my father took me down to the beach in New Jersey, carried me into the surf until the waves were crashing onto his chest, and then threw me in like a dog, to see, I suppose, whether I would sink or float.

My mother, who was from high in the Rocky Mountains, where all the water was too cold for swimming, and who had been told since birth never to get her face wet (she took only baths, never showers), got so hysterical by the water's edge that lifeguards from two different stands leapt to my rescue.

There was no need, however. By the time they arrived at my father's side I had passed the flotation test, had swum as hard and fast as my untried limbs would carry me, and my father had me up on his shoulders, smiling and smug and a little surprised.

I make Leo drive back by the Palace of the Fine Arts on the way home, though the Richmond Bridge is faster. The fog has moved in there too, and the last of the brides are worrying their hairdos while the grooms help them into big dark cars that will whisk them away to the honeymoon suite at the Four Seasons, or to the airport to board planes bound for Tokyo or Rio.

Leo stays in the car while I walk back to the pond. The sidewalk is littered with rose petals and that artificial rice that dissolves in the rain. Even the swans have paired off and are swimming that way, the feathers of their inside wings barely touching, their long necks bent slightly toward each other, the tips of their beaks almost closing the M.

I take the swans' picture, and a picture of the rose petals bleeding onto the sidewalk. I step up under the tallest of the arches and bow to my imaginary husband. He takes my hand and we turn to the minister, who bows to us, and we bow again.

"I'm scared," I say again, but this time it comes out stronger, almost like singing, as though it might be the first step — in fifty-five or a thousand — toward something like a real life, the very first step toward something that will last.

HA JIN

In the Kindergarten

FROM FIVE POINTS

SHAONA KEPT HER EYES SHUT, trying to sleep. Outside, the noonday sun was blazing, and bumblebees were droning in the shade of an elm. Time and again one of them would bump into the window's wire screen with a thud and then a louder buzz. Soon Teacher Shen's voice in the next room grew clearer.

"Oh please!" the teacher blubbered on the phone. "I'll pay the money back in three months. You've already helped me so much, why can't you help me out?"

Those words made Shaona fully awake. She moved her head closer to the wall and strained her ears to listen. The teacher begged, "Have mercy on me, Doctor Niu. I've an old mother at home. My mother and I have to live. . . . You know, I lost so much blood, because of the baby, that I have to eat some eggs to recuperate. I'm really broke now. Can you just give me another month?"

Shaona was puzzled, thinking how a baby could injure her teacher's health. Her grandmother used to say that babies were dug out from pumpkin fields in the countryside. Why did her teacher sound as though the baby had come off from her body? Why did she bleed for the baby?

Teacher Shen's voice turned desperate. "Please, don't tell anyone about the abortion! I'll try my best to pay you back . . . very soon. I'll see if I can borrow some money from a friend."

What's an abortion? Shaona asked herself. Is it something that holds a baby? What does it look like? Must be very expensive.

Her teacher slammed the phone down, then cried, "Heaven help me!"

Shaona couldn't sleep anymore. She missed her parents so much that she began sobbing again. This was her second week in the kindergarten, and she was not used to sleeping alone yet. Her small iron bed was uncomfortable, in every way different from the large soft bed at home, which could hold her entire family. She couldn't help wondering if her parents would love her the same as before, because three weeks ago her mother had given her a baby brother. These days her father was so happy that he often chanted opera snatches.

In the room seven other children were napping, one of them wheezing with a stuffy nose. Two large bronze moths, exhausted by the heat, were resting on the ceiling, their powdery wings flickering now and again. Shaona yawned sleepily but still couldn't go to sleep.

At two-thirty the bell rang, and all the nappers got out of their beds. Teacher Shen gathered the whole class of five- and six-year-olds in the corridor. Then in two lines they set out for the turnip field behind the kindergarten. It was still hot. A steamer went on blowing her horn in the north, and a pair of jet fighters were flying in the distant sky, drawing a long double curve. Shaona wondered how a pilot could stay inside those planes that looked as small as pigeons. In the air lingered a sweetish odor of dichlorvos, which had been sprayed around in the city to get rid of flies, fleas, mosquitoes. The children were excited, because seldom could they go beyond the stone wall topped with shards of dark brown glass. Today, instead of playing games within the yard as the children of the other classes were doing, Teacher Shen was going to teach them how to gather purslanes. Few of them knew what a purslane looked like, but they were all eager to search for the herb.

On the way their teacher turned around to face them, flourishing her narrow hand and saying, "Boys and girls, you'll eat sautéed purslanes this evening. It tastes great, different from anything you've ever had. Tell me, do you all want to have purslanes for dinner or not?"

"Yes, we want," a few voices cried.

The teacher smacked her lips. Her sunburned nose crinkled, a faint smile playing on her face. As she continued walking, the ends of her two braids, tied with green woolen strings, were stroking the baggy seat of her pants. She was a young woman, tall and angular, with crescent eyebrows. She used to sing a lot; her voice was fruity and clear. But recently she was quiet, her face rather pallid. It was said that she had divorced her husband the previous summer because he had been sentenced to thirteen years in prison for embezzlement.

When they arrived at the field, Teacher Shen plucked a purslane from between two turnip seedlings. She said to the children standing in a horseshoe, "Look, its leaves are tiny, fleshy, and egg-shaped. It has reddish stems, different from regular veggies and grass. Sometimes it has small yellow flowers." She dropped the purslane into her duffel bag on the ground and went on, "Now, you each take charge of one row."

Following her orders, the children spread out along the edge of the field and then walked into the turnip seedlings.

Shaona lifted up the bottom of her checked skirt to form a hollow before her stomach and set out to search. Purslanes weren't difficult to find among the turnips, whose greens were not yet larger than a palm. Pretty soon every one of the children had gathered some purslanes.

"Don't stamp on the turnips!" Uncle Chang shouted at them from time to time. Sitting under an acacia, he was puffing away at a long pipe that had a brass bowl, his bald crown coated with beads of sweat. He was in charge of a few vegetable fields and the dilapidated pump house.

Shaona noticed Dabin, a rambunctious boy, sidling up to her, but she pretended she hadn't seen him. He nudged her and asked, "How many did you get?" He sniffled — two lines of dark mucus disappeared from his nostrils, then poked out again.

She lowered the hollow of her skirt, showing him about a dozen purslanes.

He said with one eye shut, "You're no good. Look at mine." He held out his peaked cap, which was full.

She felt a little hurt, but kept quiet. He turned away to talk to other children, telling them that purslanes tasted awful. He claimed he had once eaten a bowl of purslane stew when he had had diarrhea. He would never have touched that stuff if his parents hadn't forced him. "It tastes like crap, more bitter than sweet potato vines," he assured them.

"Not true," said Weilan, a scrawny girl. "Teacher Shen told us it tastes great."

"How can you know?"

"I just know it."

"You know your granny's fart!"

"Big asshole," Weilan said, and made a face at him, sticking out her tongue.

"Say that again, bitch!" He went up to her, grabbed her shoulder, pushed her to the ground, and kicked her butt. She burst out crying.

Their teacher came over and asked who had started the fight. Shaona pointed at Dabin. To her surprise, the teacher walked up to the boy and seized him by the ear, saying through her teeth, "You can't live for a day without making trouble. Come now, I'm going to give you a trouble-free place to stay." She was dragging him away.

"Ouch!" he cried with a rattling noise in his throat. "You're pulling off my ear."

"You'll have the other one left."

Passing Uncle Chang, Teacher Shen stopped to ask him to keep an eye on the children for a short while. Then she pulled Dabin back to the kindergarten.

Shaona's mouth fell open. That boy would be "jailed" and he might get even with her after he was released. On the second floor of their building there was a room, an unused kitchen, in which three bedside cupboards sat on the cooking range. Sometimes a troublesome boy would be locked in one of them for hours. Once in a while his teacher might forget to let him out in time, so that he had to go without lunch or dinner.

About ten minutes later Teacher Shen returned, panting hard, as though she had just finished a sprint. She counted the children to make sure nobody was missing.

Shaona, immersed in looking for more purslanes, soon forgot Dabin. For most of the children this was real work. Few of them had ever tasted anything gathered by themselves, so they were searching diligently. Whenever their little skirts or caps were full, they went over to unload the purslanes into the duffel bag, from which their teacher was busy picking out grass and other kinds of herbs mixed into the purslanes. The children were amazed that in just one and a half hours the bag was filled up and that they had almost combed the entire field. Their teacher kept reminding them of the proverb they had learned lately — "Many hands provide great strength."

When they had searched the field, they were lined up hand in hand behind the pump house, ready to return to the kindergarten. But before leaving, for some reason their teacher gave several handfuls of purslanes to Uncle Chang. With grudging eyes they watched her drop almost a third of their harvest into the old man's wicker basket, but none of them made a peep. The old man went on smiling at the young woman, saying, "All right, enough, enough. Keep the rest for yourself." As he was speaking, spittle was emitted through his gapped teeth.

Shaona's mind was full, and she couldn't wait for dinner. She thought, If purslanes taste real good, I'll pick some for Mom and Dad. She knew a place in the kindergarten — inside the deserted pigsty — where she had seen a few purslanes.

To her dismay, dinner was similar to other days': corn glue, steamed sweet potatoes, and sautéed radishes. There wasn't even a purslane leaf on the table. Every one of her classmates looked upset. Not knowing what to say, some children were noisily stirring the corn glue with spoons. Shaona wanted to cry, but she controlled herself. She remembered seeing her teacher leave for home with the bulging duffel clasped on the carrier of her bicycle. At that moment Shaona had thought the green bag must contain laundry or something, because it was so full. Now she understood — their teacher took their harvest home.

Shaona liked sweet potato, but she didn't eat much. Anger and gas filled her stomach. Despite their sullen faces and disappointed hearts, none of the children mentioned purslanes. Everyone looked rather dejected except for Dabin. He had kept glaring at Shaona ever since he was let out of the cupboard for dinner. She knew he was going to take his revenge. What should she do?

In the dusk, when the children were playing in the yard, Shaona caught sight of Dabin. She called and beckoned to him. He came over and grunted, "What's up, little telltale?"

"Dabin, would you like to have these?" In her palm were two long peanuts. Her father had given her six of them when she was coming back to the kindergarten two days ago.

"Huh!" he exclaimed with pursed lips. "I never saw a peanut with four seeds in it." He snatched them from her hand and without another word cracked one. His eyes glittered and his mouth twitched like a rabbit's while he was chewing the roasted kernels.

Within a few seconds he finished the peanuts off. Then he asked, "Do you have more?"

"Uh-uh." She shook her head, her slant eyes fixed on the ground.

He touched her sweater pocket, which was empty. She had hidden the other four peanuts in her socks. He said, "You must be nice to me from now on. Remember to save lots of goodies for me, got it?"

She nodded without looking at him.

Standing below a slide, she watched him running away with his bowlegs to join the boys who were hurling paper bombers and imitating explosions. Behind the cypress hedge, near the closed front gate, a couple of children were playing hide-and-go-seek, their white clothes flickering and their ecstatic cries ringing in the twilight.

That night Shaona didn't sleep well. She was still scared of the dark room. One of her roommates, Aili, snored without stopping. An owl or a hawk went on hooting like an old man's coughing. A steam hammer in the shipyard on the riverbank pounded metal now and then. Unable to sleep, Shaona ate a peanut, though the rule didn't allow her to eat anything after she had brushed her teeth for bed. She took care to hide the shells under her pillow. How she missed her mother's warm, soft belly; again she cried quietly.

It rained the next morning, but the clouds began lifting after nine o'clock, so the children were allowed to go out and play. In the middle of the yard stood a miniature merry-go-round, sky blue and nine feet across. A ring of boys were sitting on it, revolving and yelling happily. Dabin and Shuwen, who was squint-eyed, were among them, firing wooden carbines at treetops, people, birds, smokestacks, and anything that came into sight. They were shouting out "rat-a-tat" as if the spinning platform were a tank turret. Shaona dared not go take a spin. The previous week she had ridden on that thing and had been spun giddy, sick for two days.

So instead she played court with a bunch of girls. They elected her the queen, saying she looked the most handsome among them. With four maids waiting on her, she had to sit on the wet ground all the time. Weilan and Aili were her amazons, each holding a whittled branch as a lance. The girls wished they could have made a strong boy the king, but only Dun was willing to stay with them. He was a mousy boy, and most of the girls could beat him easily. He should have been a courtier rather than the ruler. Soon Shaona couldn't stand remaining the queen anymore, because she felt silly calling him "Your Majesty" and hated obeying his orders. She begged other girls to replace her, but none of them would. She got up from the ground, shouting, "I quit!" To keep the court from disintegrating, Aili agreed to be a vice-queen.

Because of the soggy ground, many of the children had their clothes soiled by lunchtime. Teacher Shen was angry, especially with those who had played mud pies. She said that if they were not careful about their clothes, she wouldn't let them go out in the afternoon. "None of you is a good child," she declared. "You all want to create more work for me."

After lunch, while the children were napping, Teacher Shen collected their clothes to scrub off the mudstains. She was unhappy because she couldn't take a nap.

Too exhausted to miss her parents, Shaona fell asleep the moment her head touched her pillow. She slept an hour and a half. When she woke up, she was pleased to find her sweater and skirt clean, without a speck of mud. But as her hand slotted into the sweater pocket she was surprised — the three peanuts were gone. She removed the toweling coverlet and rummaged through her bedding but couldn't find any trace of them; even the shells under her pillow had disappeared. Heartbroken, she couldn't stop her tears, knowing that her teacher must have confiscated the peanuts.

The sun came out in the afternoon, and the ground in the yard turned whitish. Again Teacher Shen led the twenty-four children out to the turnip field. On their way they sang the song "Red Flowers," which they had learned the week before:

> Red flowers are blooming everywhere.
> Clapping our hands, we sing
> And play a game in the square,
> All happy like blossoms of spring.

When they arrived at the field, Uncle Chang was not in view, but the water pump was snarling, tiny streams glinting here and there among the turnip rows.

The sight of the irrigation made their teacher hesitate for a moment. Then she said loudly to the children, "We're going to gather more purslanes this afternoon. Aunt Chef couldn't cook those we got yesterday because we turned them in too late, but she'll cook them for us today. So everybody must be a good child and work hard. Understood?"

"Understood," they said, almost in unison. Then they began to search among the turnips.

Although most of the children were as high-spirited as the day before, there weren't many purslanes left in the field, which was muddy and slippery. A number of them fell on their buttocks and had their clothes soiled. Their shoes were ringed with dark mud.

Yet the hollow of Shaona's skirt was soon filled with several puny purslanes, and some children had even dropped a load into the duffel, which began to swell little by little. Unlike the silly boys and girls who were still talking about what purslanes tasted like, Shaona was sulky the whole time, though she never stopped searching.

In front of her appeared a few tufts of wormwood, among which were some brownish rocks partly covered by dried grass. A swarm of small butterflies rested on the wormwood, flapping their white wings marked with black spots. Now and then one of them took off, flying sideways to land on a rock. Shaona went over to search through the grass; her motion set the butterflies in flight all at once, like a flurry of snowflakes. Suddenly a wild rabbit jumped out, racing away toward a group of girls, who all saw it and broke out hollering. The animal, frightened by their voices, swerved and bolted away toward the back wall of the kindergarten. At the sight of the fleeing creature, Teacher Shen yelled, "Catch him! Don't let him run away!"

All at once several boys started chasing the rabbit, which turned out to have a crippled hind leg. Now their teacher was running after it too, motioning to the children ahead to intercept the animal. Her long braids swayed from side to side as she was dashing away. Within seconds all the children except Shaona joined the chase. The turnip field was being ruined, with a lot of seedlings trampled and muddy water splashing from the running feet. Shrieks and laughter were rising from the west side of the field.

Shaona was not with them because she wanted to pee. Looking around, she saw nobody near, so she squatted down over the duffel, made sure to conceal her little behind with her skirt, and peed on the purslanes inside the bag. But she dared not empty her bladder altogether; she stopped halfway, got up, and covered the wet purslanes with the dry ones she had gathered. Then with a kicking heart she ran away to join the chasers.

The rabbit had fled out of sight, but the children were still excited, boys huffing and puffing and bragging about how close they had got to the animal. Dabin swore that his toes, caged in a pair of open-headed sandals, had touched that fluffy tail. Shuwen said that the wild rabbit tasted much better than the domestic rabbit; a few children were listening to him describe how his uncle had shot a pair of wild rabbits in the mountain and how his aunt had cut them to pieces and stewed them with potato and carrot cubes. Their teacher stopped him from finishing his story. Without delay she assembled the children and led them out of the field, fearful that Uncle Chang would call her names for the trampled turnips.

Before dinner Shaona was worried for fear the chef might cook the soiled purslanes for them. To her relief, dinner turned out to be similar. She was thrilled. For the first time in the kindergarten she ate a hearty meal — three sweet potatoes, two bowls of corn glue, and many spoonfuls of fried eggplant. The whole evening she was so excited that she joined the boys in playing soldier, carrying a toy pistol, as though all of a sudden she had become a big girl. She felt that from now on she would no longer cry like a baby at night.

HEIDI JULAVITS

Marry the One Who Gets There First

Outtakes from the Sheidegger-Krupnik
wedding album

FROM ESQUIRE

Photo 1 *June Sheidegger, maid of honor, leans on the porch railing of the
Rocky Mountain Lodge.*

Violet's younger sister, June, refuses to wear a slip beneath her
sheer silk bridesmaid dress. The startling views of the Sawtooth
Range serve as only a momentary distraction from the unfettered
swell of June's behind inside the peach fabric, indicating that June
also decided to forgo underwear.

Photo 2 *Violet, half dressed, sits before a map of Idaho (circa 1921) while
her Grandma Rose pins hot rollers in her hair.*

Earlier in the week, Violet had pored over maps in the Lower
Stanley Municipal Building. Violet is a psychology student and an
advocate of an experimental method called "language therapy."
(Her first paper, "Alleviate Chronic Depression Through Positive
Word Usage," has just been accepted at an on-line 'zine called
Psyched!) Thus, she is reluctant to be wed in a place called Lower
Stanley. She hoped that a close examination of the zoning maps
would reveal that the Rocky Mountain Lodge was actually part of
the adjacent township, Diamond Heights.

While Violet fretted over fragile, unwieldy acres of paper, Louis,
her husband-to-be, entertained himself with a dirty manila file he

found marked SURVEYORS. Now that both his parents are dead, Louis runs the family business — Krupnik Bros. Photographic Supplies and Development — located on the Lower East Side of Manhattan. Unlike his fiancée, he thinks *lower* connotes the humble foundation upon which an island of steel and striving depends.

SURVEYORS contained snapshots of WPA workers from the thirties. All the images were identical save one — strangely enough, a photo of a newly wed couple on the porch of what appeared to be the Rocky Mountain Lodge. Indeed, written on the back was the inscription "I knew from the moment I saw her. Stan and Rhoda, Rocky Mountain Lodge, 9/5/33."

Louis wondered how Stan could have been so sure and pegged him as a cocky, unimaginative bastard. Still, he believed that this photograph, so out of place among the saddle-faced ditchdiggers, was meant as a sign to him, Louis Krupnik: Orphan, Pessimist, Voyeur, Liar.

He shoved the photograph into the pocket of his windbreaker.

Photo 3 *June sorts through a shoebox of letters in front of the lodge's big stone fireplace.*

As the fire crackles and the morning light grows stronger and higher through the lodge windows, June cuts the blue stationery into careful strips and returns them, gently, to the shoebox.

Photo 4 *Violet, flipping through a fashion magazine while receiving a pedicure, holds up a headline —* 15 WAYS TO LOOK GOOD NAKED AND WIN THE MAN OF YOUR DREAMS.

Louis was the sort of man who had a drawerful of T-shirts emblazoned with the names of women's fashion magazines. At first, Violet mistook this for the seething undercurrent of Louis's anima. Later, she realized there was a predatory subtext to his T-shirts that she'd chosen, optimistically, not to see. Instead of the one-word innocence of *Vogue* and *Seventeen,* it was "(I slept with a girl who works at) *Seventeen*" and "(I slept with a girl who works at) *Vogue.*" And he had. Normally, this did not bother her, except when he moved inside her and it seemed that nothing less than a vise grip could coax him into coming.

It's all those girls, she'd think. His prick was a jaded, callused bit of flesh — senseless as a carpenter's thumb. She dreamed of taking a pumice stone to that hardened knob the way the pedicurist sands away at her thick heels, flesh falling like sawdust into the metal sink. She would make it raw and new and hers.

Photo 5 *As Louis and Bart toss a football on the lodge's front lawn, Bart throws long, driving Louis backward into a bramble bush.*

Louis's first date with Violet ended well — the two of them kissing frantically between bushes in a small park near the Hudson River — though the beginning was far from promising. Talking to Violet was like talking to a wine expert, insofar as she found soaring, unlikely virtues in the most basic things. The restaurant he chose was "clerical yet stately," the minestrone soup "balmy and supine," his blue shirt "refreshingly insouciant." At first, he found her relentless chirping nauseating. The restaurant's most distinguishing feature, truth be told, was that it owed him a free dinner, the soup was obviously from a can, and the shirt was stolen.

After a few decanters of rotgut ("spirited," "tumescent") Chianti, however, Violet in her fluffy sweater became increasingly irresistible. By 2:00 A.M., they found themselves rolling around the stale city grass of a tiny park. Violet would later insist that it was her "positive speech" that made Louis change his mind about her, but he maintained, stubbornly, that it was nothing but the wine talking.

Photo 6 *A football, poorly thrown, spooks a horse.*

Norton Black, stable hand at the Rocky Mountain Lodge, is accustomed to bearing the brunt of the guests' stupidity. He picks himself out of the arroyo where his horse has just tossed him. Goddamned weddings every weekend, he thinks. Marrying soft-footed city kids who fancy themselves pioneers.

He brushes off his Wranglers and bullets back the football. It punches Mr. Shitty Quarterback square in the diaphragm.

"Hey, man, really sorry about that," Mr. Shitty Quarterback gasps, winded, obviously scared to offer Norton a hand for fear he'll tear it off.

Norton doesn't give the guy the satisfaction of an answer. He cracks his knuckles as he goes to fetch his horse. In truth, he's not mad at this skinny rich guy, or his horse, or anything. Life has never been particularly good to Norton Black, and he sees no reason why it should change its tune today.

*

Photo 7 *Grandma Rose Sheidegger, arranging flowers on the fireplace mantel, knocks a glass vase to the floor.*

Grandma Rose, like most women of her era, believed in omens and structured her life decisions respectfully around her debatable interpretations of them. She knew, for example, the morning she awoke to a squirrel noisily turning a bone around and around in the copper rain gutter outside her bedroom window that it was time to cut her long red hair. Likewise, she knew when she met Joe Sheidegger that he was to be her husband. Never mind that he smelled foreign and always would. They were drinking champagne at the Essex Hotel, and Rose, in her nervousness, knocked her flute to the floor. Joe soothed her immediately by saying, "It is better to be a crystal and be broken than to remain perfect like a tile on a housetop." She knew it as a Chinese proverb oft repeated by her own grandfather. In a world full of empty coincidences and accidents, she read this as an omen of their fated union.

Photo 8 *Louis, fresh from the shower, snaps a self-portrait in his towel.*

No man could ever accuse him of being unromantic. A thief, perhaps, a pervert, even, but not unromantic. Had he learned nothing from his father? Had he not witnessed Saul Krupnik waste his youth and health on a store, eventually succumbing to an aneurysm directly attributable to the late shipment of the new Fuji X200 telephoto lens? Had he not watched his mother, Ida, endure unloved by Saul until her heart turned small and mean and weak?

Louis was not the man his father was — the straight man, the coldly determined man, the man without lust. He began what he called the Krupnik Variation during his high school vacations, when he was responsible for slipping the sheeny new photos into yellow envelopes. At first, Louis felt guilty about flipping through the images before putting them behind the appropriate alphabetized tab. Then he became entranced by the odd pieces of the world people found worth preserving — a door with a brass street number, a tin of muffins, the mole on a woman's forearm.

It was only when he stumbled across the raven-haired girl wearing a red dress in front of a Ferris wheel that he realized his transgression had been in the service of a divine search all along. Here, the Girl of his Dreams.

*

Photo 9 *Margie Adams, covered in pastry flour, blushes as June catches her licking the buttercream frosting off the feet of a plastic bride and groom.*

In addition to being an accomplished pastry chef, Margie Adams is Grandma Rose and Grandpa Joe's live-in caretaker, a sprightly yet solidly muscular woman who June is convinced is a lesbian. It is for her sake that June has neglected to wear underwear, in hopes that it will distract Margie from the oddity of her request to bake a boxful of shredded blue paper into the wedding cake.

"Fortunes," June explains, smiling in that sweet, lying way she imagines Margie will find irresistible.

Photo 10 *Violet does the Dance of the Tacky Wedding Presents in her satin panties, holding a salad bowl over her bare breasts.*

The bowl is hand-painted with a ring of purple coyotes howling at nothing. Violet hates it.

Later, as she is composing an insincere thank-you note, Violet will think of her own family's salad bowl. She remembers also serving platters, salt and pepper shakers, pots and pans, silver trivets, all the utilitarian things that were selected, she assumed, with exquisite care by her parents. Now she realizes that her parents probably received their family salad bowl as a wedding gift, an object that neither had cared for much but that they needed and therefore kept. These were the precious relics of her childhood — these accidental, unwanted things.

Photo 11 *Louis, walking to his rented minivan to get his cufflinks, sees June on the porch, examining her reflection in the window.*

She is outside; he is inside. It is precisely as it was the first time he laid eyes on her. He almost makes the same mistake, too, thinking she is gazing with such intensity at him instead of at her own reflection. He was in a bookstore in San Francisco. June was (she defensively claimed) merely checking to make sure her earrings weren't half slipped from her ears. She had just pulled her sweater over her head, and she had lost more than a few single earrings that way. Honestly, she'd prefer to lose the pair. She was an advocate of the clean break, she informed him. Nothing to be gained by retaining the partial remainder of a previous whole, there to niggle you every time you open your jewelry box with the things you've lost in life.

He had followed her from the bookstore to a café, recognizing her as the Girl of his Dreams. He also found familiar her calculated attempts to make something different of herself.

Afterward, he wondered if she would have slept with him if he hadn't just been visiting friends for the weekend, if she'd never learned that he actually lived in New York. Suddenly, he loomed as an opportunity to be missed, a potential regret, rather than a local stranger full of possibilities.

Photo 12 *Violet and June's brother, Bart, armed with a fleur-de-lis linen napkin, flogs their mother, Tenny Sheidegger, who realized too late that the florist forgot to depistil the lilies.*

Bart will never beat his future wife, but he will spend thousands of dollars on a dominatrix service whose billed charges (poorly masquerading as a culinary-supply store called the Whip and Spoon) will be found on Bart's Visa statement by his wife, causing her to reflect lovingly on the inherent Weakness of Men.

Photo 13 *Grandma Rose Sheidegger, crying at the prenuptial luncheon.*

Joe, her husband, has refused to let her have a second helping of turkey tetrazzini and a refill of coffee. He barks and Rose starts to cry. Without a word, he lays his napkin over his uneaten lunch and leaves the dining room.

"He always makes me leave before I'm ready," Rose whimpers to Margie. "Last wedding we went to, I wanted to keep dancing."

Rose looks despondently down the lodge drive at the two wheel ruts that grow closer and closer together as they roll down the hill. Somehow they strike her as dishonest, these two lines pressed into the earth. She feels they should move farther apart as they reach for the far-off horizon. She stands to get a better look, hoping that the two ruts diverge farther on, and knocks her juice glass onto the wide-plank floor.

Rose regards the shattered bits hatefully, as if they had exposed her.

"I married the wrong man," Rose says to Margie loudly and slowly, as if she were hard of hearing, like Joe. Rose holds Margie's wrist for balance as she steps on the shards of glass with her heel, grinding them into a sharp, iridescent snow.

*

Photo 14 *Louis nicks himself shaving as he notices June in the mirror, visible on the lawn through his bathroom window.*

When did he first know? Certainly not in San Francisco. He and Violet had only just begun to date, and he didn't think he even knew she had a sister. It wasn't until he went to the Sheideggers' summer house on Lake Sunapee for the Fourth of July weekend that the two Junes merged into one spirited dark-haired girl, a bikini strap drifting down her tan shoulder and her hips bound low with a towel batiked by boat grease and wood varnish. He was looking out the picture window, and she was looking in, fiddling with her bare earlobes and appearing to be searching for no one but him.

Photo 15 *June, looking at a photograph.*

It's a self-timed picture of her and Louis in the Eagle's Nest, the small guest shack at Lake Sunapee hidden from the main house behind a tightly ivied trellis. They are both naked beneath a Hudson Bay blanket. The light in the cabin was so poor that their faces moon out from the shadows of the bunk bed, rounder and whiter than they must have been on a holiday weekend in July.

She can remember full well where Violet was — at her friend Susie Minturn's Peace Corps send-off party (two years in Botswana, an unlikely career choice for someone as committed to leg waxing as Susie). Violet asked her to "keep Louis entertained" because Violet was as blond and stupid as June was dark and wise. So there they were, in a shack that smelled of kerosene and pine needles and mold, listening to the water lap viciously at the small stone beach every time a water-skier whished by. Louis loved her then with a power that pried his ribs apart, she could tell.

It was her idea to take the picture. He was reluctant for the obvious reasons, but then his love of perversity overrode reason. Or maybe it was because June insisted so tenaciously, knowing that he would require this sort of evidence loose in the world in order to love her. Then he would be able to encounter it accidentally and spy on a framed snippet of passion. He could make it his, but only if it seemed he was stealing it from a stranger.

Photo 16 *Grandpa Joe starts the car, leaving his weepy wife behind.*

He starts these fights intentionally. He wouldn't want to hurt

Rose, so he feels it's better she doesn't know the truth. He looks at the map again to measure the distance to the nearest Indian reservation. Fifteen miles. He feels the folded bills in his pocket thick as a heart and readies himself for the quick banter around the craps table. It makes him think of the mah-jongg parlor he visited just before he took Rose on their first date. The boss, Jimmy Wong, made him memorize some Chinese saying about roof tiles. "Works ladies like charm," Jimmy assured him. It was the first and only time Jimmy hadn't cheated the daylights out of him.

Photo 17 *Violet, wearing her bathrobe, hair wet and uncombed, makes a call from an outside pay phone near the open kitchen windows.*

She can smell her own wedding feast in its nascent stages, the ghosts of wilting onions and browning garlic escaping through the greasy screens. She can hear the mindless banter of the summer lodge staff — underage, ill-at-ease college students from Massachusetts, Virginia, Vermont — as they gossip about what a slut Hope is, sleeping with the stable guy so he'll buy her beer. Norton is his name, a hayseed endowed with a penis not entirely dissimilar to that of his equestrian charges. She can't help but pick up the undertones of envy and admiration they feel for Hope the Slut, and possibly longing that she share some of her wanton-woman's bounty with them — Schlitz, Weidemann's, Old Milwaukee.

Violet imagines herself sneaking a few six-packs into the kitchen for these mean, thirsty kids in ski-resort T-shirts and Tevas, but then she stops herself. She is no fairy godmother. Violet has made a life out of knowing others' secrets and desires. She likes to be able to look through people and interpret their promises and loyalties as the ragged, halfhearted things that they are. If she can't control the way people desire her, at least she can comfort herself with the knowledge that she has spied on what lives in their hearts.

Photo 18 *Louis, buttoning his tux trousers, reaches into the back pocket and pulls out an envelope.*

Of course Louis found them. To his credit, his father was half smart about hiding the photos. But Louis discovered them anyway after Saul died, tucked in his leather account ledger. The Ferris wheel rose behind them. The woman wore a red dress and a mink stole that had once belonged to Ida, but otherwise bore scant resemblance to his mother. Looking at the photos, Louis couldn't decide which disturbed him more — the fact that his father was actually a cheating, lying bastard or that he was too damned cheap to buy the poor girl her own furs. Then he realized what bothered him most was how eerily similar the photo of his father's mistress was to that of the Girl of his Dreams and how distastefully his current situation with June and Violet Sheidegger mirrored that of his father.

He closed the ledger, feeling ill. As he left the office, he was unable to shake the echoes of his father's business mantra from his head.

"Give a man incentive to buy," his father had always told him. "Two for the price of one, boy. Two for the price of one."

Photo 19 *June in the lodge kitchen, contemplating a cockroach on the wall.*

If only June had been a fly on the wall, or even a cockroach, for that matter, just to know what had transpired to make Louis send her that Dear June letter on his signature blue stationery.

"Get rid of my letters," his final missive demanded. "Shred them. Bury them. I don't care. Just get rid of them."

June looks at the wedding cake, basking on a silver tray in all its frilly splendor, and smiles.

Such a good girl for a change. She has done exactly as he requested.

Photo 20 *Louis fingers a man's antique watch as he stares at his reflection in the dressing room mirror.*

The watch was given to his father by his mother on their wedding day. It is gold with a bracelet band. Saul stopped wearing it because it gave him a rash, so his mother wore it instead. She wore it until the day before she died, when Louis visited her at the hospital.

"Get out!" she screamed, hurling the watch at him. It hit the wall next to his head, the crystal cracking like a delicate bone.

"Mother, it's Louis," Louis said. She thought he was his dead father. It made him wince.

"The one, the one, you were *the one*. Bah!" Ida spat at him, but the saliva landed on her chin, making a dark stain on her blue paper hospital robe.

Louis put the broken watch in his coat and closed the door behind him.

He sat on a park bench across from the hospital and watched the pigeons feed on old peanut hulls. As he rummaged for the watch in his pocket, a shard of glass cut him. He sucked his finger as he flipped the watch over with his free hand. "To the one of my dreams," the inscription read. "Ida 12/3/62."

What a fucking trap, he thought. He reached into his pocket for the Girl of his Dreams, bent on tearing her to shreds, but found he had left the photo in another coat.

Suddenly he felt the glass wriggle free of his wound, along with a sweet string of blood. Without thinking twice, he swallowed the shard, feeling it scrape past his throat, his larynx, lodging, finally, somewhere near his heart.

Photo 21 *June and Susie Minturn, wearing their matching bridesmaid dresses, speak briefly as they apply their lipstick in the washroom.*

June, making small talk, asks Susie how long ago she returned from Botswana. Susie, bewildered, clarifies that she's been living in Atlanta for the past three years as a buyer for a southern department-store chain called Bink's. Susie (Susan, now) has embraced the South completely, finding it to be a far more refined existence. Even the drunks are elegant in Atlanta, she will later tell Bart as he undresses her at the EZ Sleep Motel. Bart will not be able to get it up, and Susan will lie awake as he snores, naked, beside her. She will feel strangely proud of herself, as if she'd beaten him at a game women aren't supposed to win, like one-on-one basketball. From the onset of their lives together, Susan's love for her future husband, Bart Sheidegger, is inextricably linked with pity, as well as a heady feeling of superiority.

Photo 22 *Violet at the pay phone, wearing her wedding dress, her hair still in curlers.*

Maybe it was revenge.

Maybe if she hadn't trapped them together in the Eagle's Nest, she wouldn't have exuded the sort of proud, spurned rawness that is so attractive to certain kinds of men, men composed of impulses both carnivorous and maternal.

His name was Shane, a perfectly hushed, ethereal name for a

man whose life was committed to adoring things he could never have. She began spending one night a week, then two, then three, sitting in one of Shane's cracked French-leather armchairs, listening to Frank Sinatra recordings and drinking the fine, pale West Indian rum Shane poured into her tumbler. She was intrigued by a certain saintly quality in him, an excessive goodness always verging on perversity.

She lied to Louis, telling him she'd picked up a private tutorial in Queens. Shane insisted on paying her to offset suspicions. Maybe that's why she let him touch her the way she did. He had a signet ring that he liked to press over her eyelids, branding her with his initials so that his ownership would be clear every time she blinked.

Returning to Louis on the train, she would finger the twenties Shane gave her and not feel the slightest twinge of guilt. Rather, she reasoned she was developing her own secrets, her own desires, her own darknesses, that she was no longer the obvious blond optimist, the girl with her heart on her sleeve, the girl who cheerily urged people to use words like *upper* instead of *lower,* the girl too stupid to know the thrill one can get from deception.

Photo 23 *Louis and June, arguing behind the horse stables before the ceremony.*

June, panicked, has just told Louis that Susie Minturn never went to Botswana.

"Violet framed us," June says.

Louis feels not so much guilty as foolish. She's beaten him at his own game. The thought of being watched is something he's never in his life considered happening to him. He finds it gives him a shiver of something he can't name — loathing, excitement, he isn't sure.

June looks at him all cow-eyed, petting her evening bag. Louis grabs the bag and pushes a rough hand into its silky interior. He pulls out the photo of the two of them at the Eagle's Nest.

"How dare you," he hisses, shaking the photograph in her face.

She tries to snatch it back from him, but he holds it high over his head, ripping it into tiny pieces.

The sun shines through her gauzy dress and he can see everything about her. He throws her away from him, disgusted. Just like every other fucking woman, he mutters to himself as he heads back to the lodge. It's not that Louis doesn't like women. He's just disgusted with June for advertising herself as something different.

Not like Violet, he finds himself thinking proudly as he stalks back to the chapel to be married. All along, Violet had him believing she was just another girl, when actually she was a soul cut from the same devious cloth.

Photo 24 *Violet stands at the pay phone with the wind blowing her veil over her face.*

Again the answering machine picks up, the man's voice woven through faint strains of Sinatra. *"I'm not in right now, but if you leave your name and number . . ."*

Violet starts to speak but then goes silent. Instead, she holds the receiver out toward the Sawtooth Range so that she can record for Shane the eagles circling around the snow-capped peaks, the lemony late-afternoon sunshine, the way she feels mere moments before she exchanges her wedding vows. And how *does* she feel? She isn't sure precisely, but a part of her believes she must find meaning in the fact that Shane is not home to comfort her, that she has been pushed to do the right thing despite the secret lives she and Louis lead. As she hangs up the phone, she feels claustrophobic, as if the mountains and the air are crushing in on her like a great expanse of possibilities aligning into the sudden, clear trajectory of her life.

Photo 25 *June, crying behind the stables, stabs a hole in the earth with the heel of her silver sandal.*

When the hole is deep enough, she fills it with the torn pieces of the photograph, then pushes the dirt back with her toe. She tamps the earth down. Tamp, tamp, tamp. As a child, she took clogging lessons, and the steps come back to her now. One-two-three, one-two-three, tamp-tamp-tamp, tamp-tamp-tamp.

Hands on her hips, she clogs around to the front of the stables but stops when she sees Louis leaning against the side wall. He motions to her to come toward him, quietly. He puts his hands on her shoulders and turns her, pressing himself against her back. They are looking through a large hole in the wall, staring at a man in a cowboy hat with his jeans around his boots, stroking his monstrous hardness with a dusty hand. He stands over a young girl lying naked on a horse blanket, Tevas on her tanned feet. He regards her with eyes that are as wide and blank as a horse's.

June feels Louis start to swell against her gauzy behind. He hugs her tight as if she were anything — a blanket, a pillow, just something to hold on to — as he starts, with great, silent sobs, to cry.

Photo 26 *Louis, frantic, spots June's handbag by the fireplace.*
He is just about to walk to the chapel, located in the middle of a field behind the lodge. He can hear the strains of Mendelssohn's "Wedding March" warbling through the dry grasses. Suddenly he reaches into his tux jacket. No one sees him stuff the envelope of photos inside June's forgotten handbag. No one sees the relief he seems to feel afterward, as if he had just buried a long-sick relative.

Photo 27 *Violet adjusts her garter beneath the chapel door's rough-hewn lintel.*
She can see Louis at the altar, watching her with astonishment, as if she were a statue that had just stepped off its pedestal. He looks at her and she knows, in a glance, that he knows she knows. A shiver goes through her. She enters the chapel.

Photo 28 *Hope, walking up from the stables, buckling her new, big belt.*
She smells the inside of her elbow, because that's where a person stinks of sex if they're going to. All she smells, however, is horse shit and hay. She alternates between feeling lost and victorious, between the sense that she's located something in herself that she never knew existed or lost something forever. It does not occur to her at any point during her walk up the mile-long drive to the lodge that she has experienced both things, that they are one and the same.

Photo 29 *Violet's veil, lying in the road.*
A chuck wagon drives the newlyweds around the property as the guests walk from the chapel to the lodge. Violet's veil snags on a piece of fencing, pulling with it a fake blond braid that lands, coiled and still as a sleeping rattlesnake, in a wheel rut.

Photo 30 *June crouched in the back of the chuck wagon, recently freed of its nuptial cargo.*
In her hand is what appears to be a length of Rapunzel's escape rope. June is in the process of debraiding it with her hot fingers. (It can rescue no one, certainly not her.) Suddenly, without the aid of

any reflective surface, she catches a perfect and absurd image of herself — weeping in the back of a chuck wagon, clinging to a piece of fake hair with nails painted a deep, sad red chosen because of its appropriate name (Other Woman) — and for the first time in a long time, she laughs at herself.

Photo 31 *Grandma Rose, fast asleep at the reception.*

In the background, people lunge and twirl on a parquet dance floor. Grandpa Joe has taken off his suit coat to drape around her shoulders while he goes to fetch their Lincoln from the parking lot. He imagines he will read tonight, or maybe play cribbage alone, being first himself, then Rose, trying to forget what he knows of each hand as he switches chairs in the kitchenette. Maybe, however, he will simply turn off the lights and come as close as he ever does to sleep, flipping between the talk shows and the Weather Channel, alone in the world and yet comfortably so, keeping one protective hand on the upturned hip of his sleeping wife.

Photo 32 *Louis and Violet join hands to cut the cake.*

They both notice the strange texture as the knife sinks through the frosting, like rowing a boat through seaweed.

Photo 33 *June hikes her bridesmaid dress up around her thighs.*

She is striking out, lighter, it seems, into the ocean of burnt-yellow hills behind the lodge. The heels of her shoes dip and teeter into snake holes. She whips them off, hurling them into the low-lying scrub and flushing a pair of pheasants. She searches her purse for a hair clip and finds instead three unfamiliar photos.

The first photo is of an old man who vaguely resembles Louis, his arm around a woman in furs who's young enough to be his daughter. The second is an old black-and-white photo of a just-married couple *("I knew from the moment I saw her")*. The third photo is of a young girl in a red dress at a carnival. They are meaningless pieces of somebody's life, not hers. June throws the photos into the air and watches them as they catch the air currents like birds and swoop away toward the ravine.

Her ethereal figure grows smaller and smaller as she disappears into the setting sun, the sound of the swing band now barely audible as she hears the drum roll, signaling the cutting of the cake.

*

Photo 34 *Louis and Violet chew, quizzically.*
Louis reaches into his mouth as if he's removing one of the long blond hairs Violet occasionally cooks into his dinner. He recognizes his handwriting on the strip of blue paper immediately.
"*. . . no one in the world meant for me but you, June . . .*"

Photo 35 *Louis plunges a hand into the center of the cake and emerges with a fistful of its warm, floury innards entwined with little bits of blue paper like worms around a dog's heart.*
He has a mind to suffocate June with the fucking cake, stuff every last confetti-filled piece of it down her vindictive little throat.

As his eyes pass over the crowd, Louis is alarmed to discover that he doesn't recognize a single one of the guests, as if he has arrived to be married at the wrong wedding. Strangely, nor does he recognize the woman beside him with whom he grasps a knife handle.

They avoid each other's eyes like two strangers sharing a table in a café. The guests sense their awkwardness and begin to shift and shuffle and buzz.

Suddenly this woman (his wife, he guesses) reaches over and pulls his hand to her lips, the hand that is smeared with buttercream and bits of cake and slips of blue paper. She pushes his fist into her mouth, his knuckles cutting against her sharp teeth. She eats madly — cake, frosting, paper.

At first, he is horrified. Then he finds he has the strongest urge to kiss her. He does exactly that, tasting the mess of cake and buttercream and lipstick and blood from his cut knuckles as the crowd of strangers cheers them on bawdily. He realizes he barely knows this woman with whom he now shares a name, a bed, a life. At the same time, he feels she knows and loves him for all the ways that he has always been unknowable. Though he can't be sure, he senses himself closing in on a mystery that has governed his parents, his grandparents, his great-grandparents, their loves as fated as they are accidental. After a life of spying on other people's intimacy, he is suddenly the man on the inside, slightly less bewildered, looking out.

He too takes a bite of the cake, eats his words.

Photo 36 *It is nearly dark now.*
The last dusky bits of day cling to the horizon. June trips along the arroyo that hugs the highway, feeling her way with her bare feet.

Suddenly headlights appear over the ridge. They drift across her cautiously, thinking her a ghost. She hears the gears shift and the engine idle.

"Need a lift?"

June looks up. A man in a pickup leans out his window.

"Where are you headed?" she asks.

He nods his head forward. "Up the road a piece. Going to buy some beer."

June considers this for a moment. She's rather thirsty after all her walking.

"A beer sounds good right about now," she replies, and lets herself in through the passenger-side door. The man notices her bare feet, but not in a way that indicates he finds it strange.

"Norton Black," he says, holding out a hand. "Nice dress."

"June Sheidegger," she replies, extending hers. "Thanks." She can tell by his tone that he means it.

Norton puts the truck in gear, and the two of them pull away until they are nothing but two taillights against a purpling sky. Maybe they will drive to the store and decide to grab a bite to eat at the steak house, talk about their notions of themselves. Maybe Norton will see in June a strange resemblance to his dead sister and June will admire the way he wears a pocket watch in his jeans like her Grandpa Joe. Maybe they will decide, by the time they've worked their way through their rhubarb pie, that they were made for each other and keep driving into the sunset that faded ages ago. Maybe they will marry and, more often than not, wake up next to each other lonelier than if one of them had slept on the rec-room couch.

But probably they will thrill in telling their kids about that fated evening, and their grandkids. They will talk and talk about the way that love is an obvious thing and how they just *knew*. And maybe on certain evenings — when they're looking at their carefully posed wedding photographs, and the sun is setting, and the air is like it was the night Norton found June barefoot by the road — they'll believe their own tales about how love is a fixed, unquestionable thing, written in stars and in stones.

HESTER KAPLAN

Live Life King-Sized

FROM PRESS

LATE IN THE SUMMER of 1993, a hurricane with the gentle name of Tess smashed everything I had into a million pieces. From a window in the cement cooling house where I waited out the storm, I watched the wind suck all the water from the pool, lift the thatch roof from the tiki hut, and detonate the last of the beach chairs. Square by square, the dining room patio was untiled, and just before Tess changed course, a single wave plucked out the entire length of dock.

Hours earlier, my staff had left for the main island, cramming themselves into four tiny boats, which seemed more dangerous than any hurricane. I'd told them to take what food they wanted from the kitchen freezers — we'd lose power and it would all spoil — but they still hid it in their bags and under straw hats. They yelled that I was a crazy yellow-haired man to stare a hurricane in the eye. She will think you're making fun of death, they warned, shielding themselves from the hot wind that was already blowing up their bright shirts, and death will make fun back at you. On this island, superstitions and sightings are as plentiful as the joints of coral that cut your feet in the sand, and so I waved them away.

Weeks later, a few of my staff straggled up the trashed beach looking for work, but the rest had been spooked away for good, and I never saw them again. During the next exhausting year, there wasn't a time when I wasn't picking up broken glass or scrubbing away the pocks and pecks of seawater and sand. I hammered shingles onto the roofs of twenty cabanas, quarried slabs of bluebitch stone, rebuilt the dock, spent all the money I had and borrowed more. When the repairs were almost finished, I got on the phone and begged every travel agent I'd ever had anything to do with in my fifteen years as owner of this place (at twenty-five I had taken over from my mother, now retired to the heart of Manhattan) to steer clients my way. They promised they'd do what they could.

Finally, at the height of my first season back in business, from behind the rethatched tiki bar, I stood for a moment and looked gratefully out at my guests around the pool. Five women from a book group ordered drinks from Tom, who was stiff and unsure in his khakis and flowered shirt, when he was used to carrying buckets and hammers and wearing nothing but a pair of running shorts bleached gauzy. I expected the women to start reading — the same book, of course — but they gazed at the water instead, hands under their thighs, trying on the unfamiliar work of relaxation. Three men I'd checked in the night before, when they arrived from a day of delayed flights and too many mixed drinks, were already asleep on chaises, their tight faces to the sun. The Jensen family reunion, thirteen in all, took up more than their share of space with their gear and noise. Scattered couples, including a pair on their honeymoon, filled out the small but adequate crowd. Down at the beach, an awkward man lumbered onto a jet-ski while his wife stood on the sand and shouted cautions at him.

The day was brilliant, the heat tempered by the trade winds, and for a lifting moment I heard the hymn I'd been waiting for since the day Tess tore through. Every host, every cook, every seducer, listens for his particular sound, and mine was the simple noise of my existence — people at leisure. But despite the sound, I also knew I was barely hanging on to the place I loved so much. I'd left myself no margin for another disaster, and this might be the final decisive season for me. The possibility that I could fail so easily and lose all this — my life, the only place I knew and wanted to be — made me dizzy enough to crouch down and rest my forehead against iced bottles of beer at the base of the bar.

At a sudden shift in the air, I stood again. When I looked past the pool, I saw a deathly figure moving among the shadows. He took forever on desiccated, sticklike legs to move through the low sea grape trees, some of which were badly deformed from the storm. When he stepped out, the bright glare of the sun seemed to shock him absolutely still. His thin gray lips pursed, and his eyes receded in sore, watery sockets. The hymn died instantly as eyes fixed on the man's distended belly, which urged itself against a pink shirt, and ears attuned to his labored wheeze. Men pulled their knees up, a child fussed, its mother tensed; I held my breath, stunned. Very soon, the man's wife hurried out of the shade to lead her husband to a chair; in a neon pink bathing suit, she looked obscene with health next to him.

I had checked her in the evening before — they were Cecelia and Henry Blaze, from just outside Boston. Henry, she'd explained while signing the registration slip with her own gold-capped pen, didn't travel well; they would skip dinner. Under the bougain-villeaed portico, I could just make out his bent shape among the bags Jono was piling into the cart that would buzz them to their cabana. They were staying for three weeks, Cecelia reminded me as she slipped her pen back in her purse, and she hoped the weather would hold. She was in her mid-fifties, and I could see that she'd been pretty once, but over-efficiency and some sadness had taken it out of her. Distracted by noise in the kitchen at that moment, I didn't think about the Blazes again.

Now, as Henry Blaze creaked himself onto one of the pool chairs, I anxiously waited for leisure to return poolside, but I saw from the looks on the faces of the other guests that it wasn't going to come back so easily. No one wants to see reality on vacation, and this was an awful lot of reality on such a bright day. If my first thought about Henry Blaze was to get him the hell out of here, my second was, is this death making fun back at me? Tess had nearly wiped me out. After everything, I was not going to let a dead man kill me now.

Before dinner that evening, I searched for my one remaining pair of long white pants and linen shirt. My cabana — bedroom, sitting room, bathroom — was the only place that still looked like the hurricane had just blown through. I had replaced the broken win-dows, but the roof continued to leak and the floor buckled. My bed was unmade — I didn't allow housekeeping in here — the unused half covered with papers, clothes, music tapes I ordered through the mail, a plate and coffee cup from breakfast.

Some views might be bigger, but I liked the one from my bed-room best. A blue lozenge of water glimmered at the end of a tunnel of sea grape leaves, a less-is-more equation of beauty, and for a seductive second I was stuck on it. I heard calm among the guests, the routine clink of drinks being served on the dining room patio, the two young men I'd hired the week before joking as they put away beach equipment. I had a startling flash of Blaze among the trees, and the possibility that I might lose all this — and then where would I go? — hit me for the second time that day. The outside world seemed tremulous, and without borders.

It was too late to iron my shirt once I found it, so I tried to smooth out the wrinkles as I walked to the dining room, where the guests were already attempting to outdo each other with descriptions of the sunset. Relieved that Blaze was not around — I assumed he was eating in his cabana and I was spared for the moment — I entered the room as the perfectly confident proprietor.

The book group, shiny in sundresses, ordered a bottle of wine as I stood by their table, hands behind my back. I inhaled their smells, which made me a little forgetful as I leaned over glossy shoulders to pour. One of the women had a wonderful, shocked laugh and a head of spiky hair I liked. At another table, the Jensens already had the waiters in a state of mild panic, which seemed to give Bob Jensen a feeling of great power. I'd seen this type before, entitled not by the having of money but simply by the spending of it. Still, I couldn't deny that the table exuded a kind of welcome, affluent energy.

"How are you all doing?" I said, placing my hand on Jensen's shoulder. I felt the burn on his thick skin through his shirt — I wasn't surprised he'd flipped the sun the finger. He ordered a beer, while some of the older Jensens looked like they'd slipped gently, unnoticed, into a fugue state. It is true that this business only survives on repeats and referrals, so I brought maraschino cherries for the kids and a very cold beer for Bob Jensen.

I did the room from table to table, made up for the lags the new cook and dining room staff left. This was the head-filling work I was at ease in, the careful organization of a meal, the murmurs of diners, the matte of the red tile floor which would later be mopped down for the night. I heard tones of teasing waft out from the kitchen, and I stared at the spiky-haired woman from the book group, her dress drooping on her shoulders to reveal a glistening chest. I wondered what it would be like if she came back to my wind-whipped cabana and lay on my bed. I'd done this enough

times over the years to pacify myself, but never for love. She reminded me that I hadn't stopped to read a book in a long time, but
it had been even longer since I'd slept with a woman.

There was a hiss of rubber on the tile just then, and the sound
made me recall riding my tricycle around the dining room in the
windy off-season, skirting the tables like streetcorners and stop-
lights I'd seen in the picture books my mother gave me. But the
hissing was Cecelia Blaze, or rather the portable oxygen tank she
pulled behind her on a small dolly as she entered the room, clear
tubing and the mask draped on a metal hook. She stopped to watch
her husband, in a white shirt and a pair of beltless pants, step
cautiously over the threshold of the dining room. The tufts of hair
on his alabaster scalp had been combed into temporary compliance.

I showed the Blazes to the last empty table, between the Jensens
and the book club. Cecelia ordered for both of them, and when the
bisque came, Blaze sipped his loudly and banged the bowl with a
large gold pinkie ring set with a red stone. Cecelia did not look at
her husband but stared at the view as she ate. I wondered what twist
had led her to marry this older man — and what crueler twist had
led them to plague me now.

Blaze didn't look up when I stood by their table, and I could tell
he was accustomed to not responding until he was good and ready,
that he'd once been in charge of people and things. Cecelia and I
talked about hikes she might take, and when I asked if she was
interested in a jet-ski — I was only trying to feel something out
about these people, what would stir or startle them — she laughed,
grateful, I think, for even this lame bit of flattery.

"How about me?" Blaze said.

It was more than I'd heard him say before, and the strength of his
voice was unsettling. I had expected something closer to a rasp or a
whisper. His wife pretended he hadn't spoken at all, and went back
to her soup.

The book club ordered another bottle of wine, and when Blaze
began to wheeze, I hurried to pull the cork and pour, to catch the
eye of the spiky-haired woman, to make conversation and offer
distraction. Cecelia slowly touched her mouth with a napkin and
put it by her plate before she stood. A sense of urgency had gripped
me and the room, which was now watching the scene with distaste.

She began to fumble with the tubing from the oxygen tank, and small words tumbled from her lips. Blaze's shoulders heaved in an increasingly labored way. A waiter stopped short with his tray of melting ice cream for the Jensens.

"Here, let me help you," I offered, and bent down next to Cecelia, who was now kneeling, her skin pale against the red tiles. Her skirt was unwrapped up the length of a freckled thigh, revealing sad white underpants.

"I have it," she said, but continued to pull uselessly at the tubing.

A nervous odor rose off Blaze. I was now almost cheek to cheek with his wife, and a little desperate. "The goddamn thing's taped up," I said.

Cecelia shot me a look of disapproval. She flipped her skirt shut, sat back, and with what seemed like total, prideful indifference tossed the problem to me; her husband was going to die in *my* dining room. Blaze shifted to the right then, and with a small, almost dainty cough, threw up his dinner. A moment later, he took a full, wheezeless sigh while a splatter slid off his square knees onto the floor.

I stood too fast and motioned for my staff to come clean up; suddenly they were blind to me, and I was dizzy.

"Goddamn it!" Blaze said. For the first time we looked directly at each other, and I saw from his eyes that he wasn't really old at all. I could have felt sorry for him then — all this misery in a man just sixty — but I was even less forgiving than earlier that he'd chosen my place for this freak show of his.

After some cleaning up, Cecelia slouched her husband out of the room. I assured the book group that Blaze would be fine, though I could see them rallying as concerned women now and not vacationers. I sent Jensen another beer, which he received with a verdictless shrug, and I turned on the ceiling fan to blow the death smell of Henry Blaze out to sea.

Later, the book club played poker and scattered plastic chips on the patio floor, their tone a little off, like people having a good time at a wake. I heard the clatter of bikes and mopeds behind the kitchen as the staff heckled their way home. In the front office, I checked the computer, as I did every night now, to see if new reservations had come in since I'd last looked. There was only one, and that not yet confirmed. I put my head in my hands.

"Jesus H., that was some scene with the old man tonight," Bob Jensen said, peering into the office and startling me. "Disturbing you?"

"Disturbing me? No, just shutting up for the night," I said. I wanted to tell him not to stroll where he wasn't welcome, and I knew by the way he was hanging around that I'd have to open the bar and give the guy a drink on the house pretty soon. I turned out the office light.

"So, I thought he was going to die right there," Jensen continued as we walked outside. He shivered for a second in the heat. "You know that noise he made, like a spoon went down his garbage disposal. Kind of freaked my wife and kids. Let's not even talk about the spewing."

"Let me get you a drink, Mr. Jensen," I said, and led him to the dark tiki bar. He hoisted himself onto a stool and told me what a nice place I had. With his broad back half turned to me, he watched the anoles skitter by the pool lights and sipped his cuba libre.

"Okay, what I'm wondering," he said, "is maybe the old guy could eat earlier or later or in his cabana or something. You don't think I'm being hard, do you?" Jensen said, his voice falsely sappy. "And I'm not saying he shouldn't be here at all, because hey, that's his right too. I just think he could be less here, if you see what I mean. I'm sure I speak for the other guests, and I *know* I speak for the Jensens, all fourteen of us."

"Thirteen," I corrected.

"There's a set of twins," he said, and his tongue explored the inside of his cheek as though now daring me to charge him for one more person, when I'd sat him next to death at dinner. "The ten-year-olds. You probably missed them, everyone always does. Anyway, I'd like to see what you can do about it. This is our one vacation a year, know what I mean? We plan to make it a regular thing too, come back here maybe, if all goes well."

The fat fuck was threatening me. "Can I top you off?" I said, holding up the bottle of rum. But he waved it away, finished the rest of his drink in a final gulp, and said goodnight. I saw him jump back as a tiny emerald lizard crossed his path.

The book club quit around midnight and made their way, loopy with booze and solidarity, through the trees. Finally I could go to my cabana. This not going to bed before the last guest was one of my mother's more tenacious policies. She'd also say Blaze should stay, and take him his meals herself if that's what needed to be done to keep him happy and hidden. It was a win-win situation finan-cially, she'd declare — her own uneasiness inconsequential, her eye always on business and the next season. But I simply wanted Blaze gone, off my island before he ruined it. His ghostliness, his precarious hold on things, felt too much like mine at the moment.

Though it was late and I was exhausted, I walked toward the Blazes' cabana. From the path, I could see the two defiant fist-shaped rock outcroppings that towered over an eddying, unpre-dictable pool below, shaded violet even in the dark. I know my part of the island is inspired with natural, moody beauty, and that night I noticed how a winking luminescence seemed to rise from the coral reefs. Cecelia was playing cards on the open terrace and listening to a symphony on the only radio station we got on the windward side of the island. Henry, in a white robe, was asleep in the hammock chair, his head lolled to one side. Cecelia looked up suddenly, though I don't think she saw me hidden by the curve of the path. She looked pained, as if she'd lost something. She might have simply caught a flash off the water just then that made her want to go home as desperately as I wanted them to leave. For this, for her, I decided to let them have the night.

It wasn't until I was in the light of the bathroom back in my cabana that I noticed the spattering of spew — as Jensen had put it so eloquently — on the cuffs of my pants. I had to scrub with an old toothbrush and a cracked bar of soap to get them clean.

"You want us to leave," Blaze said the next morning when I showed up on the terrace of his cabana. Alone and in the full sun, he sat in the hammock swing again, an open book on his lap. He seemed transfixed by something out on the water.

I hadn't expected to arrive at the point so quickly, and it took me a moment to catch up. "I'm concerned about you, that's all," I said. "We have no medical facilities here that I'd trust to treat anything more than a moped burn or diarrhea. We're really not equipped to handle an emergency."

"Like death, for instance, which is hardly an emergency, Mr. Thierry. I take it your guests didn't like my performance at dinner," he said. "But now Cecelia has those nice bookish women to talk to because of me. They've adopted her, I think."

"Please, Mr. Blaze." My impatience surprised him only a little — I could tell he enjoyed revving people up and letting them whirl uselessly. "I'm trying to hold on to this place, and I do know I can't afford to have guests pull out now because they're unhappy or decide to go somewhere else next year, for whatever reason. I'm not sure this is the best place for you to be."

"You mean I'm not an asset." Blaze countered my ugly lack of sympathy and squinted at the water again. "Your guests are too uptight."

"You have to understand my position." The truth was, I could only ask him to leave; I couldn't actually force him out.

"I understand your position well enough, Mr. Thierry. Now look at mine."

Blaze was not wearing a shirt, and I saw how trim and beautiful his body must have been before he got sick, before he became distended, toxic and puffy in some places, deflated in others. A bracelet of thin black leather circled his wrist, a strange touch on such a pale American. I was repulsed by his body, and when I turned away, I saw what he'd been looking at so intently while we talked. On the large sandbar not far offshore, the honeymooners from Philadelphia were bare-chested, their faces pressed tightly together. She was lying on top of him, while his hands circled the sides of her breasts and then the rise of her ass. Their bright orange kayaks sat nose first on the sand, the single palm tree fanning a wasted shade over them.

"Not exactly private, is it?" Blaze laughed, a little wistfully, I thought.

I sat down on the low wall. My eyes adjusted to the darkness of the room behind Blaze, and to the squadrons of pill bottles and inhalers on the wicker bureau. Last night's oxygen dolly stood by the unmade bed. For the first time, it occurred to me that Blaze might have AIDS, with his collection of mismatched and terrible ravages. Our island is an oil well of pleasure, and I'd seen enough sick people standing in cool and furtive doorways in town to know this particular disease.

"Why did you come here?" I asked.

"You think I singled you out."

"Seems that way," I said. "There are a million islands, Mr. Blaze. You could have gone to Club Med even — they would have given you your own bikinied nurses round the clock."

"Not my thing, Mr. Thierry." Blaze looked up at the sky. "I can see the hurricane did a lot of damage here. This was the most beautiful spot on earth, and I've been to some pretty spectacular places all over the world. I remember you. I remember your mother too."

"You've been here before?" I asked, skeptically.

"Several times, actually — last with my first wife, years and years ago. You must have been around thirteen then, miserable and pimply, performing an impressive repertoire of antisocial activities for the guests. You once stood on a rock and peed into the water while we were having dinner in the dining room. Your mother tried to distract us with shrimp cocktail. Jumbo shrimp, she kept saying, look at the size of their tails. All I saw was your skinny ass in the sunset. Still, I always thought it must have been paradise for you, growing up on this island. And now look at you — all business and good interpersonal skills to boot."

There were times I forgot how much I once hated this place, how I couldn't wait to get away. Despairingly fatherless, I had searched among each season's new arrivals for possible candidates. My mother gave me nothing to go on, though. She claimed to know little about who he was. Not because he'd knocked her up and disappeared, or was some married mystery, I was meant to understand, but because that's how she'd wanted it. Mother and child only, the picture of paradise. I was fathered by some resort guest who'd been turned on by my mother's independence and sharp business sense, her long toes, tanned face, and light eyes, the skittery sounds at night, this place so far from his home, the erotic heat in the dark. All she might have had of him was a credit card receipt in her files.

"Why did you come back?" I asked.

"I heard you were hurting for business. I thought I'd help you out a little."

"But I don't think that's what you're doing," I said. "You are definitely not good for business."

"I want to die here, Mr. Thierry," Blaze said, sounding as tired as he looked all of a sudden. "I was hoping you might be sympathetic."

Removed and up in his windy cabana on the bluff, Blaze stayed away from the other guests, and I had Tom take him his meals. With him out of my sight, I even allowed myself to feel hopeful and hear the hymn bounce off the bluebitch stone and pool's surface again. The Jensen kids napped by the pool. A man, still laughing, had to be brought back off the water when the breeze died on his windsurfer. The honeymooners slept past lunch, other guests settled into their own muted routines, while I willingly busied myself with work, the supplying of other people's pleasure. Cecelia Blaze had been encircled by the book group — they seemed a useful novelty to each other — and her appearance each morning was good news to me and a reminder that three weeks would go by quickly. Blaze would leave, sick but alive, as he had come.

So perhaps it was some blind gratitude, finally, or simply curiosity during a hopeful moment, but I decided to deliver Blaze's lunch myself one noon. Motionless and drained in the shadows indoors, he did not seem surprised to see me, though it had been days. He tentatively examined the tray with his head drawn back, as though the fish might jump up and bite him. I understood then that for someone as sick and weak as he was, the wrong food, wind, breath, dose could easily kill him.

He'd eaten some bad meat in Poona once, and had nearly died from it. "My stomach ulcerated, I shit blood," he explained. He took a bite of fruit — he was not starving himself — which he chewed with his front teeth. "You don't know where Poona is, do you, Kip?"

"I haven't done a whole lot of traveling," I said. "Look, I wanted to let you know I appreciate —"

"Northern India. That's your geography lesson for today," Blaze interrupted. Did I know he was the largest importer of Indian movies to the United States? The demand was voracious, he explained, not to be believed, and then he pushed away his plate and could barely keep his eyes open long enough to see me leave. When I delivered his dinner, he was in the same place I'd left him earlier, though this time he didn't talk. His lips were chalky from something Cecelia had administered to him, and the air had a cool, ventilated feel to it.

The next day he was a little more alert, and in painfully slow sentences described for me the time he'd spent in the backs of tiny Indian import shops in Queens, Detroit, and Los Angeles, sitting on overturned milk crates with his Indian friends, drinking yogurt shakes and nibbling on sweetened fennel seeds. He was hazy with fatigue, full of admiration for the exotic, lost in memory. I felt myself being drawn back to these places with Blaze — I had never known the kind of easy friendship he was describing — but still I was anxious to leave his dark sickroom with its sour, clinical odors.

In spite of my aversion, I fell into a routine of taking Blaze his meals, perhaps to ensure that he'd continue to stay away from the other guests by satisfying his increasing need to talk. One morning, at the end of his first week on my island, I found Blaze in bed, his skin a new shade of green. He'd been thinking of some of the many trips to India he'd made alone, he said, as though I'd always been standing there listening. I should imagine him, he urged, his hands stirring under the sheet, sweating with pleasure in a New Delhi hotel, burning his throat on spices in Madurai, lapping at the hot air with his tongue as he hung out a train window. His large house outside Boston was full of bolts of silk and painted boxes he had brought back from his trips. The closets stank of vegetal sizing and the sweat of polished copper. Cecelia and his two grown daughters had no interest in any of it.

"Can you picture it?" he asked. "Tell me, can you see it?"

I was born on this island, delivered by the cook's grandmother. A lime tree was planted over my placenta. As a child, I'd given names to crabs in the kitchen so they wouldn't be forgotten at dinnertime. I'd followed anoles around trees because I'd been told they led to diamonds. I knew the female pungency of every leaf and the taste of dirt and sun here, but nowhere else.

"Sure," I said, trying to appease his growing agitation. "I can picture it."

Blaze was energetically angry all of a sudden, frustrated that he could not describe anything to me with true accuracy anymore: touch, smell, a spinning head, what it felt like to be completely lost. He recalled words these days, he said, only from the practice of having spoken them before. Imagine, he begged, being robbed of everything in the dank of a park underpass in Bombay by a smooth, beautiful Indian boy, only moments after sharing pleasure with him. And imagine walking back to the hotel with pockets flapping empty, ribs aching from fear and a few swift kicks, spent and feeling exhilarated beyond belief, as though it was one of the great moments of life.

"I need you to understand," Blaze said.

I understood; he was talking about love. But what did I know about that, or what love would make a person do? "I have to go," I said, and turned away.

There was noise in the bathroom just then, which startled us both — the dull thump of Cecelia's wet towel dropped on the floor. Blaze's eyelids fluttered at this sudden reminder of his wife. I sat down on the side of his bed. I wondered then if it was disease itself or the shame of this disease — it was AIDS, I was sure now — that kept submerging so many of his memories; a struggle either way.

Blaze lifted his head from the pillow, moved his hand toward my wrist, and then withdrew. "Do you see why I want to die now?" he said.

Cecelia came out of the bathroom, her fingers inept at the buttons on her shirt, her face pale from what she'd obviously just heard him say. She sat in one of the wicker chairs and crossed her legs.

"Don't be such a priss," Blaze said to her, having regained full breath now. He was unkind, she was long-suffering; they seemed to accept their complicity in the situation.

"He was telling me about some of his trips," I said.

"I'm sure he was." She nodded. "Did he tell you how he once forgot to walk clockwise around a Buddhist shrine?" She began to laugh, and pulled her knees up girlishly. "They nearly arrested him. Oh, I don't know, it just seems like the strangest thing to me."

"Cece," Blaze said as though he'd been trying to get her to understand forever, "it is so much more than that."

Her face suddenly tightened as she considered him. Was she picturing at that moment her husband bent over another man, thrusting with passion? Was she wondering where his tongue and mouth had been? He must have also slept years of nights in bed with her, the comforter over them with reassuring weight, the dry kiss on the lips as equally reassuring. My husband is not queer, she would tell herself, he does not have sex with men, because he is my husband. She wasn't going to indulge or spare him now — his dying was killing her too, after all. She fiddled with her hair while her eyes watered; the love of her life was retreating, and he didn't want her to come along.

That evening, still distracted from the morning's scene with the Blazes, I wandered out onto the patio. The book group, having splintered during their week, was back together for a last dinner, looking forced and tired. The spiky-haired woman touched my hand as I walked by — too little, too late, too difficult, I thought — but she only wanted me to see something.

"Look," she said, and nodded toward the sandbar where Blaze and I had seen the half-naked honeymooners days earlier. I offered a Deserted Island Evening package — wine and lobster at sunset on the tiny island — for an extra fee. It had been my mother's idea early on, an appreciation of the romantic streak in others. At most, there had only been a few takers a season. "God, it's wonderful to see them out together," she sighed.

At the edge of the sandbar, one of the beach boys was helping Cecelia step out of the dinghy. In the evening light, her turquoise dress was diaphanous and slinked around her ankles. Blaze was hunched and uncertain as he lifted his knobby leg to climb out of the boat, one hand heavy on the boy's shoulder. He had not been farther than the terrace of his own cabana in almost a week, and this vastness must have startled him.

Cecelia smoothed a blanket on the sand as the boy left in the boat and Blaze sat down next to her. What a joke to offer up this sandbar as deserted. When you were on it, it felt alone and tiny and the single palm seemed enormous, but from the height of the patio — and from Blaze's terrace, as I had seen — it was a theater stage on which to act out this peculiar marriage. Cecelia's adjustment of her dress, Blaze's shift to one side as he removed something sharp from under himself, the splash as she clumsily poured wine — these were larger than life, lit up for all to see. Blaze had to know this.

We saw how Cecelia wanted to kiss her husband, so when he offered only a cheek, she forcefully took his face in her hands and pulled him toward her, pressing her mouth against his. No one spoke, and Jensen, with his knee bouncing at top speed, stared alternately at his own wife with her broad, peeling nose and at the Blazes. When I smelled the sizzle of garlic, shrimp, and lime juice, I hustled people in, tripping a little over my own feet.

Alone as I watched again in the almost dark, I saw Cecelia drop the dress off her shoulders to reveal her breasts. She straddled her husband, who was on his back, leaned down so her face was against his. They stayed like this for a long time, past the time I heard dinner brought to the tables and the sunset faded.

"You think they're okay?" Jensen said. He had left his family still eating and stood next to me on the patio. He smelled of steak and pepper. Jensen had continued to poke his head into my office from time to time, giving me a moronic thumbs-up and looking for something to throw his weight against. I knew he was inflated with a dangerous amount of sun and restlessness.

"I'm sure they're fine," I told him, but I wasn't sure at all, and was immobilized by the idea that Blaze was finally dead and Cecelia, in some love/grief clutch, was frozen too. A freak high tide should suck the corpse out to sea and dump it on some other island.

"Let me help you get them," Jensen offered, nodding toward the sandbar. As we went down to the beach and pulled the dinghy out, I wondered if I'd misjudged the guy all along — a man who is idle is sometimes not himself, or too much himself. Jensen easily rowed to the sandbar while I was transfixed by the napkin that bloomed from his pants pocket at each stroke.

"Jesus, her dress," Jensen said to me. "Hey there," he yelled to Cecelia. "Everything okay?" We were eddying in the water, Jensen's oars firm against the night's stronger and deeper current.

Cecelia slid off her husband ungracefully and covered herself as she rose from all fours. "I didn't want to wake him up. I guess I didn't realize how late it is."

"Time to come back." I jumped out of the boat and dragged it up to the sandbar with Jensen still sitting in it, sucking his teeth and showing no intention of getting out.

Cecelia leaned down toward her husband. When he opened his eyes, I could tell how disoriented he was by the water at eye level, the dark.

"I can't move," he said.

"Oh, come on, Henry." Cecelia put her hands on her hips. "It's late. These men are waiting. Try." She touched his leg with her foot.

"What's up?" Jensen yelled from the boat.

"I'm all gripped up, Cece," Blaze said. "I'm sorry."

Cecelia turned so closely to me, I thought she was going to collapse against my chest, but it was only so she could whisper. "This happens sometimes when he's still for a long time, so you're going to have to carry him." Then she stepped back and waited, her arms across her chest with that odd indifference again.

I knelt down and lifted Blaze's head off the sand. It was the first time I'd touched him, and I was surprised by his softness. I struggled ineffectively until I called to Jensen. His eyebrows rose as though I'd interrupted him, and then he gestured for me to come close.

"Well, shit, what's wrong with him first, Thierry?" he said. "Cancer, AIDS, something catching? What, before I get my hands all over him."

I hesitated for a second and looked at his unpleasantly red face. "I don't know, Mr. Jensen. I'm not a fucking doctor."

I stared at Jensen with obvious contempt while he considered whether or not to hit me. Finally he jumped out of the boat, brushing his shoulder against mine.

"Can you sit?" he yelled at Blaze, as though he were deaf.

Blaze narrowed his eyes even further. "What do you think?"

Jensen and I managed to haul Blaze into the dinghy and lean him against his wife. A small crowd had gathered on the beach, and then, as we were lifting him from the boat, Blaze slipped away from us like a hooked but determined fish. Cecelia and the others gasped, while I wanted to throw my head back and howl with laughter, fall to my knees while the tears streamed down my cheeks. My hands went weak, my bowels and stomach quivered, and Blaze sank fast and helplessly in the shallows. It was where he wanted to be, after all. I should just let him go.

But I grabbed him instead. Jensen was stunned, and Blaze was an even more impossible weight now. His eyes were closed as though he had decided to pass calmly through this humiliation and his failure. Someone had wheeled one of the wooden beach chairs down to the water's edge, and we managed to lay Blaze on it. His dripping clothes hung on the distorted angles of his body, making him look even worse than before. Jensen left, calling to his kids, who were gawking over the patio railing, as though he hadn't seen them in weeks. People flitted around us for a few seconds, while Cecelia sat on the end of the chair and stared out.

"I need to stay here for a minute," Blaze announced.

"I'm going to get you a blanket, a sweater, something," Cecelia said numbly. She stood and walked away.

"She's weaving — it's the wine." Blaze watched her go and then pulled a pack of still-dry cigarettes from his shirt pocket. "Have a lighter, Thierry?"

"Jesus Christ," I said, and lit his cigarette. "You're smoking?"

"Yes." He took a defiantly deep inhalation and looked pleased with himself. "Live life king-sized."

"What's that supposed to mean?"

"Something I liked in an Indian movie, *The Eighth Moon*. Seen it? A real blockbuster," he said. "Everything's about smoking in that country. The prince has just routed a coup, killed a few hundred ingrates, and so he pulls out a cigarette and lights up. 'Live life king-sized,' he declares. It sounded right."

I sat on the end of the chair where Cecelia had been. Blaze's ankle tapped at my thigh as he dragged on his cigarette.

"This outing tonight was my idea," he said, "so don't blame Cecelia. People say she's too stiff, but that's not really true. I think I didn't give her enough time when I was living — not dying, that is — but I love her. Your little island" — he waved his cigarette toward the sandbar — "seemed like it might be the right way to show her." Blaze laughed and pulled himself higher on the chair. "I have no energy to explain anything anymore, Thierry — my disease, my life, my unnatural passions, as it were. I want to die. Seems I'm not having much luck, though."

"It's a little hard to drown yourself in less than a foot of water." I turned around to look at him. "*You* live life king-sized, Blaze. My business is going under."

"Don't be such a pessimist. It shows a great lack of imagination."

"So what if I lose this place," I said, ignoring him. "I can go somewhere else."

"You don't want to do that. You'd get squashed, Thierry. You're an island boy, with your ponytail and skinny legs. Your sneakers are all wrong, too. What do you know about anything or anyone? Look, when was the last time you even watched television? Stay. Reposition yourself, that's all — change with the times. Maybe you can call this Euthanasia Island, the getaway of a lifetime. Hospice Hideaway. Offer sunset pillow smotherings, poolside morphine drips, the feeding tube extraction. Quick turnover. You haven't been in the real world — you have no idea how popular this dying thing is." Blaze tossed his cigarette into the water. "I could make it worth your while. Repeats and referrals, the blood of the business. I know everyone, I'd bring them to you, all my friends I've told you about. You help me on my way, and I'll save your business in return."

"You're asking me to kill you," I said.

Blaze tapped his foot against my thigh again. His offer was horribly simple — if I believed him at all. I thought about how many times, after Tess tore through and I was on my knees picking up the endless pieces, I said I'd do anything to save my island. I heard water slide into the sand, heat spiral in the air, the coral reef shift and settle. All my life, this sound had been my idea of a perfect night, and always would be, no matter where I ended up.

"I won't kill you, Blaze," I said absolutely. "Not even to save all this." Finally, I was surer of this than of anything else in my life.

"*Euthanize* is the word, Thierry. It's an act of mercy, not business." He sighed, defeated. "I've been trying to tell you that, to show you. I've told you all my stories now."

Their week over, the book club and other guests left the next day, and I was hardly surprised when Jensen checked out with them, a week early, bullying my office to accommodate his immediate change in plans, dragging his dopey family with him.

The time before a new group of guests arrived has always been a good break for me and my staff, and this time I fell into it, grateful for the distraction. The staff talked in full island voices again. Together we ogled the stuff people forgot under beds and in full view. We ate lunch in the kitchen and sloppy salad with our hands, whisked our bare feet across the floor. Their children, now bravely out from among the trees, wandered around and bounced on the empty beds. I had Tom take Blaze his meals again, so I wouldn't have to see him. On two evenings I saw Henry and Cecelia standing on the dirt road that led to the center of the island. I didn't know where they had been or were headed as they looked up at the canopy of trees that kept the moon from lighting their way.

By the middle of the Blazes' second week, there were several last-minute cancellations, and occupancy was at an all-time low. I must have seemed shell-shocked as I wandered around, and I felt I'd slipped into some kind of mindlessness. I wondered if this was how Blaze felt, a kind of giddiness knowing what would come next, a true dead end, for it was now pretty clear it was over for me. The few remaining guests began to assume the natural liberties that come with an enormous amount of space. Their irritations became public as they echoed off the bluebitch, and they were careless with their things, which I sometimes saw float away with the tide.

One morning I wandered aimlessly behind the kitchen. Inside, a tape played loudly, and I'd been drawn to the open door by the music to watch the women bent and swaying over counters, sweat on the backs of their thick necks, feet slipped out of shoes. I had known them forever and so I was still paying them with what little I had left, but there was almost no work to do; they were playing cards, sucking on toothpicks, talking. As I watched, I remembered how once one of the staff had come trembling to me. She swore she'd just seen her long-dead father leaning against the kitchen's back door, smoking and waiting for her to get off work, and she wanted me to shoo him away, which I pretended to do. Now I felt those eyes and a hot breath in the shade and left quickly.

That evening Tom told me the Blazes were waiting for me on the patio. Cecelia was wearing an alarmingly bright dress, huge yellow daisies with blue centers, an ugly island design my mother used to wear on Saturday nights. Henry, in a chair next to her, wasn't eating that day, she told me. First fasting, then a sunset and an enema before bed.

"Like scrubbing the ring off a bathtub," Blaze said. He looked sicker, but also strangely expectant for someone who couldn't expect much of anything anymore. "Has to be done every once in a while so the water's clean. Give it to him, Cece."

"What's this?" I asked, and took the piece of paper Cecelia held out to me. There were fifteen names on the list, all Indian, from what I could tell.

"I've invited my friends, just like I told you I would," Blaze said. "You got a few empty rooms at the moment, am I right?"

"A few," I said weakly. I needed to sit down but leaned heavily against the patio railing, my back to the water.

"Some of them won't be able to come on such short notice, of course," Cecelia said, energized by her sudden usefulness to her husband, even in this deranged task. I couldn't bring myself to look at her, to see what she might or might not understand. "They're Henry's friends, really. You know he was up late last night trying to arrange this over the phone."

"Not easy," Blaze said. "But believe me, I've arranged much more complicated deals than this one. It didn't take much convincing; I offered something for nothing. Most people are pigs." Cecelia laughed at this, and looked a little surprised at her gaiety. Blaze gave her a puzzled look.

"All these people are coming here," I said to Blaze. "Do I have that right?"

"You didn't think I was serious, did you? I can see it in your face," he said. "But a deal is a deal."

Cecelia ignored her husband, as I'd seen her do so many times before. "He's decided he wants them to be here when he dies. They love him." She slapped her hand over her mouth. The way the lowering sun caught in her eyes, I didn't know if she was horrified, thrilled, or both.

Blaze delivered on his promise, and over the next few days, fourteen of his friends came to my island. Each arrival was another weight for me, more evidence of a debt I was expected to pay back. As a group, though, these people brought with them an attractive, buoyant life I'd never seen before, a new hymn that I sometimes found myself swaying to. They enthusiastically loved the place and wandered noisily into the dining room at the last minute and stayed for hours, swam at night, slept most of the morning, talked endlessly to me about the island, the birds, and Blaze.

Sanjiv Bhargava, a large and slickly confident man, was Blaze's closest friend among the group, and often sought me out with earnest questions about natural history and my childhood on the island. Three of the guests had brought wives, who rubbed oil on their dark skin for hours and melted into each other around the pool. Cecelia looked uncomfortable around them at first, so stiff, with her mouth mimicking the curve of her arching hairline. She startled at their hands resting on her arms, her knees, the way they included her.

Blaze sat kinglike in the middle, but shut out the sudden activity that now swirled around him. Watching him from the window in the main house that overlooked the pool, I was the only one who noticed that he was in deeper trouble now, that his face contorted with spasms and he fell asleep with his mouth open. In the space of only a few days his chest had collapsed, so that a hollow preceded him, sat on his lap, sucked up his words. These friends of his — fully paid for and loving their midwinter luck — swam and teased, but they never turned their heads to check on him, as though he should be my responsibility now.

One morning Blaze's friends left him while they went down to the beach. Squinting uncomfortably, Blaze sat in the direct early heat but appeared not to have the strength to move himself. Finally, when I could no longer stand to see him purpling and swelling in the sun, I came out of the main house and moved his chair into the shade. I was quick to hurry away.

"No, don't go yet," Blaze said, and caught my arm. "Tell me, Thierry, how does my future look these days?" The strength of his voice still surprised me.

"I don't know about your future," I stalled. I saw Cecelia and Blaze's friends circling around a pair of sailboats on the beach, considering their next activity. "What do your doctors say?"

Blaze laughed. "You want to know about my doctors? All right," he said. "They are institutionally optimistic. They should all be forced to wear buttons that say 'Be hopeful,' and at night they should have to lay the buttons down next to their alarm clocks so they will be the first thing they see when they wake up, even before they take a leak. But enough already with the optimism, don't you think? It doesn't do me any good." He nodded toward the beach, his wife and friends, and his eyes teared. "Anyway, I've arranged everything. My friends will be back next year with their big brown families and business partners and silent, glaring grandmas who don't speak English — all on my nickel. So you'll be okay, Thierry, don't worry. Now put me back in the sun."

My mother called a little later. Cold as hell in New York, she said hoarsely, as though clots of snow were lodged in her throat. She'd just walked back from the museum and was thinking of buying a pair of snow pants like the ones all the kids had. Since my mother had left this island — ambivalent, but more than ready — she had gorged herself on choice.

"I hear you're running a leper colony down there, you've got people throwing up in the dining room," she said. Her friend at Columbus Travel (sister of the reservationist who'd booked the Jensen family) had called to report. Several others had apparently done the same.

"Yes, a leper colony. We've got body parts all over the place, but we can fit fifteen people in one bed." I wondered what she would make of Blaze, still alone and in the sun — if she would recognize him through his disease as someone from another time in her life.

"You can joke if you want," my mother said. "But if *I've* heard it, imagine how many other people have too. Word of mouth can kill your business in a second, Kip. I'm absolutely serious, it doesn't take much."

"I know."

My mother sighed. "This man Jensen claims he's going to report you — to whom and for what, who knows, but he's telling everyone. At the very least, he's looking for a full refund. There's an asshole in every crowd, remember that — you have to give him the Asshole Special, even if that means crawling to do it to save the business." My mother stopped short. Giving me advice made her uncomfortable, since she'd never gotten or asked for any herself. I knew she'd moved over to the window and was thinking, with enormous, familiar regret, how slowly the traffic below her was moving. "Are you in trouble, Kip?"

From my window, I saw one of Tom's young nephews creep past Blaze's chair and slip into the pool. My staff and their kids hissed at him excitedly to get out of the pool, which was off-limits, but he dunked and came up sputtering, his eyes completely round as he rubbed his hands across his nipples, electrifying himself. Blaze stirred in his chair and smiled. Some muted chaos had taken over.

"I am," I told my mother just before we hung up.

Blaze threw something into the pool then, a shell he'd had in his curled hand as though he'd been waiting for this, and the children dove for it. The commotion and the splashes that landed on his hot face pleased him, but his body seized with pain in retaliation. I thought he might die then, even if he lived for weeks or months, he was so close. Would it be so bad simply to help along the inevitable now? I wondered, for the briefest moment, how it might happen. I could slip him an overdose in a glass of papaya juice, which he would eagerly accept. In the privacy of his cabana, I could cover his face with a damp towel and look away. But I'd heard the body struggled violently on its own at the end — a thought that made me sick to my stomach — and who was I to hold this man down?

As I drove Sanjiv into town one morning, he told me that he owned a chain of twelve shoe stores in New Jersey and had at least one relative working in every shop. Earlier he had asked if he could use the kitchen that night — a meal for Henry was what he had in mind

— and if I'd show him where he could buy some of the ingredients he needed.

"Full compliance with your requirements and schedule," he had said formally, meaning that this was to take place after the regular dinner for the few other guests and that he would pay for everything. He'd toured the kitchen, walking regally among the staff with their tilted stares and white aprons, found it missing what he needed, hiked up his perfectly pressed black linen shorts, and given me a broad smile.

I parked the car off the main street, pointed out a few places he might try — though the town was a tourist rip-off and I didn't think he'd have much luck — and told him I'd meet him in the bar across from the post office. I hadn't been in Sportsman's in months, since before the season began. The place was empty, and I sat at the bar. I made conversation with Louis, the owner, whom I'd known for years, a guy who had come to the island after college and never left. Occasionally he'd show up for dinner at my place with one of his girlfriends and drive home drunk, his hand probably already between her legs.

"Hey, I hear you have some weird shit happening over at your place," Louis said in a conspiratorial whisper, though nothing on the island was secret. "Business sucks and you got all these Indians, for one thing. And a guy died?"

"Not that I know of," I said.

"That's not what I heard." Louis looked up at the planked ceiling, fingered a faded shell necklace around his neck. His face was wrinkled and a little vexed. I wondered if all of us island boys seemed alike, boyish and stunted. We were single and childless and might always be. "He died in the pool or something, right?"

Sanjiv walked in just then and put his heavy plastic bags down by the door as if they contained the most fragile flowers. He removed a thin, honey-colored wallet from his back pocket, placed it on the bar, and sat down next to me. It was unusually hot in town that day, and Sanjiv drank his beer in several gulps. He ordered another one, which he rested between his large hands, tapping the glass with his rings.

"Much better," Sanjiv said. "Now we can talk, Mr. Thierry."

"Find what you were looking for?" I asked.

"Surprisingly, yes. Completely successful." He named a few stores.

"And I poked around the video shop here as well, to see what's what in a place like this. Large porno selection, one might be surprised to know."

"It can get pretty quiet around here," I said, and Louis smirked. "Long hot winters. Long hot summers, long hot in-betweens."

Sanjiv considered this, sipped his beer slowly, and smiled condescendingly at Louis, who got the hint and backed away. "I will have to tell Henry he is well represented. It will give him great pleasure to know that he has reached even such a place as this."

"Blaze is into porno?"

"Well, he imports it, of course. You have to these days to make any money. It is a small part of his business, in fact, but a most lucrative one. He doesn't approve of the stuff."

"Art films, he told me, epics, that sort of thing," I said. "Blockbusters. *The Eighth Moon.*"

"You know that one? Ah, Henry. He's a deal maker, an orchestrator. I am aware of all his business dealings." Sanjiv laughed. His accent was subtle and covered his words in silk. "You wouldn't think Mrs. Blaze would approve either, would you. And she doesn't, of course." He turned to face me and winked. "She pretends not to know — that and other things. It is a complicated thing, very sad, all of this, AIDS now. We have been lovers, Henry and I, for many years."

We turned back to our beers for a minute, and I felt an enormous pressure to say something, my own confession. "He wants me to help him die. He said he'd bring you here in return."

"Yes, I know that. Henry keeps a promise." Sanjiv nodded, his eyes tearing. "We're all here now to say goodbye. He doesn't look good, I agree, and I imagine he will die on this island." He took a sip of his beer. "Henry has told me about you, Mr. Thierry, that he has known you since you were a little boy, and now he will save your island for you. You're a fine businessman, a proprietor, and this is a wonderful place; you'll make a good decision about things," he said knowingly.

"Jesus, killing a man is not a business deal," I said angrily.

Sanjiv shook his head. "No, of course it isn't. It was never meant to be. I love him very much, and I will be sad to see him go, but sometimes this is right. You know, I will be sadder to have him dead in the end."

*

That evening I was drawn to watch Sanjiv at work in the kitchen. Easily frustrated, he was also surprisingly awkward as he cooked, bending from the hips as though his back hurt him. The blade of the knife bit into his skin too often; he squinted unhappily at the chaos of chopped onions. His white shirt was stained, and the heft of the pans turned his wrists. When he rolled up his sleeves, I noticed that he wore a black bracelet like Blaze's, which circled tightly against his bone.

I was not used to the thick aromas and yellow scents that rose from the pots, nor were the greengaw birds loitering around the open back door, who stopped their night singing as if another hurricane were whistling toward them. Steam pulsed from the food Sanjiv and I brought out to the dining room, where Blaze, his wife, and his friends were seated around several tables pushed together. They had lit a dozen candles. The few other guests watched from their tables, where they were drinking and bored. The windows fogged up, and someone jumped to turn on the ceiling fan. A tape player, stashed under the table, hummed unfamiliar music softly.

I hadn't been invited to eat, and I had no appetite, but I saw that a place had been left at the table; they waited for me to sit down. The food was startling, and women piled it on my plate. Sweat collected under my eyes. Blaze forced small forkfuls into his mouth and chewed slowly. Every few minutes a toast would be made to him, stories of his generosity, affection, and humor. He stared at me as these testaments linked us closer together with expectation. A heavy silence fell over this farewell dinner. Some of my staff, usually long gone by that hour, smoked cigarettes on the patio and watched me. Something has happened to Kip Thierry, who sat down to eat with these lighter-dark people, they would report. I was under an island spell that had left me confused and could not be good. Nothing would ever be the same after this.

"Now we should thank our host," Blaze said, speaking for the first time that night and turning to Sanjiv.

"We appreciate your finest hospitality, Mr. Thierry." Sanjiv raised his can of Coke. "And we have made Henry the promise that we will be back next year. We will bring our families, if you will have us."

"What do you think, Sanjiv?" Blaze said. He stared at me, not unkindly. "Is a man in his position going to say no to a deal like that?"

A shadow moved behind Blaze in the darkest part of the room.

My throat slammed shut, and the shadow passed behind me like a pressing heat across my shoulders. Blaze extracted something from his mouth. Sanjiv wiped his forehead and watched him with a left-ward slide of his eyes. Two women whispered like rustling leaves. Cecelia's eyes darted. They were waiting for me to speak, but I couldn't. I thought I might fall over then, my head cleave like a melon on the table.

"Ah, it's all right," Blaze said sweetly, and raised a thin arm over the table. "Are you looking for someone?"

I thought he might help *me* now, when I could barely breathe. But he was talking to a little boy who had wandered into the room looking for his father and stood frozen, terrified by the sight of Blaze in the candlelight.

I was up earlier than anyone else the next morning, and wandered around my island, drawn finally to the path that led to the Blazes'. At the turn of the bluff, I looked up at their cabana, which had taken a particularly hard beating in the hurricane. I'd rebuilt the pointed roof overhang myself out of aged purple heartwood, which now gleamed with its oily veins. But some angles, I realized that morning, would never be fully realigned, and hints of splinter and tarnish were visible everywhere. Up on the stone terrace, I looked into the cabana and saw the single sleeping, sheeted form of Cecelia, her blond hair fanned youthfully across the pillow. At my back, the wind had picked up slightly and blew the smell of salt and the sound of Sanjiv's liquid voice up the island.

When I looked down to the pool that eddied between the two fist-shaped rock outcroppings, even more perfectly visible from this height, the shaded light was green at that hour. The water was clear down to the sand, the slow-moving parrotfish, and Sanjiv, who held Blaze in his arms like a baby just above the surface. Sanjiv said something just before he leaned down. I knew that he would drown Blaze then — and wasn't that right for these lovers? — and I would be spared. I wouldn't stop it. Sanjiv kissed Blaze on the mouth and I waited. The currents rocked them, but still Sanjiv wouldn't let Blaze go. I knew at that moment he couldn't do it; he was waiting for me.

By the time I made it down to the eddying pool, I had no idea how long Blaze had been in the water. His skin was a puckered grayish white, and he looked as bad as a person can look and still be alive. There would be no startling transformation when he died, just the relief of pain and the boredom of this. To end it now would be a mercy. Sanjiv placed Blaze, chilled and practically weightless, in my arms. Blaze didn't open his eyes, and there was no struggle as I lowered him and pulled away my hands. His body darkened the water below the surface and warmed it.

Later I watched the island police prepare to take Blaze's body away. Sanjiv had his arm around Cecelia, who told him she had felt a pinch behind her ear earlier, when she was in bed. She wanted to know if he thought it had occurred at the same moment Henry died. Sanjiv said yes, it seemed they were connected that way.

Tell me what happened, an island authority said to me.

What had I seen? Two men swimming in a dangerous spot, so I'd gone to help them. I told the authority, whom I'd known since childhood, that Blaze was sick and weak. Sanjiv watched me as though I understood everything now; I had offered my island, and an act of love is no crime. So I said that Henry had drowned, and he seemed to understand the power of the currents when I showed him the exact spot where it had happened.

SHEILA KOHLER

Africans

FROM STORY

MOTHER PREFERRED Zulu servants. She said they had been disciplined warriors. They were obedient, conscientious, and fiercely loyal. Their society was built on loyalty. They had had great, autocratic rulers who were astute military strategists and who conquered much territory in a series of bloody wars. There was Dingane. There was Dingiswayo. There was the cruel Shaka, who armed his men with short stabbing spears and made them walk barefoot for greater speed and mobility. He taught them new military tactics and obliged them to remain celibate until they were forty. He ordered his impis to walk off a cliff to prove their loyalty. They were our Prussians, Mother said.

Mother preferred the men to the women because, she said, they worked even harder, did not fall pregnant, did not indulge in unnecessary chatter, and did not hesitate to perform whatever was asked of them. They rose before dawn to brush the carpets, to polish the silver and the floors, piling all the furniture in the middle of the room. They scrubbed the kitchen floor on their knees.

When they served at table, they dressed in starched white jackets and trousers, which rustled as they floated quietly and efficiently about in soft sand-shoes. Red sashes ran slantwise across their chests from shoulder to waist and ended in tassels that dangled on their hips like decorations of valor. They wore white gloves and tapped an opener against the bottle to ask us what we would like to drink.

The Zulu my sister and I loved best was John Mazaboko. He called my sister Mk-Mk-Mkatie because of the initials on her silver christening bowl, which he polished almost into oblivion. Whenever he saw her, he would chuckle as though they shared some secret understanding. We followed him around the house and watched him as he polished the floors and the furniture and the shoes, even the soles of the shoes.

He was unusually tall, and so strong he was able to catch the ancient armoire when it fell forward and almost crushed my sister as a small child. But his hands were gentle. Mother said he could not bear to hear us cry when we were babies and would beg the severe Scottish nanny to allow him to hold us in his arms.

He taught us how to ride bicycles and ran down the bank beside my sister under the flamboyants, waving the dishcloth at her and shouting, *"Khale, khale,* Mkatie," warning her to watch out as she wobbled along.

He told us stories about the Tokolosh, the evil spirit who lived in the fish pond at the bottom of the garden. He told us all the jacarandas in the garden were good except for the last one on the left, which was bad. We never went near it.

He was the one my sister called when she accidentally stepped on her beloved little budgerigar, a small, brightly colored parrot, which lay flapping its broken wings on the floor. He took its pulsing neck between his fingers and wrung it swiftly. "Better like this," he told her.

He brought us freshly squeezed orange juice in the early mornings, entering the nursery with a tray and the newspaper for the nanny, drawing back the lined curtains to let light into the room and wishing us a good morning with a grave *Sawubona.*

Once, the Scottish nanny, a diminutive woman, known as a "white nanny" to distinguish her from the black ones, summoned him to clean the inside of a malodorous cupboard. Wrinkling her nose, she said, "It smells Zulu." He bent down from his great height onto his hands and knees and scrubbed the closet clean.

After our father's death, our mother withdrew, closed many of the rooms in the house, draped the furniture with sheets, and gradually fired all the other servants. Even the Scottish nanny was fired, for stealing Mother's knitting needles and hiding them under her mattress so that Mother would not find them. The nanny slammed the door behind her and mumbled, "These children would be better off in an orphanage." Only John remained.

It was South Africa in the forties, and he was looking after two little girls and their mother. He seemed sad. "He's not too pleased," Mother told us. "He's actually a bit of a snob, you know."

Sometimes when we came indoors we would find Mother slumped on the sofa, food trickling down her chiffon dress, a cigarette burning her fingers, an empty glass on the floor. We would call John, and he would carry her to bed.

I can see him, in a brief moment of reprieve, leaning against the whitewashed wall of the empty servants' quarters, smoking his pipe in the sun. My sister sits beside him on the red earth.

I remember my sister running into him in the narrow corridor after emerging from her bath. A slip of a girl despite all the food she consumed, she was totally naked. John lifted his eyes to the ceiling and gasped in horror.

For some years we did not see John except during the holidays. Mother sent my sister and me to a boarding school run along the lines of an English school from the last century; we wore green tunics measured four inches above the knee; we read nineteenth-century authors and studied history that stopped before the First World War, which was considered too recent to be taught objectively. We slept in long dormitories, the little ones crying out for their mothers. My sister dreamed that she had passed John on the stairs without knowing who he was.

We were kept busy. We spent most of our time after class doing sport to combat sexual urges, and to learn team spirit. My sister, who was tall and athletic, won prizes. But ambition was not considered seemly for Christian girls. We were taught meekness — for the meek would inherit the earth — as well as obedience, diligence, and, like the Zulus, loyalty. As our headmistress pointed out, most of us were destined to be mothers and wives.

When my sister first told me about her decision to marry, I was living overseas with my husband and home just for a visit. It was raining hard that afternoon and hailing, as it does so often out there, and we could hear the hailstones beating against the long windows. We were in the big kitchen with the pull-out bins where the flour and the meal were kept, near the small, dark pantry where the big sacks of oranges were stored. There was the familiar smell of wet coal from John's fire in the courtyard. The room was dimly lit, and John, as usual, was polishing the silver with a toothbrush. His head was bent, and he whistled softly as he worked, the newspaper spread before him. He lifted his head and tilted it with interest, listening to us.

"Who is he?" I asked.

"A doctor, a heart surgeon," my sister said.

"You said you wanted to be a doctor, Mkatie," John reminded her, and chuckled.

My sister hesitated. "He's an Afrikaner. You can imagine how much Mother likes that." She paced back and forth restlessly. Lightning lit up the room. "She's dead set against the match, thinks the family is *common,* and keeps talking about his mother being *too broad in the beam.* Some old girlfriend of my fiancé's called Mother and begged her not to let me marry him."

John waved the toothbrush at my sister as he had the dishcloth when she wobbled down the bank on her bicycle for the first time. "What did this woman say?" he asked.

"She just kept saying, *Please don't let her marry him.*" My sister went on, "He's really very handsome and clever. Passed his matric at sixteen. Did all his studies on scholarship. Father does something on the railways. Doesn't have any money."

"What is he like?" I asked her.

"Frank, brutally frank. It's refreshing. Do you know what I mean?" I nodded my head, and John stared down at the toothbrush in his hand.

At the wedding my sister stood in her white dress, the handsome groom and all the bridesmaids and flower girls at her side on the stone steps of the church. Naturally, John was not with them.

My sister said, "Thank goodness Mother has let me have John."

"What did he say?"

"I didn't even ask him. I can't imagine starting up housekeeping, or life, for that matter, without him. I don't know how you do without help. Mother will move to the cottage, and he will stay with us in the big house."

The next time I visited my sister, John greeted us in the driveway of the house. "*Nkosazana,*" he said, addressing my daughter with the Zulu title of honor and bowing his head, holding her hand.

My sister told me that something had happened. We were enjoying the December weather. The garden was green and filled with flowers: blue and white agapanthus grew by the pool, and the jacarandas were in bloom again. We were wearing our swimsuits and sun hats, rocking back and forth on the swing seat and sipping lemonade, the ice melting in our glasses. The shifting light from the water shimmered in the feathery leaves of the acacia tree. My sister paused, forcing me to pay attention.

"Go on. So what was it?" I said.

She had given a party for her husband's family, inviting all the brothers and sisters, uncles and aunts, and their friends. She had done the flowers, great bowls of arum lilies and peonies, and ordered champagne. John had roasted chickens, baked gem squash and apple pies. He had laid them out on the trestle table on the veranda, next to the bottles of champagne, which were lined up like soldiers on a field of damask. He was wearing his starched white uniform and the red sash with the tassel.

In the middle of it all, my sister noticed that her husband was not in the crowded room, so she went looking for him.

Her husband had seemed short-tempered that evening, as he often did, saying it was because of fatigue from the long hours in the operating room, or because of my sister's careless housekeeping. He insisted that she be at home every day for lunch and complained that there was no discipline in the house. They had argued over the state of his white linen pants. John had not pressed them properly, her husband claimed.

Now she could not find him.

It was a particularly fine night, the air warm, the sky wild with stars. She burst into his study, where she discovered him on the floor, embracing another man.

"It was such a terrible shock. His whole family was there, all of our friends. What could I do?" my sister asked me.

"Screamed," I said. "Kicked them in the balls. Turned them out of the house. Made a scandal!"

"But I couldn't, you see. He would have been ruined, struck off the doctor rolls."

My sister's husband made their boy exercise in the morning to keep slim. He had him do sit-ups and scrub his fair skin with a loofah in the bath. When the boy brought his friends home to play, his father followed them into the changing rooms by the swimming pool and stared at them and touched them. The boy grew silent and sullen.

My sister asked, "Will you go to the lawyer for me? I can't. He follows me. He will find me anywhere. I am afraid of what he will do."

"Sorrow seems incongruous here," my sister said to me as John brought us a cup of tea in the garden. It was late afternoon, and I was visiting again. All those visits, year after year, have run into one another. Only certain moments remain clear in my mind. By then my sister was keeping the shutters down and sleeping for hours in the afternoons. We could hear the flapping of wings, the cry of the swallows. Someone was singing in the bamboo. It was spring and already hot out there. The three of us, she, John, and I, strolled down into the cool of the garden together and sat in the shade of the flamboyants, where John had taught us to ride our bicycles.

He had grown thinner over the years, his face more gaunt, as though he had turned inward and was bent on polishing himself into oblivion. Life in that house had worn away at his spirit. His eyes had lost that glimmer of humor when he looked at my sister.

Now he sat beside us in his impeccable khaki trousers and shirt. Big, bulbous clouds floated across the sky. He looked at my sister and said, "Mkatie, you are not eating enough, I keep telling you. You don't listen to me anymore. You are losing too much weight."

"How can I eat?" she said. She told us she had awakened one night and found her husband digging up the rose garden outside Mother's cottage in order to plant cabbages. He had thrown a glass at her, cutting her lip, the blood streaming down her chin.

Shortly afterward, my sister left for Rome and Istanbul. She wrote to me that she had met someone there. "He was at the airport, and I watched him stride across the runway. He looks like a David, Donatello's and Michelangelo's."

When my sister arrived back home, her husband found a letter from the Turkish lover and cut his wrists and lay at the bottom of the stairs and called John and all the children to come and watch him die. John clucked his tongue and shook his head and did what he was asked to do. All the children stood in a hushed circle with John at the bottom of the stairs and watched the blood running down their father's hands. My sister found them, unmoving, the light behind them, "like a chorus of angels in some medieval painting," she wrote. They rushed her husband to a clinic, where he recuperated, and he came home to fly into rages if anyone spoke of Turkish delight.

He beat the children with a belt, especially the boy, broke his bones. He beat the eldest girl unconscious. My sister did not submit to his beating her or the children without a fight. She was stronger than he when she was angry, grabbing his hair and biting, kicking his shins.

Once she had him at her mercy. He shouted for the servant. "John, help me," he screamed.

They were in her bedroom, the long windows open onto the lawn.

"Yes, *Baas*." John came as usual, swiftly and silently, looming in the doorway, watching my sister hold her husband, his arms pinned.

"What are you standing there for, help me, for God's sake," his master cried.

John did not move.

"Do what I tell you. Put her on the bed."

John grasped my sister and held her down. At first she struggled, called out to him, "What are you doing!" But when he did not reply and she saw no glimmer of response in his eyes, she gave up.

I imagine her lying on the blue silk counterpane, her face swollen as if she has soaked up water. All the delicate colors have run. She can hear the cries of children, see the sprinkler turning, a rainbow in the spray. Her hair blows across her pale forehead, a flush spreads over her cheeks like a stain. There is a scar on her lower lip. Her small chin trembles. Her eyes are round and strained, shaded by thick lashes, awash with tears, and as soft a blue as the silk beneath her. She looks up and sees the faces bending over her, a blur of black and white.

The white *baas* takes off his belt and beats her across her legs, her breasts, her face.

JHUMPA LAHIRI

Interpreter of Maladies

FROM AGNI REVIEW

AT THE TEA STALL Mr. and Mrs. Das bickered about who should take Tina to the toilet. Eventually Mrs. Das relented when Mr. Das pointed out that he had given the girl her bath the night before. In the rearview mirror Mr. Kapasi watched as Mrs. Das emerged slowly from his bulky white Ambassador, dragging her shaved, largely bare legs across the back seat. She did not hold the little girl's hand as they walked to the restroom.

They were on their way to see the Sun Temple at Konarak. It was a dry, bright Saturday, the mid-July heat tempered by a steady ocean breeze, ideal weather for sightseeing. Ordinarily Mr. Kapasi would not have stopped so soon along the way, but less than five minutes after he'd picked up the family that morning in front of Hotel Sandy Villa, the little girl had complained. The first thing Mr. Kapasi had noticed when he saw Mr. and Mrs. Das, standing with their children under the portico of the hotel, was that they were very young, perhaps not even thirty. In addition to Tina they had two boys, Ronny and Bobby, who appeared very close in age and had teeth covered in a network of flashing silver wires. The family looked Indian but dressed as foreigners did, the children in stiff, brightly colored clothing and caps with translucent visors. Mr. Kapasi was accustomed to foreign tourists; he was assigned to them regularly because he could speak English. Yesterday he had driven an elderly couple from Scotland, both with spotted faces and fluffy white hair so thin it exposed their sunburnt scalps. In comparison, the tanned, youthful faces of Mr. and Mrs. Das were all the more striking. When he'd introduced himself, Mr. Kapasi had pressed his palms together in greeting, but Mr. Das squeezed hands like an

American so that Mr. Kapasi felt it in his elbow. Mrs. Das, for her part, had flexed one side of her mouth, smiling dutifully at Mr. Kapasi without displaying any interest in him.

As they waited at the tea stall, Ronny, who looked like the older of the two boys, clambered suddenly out of the back seat, intrigued by a goat tied to a stake in the ground.

"Don't touch it," Mr. Das said. He glanced up from his paperback tour book, which said "INDIA" in yellow letters and looked as if it had been published abroad. His voice, somehow tentative and a little shrill, sounded as though it had not yet settled into maturity.

"I want to give it a piece of gum," the boy called back as he trotted ahead.

Mr. Das stepped out of the car and stretched his legs by squatting briefly to the ground. A clean-shaven man, he looked exactly like a magnified version of Ronny. He had a sapphire-blue visor and was dressed in shorts, sneakers, and a T-shirt. The camera slung around his neck, with an impressive telephoto lens and numerous buttons and markings, was the only complicated thing he wore. He frowned, watching as Ronny rushed toward the goat, but appeared to have no intention of intervening. "Bobby, make sure that your brother doesn't do anything stupid."

"I don't feel like it," Bobby said, not moving. He was sitting in the front seat beside Mr. Kapasi, studying a picture of the elephant god taped to the glove compartment.

"No need to worry," Mr. Kapasi said. "They are quite tame." Mr. Kapasi was forty-six years old, with receding hair that had gone completely silver, but his butterscotch complexion and his unlined brow, which he treated in spare moments to dabs of lotus-oil balm, made it easy to imagine what he must have looked like at an earlier age. He wore gray trousers and a matching jacket-style shirt, tapered at the waist, with short sleeves and a large pointed collar, made of a thin but durable synthetic material. He had specified both the cut and the fabric to his tailor — it was his preferred uniform for giving tours because it did not get crushed during his long hours behind the wheel. Through the windshield he watched as Ronny circled around the goat, touched it quickly on its side, then trotted back to the car.

"You left India as a child?" Mr. Kapasi asked when Mr. Das had settled once again into the passenger seat.

"Oh, Mina and I were both born in America," Mr. Das announced with an air of sudden confidence. "Born and raised. Our parents live here now, in Assansol. They retired. We visit them every couple years." He turned to watch as the little girl ran toward the car, the wide purple bows of her sundress flopping on her narrow brown shoulders. She was holding to her chest a doll with yellow hair that looked as if it had been chopped, as a punitive measure, with a pair of dull scissors. "This is Tina's first trip to India, isn't it, Tina?"

"I don't have to go to the bathroom anymore," Tina announced.

"Where's Mina?" Mr. Das asked.

Mr. Kapasi found it strange that Mr. Das should refer to his wife by her first name when speaking to the little girl. Tina pointed to where Mrs. Das was purchasing something from one of the shirtless men who worked at the tea stall. Mr. Kapasi heard one of the shirtless men sing a phrase from a popular Hindi love song as Mrs. Das walked back to the car, but she did not appear to understand the words of the song, for she did not express irritation, or embarrassment, or react in any other way to the man's declarations.

He observed her. She wore a red-and-white-checkered skirt that stopped above her knees, slip-on shoes with square wooden heels, and a close-fitting blouse styled like a man's undershirt. The blouse was decorated at chest level with a calico appliqué in the shape of a strawberry. She was a short woman, with small hands like paws, her frosty pink fingernails painted to match her lips, and was slightly plump in her figure. Her hair, shorn only a little longer than her husband's, was parted far to one side. She was wearing large dark brown sunglasses with a pinkish tint to them, and carried a big straw bag, almost as big as her torso, shaped like a bowl, with a water bottle poking out of it. She walked slowly, carrying some puffed rice tossed with peanuts and chili peppers in a large packet made from newspapers. Mr. Kapasi turned to Mr. Das.

"Where in America do you live?"

"New Brunswick, New Jersey."

"Next to New York?"

"Exactly. I teach middle school there."

"What subject?"

"Science. In fact, every year I take my students on a trip to the Museum of Natural History in New York City. In a way we have a lot in common, you could say, you and I. How long have you been a tour guide, Mr. Kapasi?"

"Five years."

Mrs. Das reached the car. "How long's the trip?" she asked, shutting the door.

"About two and a half hours," Mr. Kapasi replied.

At this Mrs. Das gave an impatient sigh, as if she had been traveling her whole life without pause. She fanned herself with a folded Bombay film magazine written in English.

"I thought that the Sun Temple is only eighteen miles north of Puri," Mr. Das said, tapping on the tour book.

"The roads to Konarak are poor. Actually it is a distance of fifty-two miles," Mr. Kapasi explained.

Mr. Das nodded, readjusting the camera strap where it had begun to chafe the back of his neck.

Before starting the ignition, Mr. Kapasi reached back to make sure the cranklike locks on the inside of each of the back doors were secured. As soon as the car began to move the little girl began to play with the lock on her side, clicking it with some effort forward and backward, but Mrs. Das said nothing to stop her. She sat a bit slouched at one end of the back seat, not offering her puffed rice to anyone. Ronny and Tina sat on either side of her, both snapping bright green gum.

"Look," Bobby said as the car began to gather speed. He pointed with his finger to the tall trees that lined the road. "Look."

"Monkeys!" Ronny shrieked. "Wow!"

They were seated in groups along the branches, with shining black faces, silver bodies, horizontal eyebrows, and crested heads. Their long gray tails dangled like a series of ropes among the leaves. A few scratched themselves with black leathery hands, or swung their feet, staring as the car passed.

"We call them the hanuman," Mr. Kapasi said. "They are quite common in the area."

As soon as he spoke, one of the monkeys leaped into the middle of the road, causing Mr. Kapasi to brake suddenly. Another bounced onto the hood of the car, then sprang away. Mr. Kapasi beeped his horn. The children began to get excited, sucking in their breath and covering their faces partly with their hands. They had never seen monkeys outside of a zoo, Mr. Das explained. He asked Mr. Kapasi to stop the car so that he could take a picture.

While Mr. Das adjusted his telephoto lens, Mrs. Das reached into her straw bag and pulled out a bottle of colorless nail polish, which she proceeded to stroke on the tip of her index finger.

The little girl stuck out a hand. "Mine too. Mommy, do mine too."

"Leave me alone," Mrs. Das said, blowing on her nail and turning her body slightly. "You're making me mess up."

The little girl occupied herself by buttoning and unbuttoning a pinafore on the doll's plastic body.

"All set," Mr. Das said, replacing the lens cap.

The car rattled considerably as it raced along the dusty road, causing them all to pop up from their seats every now and then, but Mrs. Das continued to polish her nails. Mr. Kapasi eased up on the accelerator, hoping to produce a smoother ride. When he reached for the gearshift the boy in front accommodated him by swinging his hairless knees out of the way. Mr. Kapasi noted that this boy was slightly paler than the other children. "Daddy, why is the driver sitting on the wrong side in this car too?" the boy asked.

"They all do that here, dummy," Ronny said.

"Don't call your brother a dummy," Mr. Das said. He turned to Mr. Kapasi. "In America, you know . . . it confuses them."

"Oh yes, I am well aware," Mr. Kapasi said. As delicately as he could, he shifted gears again, accelerating as they approached a hill in the road. "I see it on *Dallas*, the steering wheels are on the left-hand side."

"What's *Dallas*?" Tina asked, banging her now naked doll on the seat behind Mr. Kapasi.

"It went off the air," Mr. Das explained. "It's a television show."

They were all like siblings, Mr. Kapasi thought as they passed a row of date trees. Mr. and Mrs. Das behaved like an older brother and sister, not parents. It seemed that they were in charge of the children only for the day; it was hard to believe they were regularly responsible for anything other than themselves. Mr. Das tapped on his lens cap and his tour book, dragging his thumbnail occasionally across the pages so that they made a scraping sound. Mrs. Das continued to polish her nails. She had still not removed her sunglasses. Every now and then Tina renewed her plea that she wanted her nails done too, and so at one point Mrs. Das flicked a drop of polish on the little girl's finger before depositing the bottle back inside her straw bag.

"Isn't this an air-conditioned car?" she asked, still blowing on her hand. The window on Tina's side was broken and could not be rolled down.

"Quit complaining," Mr. Das said. "It isn't so hot."

"I told you to get a car with air conditioning," Mrs. Das continued. "Why do you do this, Raj, just to save a few stupid rupees? What are you saving us, fifty cents?"

Their accents sounded just like the ones Mr. Kapasi heard on American television programs, though not like the ones on *Dallas*.

"Doesn't it get tiresome, Mr. Kapasi, showing people the same thing every day?" Mr. Das asked, rolling down his own window all the way. "Hey, do you mind stopping the car? I just want to get a shot of this guy."

Mr. Kapasi pulled over to the side of the road as Mr. Das took a picture of a barefoot man, his head wrapped in a dirty turban, seated on top of a cart of grain sacks pulled by a pair of bullocks. Both the man and the bullocks were emaciated. In the back seat Mrs. Das gazed out another window at the sky, where nearly transparent clouds passed quickly in front of one another.

"I look forward to it, actually," Mr. Kapasi said as they continued on their way. "The Sun Temple is one of my favorite places. In that way it is a reward for me. I give tours on Fridays and Saturdays only. I have another job during the week."

"Oh? Where?" Mr. Das asked.

"I work in a doctor's office."

"You're a doctor?"

"I am not a doctor. I work with one. As an interpreter."

"What does a doctor need an interpreter for?"

"He has a number of Gujarati patients. My father was Gujarati, but many people do not speak Gujarati in this area, including the doctor. And so the doctor asked me to work in his office, interpreting what the patients say."

"Interesting. I've never heard of anything like that," Mr. Das said.

Mr. Kapasi shrugged. "It is a job like any other."

"But so romantic," Mrs. Das said dreamily, breaking her extended silence. She lifted her pinkish brown sunglasses and arranged them on top of her head like a tiara. For the first time, her eyes met Mr. Kapasi's in the rearview mirror: pale, a bit small, their gaze fixed but drowsy.

Mr. Das craned to look at her. "What's so romantic about it?"

"I don't know. Something." She shrugged, knitting her brows together for an instant. "Would you like a piece of gum, Mr. Kapasi?" she asked brightly. She reached into her straw bag and handed him a small square wrapped in green-and-white-striped paper. As soon as Mr. Kapasi put the gum in his mouth a thick sweet liquid burst onto his tongue.

"Tell us more about your job, Mr. Kapasi," Mrs. Das said.

"What would you like to know, madam?"

"I don't know." She shrugged again, munching on some puffed rice and licking the mustard oil from the corners of her mouth. "Tell us a typical situation." She settled back in her seat, her head tilted in a patch of sun, and closed her eyes. "I want to picture what happens."

"Very well. The other day a man came in with a pain in his throat."

"Did he smoke cigarettes?"

"No. It was very curious. He complained that he felt as if there were long pieces of straw stuck in his throat. When I told the doctor, he was able to prescribe the proper medication."

"That's so neat."

"Yes," Mr. Kapasi agreed, after some hesitation.

"So these patients are totally dependent on you," Mrs. Das said. She spoke slowly, as if she were thinking aloud. "In a way, more dependent on you than the doctor."

"How do you mean? How could it be?"

"Well, for example, you could tell the doctor that the pain felt like a burning, not straw. The patient would never know what you had told the doctor, and the doctor wouldn't know that you had told the wrong thing. It's a big responsibility."

"Yes, a big responsibility you have there, Mr. Kapasi," Mr. Das agreed.

Mr. Kapasi had never thought of his job in such complimentary terms. To him it was a thankless occupation. He found nothing noble in interpreting people's maladies, assiduously translating the symptoms of so many swollen bones, countless cramps of bellies and bowels, spots on people's palms that changed color, shape, or size. The doctor, nearly half his age, had an affinity for bell-bottom trousers and made humorless jokes about the Congress party. Together they worked in a stale little infirmary where Mr. Kapasi's smartly tailored clothes clung to him in the heat, in spite of the blackened blades of a ceiling fan churning over their heads.

The job was a sign of his failings. In his youth he'd been a devoted scholar of foreign languages, the owner of an impressive collection of dictionaries. He had dreamed of being an interpreter for diplomats and dignitaries, resolving conflicts between people and nations, settling disputes of which he alone could understand both sides. He was a self-educated man. In a series of notebooks, in the evenings before his parents settled his marriage, he had listed the common etymologies of words, and at one point in his life he was confident that he could converse, if given the opportunity, in English, French, Russian, Portuguese, and Italian, not to mention Hindi, Bengali, Orissi, and Gujarati. Now only a handful of European phrases remained in his memory, scattered words for things like saucers and chairs. English was the only non-Indian language he spoke fluently anymore. Mr. Kapasi knew it was not a remarkable talent. Sometimes he feared that his children knew better English than he did, just from watching television. Still, it came in handy for the tours.

He had taken the job as an interpreter after his first son, at the age of seven, contracted typhoid — that was how he had first made the acquaintance of the doctor. At the time Mr. Kapasi had been teaching English in a grammar school, and he bartered his skills as an interpreter to pay the increasingly exorbitant medical bills. In the end the boy had died one evening in his mother's arms, his limbs burning with fever, but then there was the funeral to pay for, and the other children who were born soon enough, and the newer, bigger house, and the good schools and tutors, and the fine shoes and the television, and the countless other ways he tried to console his wife and to keep her from crying in her sleep, and so when the doctor offered to pay him twice as much as he earned at the grammar school, he accepted. Mr. Kapasi knew that his wife had little regard for his career as an interpreter. He knew it reminded her of the son she'd lost, and that she resented the other lives he helped, in his own small way, to save. If ever she referred to his position, she used the phrase "doctor's assistant," as if the process of interpretation were equal to taking someone's temperature, or changing a bedpan. She never asked him about the patients who came to the doctor's office, or said that his job was a big responsibility.

For this reason it flattered Mr. Kapasi that Mrs. Das was so intrigued by his job. Unlike his wife, she had reminded him of its intellectual challenges. She had also used the word *romantic*. She did not behave in a romantic way toward her husband, and yet she had used the word to describe him. He wondered if Mr. and Mrs. Das were a bad match, just as he and his wife were. Perhaps they too had little in common apart from three children and a decade of their lives. The signs he recognized from his own marriage were there — the bickering, the indifference, the protracted silences. Her sudden interest in him, an interest she did not express in either her husband or her children, was mildly intoxicating. When Mr. Kapasi thought once again about how she had said "romantic," the feeling of intoxication grew.

He began to check his reflection in the rearview mirror as he drove, feeling grateful that he had chosen the gray suit that morning and not the brown one, which tended to sag a little in the knees. From time to time he glanced in the mirror at Mrs. Das. In addition to glancing at her face, he glanced at the strawberry between her breasts and the golden brown hollow in her throat. He decided to tell Mrs. Das about another patient, and another: the young woman who had complained of a sensation of raindrops in her spine, the gentleman whose birthmark had begun to sprout hairs. Mrs. Das listened attentively, stroking her hair with a small plastic brush that resembled an oval bed of nails, asking more questions, for yet another example. The children were quiet, intent on spotting more monkeys in the trees, and Mr. Das was absorbed by his tour book, so it seemed like a private conversation between Mr. Kapasi and Mrs. Das. In this manner the next half hour passed, and when they stopped for lunch at a roadside restaurant that sold fritters and omelette sandwiches, usually something Mr. Kapasi looked forward to on his tours so that he could sit in peace and enjoy some hot tea, he was disappointed. As the Das family settled together under a magenta umbrella fringed with white and orange tassels, and placed their orders with one of the waiters who marched about in tricornered caps, Mr. Kapasi reluctantly headed toward a neighboring table.

"Mr. Kapasi, wait. There's room here," Mrs. Das called out. She gathered Tina onto her lap, insisting that he accompany them. And so together they had bottled mango juice and sandwiches and plates of onions and potatoes deep-fried in graham-flour batter. After finishing two omelette sandwiches, Mr. Das took more pictures of the group as they ate.

"How much longer?" he asked Mr. Kapasi as he paused to load a new roll of film in the camera.

"About half an hour more."

By now the children had gotten up from the table to look at more monkeys perched in a nearby tree, so there was a considerable space between Mrs. Das and Mr. Kapasi. Mr. Das placed the camera to his face and squeezed one eye shut, his tongue exposed at one corner of his mouth. "This looks funny. Mina, you need to lean in closer to Mr. Kapasi."

She did. He could smell a scent on her skin, like a mixture of whiskey and rosewater. He worried suddenly that she could smell his perspiration, which he knew had collected beneath the synthetic material of his shirt. He polished off his mango juice in one gulp and smoothed his silver hair with his hands. A bit of the juice dripped onto his chin. He wondered if Mrs. Das had noticed.

She had not. "What's your address, Mr. Kapasi?" she inquired, fishing for something inside her straw bag.

"You would like my address?"

"So we can send you copies," she said. "Of the pictures." She handed him a scrap of paper which she had hastily ripped from a page of her film magazine. The blank portion was limited, for the narrow strip was crowded by lines of text and a tiny picture of a hero and heroine embracing under a eucalyptus tree.

The paper curled as Mr. Kapasi wrote his address in clear, careful letters. She would write to him, asking about his days interpreting at the doctor's office, and he would respond eloquently, choosing only the most entertaining anecdotes, ones that would make her laugh out loud as she read them in her house in New Jersey. In time she would reveal the disappointment of her marriage, and he his. In this way their friendship would grow, and flourish. He would possess a picture of the two of them, eating fried onions under a magenta umbrella, which he would keep, he decided, safely tucked between the pages of his Russian grammar. As his mind raced, Mr. Kapasi experienced a mild and pleasant shock. It was similar to a feeling he used to experience long ago when, after months of translating with the aid of a dictionary, he would finally read a passage from a French novel, or an Italian sonnet, and understand the words, one after another, unencumbered by his own efforts. In those moments Mr. Kapasi used to believe that all was right with the world, that all struggles were rewarded, that all of life's mistakes made sense in the end. The promise that he would hear from Mrs. Das now filled him with the same belief.

When he finished writing his address Mr. Kapasi handed her the paper, but as soon as he did so he worried that he had either misspelled his name or accidentally reversed the numbers of his postal code. He dreaded the possibility of a lost letter, the photograph never reaching him, hovering somewhere in Orissa, close but ultimately unattainable. He thought of asking for the slip of paper again, just to make sure he had written his address accurately, but Mrs. Das had already dropped it into the jumble of her bag.

They reached Konarak at two-thirty. The temple, made of sandstone, was a massive pyramid-like structure in the shape of a chariot. It was dedicated to the great master of life, the sun, which struck three sides of the edifice as it made its journey each day across the sky. Twenty-four giant wheels were carved on the north and south sides of the plinth. The whole thing was drawn by a team of seven horses, speeding as if through the heavens. As they approached, Mr. Kapasi explained that the temple had been built between A.D. 1243 and 1255, with the efforts of twelve hundred artisans, by the great ruler of the Ganga dynasty, King Narasimhadeva the First, to commemorate his victory against the Muslim army.

"It says the temple occupies about a hundred and seventy acres of land," Mr. Das said, reading from his book.

"It's like a desert," Ronny said, his eyes wandering across the sand that stretched on all sides beyond the temple.

"The Chandrabhaga River once flowed one mile north of here. It is dry now," Mr. Kapasi said, turning off the engine.

They got out and walked toward the temple, posing first for pictures by the pair of lions that flanked the steps. Mr. Kapasi led them next to one of the wheels of the chariot, higher than any human being, nine feet in diameter.

"'The wheels are supposed to symbolize the wheel of life,'" Mr. Das read. "'They depict the cycle of creation, preservation, and achievement of realization.' Cool." He turned the page of his book. "'Each wheel is divided into eight thick and thin spokes, dividing the day into eight equal parts. The rims are carved with designs of birds and animals, whereas the medallions in the spokes are carved with women in luxurious poses, largely erotic in nature.'"

What he referred to were the countless friezes of entwined naked bodies making love in various positions, women clinging to the necks of men, their knees wrapped eternally around their lovers' thighs. In addition to these were assorted scenes from daily life, of hunting and trading, of deer being killed with bows and arrows and marching warriors holding swords in their hands.

It was no longer possible to enter the temple, for it had filled with rubble years ago, but they admired the exterior, as did all the tourists Mr. Kapasi took there, slowly strolling along each of its sides. Mr. Das trailed behind, taking pictures. The children ran ahead, pointing to figures of naked people, intrigued in particular by the Nagamithunas, the half-human, half-serpentine couples who were said, Mr. Kapasi told them, to live in the deepest waters of the sea. Mr. Kapasi was pleased that they liked the temple, pleased especially that it appealed to Mrs. Das. She stopped every three or four paces, staring silently at the carved lovers, and the processions of elephants, and the topless female musicians beating on two-sided drums.

Though Mr. Kapasi had been to the temple countless times, it occurred to him, as he too gazed at the topless women, that he had never seen his own wife fully naked. Even when they had made love she kept the panels of her blouse hooked together, the string of her petticoat knotted around her waist. He had never admired the backs of his wife's legs the way he now admired those of Mrs. Das, walking as if for his benefit alone. He had, of course, seen plenty of bare limbs before, belonging to the American and European ladies who took his tours. But Mrs. Das was different. Unlike the other women, who had an interest only in the temple and kept their noses buried in a guidebook or their eyes behind the lens of a camera, Mrs. Das had taken an interest in him.

Mr. Kapasi was anxious to be alone with her, to continue their private conversation, yet he felt nervous to walk at her side. She was lost behind her sunglasses, ignoring her husband's requests that she pose for another picture, walking past her children as if they were strangers. Worried that he might disturb her, Mr. Kapasi walked ahead, to admire, as he always did, the three life-sized bronze avatars of Surya, the sun god, each emerging from its own niche on the temple façade to greet the sun at dawn, noon, and evening. They wore elaborate headdresses, their languid, elongated eyes closed, their bare chests draped with carved chains and amulets. Hibiscus petals, offerings from previous visitors, were strewn at their gray-green feet. The last statue, on the northern wall of the temple, was Mr. Kapasi's favorite. This Surya had a tired expression, weary after a hard day of work, sitting astride a horse with folded legs. Even his horse's eyes were drowsy. Around his body were smaller sculptures of women in pairs, their hips thrust to one side.

"Who's that?" Mrs. Das asked. He was startled to see that she was standing beside him.

"He is the Astachala-Surya," Mr. Kapasi said. "The setting sun."

"So in a couple of hours the sun will set right here?" She slipped a foot out of one of her square-heeled shoes, rubbed her toes on the back of her other leg.

"That is correct."

She raised her sunglasses for a moment, then put them back on again. "Neat."

Mr. Kapasi was not certain exactly what the word suggested, but he had a feeling it was a favorable response. He hoped that Mrs. Das had understood Surya's beauty, his power. Perhaps they would discuss it further in their letters. He would explain things to her, things about India, and she would explain things to him about America. In its own way this correspondence would fulfill his dream of serving as an interpreter between nations. He looked at her straw bag, delighted that his address lay nestled among its contents. When he pictured her so many thousands of miles away he plummeted, so much so that he had an overwhelming urge to wrap his arms around her, to freeze with her, even for an instant, in an embrace witnessed by his favorite Surya. But Mrs. Das had already started walking.

"When do you return to America?" he asked, trying to sound placid.

"In ten days."

He calculated: a week to settle in, a week to develop the pictures, a few days to compose her letter, two weeks to get to India by air. According to his schedule, allowing room for delays, he would hear from Mrs. Das in approximately six weeks' time.

The family was silent as Mr. Kapasi drove them back, a little past four-thirty, to Hotel Sandy Villa. The children had bought miniature granite versions of the chariot's wheels at a souvenir stand, and they turned them round in their hands. Mr. Das continued to read his book. Mrs. Das untangled Tina's hair with her brush and divided it into two little ponytails.

Mr. Kapasi was beginning to dread the thought of dropping them off. He was not prepared to begin his six-week wait to hear from Mrs. Das. As he stole glances at her in the rearview mirror, wrapping elastic bands around Tina's hair, he wondered how he might make the tour last a little longer. Ordinarily he sped back to Puri using a shortcut, eager to return home, scrub his feet and hands with sandalwood soap, and enjoy the evening newspaper and a cup of tea that his wife would serve him in silence. The thought of that silence, something to which he'd long been resigned, now oppressed him. It was then that he suggested visiting the hills at Udayagiri and Khandagiri, where a number of monastic dwellings were hewn out of the ground, facing one another across a defile. It was some miles away, but well worth seeing, Mr. Kapasi told them.

"Oh yeah, there's something mentioned about it in this book," Mr. Das said. "Built by a Jain king or something."

"Shall we go then?" Mr. Kapasi asked. He paused at a turn in the road. "It's to the left."

Mr. Das turned to look at Mrs. Das. Both of them shrugged.

"Left, left," the children chanted.

Mr. Kapasi turned the wheel, almost delirious with relief. He did not know what he would do or say to Mrs. Das once they arrived at the hills. Perhaps he would tell her what a pleasing smile she had. Perhaps he would compliment her strawberry shirt, which he found irresistibly becoming. Perhaps, when Mr. Das was busy taking a picture, he would take her hand.

He did not have to worry. When they got to the hills, divided by a steep path thick with trees, Mrs. Das refused to get out of the car. All along the path, dozens of monkeys were seated on stones, as well as on the branches of the trees. Their hind legs were stretched out in front and raised to shoulder level, their arms resting on their knees.

"My legs are tired," she said, sinking low in her seat. "I'll stay here."

"Why did you have to wear those stupid shoes?" Mr. Das said. "You won't be in the pictures."

"Pretend I'm there."

"But we could use one of these pictures for our Christmas card this year. We didn't get one of all five of us at the Sun Temple. Mr. Kapasi could take it."

"I'm not coming. Anyway, those monkeys give me the creeps."

"But they're harmless," Mr. Das said. He turned to Mr. Kapasi. "Aren't they?"

"They are more hungry than dangerous," Mr. Kapasi said. "Do not provoke them with food, and they will not bother you."

Mr. Das headed up the defile with the children, the boys at his side, the little girl on his shoulders. Mr. Kapasi watched as they crossed paths with a Japanese man and woman, the only other tourists there, who paused for a final photograph, then stepped into a nearby car and drove away. As the car disappeared out of view some of the monkeys called out, emitting soft whooping sounds, and then walked on their flat black hands and feet up the path. At one point a group of them formed a little ring around Mr. Das and the children. Tina screamed in delight. Ronny ran in circles around his father. Bobby bent down and picked up a fat stick on the ground. When he extended it, one of the monkeys approached him and snatched it, then briefly beat the ground.

"I'll join them," Mr. Kapasi said, unlocking the door on his side. "There is much to explain about the caves."

"No. Stay a minute," Mrs. Das said. She got out of the back seat and slipped in beside Mr. Kapasi. "Raj has his dumb book anyway." Together, through the windshield, Mrs. Das and Mr. Kapasi watched as Bobby and the monkey passed the stick back and forth between them.

"A brave little boy," Mr. Kapasi commented.

"It's not so surprising," Mrs. Das said.

"No?"

"He's not his."

"I beg your pardon?"

"Raj's. He's not Raj's son."

Mr. Kapasi felt a prickle on his skin. He reached into his shirt pocket for the small tin of lotus-oil balm he carried with him at all times, and applied it to three spots on his forehead. He knew that Mrs. Das was watching him, but he did not turn to face her. Instead he watched as the figures of Mr. Das and the children grew smaller, climbing up the steep path, pausing every now and then for a picture, surrounded by a growing number of monkeys.

"Are you surprised?" The way she put it made him choose his words with care.

"It's not the type of thing one assumes," Mr. Kapasi replied slowly. He put the tin of lotus-oil balm back in his pocket.

"No, of course not. And no one knows, of course. No one at all. I've kept it a secret for eight whole years." She looked at Mr. Kapasi, tilting her chin as if to gain a fresh perspective. "But now I've told you."

Mr. Kapasi nodded. He felt suddenly parched, and his forehead was warm and slightly numb from the balm. He considered asking Mrs. Das for a sip of water, then decided against it.

"We met when we were very young," she said. She reached into her straw bag in search of something, then pulled out a packet of puffed rice. "Want some?"

"No, thank you."

She put a fistful in her mouth, sank into the seat a little, and looked away from Mr. Kapasi, out the window on her side of the car. "We married when we were still in college. We were in high school when he proposed. We went to the same college, of course. Back then we couldn't stand the thought of being separated, not for a day, not for a minute. Our parents were best friends who lived in the same town. My entire life I saw him every weekend, either at our house or theirs. We were sent upstairs to play together while our parents joked about our marriage. Imagine! They never caught us at anything, though in a way I think it was all more or less a setup. The things we did those Friday and Saturday nights, while our parents sat downstairs drinking tea . . . I could tell you stories, Mr. Kapasi."

As a result of spending all her time in college with Raj, she continued, she did not make many close friends. There was no one to confide in about him at the end of a difficult day, or to share a passing thought or a worry. Her parents now lived on the other side of the world, but she had never been very close to them anyway. After marrying so young she was overwhelmed by it all, having a child so quickly, and nursing, and warming up bottles of milk and testing their temperature against her wrist while Raj was at work, dressed in sweaters and corduroy pants, teaching his students about rocks and dinosaurs. Raj never looked cross or harried, or plump as she had become after the first baby.

Always tired, she declined invitations from her one or two college girlfriends to have lunch or shop in Manhattan. Eventually the friends stopped calling her, so that she was left at home all day with the baby, surrounded by toys that made her trip when she walked or wince when she sat, always cross and tired. Only occasionally did they go out after Ronny was born, and even more rarely did they entertain. Raj didn't mind; he looked forward to coming home from teaching and watching television and bouncing Ronny on his knee. She had been outraged when Raj told her that a Punjabi friend, someone whom she had once met but did not remember, would be staying with them for a week for some job interviews in the New Brunswick area.

Bobby was conceived in the afternoon, on a sofa littered with rubber teething toys, after the friend learned that a London pharmaceutical company had hired him, while Ronny cried to be freed from his playpen. She made no protest when the friend touched the small of her back as she was about to make a pot of coffee, then pulled her against his crisp navy suit. He made love to her swiftly, in silence, with an expertise she had never known, without the meaningful expressions and smiles Raj always insisted on afterward. The next day Raj drove the friend to JFK. He was married now, to a Punjabi girl, and they lived in London still, and every year they exchanged Christmas cards with Raj and Mina, each couple tucking photos of their families into the envelopes. He did not know that he was Bobby's father. He never would.

"I beg your pardon, Mrs. Das, but why have you told me this information?" Mr. Kapasi asked when she had finally finished speaking and had turned to face him once again.

"For God's sake, stop calling me Mrs. Das. I'm twenty-eight. You probably have children my age."

"Not quite." It disturbed Mr. Kapasi to learn that she thought of him as a parent. The feeling he had had toward her, that had made him check his reflection in the rearview mirror as they drove, evaporated a little.

"I told you, because of your talents." She put the packet of puffed rice back into her bag without folding over the top.

"I don't understand," Mr. Kapasi said.

"Don't you see? For eight years I haven't been able to express this to anybody, not to friends, certainly not to Raj. He doesn't even suspect it. He thinks I'm still in love with him. Well, don't you have anything to say?"

"About what?"

"About what I've just told you. About my secret, and about how terrible it makes me feel. I feel terrible looking at my children, and at Raj, always terrible. I have terrible urges, Mr. Kapasi, to throw things away. One day I had the urge to throw everything I own out the window — the television, the children, everything. Don't you think it's unhealthy?"

He was silent.

"Mr. Kapasi, don't you have anything to say? I thought that was your job."

"My job is to give tours, Mrs. Das."

"Not that. Your other job. As an interpreter."

"But we do not face a language barrier. What need is there for an interpreter?"

"That's not what I mean. I would never have told you otherwise. Don't you realize what it means for me to tell you?"

"What does it mean?"

"It means that I'm tired of feeling so terrible all the time. Eight years, Mr. Kapasi, I've been in pain eight years. I was hoping you could help me feel better, say the right thing. Suggest some kind of remedy."

He looked at her, in her red plaid skirt and strawberry T-shirt, a woman not yet thirty, who loved neither her husband nor her children, who had already fallen out of love with life. Her confession depressed him, depressed him all the more when he thought of Mr. Das at the top of the path, Tina clinging to his shoulders, taking pictures of ancient monastic cells cut into the hills to show his students in America, unsuspecting and unaware that one of his sons was not his own. Mr. Kapasi felt insulted that Mrs. Das should ask him to interpret her common, trivial little secret. She did not resemble the patients in the doctor's office, those who came glassy-eyed and desperate, unable to sleep or breathe or urinate with ease, unable, above all, to give words to their pains. Still, Mr. Kapasi believed it was his duty to assist Mrs. Das. Perhaps he ought to tell her to confess the truth to Mr. Das. He would explain that honesty was the best policy. Honesty, surely, would help her feel better, as she'd put it. Perhaps he would offer to preside over the discussion, as a mediator. He decided to begin with the most obvious question, to get to the heart of the matter, and so he asked, "Is it really pain you feel, Mrs. Das, or is it guilt?"

She turned to him and glared, mustard oil thick on her frosty pink lips. She opened her mouth to say something, but as she glared at Mr. Kapasi some certain knowledge seemed to pass before her eyes, and she stopped. It crushed him; he knew at that moment that he was not even important enough to be properly insulted. She opened the car door and began walking up the path, wobbling a little on her square wooden heels, reaching into her straw bag to eat handfuls of puffed rice. It fell through her fingers, leaving a zigzagging trail, causing a monkey to leap down from a tree and devour the little white grains. In search of more, the monkey began to follow Mrs. Das. Others joined him, so that she was soon being followed by about half a dozen of them, their velvety tails dragging behind.

Mr. Kapasi stepped out of the car. He wanted to holler, to alert her in some way, but he worried that if she knew they were behind her, she would grow nervous. Perhaps she would lose her balance. Perhaps they would pull at her bag or her hair. He began to jog up the path, taking a fallen branch in his hand to scare away the monkeys. Mrs. Das continued walking, oblivious, trailing grains of puffed rice. Near the top of the incline, before a group of cells fronted by a row of squat stone pillars, Mr. Das was kneeling on the ground, focusing the lens of his camera. The children stood under the arcade, now hiding, now emerging from view.

"Wait for me," Mrs. Das called out. "I'm coming."

Tina jumped up and down. "Here comes Mommy!"

"Great," Mr. Das said without looking up. "Just in time. We'll get Mr. Kapasi to take a picture of the five of us."

Mr. Kapasi quickened his pace, waving his branch so that the monkeys scampered away, distracted, in another direction.

"Where's Bobby?" Mrs. Das asked when she stopped.

Mr. Das looked up from the camera. "I don't know. Ronny, where's Bobby?"

Ronny shrugged. "I thought he was right here."

"Where is he?" Mrs. Das repeated sharply. "What's wrong with all of you?"

They began calling his name, wandering up and down the path a bit. Because they were calling, they did not initially hear the boy's screams. When they found him, a little farther down the path under a tree, he was surrounded by a group of monkeys, over a dozen of them, pulling at his T-shirt with their long black fingers. The puffed rice Mrs. Das had spilled was scattered at his feet, raked over by the monkeys' hands. The boy was silent, his body frozen, swift tears running down his startled face. His bare legs were dusty and red with welts from where one of the monkeys struck him repeatedly with the stick he had given to it earlier.

"Daddy, the monkey's hurting Bobby," Tina said.

Mr. Das wiped his palms on the front of his shorts. In his nervousness he accidentally pressed the shutter on his camera; the whirring noise of the advancing film excited the monkeys, and the one with the stick began to beat Bobby more intently. "What are we supposed to do? What if they start attacking?"

"Mr. Kapasi," Mrs. Das shrieked, noticing him standing to one side. "Do something, for God's sake, do something!"

Mr. Kapasi took his branch and shooed them away, hissing at the ones that remained, stomping his feet to scare them. The animals retreated slowly, with a measured gait, obedient but unintimidated. Mr. Kapasi gathered Bobby in his arms and brought him back to where his parents and siblings were standing. As he carried him, he was tempted to whisper a secret into the boy's ear. But Bobby was stunned, and shivering with fright, his legs bleeding slightly where the stick had broken the skin. When Mr. Kapasi delivered him to his parents, Mr. Das brushed some dirt off the boy's T-shirt and put the visor on him the right way. Mrs. Das reached into her straw bag to find a bandage, which she taped over the cut on his knee. Ronny offered his brother a fresh piece of gum. "He's fine. Just a little scared, right, Bobby?" Mr. Das said, patting the top of his head.

"God, let's get out of here," Mrs. Das said. She folded her arms across the strawberry on her chest. "This place gives me the creeps."

"Yeah. Back to the hotel, definitely," Mr. Das agreed.

"Poor Bobby," Mrs. Das said. "Come here a second. Let Mommy fix your hair." Again she reached into her straw bag, this time for her hairbrush, and began to run it around the edges of the translucent visor. When she whipped out the hairbrush, the slip of paper with Mr. Kapasi's address on it fluttered away in the wind. No one but Mr. Kapasi noticed. He watched as it rose, carried higher and higher by the breeze, into the trees where the monkeys now sat, solemnly observing the scene below. Mr. Kapasi observed it too, knowing that this was the picture of the Das family he would preserve forever in his mind.

LORRIE MOORE

Real Estate

FROM THE NEW YORKER

> And yet of course these trinkets are endearing . . .
> — "Glitter and Be Gay"

IT MUST BE, Ruth thought, that she was going to die in the spring. She felt such inexplicable desolation then, such sludge in the heart, felt the season's mockery, all that chartreuse humidity in her throat like a gag. How else to explain such a feeling? She could almost burst — could one burst with joylessness? What she was feeling was too strange, too contrary, too isolated for a mere emotion. It had to be a premonition — one of being finally whisked away after much boring flailing and flapping and the pained, purposeless work that constituted life. And in spring, no less: a premonition of death. A rehearsal. A secretary's call to remind of the appointment.

Of course, it had always been in the spring that she discovered her husband's affairs. But the last one was years ago, and what did she care about all that now? There had been a parade of flings — in the end, they'd made her laugh: Ha! Ha! Ha! Ha! Ha! Ha! Ha! Ha! Ha! Ha! Ha! Ha! Ha! Ha! Ha!

Ha! Ha! Ha! Ha! Ha! Ha! Ha! Ha! Ha! Ha! Ha! Ha!

Ha! Ha! Ha! Ha! Ha! Ha! Ha! Ha! Ha! Ha! Ha! Ha! Ha! Ha! Ha! Ha! Ha! Ha! Ha! Ha! Ha! Ha! Ha! Ha! Ha! Ha! Ha! Ha! Ha! Ha! Ha! Ha! Ha! Ha! Ha! Ha! Ha! Ha! Ha! Ha! Ha! Ha! Ha! Ha! Ha! Ha! Ha! Ha! Ha! Ha! Ha! Ha! Ha! Ha! Ha! Ha! Ha! Ha! Ha! Ha! Ha! Ha! Ha! Ha! Ha! Ha! Ha! Ha! Ha! Ha! Ha! Ha! Ha! Ha! Ha! Ha! Ha! Ha! Ha! Ha! Ha! Ha! Ha! Ha! Ha! Ha! Ha! Ha! Ha! Ha! Ha! Ha! Ha! Ha! Ha! Ha! Ha!

Ha! Ha! Ha! Ha! Ha! Ha! Ha! Ha! Ha! Ha! Ha! Ha! Ha! Ha! Ha!
Ha! Ha! Ha! Ha! Ha! Ha! Ha! Ha! Ha! Ha! Ha! Ha! Ha! Ha! Ha!
Ha! Ha! Ha! Ha! Ha! Ha! Ha! Ha! Ha! Ha! Ha! Ha! Ha! Ha! Ha!
Ha! Ha! Ha! Ha! Ha! Ha! Ha! Ha! Ha! Ha! Ha! Ha! Ha! Ha! Ha!
Ha! Ha! Ha! Ha! Ha! Ha! Ha! Ha! Ha! Ha! Ha! Ha! Ha! Ha! Ha!
Ha! Ha! Ha! Ha! Ha! Ha! Ha! Ha! Ha! Ha! Ha! Ha! Ha! Ha! Ha!
Ha! Ha! Ha! Ha! Ha! Ha! Ha! Ha! Ha! Ha! Ha! Ha! Ha! Ha! Ha!
Ha! Ha! Ha! Ha! Ha! Ha! Ha! Ha! Ha! Ha! Ha! Ha! Ha! Ha! Ha!
Ha! Ha! Ha! Ha! Ha! Ha! Ha! Ha! Ha! Ha! Ha! Ha! Ha! Ha! Ha!
Ha! Ha! Ha! Ha! Ha! Ha! Ha! Ha! Ha! Ha! Ha! Ha! Ha! Ha! Ha!
Ha! Ha! Ha! Ha! Ha! Ha! Ha! Ha! Ha! Ha! Ha! Ha! Ha! Ha! Ha!
Ha! Ha! Ha! Ha! Ha! Ha! Ha! Ha! Ha! Ha! Ha! Ha! Ha! Ha! Ha!
Ha! Ha! Ha! Ha! Ha! Ha! Ha! Ha! Ha! Ha! Ha! Ha! Ha! Ha! Ha!
Ha! Ha! Ha! Ha! Ha! Ha! Ha! Ha! Ha! Ha! Ha! Ha! Ha! Ha! Ha!
Ha! Ha! Ha! Ha! Ha! Ha! Ha! Ha! Ha! Ha! Ha! Ha! Ha! Ha! Ha!
Ha! Ha! Ha! Ha! Ha! Ha! Ha! Ha! Ha! Ha! Ha! Ha! Ha! Ha! Ha!
Ha! Ha! Ha! Ha! Ha! Ha! Ha! Ha! Ha! Ha! Ha! Ha! Ha! Ha! Ha!
Ha! Ha! Ha! Ha! Ha! Ha! Ha! Ha! Ha! Ha! Ha! Ha! Ha! Ha! Ha!
Ha! Ha! Ha! Ha! Ha! Ha! Ha! Ha! Ha! Ha! Ha! Ha! Ha! Ha! Ha!
Ha! Ha! Ha! Ha! Ha! Ha! Ha! Ha! Ha! Ha! Ha! Ha! Ha! Ha! Ha!
Ha! Ha! Ha! Ha! Ha! Ha! Ha! Ha! Ha! Ha! Ha! Ha! Ha! Ha! Ha!
Ha! Ha! Ha! Ha! Ha! Ha! Ha! Ha! Ha! Ha! Ha! Ha! Ha! Ha! Ha!
Ha! Ha! Ha! Ha! Ha! Ha! Ha! Ha! Ha! Ha! Ha! Ha! Ha! Ha! Ha!
Ha! Ha! Ha! Ha! Ha! Ha! Ha! Ha! Ha! Ha! Ha! Ha! Ha! Ha! Ha!
Ha! Ha! Ha! Ha! Ha! Ha! Ha! Ha! Ha! Ha! Ha! Ha! Ha! Ha! Ha!
Ha! Ha! Ha! Ha! Ha! Ha! Ha! Ha! Ha! Ha! Ha! Ha! Ha! Ha! Ha!
Ha! Ha! Ha! Ha! Ha! Ha! Ha! Ha! Ha! Ha! Ha! Ha! Ha! Ha! Ha!
Ha! Ha! Ha! Ha! Ha! Ha! Ha! Ha! Ha! Ha! Ha! Ha! Ha! Ha! Ha!
Ha! Ha! Ha! Ha! Ha! Ha! Ha! Ha! Ha! Ha! Ha! Ha! Ha! Ha! Ha!
Ha! Ha! Ha! Ha! Ha! Ha! Ha! Ha! Ha! Ha! Ha! Ha! Ha! Ha! Ha!
Ha! Ha! Ha! Ha! Ha! Ha! Ha! Ha! Ha! Ha! Ha! Ha! Ha! Ha! Ha!
Ha! Ha! Ha! Ha! Ha! Ha! Ha! Ha! Ha! Ha! Ha! Ha! Ha! Ha! Ha!
Ha! Ha! Ha! Ha! Ha! Ha! Ha! Ha! Ha! Ha! Ha! Ha! Ha! Ha! Ha!
Ha! Ha! Ha! Ha! Ha! Ha! Ha! Ha! Ha! Ha! Ha! Ha! Ha! Ha! Ha!
Ha! Ha! Ha! Ha! Ha! Ha! Ha! Ha! Ha! Ha! Ha! Ha! Ha! Ha! Ha!
Ha! Ha! Ha! Ha! Ha! Ha! Ha! Ha! Ha! Ha! Ha! Ha! Ha! Ha! Ha!
Ha! Ha! Ha! Ha! Ha! Ha! Ha! Ha! Ha! Ha! Ha! Ha! Ha! Ha! Ha!
Ha! Ha! Ha! Ha! Ha! Ha! Ha! Ha! Ha! Ha! Ha! Ha! Ha! Ha! Ha!
Ha! Ha! Ha! Ha! Ha! Ha! Ha! Ha! Ha! Ha! Ha! Ha! Ha! Ha! Ha!
Ha! Ha! Ha! Ha! Ha! Ha! Ha! Ha! Ha! Ha! Ha! Ha! Ha! Ha! Ha!
Ha! Ha! Ha! Ha! Ha! Ha! Ha! Ha! Ha! Ha! Ha! Ha! Ha! Ha! Ha!
Ha! Ha! Ha! Ha! Ha! Ha! Ha! Ha! Ha! Ha! Ha! Ha! Ha! Ha! Ha!
Ha! Ha! Ha! Ha! Ha! Ha! Ha! Ha! Ha! Ha! Ha! Ha! Ha! Ha! Ha!
Ha! Ha! Ha! Ha! Ha! Ha! Ha! Ha! Ha! Ha! Ha! Ha! Ha! Ha! Ha!
Ha! Ha! Ha! Ha! Ha! Ha! Ha! Ha! Ha! Ha! Ha! Ha! Ha! Ha! Ha!

Ha! Ha! Ha! Ha! Ha! Ha! Ha! Ha! Ha! Ha! Ha! Ha! Ha! Ha! Ha!
Ha! Ha! Ha! Ha! Ha! Ha! Ha! Ha! Ha! Ha! Ha! Ha! Ha! Ha! Ha!
Ha! Ha! Ha! Ha! Ha! Ha! Ha! Ha! Ha! Ha! Ha! Ha! Ha! Ha! Ha!
Ha! Ha! Ha! Ha! Ha! Ha! Ha! Ha! Ha! Ha! Ha! Ha! Ha! Ha! Ha!
Ha! Ha! Ha! Ha! Ha! Ha! Ha! Ha! Ha! Ha! Ha! Ha! Ha! Ha! Ha!
Ha! Ha! Ha! Ha! Ha! Ha! Ha! Ha! Ha! Ha! Ha! Ha! Ha! Ha! Ha!
Ha! Ha! Ha! Ha! Ha! Ha! Ha! Ha! Ha! Ha! Ha! Ha! Ha! Ha! Ha!
Ha! Ha! Ha! Ha! Ha! Ha! Ha! Ha! Ha! Ha! Ha! Ha! Ha! Ha! Ha!
Ha! Ha! Ha! Ha! Ha! Ha! Ha! Ha! Ha! Ha! Ha! Ha! Ha! Ha! Ha!
Ha! Ha! Ha! Ha! Ha! Ha! Ha! Ha! Ha! Ha! Ha! Ha! Ha! Ha! Ha!
Ha! Ha! Ha! Ha! Ha! Ha! Ha! Ha! Ha! Ha! Ha! Ha! Ha! Ha! Ha!
Ha! Ha! Ha! Ha! Ha! Ha! Ha! Ha! Ha! Ha! Ha! Ha! Ha! Ha! Ha!
Ha! Ha! Ha! Ha! Ha! Ha! Ha! Ha! Ha! Ha! Ha! Ha! Ha! Ha! Ha!
Ha! Ha! Ha! Ha! Ha! Ha! Ha! Ha! Ha! Ha! Ha! Ha! Ha! Ha! Ha!
Ha! Ha! Ha! Ha! Ha! Ha! Ha! Ha! Ha! Ha! Ha! Ha! Ha! Ha! Ha!
Ha! Ha! Ha! Ha! Ha! Ha! Ha! Ha! Ha! Ha! Ha! Ha! Ha! Ha! Ha!
Ha! Ha! Ha! Ha! Ha! Ha! Ha! Ha! Ha! Ha! Ha! Ha! Ha! Ha! Ha!
Ha! Ha! Ha! Ha! Ha! Ha! Ha! Ha! Ha! Ha! Ha! Ha! Ha! Ha! Ha!
Ha! Ha! Ha! Ha! Ha! Ha! Ha! Ha! Ha! Ha! Ha! Ha! Ha! Ha! Ha!
Ha! Ha! Ha! Ha! Ha! Ha! Ha! Ha! Ha! Ha! Ha! Ha! Ha! Ha! Ha!
Ha! Ha! Ha! Ha! Ha! Ha! Ha! Ha! Ha! Ha! Ha! Ha! Ha! Ha! Ha!
Ha! Ha! Ha! Ha! Ha! Ha! Ha! Ha! Ha! Ha! Ha! Ha! Ha! Ha! Ha!
Ha! Ha! Ha! Ha! Ha! Ha! Ha! Ha! Ha! Ha! Ha! Ha! Ha! Ha! Ha!
Ha! Ha! Ha! Ha! Ha! Ha! Ha! Ha! Ha! Ha! Ha! Ha! Ha! Ha! Ha!
Ha! Ha! Ha! Ha! Ha! Ha! Ha! Ha! Ha! Ha! Ha! Ha! Ha! Ha! Ha!
Ha! Ha! Ha! Ha! Ha! Ha! Ha! Ha! Ha! Ha!

Holding fast to her little patch of marital ground, she'd watched
as his lovers floated through like ballerinas, or dandelion down,
all of them sudden and fleeting, as if they were calendar girls
ripped monthly by the same mysterious calendar-ripping wind that
hurried time along in old movies. Hello! Goodbye! Ha! Ha! Ha!
What did Ruth care now? Those girls were over and gone. The key
to marriage, she concluded, was just not to take the thing too
personally.

"You *assume* they're over and gone," said her friend Carla, who, in
Ruth's living room, was working on both her inner child and her
inner thighs, getting rid of the child but in touch with the thighs;
Ruth couldn't keep it straight. Carla sometimes came over and did

her exercises in the middle of Ruth's Afghan rug. Carla liked to blurt out things and then say, "Oops, did I say that?" Or sometimes: "You know what? Life is short. Dumpy, too, so you've got to do your best: no Empire waists." She lay on her back and did breathing exercises and encouraged Ruth to do the same. "I can't. I'll just fall asleep," said Ruth, though she suspected she wouldn't really.

Carla shrugged. "If you fall asleep, great. It's a beauty nap. If you almost do but don't actually, it's meditation."

"*That's* meditation?"

"That's meditation."

Two years ago, when Ruth was going through chemo — the oncologist in Chicago had set Ruth's five-year survival chances at fifty-fifty; how mean not to lie and say sixty-forty! — Carla had brought over lasagnas, which lasted in their various shrinking incarnations in Ruth's refrigerator for weeks. "Try not to think of roadkill when you reheat," Carla said. She also brought over sage and rosemary soaps, which looked like slabs of butter with twigs in them. She brought Ruth a book to read, a collection of stories entitled *Trust Me,* and she had, on the jacket, crossed out the author's name and written in her own: Carla McGraw. Carla was a friend. Who had many friends these days?

"I do assume," Ruth said. "I have to." Terence's last affair, two springs ago, had ended badly. He'd told Ruth he had a meeting that would go on rather late, until ten or so, but then he arrived home, damp and disheveled, at seven-thirty. "The meeting's been canceled," he said, and went directly upstairs, where she could hear him sobbing in the bathroom. He cried for almost an hour, and as she listened to him, her heart filled up with pity and a deep, sisterly love. At all the funerals for love, love had its neat trick of making you mourn it so much it reappeared. Popped right up from the casket. Or, if it didn't reappear itself, it sent a relative of startling resemblance, a thin and charming twin, which you took back home with you to fatten and cradle, nuzzle and scold.

Oh, the rich torment that was life. She just didn't investigate Terence's activities anymore. No steaming open credit-card statements, no "accidentally" picking up the phone extension. As the doctor who diagnosed her now fully remissioned cancer once said to her, "The only way to know absolutely everything in life is via an autopsy."

Nuptial forensics. Ruth would let her marriage live. No mercy killing, no autopsy. She would let it live! Ha! She would settle, as a person must, for not knowing everything: ignorance as mystery; mystery as faith; faith as food; food as sex; sex as love; love as hate; hate as transcendence. Was this a religion or some weird kind of math?

Or was this, in fact, just spring?

Certain things helped: the occasional Winston (convinced, as Ruth was, despite the one lung, the lip blisters, and the keloidal track across her ribs, that at the end she would regret the cigarettes she hadn't smoked more than the ones she had; besides, she no longer coughed much at all, let alone so hard that her retinas detached); pots of lobelia ("Excuse me, gotta go," she had said more than once to a loquacious store clerk, "I've got some new lobelia sitting in a steaming hot car"); plus a long, scenic search for a new house.

"A move . . . yes. A move will be good. We've soiled the nest, in many respects," her husband had said, in the circuitous syntax and ponderous Louisiana drawl that, like so much else about him, had once made her misty with desire and now drove her nuts with scorn. "Think about it, honey," he'd said after the reconciliation, the first remission, and the initial reconnaissance through the realtors — after her feelings had gone well beyond rage into sarcasm and carcinoma. "We should probably consider leaving this home entirely behind. Depending on what you want to do — or, of course, if you have another home in mind, I'm practically certain I'd be amenable. We would want to discuss it, however, or anything else you might be thinking of. I myself — though it may be presumptuous of me, I realize — but then, hey, it wouldn't be the first time, now would it? I myself was thinking that, if you were inclined —"

"Terence!" Ruth clapped her hands twice, sharply. "Speak more quickly! I don't have long to live!" They'd been married for twenty-three years. Marriage, she felt, was a fine arrangement generally, except that one never got it generally. One got it very, very specifically. "And please," she added, "don't be fooled by the euphemisms of realtors. This was never a home, darling. This is a *house.*"

In this way — a wedding of emotionally handicapped parking spaces, an arduously tatted lace of property and irritation — they'd managed to stay married. He was not such a bad guy! — just a handsome country boy, disbelieving of his own luck, which came to him imperfectly but continually, like crackers from a cookie jar. She had counted on him to make money — was that so wrong? — and he had made some, in used-car dealerships and computer software stock. With its sweet, urgent beginnings and grateful, hand-holding end, marriage was always its worst in the middle: it was always a muddle, a ruin, an unnavigable field. But it was not, she felt, a total wasteland. In her own marriage there was one sweet little recurrent season, one tiny, nameless room, that suited and consoled her. She would lie in Terence's arms and he would be quiet and his quietness would restore her. There was music. There was peace. That was all. There were no words in it. But that tiny spot — like any season, or moon, or theater set; like a cake in a rotary display — invariably spun out of reach and view, and the quarreling would resume and she would have to wait a long time for the cake to come round again.

Of course, their daughter, Mitzy, adored Terence — the hot, lucky fire of him. In Ruth, on the other hand, Mitzy seemed to sense only the chill spirit of a woman getting by. But what was a person in Ruth's position *supposed* to do, except rebuild herself, from the ground up, as an iceberg? Ruth wanted to know! And so, in the strange, warm dissolutions that came over her these May nights silently before sleep, a pointillist's breaking up of the body and self and of the very room, Ruth began, again, to foresee her own death.

At first, looking at other houses on Sunday afternoons — wandering across other people's floors and carpets, opening the closets to look at other people's shoes — gave Ruth a thrill. The tacky photos on the potter's piano. The dean with no doorknobs. The orthodontist with thirty built-in cubbyholes for his thirty tennis shoes. Wallpaper peeling like birch skin. Assorted stained, scuffed floors and misaligned moldings. The Dacron carpets. The trashy magazines on the coffee table. And those economy snacks! People had pretzel boxes the size of bookcases. And no bookcases. What would they do with a book? Just put it in the pretzel box! Ruth took an unseemly interest in the faulty angles of a staircase landing, or the contents of a room: the ceramic pinecone lamps, the wedding photo of the dogs. Was the town that boring that this was now what amused her? What was so intriguing to her about all this homeowning thrown open to the marketplace? The airing of the family vault? The peek into the grave? Ruth hired a realtor. Stepping into a house, hunting out its little spaces, surveying its ceiling stains and roof rot, exhilarated her. It amazed her that there was always something wrong with a house, and after a while, her amazement became a kind of pleasure; it was pleasing that there should always be something wrong. It made the house seem more natural that way.

But soon she backed off. "I could never buy a house that had that magazine on the coffee table," she said once. A kind of fear overtook her. "I don't like that neo-Georgian thing," she said now, before the realtor, Kit, had even turned off the car, forcing Kit to back out again from the driveway. "I'm sorry, but when I look at it," Ruth added, "my eye feels disorganized, and my heart just empties right out."

"I care about you, Ruth," said Kit, who was terrified of losing clients and so worked hard to hide the fact that she had the patience of a gnat. "Our motto is 'We Care,' and that is just so true: we really, really care, Ruth. We care about you. We care about your feelings and desires. We want you to be happy. So, here we are driving along. Driving toward a thing, then driving past. You want a house, Ruth, or shall we just go to the goddamn movies?"

"You think I'm being unrealistic."

"Aw, I get enough realism as it is. Realism's overrated. I mean it about the movies."

"You do?"

"Sure!" And so that once, Ruth went to the movies with her realtor. It was a preseason matinee of *Forrest Gump,* which made her teary with weariness, hurt, and bone-thinning boredom. "Such a career-ender for poor Tom Hanks. Mark my words," Ruth whispered to her realtor, candy wrappers floating down in the dark toward her shoes. "Thank God we bought toffees. What would we do without these toffees?"

Eventually, not even a month later, in Kit's white Cabriolet, the top down, the wind whipping everyone's hair in an unsightly way, Ruth and Terence took a final tour of the suburbanized cornfields on the periphery of town and found a house. It was the original ancient four-square farmhouse in the center of a 1979 subdivision. A manmade pond had been dug into the former field that edged the side yard. A wishing well full of wildflowers stood in the front yard.

"This is it," Terence said, gesturing toward the house.

"It is?" said Ruth. She tried to study it with an open mind — its porch and dormers angled as if by a Cubist, its chimney crumbling on one side, its cedar shingles ornately leprous with old green paint. "If one of us kisses it, will it turn into a house?" The dispiriting white ranches and split-levels lined up on either side at least possessed a geometry she understood.

"It needs a lot of work," admitted Kit.

"Yes," said Ruth. Even the FOR SALE sign had sprouted a shock of dandelions at its base. "Unlike chocolates, houses are predictable: you always know you're getting rot and decay and a long, tough mortgage. Eat them or put them back in the box — you can't do either without a lawsuit or an ordinance hearing."

"I don't know what you're talking about," said Terence. He took Ruth aside.

"This is it," he hissed. "This is our dream house."

"*Dream* house?" All the dreams she'd been having were about death — its blurry pixilation, its movement through a dark, soft sleep to a hard, bright end.

"I'm surprised you can't see it," said Terence, visibly frustrated.

She squinted again toward the soffits, the Picasso porch, the roof mottled with moss and soot. She studied the geese and the goose poop, moist, mashed cigars of which littered the stony shore of the pond. "Ah, maybe," she said. "Maybe yes. I think I'm beginning to see it. Who owns it again?"

"A Canadian. He's been renting it out. It's a nice neighborhood. Near a nature conservatory and the zoo."

"The zoo?"

Ruth thought about this. They would have to hire a lot of people, of course. It would be like running a company to get this thing back in shape, bossing everybody around, monitoring the loans and payments. She sighed. Such entrepreneurial spirit did not run in her family. It was not native to her. She came from a long line of teachers and ministers — employees. Hopeless people. People with faith but no hope. There was not one successful small business anywhere in her genes. "I'm starting to see the whole thing," she said.

On the other side of town, where other people lived, a man named Noel and a woman named Nitchka were in an apartment, in the kitchen, having a discussion about music. The woman said, "So you know nothing at all? Not a single song?"

"I don't think so," said Noel. Why was this a problem for her? It wasn't a problem for him. So he didn't know any songs. He had always been willing to let her know more than he did; it didn't bother him, until it bothered her.

"Noel, what kind of upbringing did you have, anyway?" He knew she felt he had been deprived and that he should feel angry about it. But he did! He did feel angry about it! "Didn't your parents ever sing songs to you?" she asked. "Can't you even sing one single song by heart? Sing a song. Just any song."

"Like what?"

"If there was a gun to your head, what song would you sing?"

"I don't know!" he shouted, and threw a chair across the room. They hadn't had sex in two months.

"Is it that you don't even know the *name* of a song?"

At night, every night, they just lay there with their magazines and Tylenol PM and then, often with the lights still on, were whisked quickly down into their own separate worlds of sleep — his filled with lots of whirling trees and antique flying machines and bouquets of ferns. He had no idea why.

"I know the name of a song," he said.

"What song?"

"'Open the Door, Richard.'"

"What kind of song is that?"

It was a song his friend Richard's mother had sung when he was twelve and he and Richard were locked in the bedroom, flipping madly through magazines: *Breasts and the Rest, Tight Tushies,* and *Lollapalooza Ladies.* But it was a real song, which still existed — though you couldn't find those magazines anymore. Noel had looked.

"See? I know a song that you don't!" he exclaimed.

"Is this a song of spiritual significance to you?"

"Yup, it really is." He picked up a rubber band from the counter, stretched it between his fingers, and released it. It hit her on the chin. "Sorry. That was an accident," he said.

"Something is deeply missing in you!" Nitchka shouted, and stormed out of the apartment for a walk.

Noel sank back against the refrigerator. He could see his own reflection in the window over the sink. It was dim and translucent, and a long twisted cobweb outside, caught on the eaves, swung back and forth across his face like a noose. He looked crazy and ill — but with just a smidgen of charisma! "If there was a gun to your head," he said to the reflection, "what song would you sing?"

Ruth wondered whether she really needed a project this badly. A diversion. A resurrection. An undertaking. Their daughter, Mitzy, grown and gone — was the whole empty nest thing such a crisis that they would devote the rest of their days to this mortician's delight? Was it that horribly, echoey quiet and nothing-nothing not to have Mitzy and her struggles furnishing their lives? Was it so bad no longer to have a daughter's frustrated artistic temperament bleeding daily on the carpet of their brains? Mitzy, dear Mitzy, was a dancer. All those ballet and tap lessons as a child — she wasn't supposed to have taken them seriously! They had been intended as middle-class irony and window dressing — you weren't actually supposed to *become* a dancer. But Mitzy had. Despite that she was the fattest in the troupe every time, never belonging, rejected from every important company, until one day a young director saw how beautifully, soulfully she danced — "How beautifully the fat girl dances!" — and ushered her past the corps, set her center stage, and made her a star. Now she traveled the world over and was the darling of the critics. "Size fourteen yet!" crowed one reviewer. "It is a miracle to see!" She had become a triumph of feet over heft, spirit over matter, matter over doesn't-matter, a figure of immortality, a big fat angel really, and she had "many, many homosexual fans," as Terence put it. As a result, she now rarely came home. Ruth sometimes got postcards, but Ruth hated postcards — so careless and cheap, especially from this new angel of dance writing to her own sick mother. But that was the way with children.

Once, over a year and a half ago, Mitzy had come home, but it was only for two weeks — during Ruth's chemotherapy. Mitzy was, as usual, in a state of crisis. "Sure they like my work," she wailed as Ruth adjusted that first itchy acrylic wig, the one that used to scare people. "But do they like *me*?" Mitzy was an only child, so it was natural that her first bout of sibling rivalry would be with her own work. When Ruth suggested as much, Mitzy gave her a withering look accompanied by a snorting noise, and after that chat, with a cocked eyebrow and a wince of a gaze, Mitzy began monopolizing the telephone with moving and travel plans. "You seem to be doing *extremely well*, Mom," she said, looking over her shoulder, jotting things down. Then she'd fled.

At first Terence, even more than she, seemed enlivened by the prospect of new real estate. The simplest discussion — of doorjambs or gutters — made his blood move around his face and neck like a lava lamp. Roof-shingle samples — rough, grainy squares of sepia, rose, and gray — lit his eyes up like love. He brought home doorknob catalogues and phoned a plasterer or two. After a while, however, she could see him tire and retreat, recoil even — another fling flung. "My God, Terence. Don't quit on me now. This is just like the Rollerblades!" He had last fall gone through a Rollerblade period.

"I'm way too busy," he said.

And before Ruth knew it, the entire house project — its purchase and renovation — had been turned over to her.

First Ruth had to try to sell their current house. She decided to try something called a "fosbo." FOSBO: a "For Sale by Owner." She put ads in papers, bought a sign for the front yard, and planted violet and coral impatiens in the flowerbeds for the horticulturally unsuspecting, those with no knowledge of perennials. Gorgeous yard! Mature plantings! She worked up a little flyer describing the moldings and light fixtures, all "original to the house." Someone came by to look and sniff. He fingered one of the ripped window shades. *"Original to the house?"* he said.

"All right, you're out of here," she said. To subsequent prospective buyers, she abandoned any sales pitch and went for candor. "I admit, this bathroom's got mildew. And look at this *stupid* little hallway. This is why we're moving! We hate this house." She soon hired back her Forrest Gump realtor, who, at the open house, played Vivaldi on the stereo and baked banana bread, selling the place in two hours.

The night after they closed on both houses, having sat silently through the two proceedings, like deaf-mutes being had, the mysterious Canadian once more absent and represented only by a purple-suited realtor named Flo, Ruth and Terence stood in their empty new house and ate takeout Chinese straight from the cartons. Their furniture was sitting in a truck, which was parked in a supermarket parking lot on the east side of town, and it all would be delivered the next day. For now, they stood at the bare front window of their large, echoey new dining room. A small lit candle on the floor cast their shadows up on the ceiling, gloomy and fat. Wind rattled the panes, and the boiler in the cellar burst on in small frightening explosions. The radiators hissed and smelled like cats, burning off dust as they heated up, vibrating the cobwebs in the ceiling corners above them. The entire frame of the house groaned and rumbled. There was scampering in the walls. The sound of footsteps — or something like footsteps — thudded softly in the attic, two floors above them.

"We've bought a haunted house," said Ruth. Terence's mouth was full of hot cabbagy egg roll. "A ghost!" she continued. "Just a little extra protein. Just a little amino-acid bonus." It was what her father had always said when he found a small green worm in his bowl of blueberries.

"The house is settling," said Terence.

"It's had a hundred and ten years to settle; you would think it had gotten it done with by now."

"Settling goes on and on," said Terence.

"We would know," said Ruth.

He looked at her, then dug into the container of lo mein.

A scrabbling sound came from the front porch. Terence chewed, swallowed, then walked over to turn the light on, but the light didn't come on. "Was this disclosed?" he shouted.

"It's probably just the light bulb."

"All new light bulbs were just put in, Flo said." He opened the front door. "The light's broken, and it should have been disclosed." He was holding a flashlight with one hand and unscrewing the front light with the other. Behind the light fixture gleamed three pairs of masked eyes. Dark raccoon feces were mounded up in the crawlspace between the ceiling and the roof.

"What the *hell?*" shouted Terence, backing away.

"This house is *infested!*" said Ruth. She put down her food.

"How did those creatures get up there?"

She felt a twinge in her one lung. "How does anything get anywhere — that's what I want to know." She had only ever been the lightest of smokers, never in a high-risk category, but now every pinch, prick, tick, or tock in her ribs, every glitch in the material world anywhere, made her want to light up and puff.

"Oh, God, the stench."

"Shouldn't the inspector have found this?"

"Inspectors! Obviously, they're useless. What this place needed was an MRI."

"Ah, jeez. This is the worst."

Every house is a grave, thought Ruth. All that life-stealing fuss and preparation. Which made moving from a house a resurrection — or an exodus of ghouls, depending on your point of view — and made moving *to* a house (yet another house!) the darkest of follies and desires. At best, it was a restlessness come falsely to rest. But the inevitable rot and demolition, from which the soul eventually had to flee (to live in the sky or disperse itself among the trees?), would necessarily make a person stupid with unhappiness.

Oh, well!

After their furniture arrived and was positioned almost exactly the way it had been in their old house, Ruth began to call a lot of people to come measure, inspect, capture, cart away, clean, spray, bring samples, provide estimates and bids, and sometimes they did come, though once people had gotten a deposit, they often disappeared entirely. Machines began to answer instead of humans, and sometimes phone numbers announced themselves disconnected altogether. "We're sorry. The number you have reached . . ."

The windows of the new house were huge — dusty, but bright because of their size — and because the shade shop had not yet delivered the shades, the entire neighborhood of spiffy middle management could peer into Ruth and Terence's bedroom. For one long, bewildering day, Ruth took to waving, and only sometimes did people wave back. More often, they just squinted and stared. The next day, Ruth taped bed sheets up to the windows with masking tape, but invariably the sheets fell off after ten minutes. When she bathed, she had to crawl naked out of the bathroom down the hall and into the bedroom and then into the closet to put her clothes on. Or sometimes she just lay there on the bathroom floor and wriggled into things. It was all so very hard.

*

In their new back yard, crows the size of suitcases cawed and bounced in the branches of the pear tree. Carpenter ants — like shiny pieces of a child's game — swarmed the porch steps. Ruth made even more phone calls, and finally a man with a mottled, bulbous nose and a clean white van with a cockroach painted on it came and doused the ants with poison.

"It looks just like a fire extinguisher, what you're using," said Ruth, watching.

"Ho no, ma'am. Way stronger than that." He wheezed. His nose was as knobby as a pickle. He looked underneath the porch and then back up at Ruth. "There's a whole lot of dying going on in there," he said.

"There's nothing you can do about the crows?" Ruth asked.

"Not me, but you could get a gun and shoot 'em yourself," he said. "It's not legal, but if your house were one hundred yards down that way, it would be. If it were one hundred yards down that way, you could bag twenty crows a day. Since you're where you are, within the town limits, you're going to have to do it at night, with a silencer. Catch 'em live in the morning with nets and corn, then at sunset take 'em out behind the garage and put 'em out of your misery."

"Nets?" said Ruth.

She called many people. She collected more guesstimates and advice. A guy named Noel from a lawn company advised her to forget about the crows, worry about the squirrels. She should plant her tulips deeper, and with a lot of red pepper, so that squirrels would not dig them up. "Look at all these squirrels!" he said, pointing to the garage roof and to all the weedy flowerbeds. "And how about some ground cover in here, by the porch, some lilies by the well, and some sunflowers in the side yard?"

"Let me think about it," said Ruth. "I would like to keep some of these violets," she said, indicating the pleasant-looking leaves throughout the irises.

"Those aren't violets. That's a weed. That's a very common, tough little weed."

"I always thought those were violets."

"Nope."

"Things can really overtake a place, can't they? This planet's just one big divisive cutthroat competition of growing. I mean, they look like violets, don't they? The leaves, I mean."

Noel shrugged. "Not to me. Not really."

How could she keep any of it straight? There was spirea and then there was false spirea — she forgot which was which. "Which is the spirea again?" she asked. Noel pointed to the bridal-wreath hedge, which was joyously blooming from left to right, from sun to shade, and in two weeks would sag and brown in the same direction. "Ah, marriage," she said aloud.

"Pardon?" said Noel.

"Are you married?" she asked.

He gave her a tired little smile and said, "No. Trying to make it happen with a girlfriend, but no, not married."

"That's probably better," said Ruth.

"How about this vegetable garden?" he asked nervously.

"It's just a lot of grass with a rhubarb in it," said Ruth. "I'd like to dig the whole thing up and plant roses — unless you think it's bad luck to replace food with flowers. Vanity before the Lord, or something."

"It's up to you," he said.

She called him back that night. He personally, no machine, answered the phone. "I've been thinking about the sunflowers," she said.

"Who is this?" he said.

"Ruth. Ruth Aikins."

"Oh, say, Ruth. Ruth! Hi!"

"Hi," she said in a worried way. He sounded as if he'd been drinking.

"Now what about those sunflowers?" he asked. "I'd like to plant those sunflowers real soon, you know that? Here's why: my girlfriend's talking again about leaving me, and I've just been diagnosed with lymphoma. So I'd like to see some sunflowers come up end of August."

"Oh, my God. Life stinks!" cried Ruth.

"Yup. So I'd like to see some sunflowers. End of summer, I'd like something to look forward to."

"What kind of girlfriend talks about leaving her beau at a time like this?"

"I don't know."

"I mean — good riddance. On the other hand, you know what you should do? You should make yourself a good cup of tea and sit down and write her a letter. You're going to need someone to care for you through all this. Don't let her call all the shots. Let her understand the implications of her behavior and her responsibilities to you. I know whereof I speak."

Ruth was about to explain further, when Noel cleared his throat hotly. "I don't think it's such a great idea for you to go get personal and advising. I mean, look. *Ruth,* is it? You see, I don't even know your name, Ruth. I know a lot of Ruths. You could be goddamned anyone. Ruth this, Ruth that, Ruth who knows. As a matter of fact, the lymphoma thing I just made up, because I thought you were a totally different Ruth." And with that, he hung up.

She put out cages for the squirrels — the squirrels that gnawed the hyacinth bulbs, giving their smooth surfaces runs like stockings, the squirrels that utterly devoured the crocuses. From the back porch, she watched each squirrel thrash around in the cage for an hour, hurling itself against the cage bars and rubbing bald spots into its head, before she finally took pity and drove each one to a faraway quarry to set it free. The quarry was a spot that Terence had recommended as "a beautiful seclusion, a rodent Eden, a hillside of oaks above a running brook." Such poetry: probably he'd gotten laid there once. Talk about your rodent Eden! In actuality, the place was a depressing little gravel gully, with a trickle of brown water running through it, a tiny crew of scrub oaks manning the nearby incline. It was the kind of place where the squirrel mafia would have dumped their offed squirrels.

She lifted the trap door and watched each animal scurry off toward the hillside. Did they know what they were doing? Would they join their friends, or would every last one of them find its way back to the hollow walls of her house and set up shop again?

The bats — bats! — arrived the following week, one afternoon during a loud, dark thundershower, like a horror movie. They flew back and forth in the stairwells, then hung upside down from the picture-frame molding in the dining room, where they discreetly defecated, leaving clumps of shiny black guano pasted to the wall.

Ruth phoned her husband at his office but only got his voice mail, so she then phoned Carla, who came dashing over with a tennis racket, a butterfly net, and a push broom, all with ribbons tied around their handles. "These are my housewarming presents," she said.

"They're swooping again! Look out! They're swooping!"

"Let me at those sons of bitches," Carla said.

From her fetal position on the floor, Ruth looked up at her. "What did I ever do to get such a great friend as you?"

Carla stopped. Her face was flushed with affection, her cheeks blotched with pink. "You think so?" A bat dive-bombed her hair. The old wives' tale — that bats got caught in your hair — seemed truer to Ruth than the new wives' tale — that bats getting caught in your hair was just an old wives' tale. Bats possessed curiosity and arrogance. They were little social scientists. They got close to hair — to investigate, measure, and interview. And when something got close — a moth to a flame, a woman to a house, a woman to a grave, a sick woman to a fresh, wide-open grave like a bed — it could fall in and get caught.

"You gotta stuff your dormer eaves with steel wool," said Carla.

"Hey. Ain't it the truth," said Ruth.

They buried the whacked bats in tabouli containers, in the side yard: everything just tabouli in the end.

With the crows in mind, Ruth started to go with Carla to the shooting range. The geese, Carla said, were not that big a problem. The geese could be discouraged simply by shaking up the eggs in their nests. Carla was practical. She had a heart the shape of an ax. She brought over a canoe and paddled Ruth out into the cattails to find the goose nests, and there she took each goose egg and shook it furiously. "If you just take and toss the egg," explained Carla, "the damn goose will lay another one. This way, you kill the gosling, and the goose never knows. It sits there warming the damn eggnog until the winter comes, and then the goose just leaves, heartbroken, and never comes back. With the crows, however, you just have to blow their brains out."

At the shooting range, they paid a man with a green metal money box twenty dollars for an hour of shooting. They got several cans of Diet Coke, which they bought from a vending machine outside near the restrooms, and which they set at their feet, at their heels, just behind them. They each had pistols, Ruth's from World War I, Carla's from World War II, which they had bought in an antique-gun store. "Anyone could shoot birds with a shotgun," Carla had said. "Let's be unique."

"That's never really been a big ambition of mine," said Ruth.

They were the only ones there at the range and stood fifty yards from three brown sacks of hay with red circles painted on them. They fired at the circles — one! two! three! — then turned, squatted, set their guns down, and sipped their Cokes. The noise was astonishing, bursting through the fields around them, echoing off the small hills and back out of the sky, mocking and retaliatory. "My Lord!" Ruth exclaimed. Her gun felt hard and unaimable. "I don't think I'm doing this right," she said. She had expected a pistol to seem light and natural — a seamless extension of her angry feral self. But instead, it felt heavy and huge and so unnaturally loud she never wanted to fire such a thing again.

But she did. Only twice did she see her hay sack buckle. Mostly she seemed to be firing too high, into the trees behind the targets, perhaps hitting squirrels — perhaps the very squirrels she had caught in her have-a-heart cage, now set free and shot dead with her have-a-house gun. "It's all too much," said Ruth. "I can't possibly be doing this right. It's way too complicated and mean."

"You've forgotten about the damn crows," said Carla. "Don't forget them."

"That's right," said Ruth, and she picked up the gun again. "Crows." Then she lowered her gun. "But won't I just be shooting them at close range, after I catch them in nets?"

"Maybe," said Carla. "But maybe not."

When Nitchka finally left him, she first watched her favorite TV show, then turned off the television, lifted up her CD player and her now-unhooked VCR, and stopped to poise herself dramatically in the front hall. "You know, you haven't a clue what the human experience is even about," she said.

"This song and dance again," he said. "Are you taking it on the road?" She set her things down outside in the hall so she could slam the door loudly and leave him — leave him, he imagined, for some new, handsome man she had met at work. Dumped for Hunks. That was the title of his life. In heaven, just to spite her, that would be the name of his goddamned band.

He drank a lot that week, and on Friday his boss, McCarthy, called to say Noel was fired. "You think we can run a lawn store this way?" he said.

"If there was a gun to your head," said Noel, "what song would you sing?"

"Get help," said McCarthy. "That's all I have to say." Then there was a dial tone.

Noel began to collect unemployment, getting to the office just before it closed. He began to sleep in the days and stay up late at night. He got turned around. He went out at midnight for walks, feeling insomniac and mocked by the dark snore of the neighborhood. Rage circled and built in him, like a saxophone solo. He began to venture into other parts of town. Sidewalks appeared, then disappeared again. The moon shone on one side and then on the other. Once he took duct tape with him and a ski mask. Another time he took duct tape, a ski mask, and a gun one of his stepfathers had given him when he was twenty. If you carefully taped a window from the outside, it could be broken quietly: the glass would stick to the tape and cave gently outward.

"I'm not going to hurt you," he said. He turned on the light in the bedroom. He taped the woman's mouth first, then the man's. He made them get out of bed and stand over by the dresser. "I'm going to take your TV set," said Noel. "And I'm going to take your VCR. But before I do, I want you to sing me a song. I'm a music lover, and I want you to sing me one song, any song. By heart. You first," he said to the man. He pressed the gun to his head. "One song." He pulled the duct tape gently off the man's mouth.

"Any song?" repeated the man. He tried to look into the eyeholes of Noel's ski mask, but Noel turned abruptly and stared at the olive-gray glass of the TV.

"Yeah," said Noel. "Any song."

"Okay." The man began. "'O beautiful for spacious skies, for amber waves of grain . . .'" His voice was deep and sure. "'For purple mountain majesties . . .'" Noel turned back and studied the man carefully. How had he learned it all by heart? "You want *all* the verses?" the man stopped and asked, a bit too proudly, Noel thought, for someone who had a gun aimed his way.

"Nah, that's enough," Noel said irritably. "Now you," he said to the woman. He pulled the duct tape off her mouth. Her upper lip was moistly pink, raw from the adhesive. He glanced down at the tape and saw the spiky glisten of little mustache hairs. She began immediately, anxiously, to sing. "'You are my lucky star. I'm lucky where you are / Two lovely eyes at me that were —'"

"What kind of song is this?"

She nervously ignored him, kept on: "'. . . beaming, gleaming, I was starstruck." She began to sway a little, move her hands up and down. She cleared her throat and modulated upward, a light, chirpy warble, though her face was stretched wide with fright, like heated wax. "'You're all my lucky charms. I'm lucky in your arms . . .'" Here her hands fluttered up to her heart.

"All right, that's enough. I'm taking the VCR now."

"That's practically the end anyway," said the woman.

At the next house he did, he got a Christmas carol, plus "La Vie en Rose." At the third house, the week following, he got one nursery rhyme, half a school song, and "Memory" from *Cats*. He began to write down the titles and words. At home, looking over his notepad, he realized he was creating a whole new kind of songbook. Still the heart of these songs eluded him. Looking at the words the next day, a good, almost new VCR at his feet, he could never conjure the tune. And without the tune, the words seemed stupid and half mad.

To avoid the chaos of the house entirely, Ruth took to going to matinees. First-run movies, second-run — she didn't care. Movies were the ultimate real estate: you stepped in and looked around and almost always bought. She was especially stirred by a movie she saw about a beautiful widow who fell in love with a space alien who had assumed human form — the form of the woman's long-lost husband! Eventually, however, the man had to go back to his real home, and an immense and amazing spaceship came to get him, landing in a nearby field. To Ruth it seemed so sad and true, just like life: someone assumed the form of the great love of your life, only to reveal himself later as an alien who had to get on a spaceship and go back to his planet. Certainly it had been true for Terence. Terence had gotten on a spaceship and gone back long ago. Although, of course, in real life you seldom saw the actual spaceship. Usually there was just a lot of drinking, mumbling, and some passing out in the family room.

Sometimes on the way back from the movies, she would drive by their old house. They had sold it to an unmemorable young couple, and now, driving past it slowly, eyeing it like a pervert, she began to want it back. It was a good house. They didn't deserve it, that

couple: look how ignorant they were — pulling out all those for-
sythia bushes as if they were weeds.

Or maybe they *were* weeds. She never knew anymore what was
good life and what was bad, what was desirable matter and what was
antimatter, what was the thing itself and what was the death of the
thing: one mimicked the other, and she resented the work of having to distinguish.

Which, again, was the false spirea and which was the true?

The house was hers. If it hadn't been for that damn banana
bread, it still would be hers.

Perhaps she could get arrested creeping slowly past in her car
like this. She didn't know. But every time she drove by, the house
seemed to see her and cry out, It's you! Hello, hello! You're back!
So she tried not to do it too often. She would speed up a little, give
a fluttery wave, and drive off.

At home, she could not actually net the crows, though their old
habitat, the former cornfield that constituted the neighborhood,
continued to attract them like an ancestral land or a good life
recalled over gin. They hovered in the yards, tormented the cats,
and ate the still wet day-old songbirds right out of their nests. How
was she supposed to catch such fiends? She could not. She draped
nets in the branches of trees to snag them, but always a wind caused
the nets to twist or drop, or pages of old newspaper blew by and got
stuck inside, plastering the nets with op-ed pages and ads. From the
vegetable garden now turning flowerbed came the persistent on-
iony smell of those chives not yet smothered by the weed barrier.
And the rhubarb too kept exploding stubbornly through, no matter how she plucked at it, though each clutch of stalks was paler and
spindlier than the last.

She began generally not to feel well. Never a temple, her body
had gone from being a home, to being a house, to being a phone
booth, to being a kite. Nothing about it gave her proper shelter.
When she went for a stroll or was out in the yard throwing the nets
up into the oaks, other people in the neighborhood walked briskly
past her. The healthy, the feeling well, when they felt that way,
couldn't remember feeling any other, couldn't imagine it. They
were niftily in their bodies. They were not only out of the range of
sympathy; they were out of the range of mere imagining. Whereas
the sick could only think of being otherwise. Their hearts, their

every other thought, went out to that well person they hated a little but wanted to be. But the sick were sick. They were not in charge. They had lost their place at the top of the food chain. The feeling well were running the show, which was why the world was such a savage place. From her own porch she could hear the PA announcements from the zoo. They were opening; they were closing; would someone move their car. She could also hear the elephant, his sad bluesy trumpet, and the Bengal tiger roaring his heartbreak: all that animal unhappiness. The zoo was a terrible place and a terrible place to live near: the pacing ocelot, the polar bear green with fungus, the zebra demented and hungry and eating the fence, the children taken there to taunt the animals with paper cups and their own clean place in the world, the vulture sobbing behind his scowl.

Ruth began staying inside, drinking tea. She felt tightenings, pain, and vertigo, but then, was that so new? It seemed her body, so mysterious and apart from her, could only produce illness. Though once, of course, it had produced Mitzy. How had it done that? Mitzy was the only good thing her body had ever been able to grow. She was a real chunk of change, that one, a gorgeous george. How had her body done it? How does a body ever do it? Life inhabits life. Birds inhabit trees. Bones sprout bones. Blood gathers and makes new blood.

A miracle of manufacturing.

On one particular afternoon that was too cool for spring, when Ruth was sitting inside drinking tea so hot it skinned her tongue, she heard something. Upstairs, there was the old pacing in the attic that she had come to ignore. But now there was a knock on the door — loud, rhythmic, urgent. There were voices outside.

"Yes?" Ruth called, approaching the entryway, then opening the door.

Before her stood a girl, maybe fourteen or fifteen years old. "We heard there was a party here," said the girl. She had tar-black hair and a silver ring through her upper lip. Her eyes looked meek and lost. "Me and Arianna heard down on State Street that there was a party right here at this house."

"There's not," said Ruth. "There's just not." And then she closed the door, firmly.

But looking out the window, Ruth could see more teenagers

gathering in front of the house. They collected on the lawn like fruit flies on fruit. Some sat on the front steps. Some roared up on mopeds. Some hopped out of station wagons crowded with more kids just like themselves. One carload of kids poured out of the car, marched right up the front steps, and without ringing the bell opened the unlocked door and walked in.

Ruth put her tea down on the bookcase and walked toward the front entryway. "*Excuse* me!" she said, facing the kids in the front hall.

The kids stopped and stared at her. "May I help you?" asked Ruth.

"We're visiting someone who lives here."

"*I* live here."

"We were invited to a party by a *kid* who lives here."

"There's no kid who lives here. And there is no party."

"There's no kid who lives here?"

"No, there isn't."

A voice suddenly came from behind Ruth. A voice more proprietary, a voice from deeper within the house than even she was. "Yes, there is," it said.

Ruth turned and saw standing in the middle of her living room a fifteen-year-old boy dressed entirely in black, his head shaved spottily, his ears, nose, lips, and eyebrows pierced with multiple gold and copper rings. The rim of his left ear held three bronze clips.

"Who are you?" Ruth asked. Her heart flapped and fluttered, like something hit sloppily by a car.

"I'm Tod."

"Tod?"

"People call me Ed."

"Ed?"

"I live here."

"No, you don't. You don't! What do you mean, you live here?"

"I've been living in your attic."

"You have?" Ruth felt sweat burst forth from behind the wings of her nose. "You're our ghost? You've been pacing around upstairs?"

"Yeah, he has," said one of the kids at the door.

"But I don't understand." Ruth reached over and plucked a Kleenex from the box on the mail table, and wiped her face with it.

"I ran away from my own home months ago. I have a key to this house from the prior owner, who was a friend. So from time to time I've been sleeping upstairs in your attic. It's not so bad up there."

"You've been what? You've been living here, going in and out? Don't your parents know where you are?" Ruth asked.

"Look, I'm sorry about this party," said Tod. "I didn't mean for it to get this out of hand. I only invited a few people. I thought you were going away. It was supposed to be a small party. I didn't mean for it to be a big party."

"No," said Ruth. "You don't seem to understand. Big party, little party: you weren't supposed to have a party here at all. You were not even supposed to be *in* this house, let alone invite others to join you."

"But I had the key. I thought — I don't know. I thought it would be all right."

"Give me the key. Right now. Give me the key."

He handed her the key, with a smirk. "I don't know if it'll do you any good. Look." Ruth turned, and all the kids at the door held up their own shiny brass keys. "I made copies," said Tod.

Ruth began to shriek. "Get out of here! Get out of here right now! All of you! Not only will I have these locks changed, but if you ever set foot in this neighborhood again, I'll have the police on you so fast you won't know what hit you."

"But we need *some*place to drink, man," said one of the departing boys.

"Go to the damn park!"

"The cops are all over the park," one girl whined.

"Then go to the railroad tracks like we used to do, for God's sake!" she yelled. "Just get the hell out of here." She was shocked by the bourgeois venom and indignation in her own voice. She had, after all, once been a hippie. She had taken a lot of windowpane and preached about the evils of private ownership from a red Orlon blanket on a streetcorner in Chicago.

Life: what an absurd little story it always made.

"Sorry," said Tod. He touched her arm and, swinging a cloth satchel over his shoulder, walked toward the front door with the rest of them.

"Get the hell out of here," she said. "Ed."

*

The geese, the crows, the squirrels, the raccoons, the bats, the ants, the kids: Ruth now went to the firing range with Carla as often as she could. She would stand with her feet apart, both hands grasping the gun, then fire. She concentrated, tried to gather bits of strength in her, crumbs to make a loaf. She had been given way too much to cope with in life. Did God have her mixed up with someone else? Get a Job, she shouted silently to God. Get a real Job. I have never been your true and faithful servant. Then she would pull the trigger. When you told a stupid joke to God and got no response, was it that the joke was too stupid or not quite stupid enough? She narrowed her eyes. Mostly she just tried to squint, but then dread closed her eyes entirely. She fired again. Why did she not feel more spirited about this, the way Carla did? Ruth breathed deeply before firing, noting the Amazonian asymmetry of her breath, but in her heart she knew she was a mouse. A mouse bearing firearms, but a mouse nonetheless.

"Maybe I should have an affair," said Carla, who then fired her pistol into the gunnysacked hay. "I've been thinking: maybe you should too."

Now Ruth fired her own gun, its great storm of sound filling her ears. An affair? The idea of taking her clothes off and being with someone who wasn't a medical specialist just seemed ridiculous. Pointless and terrifying. Why would people do it? "Having an affair is for the young," said Ruth. "It's like taking drugs or jumping off cliffs. Why would you want to jump off a cliff?"

"Oh," said Carla. "You obviously haven't seen some of the cliffs *I've* seen."

Ruth sighed. Perhaps, if she knew a man in town who was friendly and attractive, she might — what? What might she do? She felt the opposite of sexy. She felt busy, managerial, thirsty, crazy; everything, when you got right down to it, was the opposite of sexy. If she knew a man in town she would — would go on a diet for him! But not Jenny Craig. She'd heard of someone who had died on Jenny Craig. If she had to go on a diet with a fake woman's name on it, she would go on the Betty Crocker diet, her own face ladled right in there with Betty's, in that fat red spoon. Yes, if she knew a man in town, perhaps she would let the excitement of knowing him seize the stem of her brain and energize her days. As long as it was only the stem; as long as the petals were left alone. She needed all her petals.

But she didn't know any men in town. Why didn't she know one?

In mid-June, the house he chose was an old former farmhouse in the middle of a subdivision. It was clearly being renovated — there were ladders and tarps in the yard — and in this careless presentation it seemed an easy target. Music lovers! he thought. They go for renovation! Besides, in an old house there was always one back window that, having warped into a trapezoid, had then been sanded and resanded and could be lifted off the frame like a lid. When he worked for the lawn company, he'd worked on many houses like these. Perhaps he'd even been here before, a month ago or so — he wasn't sure. Things looked different at night, and tonight the moon was not as bright as last time, less than full, like the face beneath a low slant hat, like a head scalped at the brow.

Noel looked at the couple. They had started singing "Chattanooga Choo-Choo." Lately, to save time, inspire the singers, and amuse himself, Noel had been requesting duets. "Wait a minute," he interrupted. "I wanna write this one down. I've just started to write these things down." And, like a fool, he left them to go into the next room to get a pen and a piece of paper.

"You have a sweet voice," the woman said when he returned. She was standing in front of the nightstand. He was smoothing a creased piece of paper against his chest. "A sweet speaking voice. You must sing well too."

"Nah, I have a terrible voice," he said. He felt his shirt pocket for a pen. "I was always asked to be quiet when the other children sang. The music teacher in grade school always asked me just to move my lips. 'Glory in eggshell seas,' she would say. 'Just mouth that.'"

"No, no. Your voice is sweet. The timbre is sweet. I can hear it." She took a small step sideways. The man, the husband, stayed where he was. He was wearing a big red sweatshirt and no underwear. His penis hung beneath the shirt hem like a long jewel yam. *Ah, marriage.* The woman, thrusting her hands into the pockets of her nightgown, took another small step. "It's sweet, but with weight."

Noel thought he could hear some people outside calling a dog by clapping their hands. "Bravo," said the owner of the dog, or so it sounded. "Bravo."

"Well, thank you," said Noel, his eyes cast downward.

"Surely your mother must have told you that," she said, but he decided not to answer that one. He turned to write down the words to "Chattanooga Choo-Choo," and with the beginning of the tune edging into his head — *pardon me, boys* — something exploded in the room. Suddenly, he thought he felt the yearning heart of civilization in him, felt at last, oh, Nitchka, what human experience on this planet was all about: its hard fiery center, a quick rudeness in its force; he could feel it catching him, a surprise, like a nail to the brain. A dark violet, then light washed over him. Everything went quiet. Music, he saw now, led you steadily into silence. You followed the thread of a song into a sudden sort of sleep. The white paper leapt up in a blinding flash, hot and sharp. The dresser edge caught his cheekbone in a gash, and he seemed no longer to be standing. His shoes slid along the rug. His hands reached up, then down again, then up along the dresser knobs, then flung themselves through the air and back against the floor. His brow, enclosing, then devouring his sight, finally settled darkly against his own sleeve.

Heat drained from his head, like a stone.

A police car pulled up quietly outside, with its lights turned off. There was some distant noise from geese on the pond.

There was no echo after the explosion. It was not like at the range. There had been just a click and a vibrating snap that had flown out before her toward the mask, and then the room roared and went silent, giving back nothing at all.

Terence gasped. "Good God," he said. "I suppose this is just what you've always wanted: a dead man on your bedroom floor."

"What do you mean by that? How can you say such a heartless thing?" Shouldn't her voice have had a quaver in it? Instead, it sounded flat and dry. "Forget being a decent man, Terence. Go for castability. Could you even play a decent man in a movie?"

"Did you have to be such a good shot?" Terence asked. He began to pace.

"I've been practicing," she said. Something immunological surged in her briefly, like wine. For a minute she felt restored and safe — safer than she had in years. How dare anyone come into her bedroom! How much was she expected to take? But then it all left her, wickedly, and she could again feel only her own abandonment and disease. She turned away from Terence and started to cry. "Oh, God, let me die," she finally said. "I am just so tired." Though she could hardly see, she knelt down next to the masked man and pressed his long, strange hands to her own small ones. They were not yet cold — no colder than her own. She thought she could feel herself begin to depart with him, the two of them rising together, translucent as jellyfish, leaving through the air, floating out into a night sky of singing and release, flying until they reached a bright, bright spaceship — a set of teeth on fire in the dark — and, absorbed into the larger light, were taken aboard for home. "And what on earth was all that?" she could hear them both say merrily of their lives, as if their lives were now just odd, noisy, and distant, as in fact they were.

"What have we here?" she heard someone say.

"Look for yourself, I guess," said someone else.

She touched the man's black knit mask. It was pilled with gray, like the dotted swiss of her premonitions, but it was askew, misaligned at the eyes — the soft turkey white of a cheekbone where the eye should be — and it was drenched with water and maroon. She could peel it off to see his face, see who he was, but she didn't dare. She tried to straighten the fabric, tried to find the eyes, then pulled it tightly down and turned away, wiping her hands on her nightgown. Without looking, she patted the dead man's arm. Then she turned and started out of the room. She went down the stairs and ran from the house.

Her crying now came in a stifled and parched way, and her hair fell into her mouth. Her chest ached and all her bones filled with a sharp pulsing. She was ill. She knew. Running barefoot across the lawn, she could feel some chaos in her gut — her intestines no longer curled neat and orderly as a French horn, but heaped carelessly upon one another like a box of vacuum-cleaner parts. The cancer, dismantling as it came, had begun its way back. She felt its poison, its tentacular reach and clutch, as a puppet feels a hand.

"Mitzy, my baby," she said in the dark. "Baby, come home."

Though she would have preferred long ago to have died, fled, gotten it all over with, the body — Jesus, how the body! — took its time. It possessed its own wishes and nostalgias. You could not just turn neatly into light and slip out the window. You couldn't go like that. Within one's own departing but stubborn flesh, there was only the long, sentimental, piecemeal farewell. *Sir? A towel. Is there a towel?* The body, hauling sadnesses, pursued the soul, hobbled after. The body was like a sweet, dim dog trotting lamely toward the gate as you tried slowly to drive off, out the long driveway. *Take me, take me too,* barked the dog. *Don't go, don't go,* it said, running along the fence, almost keeping pace but not quite, its reflection a shrinking charm in the car mirrors as you trundled past the viburnum, past the pine grove, past the property line, past every last patch of land, straight down the swallowing road, disappearing and disappearing. Until at last it was true: you had disappeared.

ALICE MUNRO

Save the Reaper

FROM THE NEW YORKER

THE GAME Eve was playing with her daughter Sophie's children was almost the same one that she had played with Sophie on long, dull car trips when Sophie was a little girl. Then the game was spies — now it was aliens. Sophie's children were in the back seat. Daisy was barely three and could not understand what was going on. Philip was seven, and in control. He was the one who picked the car they were to follow, in which there were newly arrived space travelers on their way to the secret headquarters, the invaders' lair. The aliens got their directions from the signals sent by plausible-looking people in other cars, or from somebody standing by a mailbox or even riding a tractor in a field. Many aliens had already arrived on Earth and been translated — this was Philip's word — so that anybody might be one: gas-station attendants or women pushing baby carriages or even the babies riding in the carriages.

Eve ventured to say that they might have to switch from following one vehicle to following another, because some were only decoys, not heading for the hideaway at all but leading you astray.

"No, that isn't it," said Philip. "What they do, they suck the people out of one car into another car, just in case anybody is following. They go into different people all the time, and the people never know what was in them."

"Really?" Eve said. "So how do we know which car?"

"The code's on the license plate," Philip said.

He sat as far forward as he could with his seat belt on, tapping his teeth sometimes in urgent concentration and making light whistling noises as he cautioned her.

"Uh-uh, watch out here," he said. "I think you're going to have to turn around. Yeah. Yeah. I think this may be it."

They had been following a white Mazda and were now, apparently, to follow an old green pickup truck, a Ford. Eve said, "Are you sure?"

"Sure."

What Eve had originally planned was to have the headquarters turn out to be in the village store that sold ice cream. But Philip had taken charge so thoroughly that now it was hard to manage the outcome. The pickup truck was turning off the paved country road onto a graveled side road. It was a decrepit truck with no topper, its body eaten by rust — it would not be going far. Home to some farm, most likely. They might not meet another vehicle to switch to before the destination was reached.

"You're positive this is it?" said Eve. "It's only one man by himself, you know. I thought they never traveled alone."

"The dog," said Philip.

For there was a dog riding in the open back of the truck, running back and forth from one side to the other as if there were events to be kept track of everywhere.

"The dog's one too."

Eve had come home from the village the day before laden with provisions. The village store was actually a classy supermarket these days. You could find almost anything — coffee, wine, rye bread without caraway seeds because Philip hated caraway, a ripe melon, fresh shrimp for Sophie, the dark cherries they all loved though Daisy had to be watched with the stones, a tub of chocolate-fudge ice cream, and all the regular things to keep them going for another week.

Sophie was clearing up the children's lunch. "Oh," she cried. "Oh, what'll we do with all that stuff?"

Ian had phoned, she said. Ian had phoned to say he was flying in to Toronto tomorrow. Work on his book had progressed more quickly than he had expected, so he had changed his plans. Instead of waiting for the three weeks to be up, he was coming tomorrow to collect Sophie and the children and take them on a little trip. He wanted to go to Quebec City. He had never been there, and he thought the children should see the part of Canada where people spoke French.

"He got lonesome," Philip said.

Sophie laughed. She said, "Yes. He got lonesome for us."

Twelve days, Eve thought. Twelve days had passed of the three weeks. She had had to take the house for a month. It was a cramped little house, fixed up on the cheap for summer rental. Eve's idea had been to get a lakeside cottage for the holiday — Sophie and Philip's first visit with her in nearly five years and Daisy's first ever. She had settled on this stretch of the Lake Huron shore because her parents used to bring her here, with her brother, when they were children. Things had changed — the cottages were all like suburban houses, and the rents were out of sight. This house, half a mile inland from the rocky, unfavored north end of the usable beach, had been the best she could manage. It stood in the middle of a cornfield. She had told the children what her father had once told her — that at night you could hear the corn growing. When she took the sheets off the line she had to shake out the corn bugs.

Sophie said that she and Ian and the children would drive to Quebec City in the rented car, then drive straight back to the Toronto airport, where the car was to be turned in. No mention of Eve's going along. There wasn't room in the rented car. But couldn't she have taken her own car? Ian could take the children, if he was so lonesome for them, give Sophie a rest. Eve and Sophie could ride together, as they used to in the summer, traveling to towns they had never seen before, where Eve had got parts in various summer-theater productions.

That was ridiculous. Eve's car was nine years old and in no condition to make a long trip. And it was Sophie Ian had got lonesome for — you could tell that by her warm, averted face.

"Well, that's wonderful," Eve said. "That he's got along so well with his book."

"It is," said Sophie. She always had an air of careful detachment when she spoke of Ian's book, and when Eve asked what it was about she had merely said, "Urban geography." Perhaps this was the correct behavior for academic wives — Eve had never known any.

"Anyway, you'll get some time by yourself," Sophie said. "After all this circus."

Maybe they'd had a tiff, thought Eve. This whole visit might have been tactical. Sophie might have taken the children off just to show him something. Planning holidays without him, to prove to herself that she could do it.

And the burning question was, who did the phoning?

"Why don't you leave the children here?" she said. "Just while you drive to the airport? Then drive back and pick them up and take off. That way, you'd have a little time alone, and a little time alone with Ian. It'll be hell with them at the airport."

"I'm tempted," Sophie said.

So in the end that was what she did.

Now Eve had to wonder if she herself had planned that change so that she could question Philip, which she must not do.

("Wasn't it a big surprise when your dad phoned from California?"

"He didn't phone. My mom phoned him."

"Did she? Oh, I didn't know. What did she say?"

"She said, 'I can't stand it here, I'm sick of it, let's figure out some plan to get me away.'")

When Sophie had called from California to say that she and Ian were getting married, Eve had asked her if it wouldn't be smarter just to live together first.

She had not thought Ian was any sort of contender — not so serious, even, as the Irish boy who had passed through a couple of years before, leaving Sophie pregnant with Philip, who initially looked a lot like Samuel Beckett.

"Oh, no," Sophie said. "Ian's weird, he doesn't believe in that."

And from then until now it had not been feasible for Eve to get to California. Invitations to visit had not been all that urgent, or even specific. Sophie had walked out of Eve's household a girl student with a toddling son — a winter-pale girl, harassed but high-spirited — and come back a self-contained full-bodied married woman with two children, a creamed-coffee skin, and lilac crescents of a permanent mild fatigue beneath her eyes. Also with a certain aversion to memories of the life she'd shared with Eve, of her blithe childhood (as Eve recalled it) or her adventurous days as a young mother. During this visit they had maintained a pleasant puttering routine of morning chores, beach afternoons, wine and movies when the children were in bed. And had avoided what seemed to be some mysterious disagreement or irreparable change of heart.

When Eve was a child staying in the village with her brother and her parents, they didn't have a car — it was wartime, they had come here on the train. The woman who ran the hotel was friends with Eve's mother, and they would be invited along when she drove to the country to buy corn or raspberries or tomatoes. Sometimes they would stop to have tea and look at the old dishes and bits of furniture for sale in some enterprising farm woman's front parlor. Eve's father preferred to stay behind and play checkers with some of the other men on the beach, while her brother watched them or went swimming unsupervised — he was older. The old hotel with its verandas extending over the sand was gone now, and the railway station with its flowerbeds spelling out the name of the village. The railway tracks, too. Instead, there was a fake old-fashioned mall with the satisfactory new supermarket and boutiques for leisure wear and country crafts.

When Eve was quite small and wore a great hair bow on top of her head, she was fond of these country expeditions. She ate tiny jam tarts and cakes whose frosting was stiff on top and soft underneath, topped with a bleeding maraschino cherry. She was not allowed to touch the dishes or the lace-and-satin pincushions or the sallow-looking old dolls, and the women's conversations passed over her head with a temporary and mildly depressing effect, like the inevitable clouds. But she enjoyed riding in the back seat, imagining herself on horseback or in a royal coach. Later on she refused to go. She began to hate trailing along with her mother and being identified as her mother's daughter. My daughter Eva. How richly condescending, and mistakenly possessive, that voice sounded in her ears. (She herself would use it, or some version of it, for years as a staple in some of her broadest, least accomplished acting.) She also detested her mother's habit of wearing large hats and gloves in the country, and sheer dresses on which there were raised flowers, like scabs. The oxford shoes, on the other hand — worn to favor her mother's corns — appeared embarrassingly stout and shabby. "What did you hate most about your mother?" was a game that Eve played with her friends in her first years free of home. "Corsets," one girl would say, and another said, "Wet aprons." Hairnets. Fat arms. Bible quotations. The way she sang "Danny Boy," Eve always said. Her corns.

She had forgotten all about this game until recently. The thought of it now was like touching a bad tooth.

Ahead of them the truck slowed and, without signaling, turned into a long tree-lined lane. Eve said, "I can't follow them any farther, Philip. That truck just belongs to some farmer who's headed home."

Philip said, "You're wrong. We have to." Eve drove on all the same, but as she passed the lane she noticed the gateposts. They were unusual, being shaped something like crude minarets and decorated with whitewashed pebbles and bits of colored glass. Neither one of them was straight, and they were half hidden by goldenrod and wild carrot, so that they had lost all reality as gateposts and looked instead like abandoned stage props from some gaudy operetta. The minute Eve saw them she remembered something else — a whitewashed outdoor wall in which pictures were set. The pictures were stiff, fantastic, childish scenes. Churches with spires, castles with towers, square houses with square, lopsided yellow windows. Triangular Christmas trees and tropical-colored birds half as big as the trees, a fat horse with dinky legs and burning red eyes, curly blue rivers of unvarying width, like lengths of ribbon, a moon and drunken stars and fat sunflowers nodding over the roofs of houses. All this made of pieces of colored glass set into cement, or plaster. She had seen it, and it wasn't in any public place. It was out in the country, and she was with her mother. The shape of her mother loomed in front of the wall — she was talking to an old farmer. He might only have been her mother's age, of course, and just looked old to Eve.

They went to look at odd things on those trips; they didn't just look at antiques. They had gone to see a shrub cut to resemble a bear, and an orchard of dwarf apple trees.

She didn't remember the gateposts at all, but it seemed to her that they could not have belonged to any other place. She backed the car up and swung around into the narrow track beneath the trees. The trees were heavy old Scotch pines, probably dangerous — you could see dangling dead and half-dead branches, and branches that had already blown or fallen down were lying in the grass and weeds on either side of the track. The car rocked back and forth in the ruts, and it seemed that Daisy approved of this motion. She began to make an accompanying noise: "Whoppy. Whoppy. Whoppy."

Here was something Daisy might remember — all she might remember — of this day. The arched trees, the sudden shadow, the interesting motion of the car. Maybe the white faces of the wild car-

rot that brushed at the windows. The sense of Philip beside her —
his incomprehensible serious excitement, the tingling of his childish voice brought under unnatural control. A much vaguer sense
of Eve — bare, freckly, sun-wrinkled arms, gray-blond frizzy curls
held back by a black hair band. Maybe a smell. Not of cigarettes
anymore, or of the touted creams and cosmetics on which Eve
had once spent so much of her money. Old skin? Garlic? Wine?
Mouthwash? Eve might be dead when Daisy remembered this.
Daisy and Philip might be estranged. Eve had not spoken to her
own brother for three years. Not since he said to her on the phone,
"You shouldn't have become an actress if you weren't equipped to
make a better go of it."

There wasn't any sign of a house ahead, but through a gap in the
trees the skeleton of a barn rose up, walls gone, beams intact, roof
whole but flopping to one side like a funny hat. There seemed to be
pieces of machinery, old cars, or trucks scattered around it, in the
sea of flowering weeds. Eve didn't have much leisure to look — she
was busy controlling the car on this rough track. The green truck
had disappeared ahead of her — how far could it have gone? Then
she saw that the lane curved. It curved, and they left the shade of
the pines and were out in the sunlight. The same sea foam of wild
carrot, the same impression of rusting junk strewn about, a high
wild hedge to one side, and there was the house, finally, behind it. A
big house, two stories of yellowish gray brick, an attic story of wood,
its dormer windows stuffed with dirty foam rubber. One of the
lower windows shone with the tinfoil that covered it on the inside.

She had come to the wrong place. She had no memory of this
house. There was no wall here around mowed grass. Saplings grew
up at random in the weeds.

The truck was parked ahead of her. And ahead of that she could
see a patch of cleared ground where gravel had been spread and
where she could have turned the car around. But she couldn't get
past the truck to do that. She had to stop too. She wondered if the
man in the truck had stopped where he had on purpose, so that she
would have to explain herself. He was now getting out of the truck
in a leisurely way. Without looking at her, he released the dog,
which had been running back and forth and barking with a great
deal of angry spirit. Once on the ground, it continued to bark but

didn't leave the man's side. The man wore a cap that shaded his face, so that Eve could not see his expression. He stood by the truck looking at them, not yet deciding to come any closer.

Eve unbuckled her seat belt.

"Don't get out," Philip said in a shrill voice. "Stay in the car. Turn around. Drive away."

"I can't," said Eve. "It's all right. That dog's just a yapper — he won't hurt me."

"Don't get out."

She should never have let the game get so far out of control. Philip was too excitable. "This isn't part of the game," she said. "He's just a man."

"I know," said Philip. "But don't get out."

"Stop that," said Eve, and got out and shut the door.

"Hi," she said. "I'm sorry. I made a mistake. I thought this was somewhere else."

The man said something like "Hey."

"I was actually looking for another place," Eve said. "It was a place I came to once when I was a little girl. There was a wall with pictures on it all made with pieces of broken glass. A cement wall, I think, whitewashed. When I saw those pillars by the road, I thought this must be it. You must have thought we were following you. It sounds so silly."

She heard the car door open. Philip got out, dragging Daisy behind him. Eve thought he had come to be close to her, and she put out her arm to welcome him. But he detached himself from Daisy and circled round Eve and spoke to the man. He had been almost hysterical a moment before, but now he said in a challenging way, "Is your dog friendly?"

"She won't hurt you," the man said. "Long as I'm here, she's okay. She gets in a tear because she's really a pup. She's still a pup."

He was a small man, no taller than Eve. He was wearing jeans and one of those open vests of colorful weave, made in Peru or Guatemala. Gold chains and medallions sparkled on his hairless, tanned, and muscular chest. When he spoke, he threw his head back and Eve could see that his face was older than his body. Some front teeth were missing.

"We won't bother you anymore," she said. "Philip, I was just telling this man we drove down this road looking for a place I came to when I was a little girl, and there were pictures made of colored glass set in a wall. But I made a mistake, this isn't the place."

"What's her name?" said Philip.

"Trixie," the man said, and on hearing her name the dog jumped up and bumped his arm. He swatted her down. "I don't know about no pictures. I don't live here. Harold, he's the one would know."

"It's all right," said Eve, and hoisted Daisy up on her hip. "If you could just move the truck ahead, then I could turn around."

"I don't know no pictures. See, if they was in the front part of the house I never would've saw them because Harold, like, he's got the front part of the house shut off."

"No, they were outside," said Eve. "It doesn't matter. This was years and years ago."

"Yeah. Yeah. Yeah," the man said, warming to the conversation. "You come in and get Harold to tell you about it. You know Harold? He's who owns it here. Mary, she owns it like, but Harold he put her in the Home, so now he does. It wasn't his fault — she had to go there." He reached into the truck and took out two cases of beer. "I just had to go to town. Harold sent me into town. You go on. You go in. Harold be glad to see you."

"Here, Trixie," Philip said sternly. Eve didn't believe he even cared about dogs — he was just asserting himself.

The dog came yelping and bounding around them. Daisy squealed with fright and pleasure — she was the one who was more of an animal lover — and somehow they were all en route to the house, Eve carrying Daisy and Philip and Trixie scrambling around her up some earthen bumps that had once been porch steps. The man came close behind them, smelling of the beer that he must have been drinking in the truck.

"Open it up, go ahead in," he said. "Make your way through. You don't mind it's got a little untidy here? Mary's in the Home, nobody to keep it organized like it used to be."

Massive disorder was what they had to make their way through — the kind that takes years to accumulate. The bottom layer of it was made up of chairs and tables and couches and perhaps a stove or two, with old bedclothes and newspapers and window shades and dead potted plants and ends of lumber and empty bottles and broken lighting fixtures and curtain rods piled on top of that, up to the ceiling in some places, blocking nearly all the light from outside. To make up for that, a light was burning by the inside door.

The man shifted the beer and got that door open, and shouted for Harold. It was hard to tell what sort of room they were in now — there were kitchen cupboards with the doors open, some cans on the shelves, but there were also a couple of cots with bare mattresses and rumpled blankets. The windows were so successfully covered up with furniture or hanging quilts that you couldn't tell where they were, and the smell was that of a junk store, a plugged sink, or maybe a plugged toilet, of cooking and grease and cigarettes and human sweat and dog mess and unremoved garbage.

Nobody answered the shouts. Eve turned around — there was room to turn around here, as there hadn't been on the porch — and said, "I don't think we should." But Trixie got in her way and the man ducked round her to bang on another door.

"Here he is," he said, still at the top of his voice, though he had opened the door. "Here's Harold, in here." At the same time, Trixie rushed forward and another man's voice said, "Fuck. Get that dog out of here."

"Lady here wants to see some pictures," the little man said. Trixie whined in pain — somebody had kicked her. Eve had no choice but to go on into the room.

This was a dining room. There was a heavy old dining room table and substantial chairs. Three men were sitting, playing cards. The fourth man had got up to kick the dog. The temperature in the room was about ninety degrees.

"Shut the door, there's a draft," one of the men at the table said.

The little man hauled Trixie out from under the table and threw her into the outer room, then closed the door behind Eve and the children.

"Christ. Fuck," said the man who had got up. His chest and arms were so heavily tattooed that he seemed to have purple or bluish skin. He shook one foot as if it hurt. Perhaps he had also kicked a table leg when he kicked Trixie.

Sitting with his back to the door was a young man with sharp shoulders and a delicate neck. At least Eve assumed he was young, because he wore his hair in dyed golden spikes and had gold rings in his ears. He didn't turn around. The man across from him was as old as Eve herself, and had a shaved head, a tidy gray beard, and bloodshot blue eyes. He looked at Eve without any friendliness but with some intelligence or comprehension, and in this he was unlike the tattooed man, who had looked at her as if she were some kind of hallucination that he had decided to ignore.

At the end of the table, in the host's or the father's chair, sat the man who had given the order to close the door but who hadn't looked up or otherwise paid any attention to the interruption. He was a large-boned, fat, pale man with sweaty brown curls, and as far as Eve could tell, he was entirely naked. The tattooed man and the blond man were wearing jeans, and the gray-bearded man was wearing jeans and a checked shirt buttoned up to the neck and a string tie. There were glasses and bottles on the table. The man in the host's chair — he must be Harold — and the gray-bearded man were drinking whiskey. The other two were drinking beer.

"I told her maybe there was pictures in the front, but she couldn't go in there, you got that shut up," the little man said.

Harold said, "You shut up."

Eve said, "I'm really sorry." There seemed to be nothing to do but go into her spiel, enlarging it to include staying at the village hotel as a little girl, drives with her mother, the pictures in the wall, her memory of them today, the gateposts, her obvious mistake, her apologies. She spoke directly to the graybeard, since he seemed to be the only one willing to listen or capable of understanding her. Her arm and shoulder ached from the weight of Daisy and from the tension that had got hold of her entire body. Yet she was thinking how she would describe this — she'd say it was like finding yourself in the middle of a Pinter play. Or like all her nightmares of a stolid, silent, hostile audience.

The graybeard spoke when she could not think of any further charming or apologetic thing to say. He said, "I don't know. You'll have to ask Harold. Hey. Hey, Harold. Do you know anything about some pictures made out of broken glass?"

"Tell her when she was riding around looking at pictures I wasn't even born yet," said Harold, without looking up.

"You're out of luck, lady," said the graybeard.

The tattooed man whistled. "Hey you," he said to Philip. "Hey, kid. Can you play the piano?"

There was a piano behind Harold's chair. There was no stool or bench — Harold himself taking up most of the room between the

piano and the table — and inappropriate things, such as plates and
overcoats, were piled on top of it, as they were on every surface in
the house.

"No," said Eve quickly. "No, he can't."

"I'm asking him," the tattooed man said. "Can you play a tune?"

"Let him alone," the graybeard said.

"Just asking if he can play a tune, what's the matter with that?"

"Let him alone."

"You see, I can't move until somebody moves the truck," Eve said.
She thought, There is a smell of semen in this room.

"If you could just move —" she said, turning and expecting to
find the little man behind her. She stopped when she saw he wasn't
there, he wasn't in the room at all, he had got out without her
knowing when. What if he had locked the door?

She put her hand on the knob and it turned. The door opened
with a little difficulty and a scramble on the other side. The little man had been crouched right there, listening. She went out
without speaking to him, out through the kitchen, Philip trotting
along beside her like the meekest little boy in the world. Along the
narrow pathway in the porch, through the junk, and when they
reached the open air she sucked it in, not having taken a real
breath for a long time.

"You ought to go along down the road, ask down at Harold's
cousin's place," the little man's voice came after her. "They got a
nice place. They got a new house, she keeps it beautiful. They'll
show you pictures or anything you want, they'll make you welcome.
They'll sit you down and feed you, they don't let nobody go away
empty."

He couldn't have been crouched against the door all the time,
because he had moved the truck. Or somebody had. It had disappeared altogether, been driven away to some shed or parking spot
out of sight.

"Thanks for telling me," Eve said. She got Daisy buckled in.
Philip was buckling himself in, without having to be reminded.
Trixie appeared from somewhere and walked around the car in a
disconsolate way, sniffing at the tires.

Eve got in and closed the door, put her sweating hand on the key.
The car started, she pulled ahead, onto the gravel — a space that
was surrounded by thick bushes, berry bushes, she supposed, and
old lilacs, as well as weeds. In places, these bushes had been flat-

tened by piles of old tires and bottles and tin cans. It was hard to believe that things had been thrown out of that house, considering all that was left in it, but apparently they had. And as Eve swung the car around she saw, revealed by this flattening, some fragment of a wall, to which bits of whitewash still clung. She thought she could see pieces of glass embedded there, glinting.

She didn't slow down to look. She hoped Philip hadn't noticed. She got the car pointed toward the lane and drove past the dirt steps leading to the porch. The little man stood there waving with both arms, and Trixie was wagging her tail, sufficiently roused from her scared docility to bark farewell and chase them partway down the lane. The chase was only a formality, she could have caught up with them if she'd wanted to. Eve had to slow down at once when she hit the ruts.

She was driving so slowly that it was possible — easy — for a figure to rise up out of the tall weeds on the passenger side of the car and open the door, which Eve had not thought of locking, and jump in.

It was the blond boy who had been sitting at the table, the one whose face she had never seen.

"Don't be scared. Don't be scared, anybody. I just wondered if I could hitch a ride with you guys, okay?"

It wasn't a man or a boy. It was a young girl. A girl now wearing a dirty sort of undershirt.

"Okay," Eve said. She had just managed to hold the car in the track.

"I couldn't ask you back in the house," the girl said. "I went in the bathroom and got out the window and run out here. They probably don't even know I'm gone yet. They're boiled." She grabbed a handful of the undershirt, which was much too large for her, and sniffed at it. "Stinks," she said. "I just grabbed this of Harold's was in the bathroom. Stinks."

Eve left the ruts, the darkness of the lane, and turned onto the ordinary road. "Jesus, I'm glad to get out of there," the girl said. "I didn't know nothing about what I was getting into. I didn't know even how I got there. It was night. It wasn't no place for me. You know what I mean?"

"They seemed pretty drunk, all right," Eve said.

"Yeah. Well, I'm sorry if I scared you."

"That's okay."

"If I hadn't've jumped in I thought you wouldn't stop for me.
Would you?"

"I don't know," said Eve. "I guess I would have if it got through to
me you were a girl. I didn't really get a look at you before."

"Yeah, I don't look like much now. I look like shit now. I'm not
saying I don't like to party. I like to party. But there's party and
there's party, you know what I mean?"

She turned in the seat and looked at Eve so steadily that Eve had
to take her eyes off the road for a moment and look back. And what
she saw was that this girl was much drunker than she sounded. Her
dark-brown eyes were glazed but wide open, rounded with effort,
and they had the imploring yet distant expression that drunks' eyes
get — a kind of last-ditch insistence on fooling you. Her skin was
blotched in some places and ashy in others, her whole face crumpled with the effects of a mighty binge. She was a natural brunette
— the gold spikes were intentionally and provocatively dark at the
roots — and pretty enough, if you disregarded her present dingi-
ness, to make you wonder how she had ever got mixed up with
Harold and his crew. Her shoulders were broad for a girl and her
chest lean — her way of living and the style of the times must have
taken ten or fifteen pounds off her — but she wasn't tall, and she
really wasn't boyish. Her true inclination was to be a cuddly chunky
girl, a darling dumpling.

"Herb was crazy bringing you in there like that," she said. "He's
got a screw loose, Herb."

Eve said, "I gathered that."

"I don't know what he does around there, I guess he works for
Harold. I don't think Harold uses him too good, neither."

Eve had never believed herself to be attracted to women in a
sexual way, and her idea of attractiveness in another woman had
never been this soiled and wayward charm. But perhaps the girl did
not believe this possible — she must be so used to appealing to
people. At any rate, she slid her hand along Eve's bare thigh, just
getting a little way beyond the hem of her shorts. It was a practiced
move, drunk as she was. To spread the fingers, to grasp flesh on the
first try, would have been too much. A practiced, automatically
hopeful move, yet so lacking in any true, strong, squirmy, com-
radely lust that Eve felt the hand might just as easily have fallen
short and caressed the car upholstery instead.

"I'm okay," the girl said, and her voice, like the hand, struggled to put herself and Eve on a new level of intimacy. "You know what I mean? You understand me. Okay?"

"Of course," Eve said brightly, and the hand trailed away, its whore's courtesy finished. But it had not failed altogether. Blatant and halfhearted as it was, it had been enough to set some old wires twitching. And the fact that it could be effective in any way filled Eve with misgiving, flung a shadow from this moment over all the rowdy and impulsive, as well as all the hopeful and serious, the more or less unrepented-of, couplings of her life. Not a real flare-up of shame, a sense of sin — just a shadow. What a joke on her, if she started to hanker now after a purer past and a cleaner slate.

No. It was possible that she just hankered after love.

Sophie's father was from Kerala, in the south of India. Eve had met him, and spent her whole time with him, on a train going from Vancouver to Toronto. He was a young doctor studying in Canada on a fellowship. He had a wife already, and a baby daughter, at home in India.

The train trip took three days. There was a half-hour stop in Calgary. Eve and the doctor ran around looking for a drugstore where they could buy condoms. They didn't find one. By the time they got to Winnipeg, where the train stopped for a full hour, it was too late. In fact, Eve always said, when she told their story, by the time they left the Calgary city limits it was probably too late.

He was traveling in the day coach — his school fellowship was not generous. But Eve had splurged and got herself a roomette. It was this extravagance — a last-minute decision — it was the convenience and privacy of the roomette that was responsible, Eve said, for the existence of Sophie and the greatest change in her, Eve's, life. That, and the fact that you couldn't get condoms anywhere around the Calgary station, not for love or money.

In Toronto, she waved goodbye to her lover from Kerala, as you would wave to any train acquaintance, because she was met there by the man who was at that time the serious interest and the main trouble in her life. The whole three days had been underscored by the swaying and rocking of the train — their motions were never just what they contrived themselves, and perhaps for that reason seemed guiltless, irresistible. Their feelings and conversations must

have been affected too. Eve remembered these as sweet and generous, never solemn or desperate.

She told Sophie his Christian name — Thomas, after the saint.
Until she met him, Eve had never heard about the ancient Chris-
tians in southern India. For a while, when she was in her teens,
Sophie had taken an interest in Kerala. She brought home books
from the library and took to going to parties in a sari. She talked
about looking her father up when she got older. The fact that
she knew his first name and his special study — diseases of the
blood — seemed to her possibly enough. Eve stressed to her the
size of the population of India and the chance that he had not
even stayed there. What she could not bring herself to explain was
how incidental, how nearly unimaginable, the existence of Sophie
would be, necessarily, in her father's life. Fortunately, the idea
faded, and Sophie gave up wearing the sari when all those dramatic
ethnic costumes became too commonplace. The only time she
mentioned her father, later on, was when she was carrying Philip
and making jokes about keeping up the family tradition of fly-by
fathers.

Eve said to the girl, "Where is it you want to go?"

The girl jerked backward, facing the road. "Where are you going?" she said. "You live around here?" The blurred, tired tones of
seduction had changed, as no doubt they would after sex, into a
tone of exhausted contempt and vague threat or challenge.

"There's a bus goes through the village," Eve said. "It stops at the
gas station. I've seen the sign."

"Yeah, but just one thing," the girl said. "I got no money. See, I
got away from there in such a hurry I never got to collect my
money. So what use would it be me getting on a bus without no
money?"

The thing to do was not to recognize a threat. Tell her that she
could hitchhike if she had no money. It wasn't likely that she had a
gun in her jeans. She just wanted to sound as if she might have one.

But a knife?

The girl turned for the first time to look into the back seat.

"You kids okay back there?" she said.

No answer.

"They're cute," she said. "They shy with strangers?"

How stupid to think about sex when the reality, the danger, was elsewhere.

Eve's purse was on the floor of the car in front of the girl's feet. She didn't know how much money was in it. Sixty, seventy dollars. Hardly more. If she offered money for a ticket, the girl would name an expensive destination. Montreal. Or at least Toronto. If she said, "Just take what's there," the girl would see capitulation. She would sense Eve's fear and might try to push further. What was the best she could do? Steal the car? If she left Eve and the children beside the road, the police would be after her in a hurry. If she left them dead in some thicket, she might get farther. Or if she took them along while she needed them, a knife against Eve's side or a child's throat.

Such things happen. But not as often as in the movies. Such things don't often happen.

Eve turned onto the county road, which was fairly busy. Why did that make her feel better? Safety there was an illusion. She could be driving along the highway in the midst of the day's traffic, taking herself and the children to their deaths.

The girl said, "Where's this road go?"

"It goes out to the main highway."

"Let's drive out there."

"That's where I'm driving," Eve said.

"Which way's the highway go?"

"It goes north to Owen Sound or up to Tobermory, where you get the boat. Or south to — I don't know. But it joins another highway that would get you to Sarnia. Or London. Or Detroit or Toronto if you keep going."

Nothing more was said until they reached the highway. Eve turned onto it and said, "This is it."

"Which way you heading now?"

Couldn't she tell by the sun?

"I'm heading north," Eve said.

"That the way you live, then?"

"I'm going to the village. I'm going to stop for gas."

"You got gas," the girl said. "You got over half a tank."

That was stupid. Eve should have said groceries.

Beside her the girl let out a long groan of decision, maybe of relinquishment.

"You know," she said. "You know, I might as well get out here if I'm going to hitch a ride. Get a ride here as easy as anyplace."

Eve pulled over onto the gravel. Relief was turning into something like shame. What was it like to be drunk, wasted, with no money, at the side of the road?

"Which way you said we're going?"

"North," Eve told her again.

"Which way you said to Sarnia?"

"South. Just cross the road, the cars'll be headed south. Watch out for the traffic."

"Sure," the girl said. Her voice was already distant, she was calculating new chances. She was half out of the car as she said, "See you." And into the back seat, "See you guys. Be good."

"Wait," Eve said. She leaned over and felt in her purse for her wallet, and took out a twenty-dollar bill. She got out of the car and went round to where the girl was waiting. "Here," she said. "This'll help you."

"Yeah, thanks," the girl said, stuffing the bill in her pocket, her eyes on the road.

"Listen," said Eve. "If you're stranded, I'll tell you where my house is. It's about two miles north of the village, and the village is about half a mile north of here. North. This way. It's all by itself in the middle of a field. It's got one ordinary window on one side of the front door and a funny-looking little window on the other. That's where they put in the bathroom."

"Yeah," the girl said.

"It's just that I thought, if you don't get a ride —"

"Okay," the girl said. "Sure."

When they had started driving again, Philip said, "Yuck. She smelled like vomit."

A little farther on he said, "She didn't even know you should look at the sun to tell directions. She was stupid. Wasn't she?"

"I guess so," Eve said.

"Yuck. I never ever saw anybody so stupid."

As they went through the village, he asked if they could stop for ice cream cones. Eve said no.

"There's so many people stopping for ice cream it's hard to find a place to park," she said. "We've got scads of ice cream at home."

"You shouldn't say 'home,'" said Philip. "It's just where we're staying. You should say 'the house.'"

The big hay rolls in a field to the east of the highway were facing ends on into the sun, so tightly packed they looked like shields or gongs or faces of Aztec metal. Past that was a field of pale soft gold. Barley.

"That's called barley, that gold stuff with the tails on it," she said to Philip.

"I know," he said.

"The tails are called beards sometimes." She began to recite, "But the reapers, reaping early, in among the bearded barley —"

Daisy said, "What does mean pearly?"

Philip said, "Bar-ley."

"Only reapers, reaping early," Eve said. She tried to remember. "Save the reapers, reaping early —"

That was the one she liked best. Save the reaper.

Sophie and Ian had bought corn at a roadside stand. It was for dinner. Plans had changed — they weren't leaving until morning. And they had bought a bottle of gin and some limes. Ian made the drinks while Eve and Sophie sat husking the corn.

"Two dozen. That's crazy," Eve said.

"Wait and see," said Sophie. "Ian loves corn."

Ian bowed when he presented Eve with her drink, and after she had tasted it she said, "This is most heavenly."

Ian wasn't much as she had remembered or pictured him. He was not tall, Teutonic, humorless. He was a slim fair-haired man of medium height, quick-moving, companionable. Sophie was less assured, more eager in all she said and did, than she had seemed in the last two weeks. But happier too.

Eve told her story. She began with the checkerboard on the beach, the vanished hotel, the drives into the country. It included her mother's city-lady outfits, her sheer dresses and matching slips, but not the older Eve's feelings of repugnance. And the things they went to see — the dwarf orchard, the shelf of old dolls, the marvelous pictures made of colored glass.

"They were a little like Chagall?" Eve said.

Ian said, "Yep, even us urban geographers know about Chagall."

"Sor-ry," Eve said. Both laughed.

Now the gateposts, the sudden memory, the dark lane and ruined barn and rusted machinery, the house a shambles.

"The owner was in there playing cards with his friends," Eve said.

"He didn't know anything about it. Didn't know or didn't care. And my God, it could have been sixty years ago, think of that."

Sophie said, "Oh, Mom. What a shame." She was glowing with relief to see Ian and Eve getting on so well together.

(She's not so awful, couldn't we stay one night?)

"Are you sure it was even the right place?" she said.

"Maybe not," said Eve. "Maybe not."

She would not mention the fragment of wall she had seen beyond the bushes. Why bother, when there were so many things she thought it best not to mention? First, the game that she had got Philip playing, overexciting him. And nearly everything about Harold and his companions. Everything, every single thing about the girl who had jumped into the car.

There are people who carry decency and optimism around with them, who seem to cleanse every atmosphere they settle in, and you can't tell such people things, it is too disruptive. Ian struck Eve as being one of those people, in spite of his present graciousness, and Sophie as being someone who thanked her lucky stars that she had found him. Eve could say that the house had smelled vile, and that the owner and his friends looked boozy and disreputable, but not that Harold was naked and never that she herself had been afraid. And never what she had been afraid of.

Philip was in charge of gathering up the cornhusks and carrying them outside to throw them along the edge of the field. Occasionally Daisy picked up a few on her own and took them off to be distributed around the house. Philip had added nothing to Eve's story and had not seemed to be concerned with the telling of it. But once it was told, and Ian (interested in bringing this local anecdote into line with his professional studies) was asking Eve what she knew about the breakup of older patterns of village and rural life, about the spread of what was called agribusiness, Philip did look up from the stooping and crawling he was doing around the adults' feet. He looked at Eve — a flat look, a moment of conspiratorial blankness, a buried smile, that passed before there could be any demand for recognition of it. It seemed to mean that, however much or little he knew, he knew about the importance of keeping things to yourself. Eve got a jolt from that. She wished to deny that she was in any way responsible for it, but she couldn't disclaim it.

If the girl came looking for her, they would all still be here. Then Eve's carefulness would go for nothing.

The girl wouldn't come. Much better offers would turn up before she'd stood ten minutes by the highway. More dangerous offers, perhaps, but more interesting, likely to be more profitable.

The girl wouldn't come. Unless she found some homeless, heartless wastrel her own age. (I know where there's a place we can stay, if we can get rid of the old lady.)

Not tonight but tomorrow night, Eve would lie down in this hollowed-out house, its board walls like a paper shell around her. She would will herself to grow light, free of consequence, and hope to go to sleep with nothing in her head but the deep, live rustle of the corn.

ANNIE PROULX

The Bunchgrass Edge
of the World

FROM THE NEW YORKER

THE COUNTRY appeared as empty ground, big sagebrush, rabbit-brush, intricate sky, flocks of small birds like packs of cards thrown up in the air, and a faint track drifting toward the red-walled horizon. Graves were unmarked, fallen house timbers and corrals burned up in old campfires. Nothing much but weather and distance, the distance punctuated once in a while by ranch gates, and to the north the endless murmur and sun-flash of semis rolling along the interstate.

In this vague region the Touheys ranched — old Red, ninety-six years young, his son Aladdin, Aladdin's wife, Wauneta, their boy, Tyler, object of Aladdin's hopes, the daughters, Shan and (the family embarrassment) Ottaline.

Old Red, born in Lusk in 1902, grew up in an orphan home, a cross-grained boy — wrists knobby and prominent, red hair parted in the middle — and walked off when he was fourteen to work in a tie-hack camp. The year the First World War ended he was in Medicine Bow timber. He quit, headed away from the drought burning the West, drilled wells, prodded cattle in railroad stockyards, pasted up handbills, cobbled a life as though hammering two-bys. In 1930 he was in New York, shoveling the Waldorf-Astoria off the side of a barge into the Atlantic Ocean.

One salty morning, homesick for hard, dry landscape, he turned west again. He found a wife along the way and soon enough had a few dirty kids to feed. In Depression Oklahoma he bombed roosting crows and sold them to restaurants. When crows went scarce, they moved to Wyoming, settled a hundred or two miles from where he'd started.

They leased a ranch in the Red Wall country — log house, straggle of corrals that from a distance resembled dropped sticks. The wind isolated them from the world. To step into that reeling torrent of air was to be forced back. The ranch was adrift on the high plain.

There was the idea of running a few sheep, his wife's idea. In five years they built the sheep up into a prime band. The Second World War held wool prices steady. They bought the ranch for back taxes.

In August of 1946 a green-shaded lamp from Sears, Roebuck arrived the same day the wife bore their last child. She named the kid Aladdin.

Peace and thermoplastic resin yarns ruined the sheep market and they went to cattle. The wife, as though disgusted with this bovine veer, complained of nausea as they unloaded the first shipment of scrubby calves. She stayed sick three or four years, finally quit. Red was a hard driver, and of the six children only Aladdin remained on the dusty ranch, the giant of the litter, stubborn and abusive, bound to have everything on the platter, whether bare bones or beefsteak.

Aladdin came back from Vietnam, where he flew C-123 Bs, spraying defoliants. Now he showed a hard disposition, a taste for pressing on to the point of exhaustion, then going dreamy and stuporous for days. He married Wauneta Hipsag on a scorching May morning in Colorado, the bride's home state. A tornado funnel hung from a green cloud miles away. Wauneta's abundant hair was rolled in an old-fashioned French knot. The wedding guests were her parents and eleven brothers, who threw handfuls of wheat, no rice available. During the ceremony, Wauneta's father smoked cigarette after cigarette. That evening at the Touhey ranch a few kernels of wheat shot from Aladdin's pants cuffs when he somersaulted off the porch, exuberant and playful before his new wife. The grains fell to the ground and in the course of time sprouted, grew, headed out, and reseeded. The wheat seized more ground each year until it covered a quarter-acre, the waving grain ardently protected by Wauneta. She said it was her wedding wheat and if ever cut the world would end.

*

When he was twenty-six, Aladdin wrenched the say of how things should go from old Red. Aladdin had been in the mud since blue morning digging out a spring. The old man rode up on his one-eyed mare. The son slung a shovelful of wet dirt.

"You ain't got it dug out yet?" the old man asked. "Not too swift, are you? Not too smart. Shovel ain't even sharp, I bet. How you got a woman a marry you I don't know. You must a got a shotgun on her. Must a hypatized her. Not that she's much, but probably beats doin it with livestock, that right?" The mud-daubed son climbed out of the hole, picked up clods, pelted his father until he galloped off, pursued him to the house, and continued the attack with stones and sticks of firewood snatched up from the woodpile, hurled the side-cutters he always carried in a back pocket, the pencil behind his ear, the round can filled not with tobacco but the dark green of homegrown.

Red, knot-headed and bleeding, raised one arm in surrender, backed onto the porch. He was seventy-one then and called out his age as a defense. "I made this ranch and I made you." His spotted hand went to his crotch. Aladdin gathered can, pencil, and side-cutters and put the old man's horse away. He went back to the spring, head down, picked up the shovel, and dug until his hands went nerveless.

Wauneta moved old Red's belongings out of the big upstairs bedroom and into a ground-floor room off the kitchen, once a pantry and still smelling of raisins and stale flour. A strip of adhesive tape held the cracked window glass together.

"You'll be closer to the bathroom," she said in a voice as smooth as gas through a funnel.

Wauneta taught her two girls to carry pie on a white plate to their grandfather, kiss him goodnight, while Tyler played with plastic cows and stayed up late. One forenoon she came in from hanging clothes and found four-year-old Ottaline gripped astraddle over old Red's lap and squirming to get down. She ripped the child from him, said, "You keep your dirty old prong away from my girls or I'll pour boilin water on it."

"What? I wasn't —" he said. "Not — never did —"

"I know old men," she said.

"Potty!" screamed Ottaline, too late.

Now she warned the daughters from him, spoke of him in a dark tone, fine with her to let him sit alone in the straight-backed chair, let him limp unaided from porch to kitchen to fusty room. The sooner he knocked on the pearly gates, the better, she told Aladdin, who groaned and rolled to his side, fretted by the darkness that kept him from work, a quick-sleeping man who would be up at three, filling the kettle, opening the red coffee can, impatient to start.

"Wauneta, what a you want me a do about it?" he said. "Drown him in the stock tank? He will kick off one a these days."

"You been sayin that for five years. He is takin the scenic route."

Time counted out in calving; first grass; branding; rainfall; clouds; roundup; the visit from old Amendinger the cattle buyer; shipping; early snow; late blizzard. The children grew up. Aladdin got an old Piper Cub, swapping it for two bulls, a set of truck tires, a saddle, the rusted frame and cylinder of an 1860 Colt .44 he'd found at the root of a cedar. Wauneta's sandy hair grayed, and every few months she went into the bathroom and gave it a maroon color treatment. Only old Red watched the progression of dates on his little feed-store calendar. He was older than kerosene now and strong to make his century.

Shan, the younger daughter, graduated from high school, moved to Las Vegas. She took a job in the package-design department of a manufacturer of religious CDs, quickly grasped the subtleties of images: breaking waves, shafts of sunlight denoted godly favor, while dark clouds with iridescent edges, babies smiling through tears represented troubles that would soon pass with the help of prayer. Nothing was hopeless and the money came in on wheels.

Ottaline was the oldest, distinguished by a physique approaching the size of a propane tank. She finished school a year behind her younger sister, stayed home. She plaited her reddish pink hair in two braids as thick as whip handles. In conversation a listener would look back and forth between the pillowy, dimpled mouth and crystal-crack blue eyes and think it a pity she was so big. The first year at home she wore gaily colored XXL skirts and helped out around the house. But her legs were always cold and she suffered from what Wauneta called "minstrel problems," a sudden flow that sent her running for the bathroom, leaving a trail of dark round blood spots behind her varying in size from a dime to a half-dollar. After bare-legged wades through snow, after scaly chilblain, she gave up drafty skirts and housework, changed to ranch chores with Aladdin. Now she wore manure-caked roper boots, big jeans, and T-shirts that hung to her thighs.

"Yes, keep her out a the house," said Wauneta. "What she don't break she loses, and what she don't lose she breaks. Her cookin would kill a pig."

"I hate cookin," said Ottaline. "I'll help Dad." It was a fallback position. She wanted to be away, wearing red sandals with cork soles, sitting in the passenger seat of a pearl-colored late-model pickup, drinking from a bottle shaped like a hula girl. When would someone come for her? She was not audacious, not like her younger sister. She knew her appalling self and there was no way to evade it.

Aladdin saw she was easy with the stock, where the boy Tyler whooped and whistled and rode like a messenger reporting a massacre.

"Had my way, ever hand'd be a woman. A woman got a nice disposition with animals." He intended the remark to sting.

"Oh, Daddy," said Tyler in comic falsetto. He was the horseman of the family, had slept out in the dilapidated bunkhouse since he was thirteen, Wauneta's edict.

"My brothers slept in the bunkhouse." There was in that flat remark all of Wauneta's childhood, sequestered, alert, surrounded by menace.

This only son, Tyler, was a huge, kit-handed youth of nineteen, stout enough to frighten any father except Aladdin. The kid stamped around in dirty jeans and a brown hat. He was slack-mouthed in reverie, sported a young man's cat-fur mustache, cheeks marred by strings of tiny pimples. He was only one percent right about anything, alternated between despondency and quick fury. On Aladdin's birthday, Tyler presented him with two coyote ears, the result of weeks of cunning stalk. Aladdin unwrapped them, laid them on the tablecloth, and said, "Aw, what am I supposed a do with two coyote ears?"

"By God," screamed Tyler, "set one a them on your dick and say it won a fur hat in the church raffle. You are all against me." He swept the ears to the floor and walked out.

"He will be back," said Wauneta. "He will be back with dirty clothes and his pockets turned inside out. I know boys."

"I was the wanderin boy," old Red mumbled. "He won't be back. Takes after me. I cowboyed. I killed hogs. I made it through. Worked like a man since I was fourteen. Ninety-six years young. Never knowed my father. Carry you all to hell and spit on you." His finger dragged across the tablecloth, the long-ago self making a way. The old man showed a terrible smile, fumbled with his can of snoose.

Aladdin, face like a shield, curly hair springing, tipped his head toward the tablecloth, mumbled, "O bless this food." Heavy beef slices, encircled by a chain of parsnips and boiled potatoes, slumped on the platter. He had discovered two long-dead cows that afternoon, one bogged, the other without a mark of cause. He lifted a small potato and transferred it to his father's plate without looking at him, ignored the rattling of the old man's fork, though Wauneta, pouring coffee into heavy cups, frowned and said, "Watch it, John Wayne." A pastel envelope lay between her knife and a flat cake with sugar icing so thin it appeared blue.

"Somethin come from Shan."

"She comin back?" Aladdin crushed his potatoes, flooded them with skim milk. Game and Fish would pay for stock killed by grizzlies or lions. He had not seen lion sign for a decade, and grizzly never.

"Didn't open it yet," she said, tearing the end. There was a short and vague letter that she read aloud and, clipped to it, an astonishing photograph. It showed his daughter in a black bikini, greased muscles starkly outlined, exhibiting bulging biceps and calves, spiky crewcut hair whitened with bleach, her rolling, apricot-size eyes frozen wide open. In the letter she had written, "Got into bodybuilding. A lot of girls here do it!"

"Whatever she has done to her hair," said Wauneta, "somebody talked her into it. I know Shan and that would not be her idea." When Shan left she had been an ordinary young woman with thin arms, blondish chew-ended hair. Her glancing unlevel eyes ricked from face to face. When she spoke, her hands revolved, the fingers flung out. The yearbook had named her "most animated."

"Bodybuildin." Aladdin's tone was neutral. He had the rancher's expectation of disaster, never believed in happy endings. He was satisfied that she was alive, not building bombs or winking at drive-by johns.

Ottaline stared at her coffee. Floating on the surface was a spread-wing moth the shape of a tiny arrowhead. It pointed at her sister's empty chair.

Aladdin wore boots and a big hat but rarely mounted a horse. He missed the Piper Cub, which had seemed to him very like a horse. Someone had stolen it two years earlier, had unbolted the wings and hauled it away on a flatbed while he slept. He suspected Mormons. Now he was welded to the driver's seat of his truck, tearing over the dusty roll of land, and sometimes, drugged and fallen, he spent the night out in a draw, cramped on the front seat. The windshield glass, discolored by high-altitude light, threw down violet radiance. He had made the headache rack from poles cut on the ranch. He kept a bottle of whiskey, a rope behind the seat. The open glove compartment carried kindling, wrenches, bolts and nuts, several hundred loose fence staples, and a handleless hammerhead. Wauneta tossed an old quilt in the cab and told him to wind up the windows when it rained.

"I know you," she said. "You will let the weather get you."

Every ten days or so Ottaline reared up and said she wanted to go to town and look for a job. Aladdin would not take her. Her weight, he said, ruined the springs on the passenger side. Anyway, there were no jobs, she knew that. She had better stay on the ranch where she didn't know how good she had it.

"I don't know why you would want a leave this ranch."

She said he should let her drive in alone.

"I will tell you when I am ready for advice," he said. "I am steerin my own truck for now. If you want a drive a truck then buy one."

"I am about a million dollars short." It was all hopeless.

"What a you want me a do, rob a bank for you?" he said. "Anyway, you're comin a the bull sale. And I'll give you a pointer you don't want a forget. Scrotal circumference is damn important."

What was there for Ottaline when the work slacked off? Stare at indigo slants of hail forty miles east, regard the tumbled clouds like mechanics' rags, count out he loves me, he loves me not, in nervous lightning crooked as branchwood through all quarters of the sky.

That summer the horses were always wet. It rained uncommonly, the southwest monsoon sweeping in. The shining horses stood out on the prairie, withers streaming, manes dripping, and one would suddenly start off, a fan of droplets coming off its shoulders like a cape. Ottaline and Aladdin wore slickers from morning coffee to goodnight yawn. Wauneta watched the television weather while she ironed shirts and sheets. Old Red called it drip and dribble, stayed in his room chewing tobacco, reading Zane Grey in large-print editions, his curved fingernail creasing the page under every line. On the Fourth of July they sat together on the porch watching a distant storm, pretending the thick, ruddy legs of lightning and thunder were fireworks.

Ottaline had seen most of what there was to see around her, with nothing new in sight. Brilliant events burst open not in the future but in the imagination. The room she had shared with Shan was a room within a room. In the unshaded moonlight her eyes shone oily white. The calfskin rug on the floor seemed to move, to hunch and crawl a fraction of an inch at a time. The dark frame of the mirror sank into the wall, a rectangular trench. From her bed she saw the moon-bleached grain elevator and behind it immeasurable range flecked with cows like small black seeds. She was no one but Ottaline in that peppery, disturbing light that made her want everything there was to want. The raw loneliness then, the silences of the day, the longing flesh led her to press her mouth into the crook of her own hot elbow. She pinched and pummeled her fat flanks, rolled on the bed, twisted, went to the window a dozen times, heels striking the floor until old Red in his pantry below called out, "What is it? You got a sailor up there?"

Her only chance seemed the semiliterate, off-again, on-again hired man, Hal Bloom, tall legs like chopsticks, T-shirt emblazoned *Aggressive by Nature, Cowboy by Choice.* He worked for Aladdin in short bursts between rodeo roping, could not often be pried off his horse (for he cherished a vision of himself as an 1870s cowboy just in from an Oregon cattle drive). Ottaline had gone with him down into the willows a dozen times, to the damp soil and nests of stinging nettles, where he pulled a pale condom over his small, hard penis and crawled silently onto her. His warm neck smelled of soap and horse.

But then, when Ottaline began working on the ranch for hard money, Aladdin told Hal Bloom to go spin his rope.

"Yeah, well, it's too shit-fire long a haul out here anyways," Bloom said, and was gone. That was that.

Ottaline was dissolving. It was too far to anything. Someone had to come for her. There was not even the solace of television, for old Red dominated the controls, always choosing Westerns, calling out to the film horses in his broken voice, "Buck him off, kick his brains out!"

Ottaline went up to her room, listened to cell-phone conversations on the scanner.

"The balance on account number seven three five five nine is minus two hundred and oh four. . . . "

"Yes, I can see that, maybe. Are you drinkin beer already?" "Ha-ha. Yes. "

"I guess maybe you didn't notice." "It wasn't all smashed flat like that, all soft. I took it out of the bag and it was — you goin a carve it?" "Not that one. It's nasty. "

"Hey, is it rainin there yet?"

"Is it rainin yet?" she repeated. It was raining everywhere, and people were alive in it except in the Red Wall country.

Ottaline studied Shan's photograph, said to her mother, "If it kills me I am goin a walk it off."

"Haven't I heard that before?" said Wauneta. "I know you."

Ottaline marched around outside the house for a few days, then widened the loop to take in the corrals, the toolshed, the root cellar, circumambulated the defunct gravel quarry where Aladdin dragged worn-out equipment, a sample of tractors, one a 1928 blue Rumely OilPull tractor on steel with a chokecherry tree growing through the frame, beside it old Red's secondhand 1935 AC with the four-cylinder overhead valve engine, paint sun-scalded white. Half buried at the foot of a caving bank lay the remains of a stripped Fordson Major, grille and radiator shroud smashed in, and next to a ruined stock tank stood the treacherous John Deere 4030.

She was walking through the rain-slicked wrecks when a voice spoke, barely audible. "Sweetheart, lady-girl."

The low sun poured slanting light under the edge of a cloud mass so dark it seemed charred, the prairie, the tractors, her hand beyond the wrist hem of the yellow slicker, all gilded with saffron brilliance. Colors of otherworld intensity blazed in the washed air, the distant Red Wall a bed of coals.

"Sweet," the voice breathed.

She was alone, there were no alien spacecraft in the sky. She stood quite still. She had eaten from a plateful of misery since childhood, suffered avoirdupois, unfeeling parents, the hard circumstances of the place. Looniness was possible, it could happen to anyone. Her mother's brother Mapston Hipsag had contracted a case of lumpy jaw from the stock, and the disease took him by stages from depressive rancher to sniggering maniac. The light glided down to a dying hue and the wrecked machines sank into their own coffee-brown shadows. She heard nothing but mosquito whine, small wind that comes with approaching darkness.

That night, listening to the ramble of talk on the scanner, she wondered if hunger had prompted an invisible voice, went to the kitchen, and ate all of the leftover pork roast.

"I'm worried about you. I hope nobody tries to kill you or something."
"Don't miss me too much."

"Nothin been hit." "It just rained like a bastard up here." "Rained like shit here too." "No point stayin here."

Nothing happened for weeks, common enough in that part of the state. On a roaring noon she went again to the gravel pit.

"Hello, sweetheart. Come here, come here." It was the 4030, Aladdin's old green tractor, burly but with forward-raking lines that falsely indicated an eagerness to run. The machine had killed a ranch hand years earlier in a rollover accident at the weed-filled irrigation ditch — Maurice Ramblewood, or what? Rambletree, Bramblefood, Rumbleseat, Tumbleflood? She was a kid but he always flashed her a smile, asked her what was cooking, and on the fatal day tossed her a candy bar, pliable and warm from his shirt pocket, said she could borrow his sunglasses that turned the world orange. In late afternoon he was dead in bristle grass and spiny clotbur. His ghost.

"Maurice? That you?"

"No. No. It ain't him. That boy's a cinder."

"Who is talkin?"

"Two steps closer."

She stretched out her hand to the side grille. Yellow jackets had built a nest in it and were creeping in and out of the grille's interstices, palping the air suspiciously. She stared fixedly at the insects.

"That is good," said the voice inside the tractor. "Get you a little stick and scratch where all that paint is blistered up." But she backed off.

"I'm just scared to pieces," she said, looking at the sky, the rise and fall of crested prairie, the bunchgrass edge of the world that flared like burning threads.

"Naw, now, don't be. This old world is full a wonders, ain't it? Come on, get up in the cab. Plenty a bounce left. The seat's still good. Pretend you're drivin right through L.A." The voice was hoarse and plangent, just above an injured whisper, a movie gangster's voice.

"No," she said. "I don't like this. I already got enough problems, not makin it worse by gettin in a old tractor cab that's ready to collapse."

"Aw, you think you got problems? Look at me, sweetheart, settin out here in the bakin sun, blizzards and lizards, not even a tarpolean over me, brakes wrecked, battery gone, workin parts seized up, no gas, surrounded by deadheads, covered with birdshit and rust. Here you are at last, won't even give me the time a day."

"It's six-twelve," she said and walked off, fingertips pressing her eyebrows. This was hallucination.

The voice called after her, "Sweetheart, lady-girl, don't go."

She craved to know something of the world, but there was only the scanner.

"Broken, threads stripped, had to take it up and get it welded. You know that fucker used a do that shit but he don't hang around here no more."

"— horns off the steers. I stopped by to see her." *"Yeah? They told me you left before three."* *"I was there at three to change my clothes."* *"You know you're full a bullshit."*

"It's fuckin pourin here, man." *"I don't know what else. It was like — Whoa! Oh my God that was a big lightnin! Whoa! I got a get off the fuckin phone."*

"I want a be with you, but I look at reality and I say to myself this fuckin woman wants a fuck everybody, I can't even get it on the couch, got a go in the fuckin bedroom." *"Yeah, it's all my fault, right?"*

It made her sick, it made her jealous to hear those quarrelsome but coupled voices.

*

She went again to the gravel pit. The choking rasp began when she was twenty feet distant.

"Maurice Stumblebum? Just forget him. Wrench your steerin wheel, jam the brakes, rev, rev, rev. Never change oil or filter, never check brake fluid, never got the ballast right, didn't bother a check the front-wheel toe-in, used a ride the clutch unmerciful, run in heavy mud and never think a the front wheel bearins. They're ground a dust. Jump around in the seat until it made me crazy. Aw, don't drum your fingers like that, take me serious."

She looked away to the Red Wall, something best kept at a distance. It was not a place to go. The distant highway flashed, the reflection from a bottle pitched out of a tourist's car.

"But that ain't why I killed him."

"Then why?"

"Over you," said the tractor. "Over you. I saved you from him. He was goin a get you."

"I could a saved myself," she said, "if I'd a wanted to."

At supper Wauneta opened a pink envelope from Shan.

"What I thought," she said. "I knew it. I knew Tyler'd show up." Shan wrote that Tyler had been living with her and her roommate for a month, that he was trying for a job with the BLM rounding up wild horses and, while he waited to hear, holding down a telephone job for a bill collector. He had bought himself a computer and in the daytime seemed to be studying electronics — the table was covered with bits of wire and tape and springs when she came home from the gym. They had become vegetarians, except Tyler, who ate shrimp and crab legs, foods he had never tasted until Las Vegas. He could not get enough of them. He had, wrote Shan, spent sixty-five dollars for a four-pound box of jumbo shrimp, had cooked and eaten them in solitary gluttony. "Ha-ha, not much has changed. He is still a pig," the letter ended.

Aladdin put a parsnip on old Red's plate.

"Shrimps'll make your pecker curl," said the old man. "Sounds like he's buildin a bomb with them wires."

"He's not doin no such thing," said Wauneta.

After supper Ottaline scraped the dishes, began to snivel. Wauneta slung her hip against her, put her arm around the soft shoulders.

"What are you cryin about? That weight not comin off? Make up your mind to it, you are one a them meant to be big. My mother was the same."

"Not that. It seems like somebody is makin fun a me."

"Who? Who is makin fun a you?"

"I don't know. Somebody." She pointed at the ceiling.

"Well, let me tell you, that Somebody makes fun a everbody. Somebody's got a be laughin at the joke. Way I look at it."

"It's lonesome here."

"There's no lonesome, you work hard enough."

Ottaline went upstairs, set the scanner to rove and seek.

"Please enter your billing number now. I'm sorry, you have either mis-dialed or dialed a billing number we cannot accept. Please dial again."

"Why would it do that?" "Turn it off, turn it off."

"Hey, git doughnuts. And don't be squirtin around with twelve of em. Git a bunch. Don't be squirtin around, git two boxes."

"If that's fuckin all you have to say — then dang!"

Every day the tractor unloaded fresh complaints, the voice rough and urgent.

"Lady-girl, your daddy is a cocklebur. Get up and he don't get down. Stay in the seat sixteen hours. Aw, come here, I want to show you somethin. Look to the left a the cowl there, yeah, down there. What do you see?"

"Patch a rust. Big patch a rust."

"That's right. A big patch a rust. I won't tell you how that got there. I don't like to tell a girl somethin bad about her daddy. But in all the years I worked for your daddy I only once had a sweet day and that was the day I come here straight off the dealer's yard, fourth-hand and abused, and you was ten years old, your birth-day. You patted me and said, 'Hello, Mr. Tractor.' Your daddy put you up in the seat, said, 'You can be the first one a sit there,' and your little hand was sticky with frostin and you wiggled around in the seat and I thought — I thought it was goin a be like that ever day and it never happened again, you never touched me again, never come near me, just that damn bony-assed Maurice couldn't be bothered a use the rock-shaft lever, I got him with hydraulic oil under pressure, he got a infection. And your dirty dad. Broke my heart until now. But I'll tell you the truth. If your daddy was a get up here today I would hurt him for what he done a my brake system. I will tell you sometime about the beer and what he done with it."

"What?"

"I'd tell you, but I think it would disgust you. I won't turn a lady-girl against her family. I know you'd hold it against me and I don't want that. Tell you some other time."

"You tell me now. Don't go around talkin blah-blah. I hate that."

"All right. You asked for it. Stumblebum never bothered a check nothin. Finally brake fluid's gone. I'm out there with your daddy, on the slope, we was haulin a horse trailer. He's got his old six-pack with him, way he drinks he's alcoholic. He mashes his foot on the brake and we just keep rippin. No way he could stop me, not that I wanted a stop. I didn't care. Slowed only when we come at a rise. He jumped off before the rollback, kicked a rock under a back wheel. What he done — poured warm beer in my master-brake-cylinder reservoir, pumped that beer down the brake lines. Yeah, he got enough pressure. But it ruined me. That's why I'm here. You hate me for tellin you, don't you?"

"No. I heard a worse crimes. Like killin somebody in a ditch."

"You goin a pout?"

Another day she stormed out to the gravel pit.

"Shut up," she said. "Don't you see I'm fat?"

"What I like."

"Why don't you fix your attentions on another tractor? Leave me alone."

"Now, think about it, lady-girl. Tractors don't care nothin about tractors. Tractors and people, that's how it is. Ever tractor craves some human person, usually ends up with some big old farmer."

"Are you like an enchanted thing? A damn story where some girl lets a warty old toad sleep in her shoe and in the mornin the toad's a good-lookin dude makin omelettes?"

"Naw. I could tell you they had a guy work at Deere a few years ago got fired out a the space program for havin picnics with foreigners and drinkin vodka but they couldn't prove nothin. He was cross-wired about it. It was around when they started foolin with computers and digital tapes. Remember them cars that told you to shut the door? Like that. Simple. Computers. He worked me up, fifteen languages. I could tell you that. Want a hear me say somethin in Urdu? Skivelly, skavelly —"

"You could tell me that, but I would not believe it. Some lame story." And it seemed to her that the in-built affection for humans the tractor harped on was balanced by vindictive malevolence.

"That's right, I was lyin."

"You got any kind a sense," she said, "you'd know people don't go crazy over tractors."

"Where you're wrong. Famous over in Iowa, Mr. Bob Ladderrung got himself buried with his tractor. Flat-out loved each other, he didn't care who knew it. And I don't just mean Iowa farmers. There's fellas can't keep away from us. There's girls fell in love with tractors all over this country. There is girls married tractors."

"I'm goin in," she said, turning away. "I'm goin in." She looked at the house, her mother's wedding wheat swaying yellow, old Red's face like a hanging skull in the window. "Oh, please," she said to herself, weeping, "not a tractor or nothin like it."

After supper, in her room, she wished for a ray gun to erase the brilliant needles of light from the isolate highway, silence the dull humming like bees in a high maybush. She wanted the cows to lie down and die, hoped for a tornado, the Second Coming, violent men in suits driving a fast car into the yard. There was the scanner.

"You think he's normal until you start to talk to him."

"I should a called the police, as mean and horrible as he is, but I'm not goin a do that. And this is what I'm thinkin. I'm goin a go after him even though we haven't been married that long. He's goin a pay. He's got it! He's makin two thousand a month. Anyway, I got a headache every day a my life over this. But I'm fine. Just a little insane. Don't worry, I'm fine."

Aladdin lifted a wad of turnip greens from the bowl, lowered it onto Ottaline's plate.

"What are you doin out there in the gravel pit with them tractors? I was lookin for you half a hour."

"Thinkin," she said, "of maybe try a fix up that Deere. Like just mess around with it." That day she had climbed up into the cab, sat on the seat, feeling an awful thrill.

"I wouldn't spend a dime on that damn thing. It never run good."

"I'd spend my own money on parts. I don't know, maybe a foolish idea. Thought I might try."

"We had trouble with that machine from day one. Damn Maurice Gargleguts got done, it wouldn't go much. We hauled that thing to

Dig Yant, he replaced some a the wirin, cleaned the fuel tank, blew
out the gas line, ten other things, rebuilt the carburetor. Then
somethin else went wrong. Ever time they fixed it, it'd blow up
somewhere else. They give me a hot iron on that one. I went to
raisin heck and the dealer finally admitted it was a lemon. Give me
a real good deal on the Case. Now, that's a tractor that's held up.
You know, that 4030, you will be strippin it down to grit." He ate his
meat loaf. He thought, said, "I could — might give you a hand.
Haul it in that blue-door shed. Put a stove out there, run a pipe."
He saw himself rising in the black wintry morning while his family
slept, going out to the shed to stoke the fire, take a little smoke, and
in the cozy warmth breaking loose rusty bolts, cleaning mucky
fittings, pins, studs, screws, nuts soaking in a tub of kerosene while
he waited for daylight and the start of the real day. "We'll get her in
there tomorrow."

"Him," said Ottaline.

"You won't fix it," said old Red. "What you are tryin a fix ain't
fixable."

"Okay," she said, walking up to the tractor. "We are goin a move you
into the blue-door shed and operate. My dad is goin a help me and
you better stay hunderd percent quiet or it's all over."

"You want a know my problems? Brakes. Belts shot, block
cracked, motor seized, everthing rusted hard, sludge, dirt, lifters
need replacin, water pump's shot, camshaft bearings shot, seals
shot, magneto, alternator fried — you look inside that clutch
housin you'll see a nightmare. Clutch plate needs a be relined, got
a replace the tie-rod ends, the fuel shut-off line is bust, the steerin-
gear assembly wrecked, the front axle bushings, spindle bushings
all bananas and gone, you want a talk differential you'll be listin
parts for fifteen minutes. The transmission clutch slipped bad before everthing went blank. I don't want your dirty dad a work on
me. He already done that and look at me."

"Different now. Anyway, goin a be mostly me. I'm doin this. What
gears was that tranny clutch slippin in?"

"You? You don't know nothin about tractor repair. I don't want
you workin on me. I want you should take me a Dig Yant — he's a
tractor man. It's men that fixes tractors, not no woman. First and
third."

"You don't got much choice. Tell you one thing, I didn't take

home ec. I took mechanics and I got a B. First and third? Seal on
the underdrive brake piston or more likely the disks bad worn." She
had brought a can of penetrating oil with her and began to squirt it
on studs, bolts, and screws, to rap on the rusted bolts with a heavy
wrench.

"You make a wrong move I might hurt you."

"You know what? I was you I'd lay back and enjoy it." Something
Hal Bloom had said.

The rain quit in September and the prairie began to yellow out.
There were a few heated days; then the weather cooled and an early
storm hoop-rolled out of the northwest, slinging a hash of snow,
before they got the tractor dismantled to frame, motor, and transmission.

"We got a get a engine hoist in here," said Aladdin, coughing.
The first night of the storm he had got wasted and slept out in his
pickup, window down, the snow carousing over him. He woke shuddering, drove home, heard they were out of coffee, drank a glass of
cold water, told Wauneta he could not eat any breakfast. By noon
he was feverish and strangling, took to the bed.

"That coughin drives me into the water and I don't swim," said
old Red. "Better off just smother him, be done with it."

"There is somebody else at the top a my smotherin list," said
Wauneta. "I knew this was goin a happen. Sleep in a truck." Aspirin,
poultices, glasses of water, steam tent, hot tea were her remedies,
but nothing changed. Aladdin roasted in his own dry heat.

"What's tomorrow," he said, rolling his aching head on the hot
pillow.

"Friday."

"Bring me my calendar." With swimming eyes he studied the
scrawled notes, called for Ottaline.

"She's out feedin. It snowed wet, froze hard crust out there, they
can't hardly get grass. Supposed a warm up this weekend."

"God damn it," he whispered, "when she comes in, send her
here." He shivered and retched.

The snow rattled down on Ottaline in the cab of Aladdin's big Case
tractor, a huge round bale on the hydraulic-lift spear. It could keep
snowing until June the way it was coming down. At noon she drove

back to the house, ravenous, hoping for macaroni and cheese. She left the Case idling.

"Dad wants you," said Wauneta. It was beef and biscuits. Ottaline took a pickle from the cut-glass dish.

She sidled into her parents' bedroom. She was one of those who could not bear sick people, who did not know where to look except away from the bloodshot eyes and swollen face.

"Look," he said. "It's first Friday a the month tomorrow. I got Amendinger comin out at eight o'clock. If I ain't better" — he coughed until he retched — "you are goin a deal with him, take him out there, he can look them over, see what we got, make you a offer." Amendinger, the cattle buyer, was a dark-complexioned man with sagging eyes, a black mustache whose ends plunged down to his jawline like twin divers. He wore black shirts and a black hat, gave off an air of implacable decision and control. He had no sense of humor, and every rancher cursed him behind his back.

"Dad, I am scared a death a that man. He will get the best a me. He will make us a low offer and I will get rattled and say yes. Why not Ma? Nobody gets on her bad side."

"Because you know the animals and she don't. If Tyler was here — but he ain't. You're my little cowgirl. You don't have to say nothin. Just take him around, hear his offer, and tell him we'll get back to him." He knew that Amendinger did business on the spot; there was no getting back to him. "I get better of this I am goin a buy a plane I been lookin at. It's the only way to work this big of a ranch. A truck ain't no good, windows and all."

"I could bring him in here, Dad."

"Nobody outside a my family sees me layin flat. God damn it." He coughed. "Ain't that how it goes, first your money and then your clothes."

She had the poorest kind of night and in the morning rose groggy and in a mood. The snow had quit and a warm Chinook blew. Already the plain was bare, the shrinking drifts lingering in cuts and folds of land. They were still out of coffee. Upstairs Aladdin wheezed and panted.

"He don't look good," said Wauneta.

By eight the cattle dealer had not arrived. Ottaline ate two oatmeal cookies, another slice of ham, drank a glass of milk. It was past nine when the dealer's black truck pulled in, Amendinger's black hat bent down as he reached for papers. There were three hound dogs in the back. He got out with the clipboard in his hand, already punching figures on a handheld calculator. Ottaline went outside.

It was not the cattle dealer but his son, Flyby Amendinger, big-nostriled, heavyset, a cleft in his stubbly chin, as quiet as three in the morning.

"Mr. Touhey around?" he asked, looking at his boots.

"I'm showin you the stock," she said. "He got the flu. Or some kind a thing. We thought you would come at eight. We thought you was goin a be your father."

"I missed a couple turns. Dad's over in Hoyt." He fished in his shirt pocket, drew out newspaper clippings, showed her an ad, Amendinger & Son Livestock Dealers. "I been workin with Dad almost nine years, guess I got a idea what I am doin by now."

"I didn't mean you didn't," she said. "I'm glad it's you. Your dad's mustache scares me." She pictured him driving the red roads to the ranch, roads like heavy red marker traced over the map, cutting the circle of horizon.

"Scare the hell out a me too, when I was a little kid." He looked at the porch, the house, the wedding wheat, the blue-door shed.

"Well," she said. "Here we go."

"That wheat needs cuttin," he said.

She drove and he stared at the far horizon visible beneath the bellies of cows. They bounced over pasture, the dust in the truck cab shaken loose and suspended in a fine sparkling haze as though an emanation from their private thoughts that might coalesce into audible statement. He opened the gates. Ottaline thanked him, pointed out the good qualities of the cattle, the trim, heavily mus-cled bodies on straight legs, the rib-eye bulge on each side of the backbone, their large size. He murmured at a coarse-fronted cow with a steery look to her, pointed out some small and sickle-hocked steers with flat loins. He counted, made notes and added figures, offered a fair price.

"You are a knowledgeable girl," he said, "and a damn good-lookin one, though upholstered. Care for a beer?"

Ottaline spent the morning tipping back beer bottles with Flyby, who described the lonely life of a cattle dealer's son, illustrating his sad sentences with long, flat gestures of his hand. It was noon when he left.

She gave the figures to Aladdin from the bedroom doorway, hanging back. Dazed and fiery, bursting with tea, he nodded, said all right. It was all right. He did not need a computer to know the margin to a penny. It was all right, and wasn't that a sad relief. He couldn't say as much for himself.

That night old Red woke from his shallow sleep to a stiff, whistling risp he dreaded to hear. His heart beat, he rose and felt his way to the pantry window. The dirty moonlight fizzed through shredded clouds, glanced off a swinging scythe blade, though it was not Death come for him this time but a man in a dark hat cutting the wedding wheat in hissing swaths, stopping at the end of every row to swig from a bottle. He saw his granddaughter Ottaline, mouth cracked wide, her hundred teeth glinting like a mica bed, leaning against the doorframe of the blue-door shed. She hurled a piece of oily metal into the sky, where it twisted and fell, stooped for another, sent it flying.

Old Red watched, summed it up. "I drove teams. I cowboyed. Worked since I was a kid. Run sheep and run cows. Still present, fork end down, ready as a dog with two dicks. I ain't finished my circle yet."

Tyler and Shan were far away hoping for good luck, but here was Ottaline and her haymaker. He wouldn't waste his dear breath laughing.

There was a wedding in September and a tremendous picnic under the Amendinger cattle-sale canopy, red and white stripes that cast a rose flush, trestle tables in the side yard, pork barbecue, a baron of beef pit-roasted, spitted lamb, prairie oysters, sweet corn, giant shrimp in Tyler's ketchup sauce, oven rolls, a keg of sour pickles, melons, ripe Oregon peaches made into deep-dish pies, and a three-tier wedding cake with pale-blue frosting topped by a tiny plastic bull and cow. The day was hot and clear and the Red Wall trembled on the horizon. Out beyond the fence the stripped frame of the 4030 lay where Aladdin had dragged it, on its side in the sagebrush. Wauneta wept, not for her daughter but for the cut wheat. Tyler inspected the ranch, looking it over with a displeased eye. Everything was smaller and shabbier. Why had he wanted this? He had a cell phone and sat on his horse talking to someone far away. Wauneta told Shan she intended to come out to Las Vegas and visit one of these days.

"Not if I got somethin to say about it," said Aladdin.

The guests dragged the folding chairs back and forth, and when Ottaline smoothed the rayon satin of her dress over her knees she felt the grit, saw the glinting dust caught in the weft. A spot of barbecue sauce marked the bosom. At last she changed into the new aquamarine pants suit and drove away with Flyby Amendinger for a four-day honeymoon among the motels of Nebraska.

Where wheat once grew a row of doghouses stood. There were two trucks in the driveway. Old Red in his pantry wished for deafness when the bedsprings sang above. Otherwise all was the same.

Aladdin applied for a bank loan for another plane. "I said if the Lord spared me I'd get it." He was dreaming of a 1948 Aeronca Sedan, a loose, big-cabined thing with feminine curves and a split crankcase to be replaced with an undamaged one from Donald's Cowboy Junkyard.

"She's so roomy, if I had to I could put a couple calves in her, bales a hay, cake, just about anything, even Ottaline, ha-ha."

The bank approved the loan, and on a quiet and gray morning, the wind lying low, Aladdin started his truck, got halfway down the drive, backed up, parked, and came into the kitchen. Old Red dunked his toast in black coffee.

"I am goin a fly that plane home," he said. "I will land in the Triangle pasture. Preciate it you was all out there watchin. You too, bubba," he said to his son-in-law.

"I got a go look at Trev's cows this mornin." Flyby Amendinger did not like living under the thumb of Aladdin Touhey. In the night he complained to Ottaline that Aladdin was worse than his mustachioed father.

"My block don't fit his tackle," he whispered.

"It sure fits mine," she whispered back.

"Call Trev up. Say you'll come a little later. He won't give a shit. I want a see everbody out wavin. Cause for celebration get a plane on this damn place again. Goin a teach Ottaline how to fly it."

It was midmorning when they heard the drone of the engine.

"Ma!" shouted Ottaline into the house. "He's comin!"

Wauneta came outside and stood with Ottaline and Flyby staring at the horizon. Old Red hobbled onto the porch. The wind had come up and was gusty and chill, the distant line of cliff marking a dull red break in the sere plain. Wauneta ran back into the house for her jacket.

The plane flew over and headed toward the Red Wall, turned, and came again in their direction, very much lower. It passed over them twenty feet off the ground. Aladdin's head was barely visible in the smoke from homegrown that clouded the cabin. The plane soared up, shaking in the wind. It rose in a steep climb, leveled out, and sailed away. When it was only a distant speck it turned and came toward the ranch again, curving and sliding, coming low. At a certain angle it resembled a billboard in the sky.

"He is actin up," said Wauneta. She watched the plane roar in low like a crop duster.

"I think he is goin a land," said Flyby, "or take a soil sample. Or stake out a homestead."

"He is actin up. I know him. YOU GET DOWN HERE!" Wauneta shouted at the plane.

As though obeying her, it touched the ground, sending up a puff of dust, bounced back into the air, and made two more prodigious hops before the left wheel caught the iron frame of the abandoned tractor and the plane fell on its face, crumpled into a mash of cloth, metal, and rancher. There was an explosion like a mighty backfire, but no flame. A ball of dust rose.

Flyby dragged Aladdin to safe ground. His father-in-law's head lolled at an unusual angle.

"He is dead, I think. I think he is dead. Yes, he is dead. His neck is broke."

Wauneta shrieked.

"Look what you done," said Ottaline to her. "You killed him."

"Me! That's what cuttin the wheat's done."

"He done it hisself," called old Red from the porch. It was clear to him the way things had to go. They'd plant Aladdin. Ottaline and her scytheman would run the ranch. Wauneta would pack her suitcase and steer for the slot machines. The minute she was out of sight he intended to move out of the pantry and back upstairs. The main thing in life was staying power. That was it: stand around long enough, you'd get to sit down.

JAMES SPENCER

The Robbers of Karnataka

FROM THE GETTYSBURG REVIEW

THE PILGRIMS are waiting for lunch in the dining room of the Ashreya Hotel in Bangalore, South India. Their leader, Pearl, sits at one end of the banquet table, with eleven pilgrims on one side and thirteen on the other. Bannister has counted. Bannister will count the number of cars parked in a block, the number of windows in a hotel, the number of chapatis on a plate. Greta has offered to let him count the hairs on her head. Greta is a heavy-breasted woman with a bleached permanent that makes her large head appear even larger. Today Bannister waited until she was seated, then found an empty chair at the other end of the table near Pascal.

Down the middle of the white linen tablecloth, condiments and plates of appetizers are arranged in a sumptuous row. There are vases of flowers. The small windows, polished brass, and dark paneled walls create a shipboard atmosphere. The first time Bannister sat in this room he felt a slight vertigo, as if the floor had tilted under him. It was not pleasant. Bannister likes things to behave the way they're supposed to. Greta has told him that in India nothing behaves the way it's supposed to. He will learn to let go of his expectations.

Pascal is a tall, narrow-shouldered mathematician with a passion for Fibonacci numbers. He has come to the lunch table in a state of excitement that has nothing to do with Fibonacci numbers. Pascal waves the front page of the *Bangalore Herald* for all to see. The two-inch headline reads, DACOITS ATTACK IN KARNATAKA. Dacoits are the bandit terrorists of India. They prey on the rich, usually in country mansions and along isolated roads. They rob and kill and sometimes rape. Pascal reads the article aloud. The dacoits have shot a whole family in the Melagiri Hills. Zizi cries out and claps a hand over her mouth. All faces turn toward her.

"That's near where we're going," she says.

Bannister is surprised that Zizi has any idea where they're going. Zizi's attention is usually limited to the problems of her small, squirmy body. On the nine-hour flight from Seattle to Tokyo, Bannister wrestled Zizi's suitcase out of the overhead rack five times. First she needed her inflatable cushion for her lower back, then a pill for her kidneys, then something for her migraine. She needed her Chinese herbs to shrink her fibroid. Then she told Bannister her silicone implants were leaking into her body and taking energy away and she needed her blue-green algae to give it back. Bannister has been called on to help other women too. Of the twenty-five pilgrims, only six are men. Greta says this is because women have a more highly developed spiritual nature.

All faces are now turned toward Pearl, a heavy, slow-moving woman of seventy-one who handles the complaints of her charges with unflagging patience. Pearl has made nineteen trips to India. She speaks soothingly.

"Nobody has ever been hurt going to see Swami."

It is not the first time Bannister has heard this. When they lifted off the runway at Madras, the Boeing 737 had banked like a fighter making a combat takeoff. Bannister had looked past Zizi at a wing angled so far down that he expected to see the wingtip clipping coconuts out of the treetops. Zizi screamed. Greta had leaned her bulk across Bannister to reassure Zizi. One large breast had rested heavily on Bannister's wrist. "Swami looks after us," Greta said. "Though he says Air India keeps him busy." She peered into Bannister's face at close range. "You don't believe me?"

"I didn't say anything," Bannister said.

"You'll see," she said, and sat back in her seat with a knowing smirk.

Don, a bespectacled, humorous man across the table from Bannister, also seems to take the dacoits in his stride. India is an enormous Petri dish, he says, a brew of cholera, typhoid, leprosy, malaria, meningitis — you name it. You take your life in your hands just breathing.

Pascal hands the newspaper to Zizi. Her cute, squirrel-like face puckers. The paper crashes to the table.

"We can't go to Mysore!" she cries. "We'll all be killed!"

In addition to her somatic problems, Zizi is afflicted by a psychic ability. She has told stories about events she's foreseen and the terrible things that befell people who had not listened to her.

"We've already paid for the bus and the driver," Pearl says. "I'm sure the army is patrolling the hills. There is nothing to fear."

"Anyway," Greta says, "*we* are the real robbers. Americans. Five percent of the people on this planet use forty percent of its resources."

Greta has made several trips to India. To hear her talk, she is very close to Swami. The pilgrims have heard lectures about compassion, chastity, service, right thinking. Bannister has trouble reconciling the chastity part with the heavy breast on his wrist. He wishes he hadn't mentioned his divorce on the flight from Seattle. Greta tries to sit next to him in restaurants and taxis. Even if he were attracted, he's not ready for the complications. He's heard that men and women at the ashram sit on different sides of the courtyard and eat in separate dining rooms. Bannister thinks he'd welcome that arrangement for a while.

When the pilgrims arrived in Bangalore, they discovered that Swami was not at the ashram. He'd left town on an errand of mercy and would not return for five or six days. Many of the pilgrims were sorely disappointed. They have only three weeks in India.

"Sometimes Swami pulls the rug out from under us," Greta said brightly. "To keep us awake."

Pearl revised their schedule. They'll spend two days in Bangalore shopping, visiting temples, and having their akashic records read from inscriptions on ancient palm leaves. Then they'll board a bus and drive across the state of Karnataka to Mysore, where shopping is even more interesting. Most of the women brightened. The men grumbled. Pearl promised them a trip to a jungle game preserve. They'll return to Bangalore in time for Swami's arrival.

An hour after lunch, Bannister is sitting on a pile of folded rugs in the open front of Gopal Fabrics, three steps up from the sidewalk on Commercvfial Street in Bangalore. The pilgrims are scattered up and down the street, shopping for sandals, clothing, jewels, musical instruments, wood carvings, and extra suitcases in which to carry their treasures home. Bannister has bought nothing. Bannister does not like possessions. It was a major conflict between him and his wife. He did not even want to own a house.

Don too is an indifferent shopper. Down the street his white straw hat bobs among the polished Ambassadors and the occasional Hillman or Toyota parked side by side along the curb. Don examines car doors for chipped paint caused by other doors flung open against them. On sixty-eight cars he's found only five small nicks. He stops to tell Bannister. "Do you remember what car doors looked like at home before we had protective strips? In our country a car is junk the day it rolls out of the factory. Here, you see, the automobile is replacing the sacred cow." Don also has a theory that Indians in traffic are telepathic with each other and their animals. "Just watch for a while," he says, pointing to the intersection, where taxis, buses, trucks, bicycles, and motorized rickshaws weave among donkey carts, chickens, cows, pigs, and people crossing each other's paths without appearing to slow down. Bannister is as skeptical about the telepathy as he is about Swami's protection. During two days in Madras he'd seen a truck rear-end a taxi, a dead man lying under a crushed bicycle, and four children fighting over the flattened corpse of a chicken.

On the far side of the narrow street, Greta and Angeline emerge from a clothing shop. In a gauzy lavender sari, Greta looks like a huge ball of cotton candy. At least the sari conceals the black hair on her unshaven legs, and shoes that suspiciously resemble combat boots. Angeline wears a yellow Punjabi. She navigates the three steps down to the sidewalk with the delicacy of a deer at the riverbank. Dark faces turn to stare at her mother-of-pearl skin. Only yesterday Greta caught Bannister staring at Angeline and told him not to get his hopes up. Angeline has a rare blood disease. She'll be dead in three months unless Swami heals her.

Whenever Bannister sits near Angeline he notices the porcelain skin of her small, tapering fingers, how she speaks in a quality of voice he associates with singing, and how she has a compliment for everyone around her — even for Bannister. She's noticed that he carries only one small duffel bag and a day pack. She is awed, she told him, by people who can travel light. She would guess that, like herself, he's not much attached to property. His eyes follow her down the street until the last flicker of the yellow Punjabi disappears in the crowd and he can no longer see her curly ash-brown hair among the sea of bobbing heads.

The intersection is so crowded that a taxi must move at a crawl. Commerce hums everywhere. A skeletal old man with a pushcart displays pathetic wares — a few loose cigarettes, a stained necktie, a souvenir ashtray, other items hard to describe. Amazingly, somebody is digging into his pocket as if to make a transaction. A man in a dhoti leans over with a racking cough and launches a goober the size of a fried egg. A pig and a chicken run to gobble it. The pig wins. As elsewhere in India, there is no problem with garbage. It is thrown into the street, where it is picked over by animals and the poorest of the poor. Here on Commercial Street, Greta says, at the end of the day the merchants remove what all creatures have rejected, so as not to offend foreign tourists.

The pilgrims load their bundles into the waiting taxis. There are two harmoniums. Drums. A voluptuous carving of Kali in sexual embrace with Shiva. A heavy bronze of six-armed Krishna dancing. There are bundles of bath towels, rolls of silk and wool, packages of clothing, bargains at prices unheard of in the United States. What will not fit into the taxi trunks the pilgrims hold on their laps. Beggars crowd around the taxis as fast as the drivers chase them away. Ragged men and women reach into the car to tap Bannister's shoulder. Children pluck at his shirtsleeves, pleading in a tongue he doesn't recognize. He feels the impact of a heavy thigh. He turns to find Greta sitting beside him, where Pascal had sat earlier. Pascal climbs in behind her. "Roll up the windows," Greta says, wriggling her hip tighter against Bannister. "Swami doesn't want us to give them money. It only encourages them."

The closed car is a furnace. Sweat drips from Bannister's eyes and trickles in rivulets under his shirt. The beggars run alongside the car, knocking on windows, pointing to their open mouths. A toothless woman holds a child with legs so crippled that it will never walk. Bannister rolls down the window and hands the woman two one-hundred-rupee notes. She stops and brings her hands together in a semblance of *namaste* as the car picks up speed.

Greta clucks disapprovingly.

"The parents broke the child's legs so they could use it for begging."

"The child has to eat," Bannister says, "no matter how it got that way."

"If you reward them for it," Greta says, "other parents will cripple their children too."

"I don't have the answer," he says brusquely. "Do you?"

She flounces, adjusting her sari over her legs.

"My goodness," she says, "I think we've just had our first argument."

The implications of this are alarming. Bannister stares out his side window. He does not want to be uncivil, but this woman seems to take civility as encouragement. On the plane from Seattle a warning light had gone off in his head when he discovered her ruddy full-moon face turned toward him in the next seat. For a while he'd answered her pushy questions in monosyllables. He'd tried to sleep, but when he awoke he found her face still turned toward him, as if she'd been watching him all the time. "Why are you so attached to sleep?" she said, as if sleep were a character defect. When he escaped to the toilet too many times, she asked if he had diarrhea or a bladder infection. "Don't you ever smile?" she said. "You're probably over fifty years old and there are no lines in your face. It's as if your character never formed." Early in the flight, in an unguarded moment, he'd told her that for the past three years he'd entered the events of every day into his computer. "My God!" Greta had cried. "If your computer crashes, how will you know who you are?"

How different the nine-hour flight to Tokyo would have been, listening to Angeline's voice in the seat beside him. It would hardly have made any difference what she said. Bannister had been struck by her voice the first time he'd heard it, in the ticket line in Seattle. She'd been talking to someone farther along in line. He'd been able to catch only a word here and there, but the sound of her voice had started subtle and complex vibrations like the response of all the strings to a single struck note on a piano.

The last phase of their shopping foray is a stop in a more suburban part of the city. The taxis find parking spaces along the block and the pilgrims converge on a yellow stucco house where an Indian devotee sells photographs of Swami. There are hundreds of photos, many of them beautiful: Swami in saffron robe, walking through a sea of seated devotees. Swami on the balcony of his *mandir.* Swami in his temple, dwarfed by the marble sculpture of Krishna and Arjuna in the war chariot. The pilgrims sort through the pictures in a buying frenzy. Even Bannister chooses a few photos. His favorite is an eight-by-ten glossy of Swami standing under the chin of his pet elephant. The elephant's oak-bark trunk delicately encircles Swami's body. Bannister had never heard of this Swami until he walked into the travel agency in Seattle. Swamis in general had not caught his attention, except for scandals about sex and money. Up to that time his impression was that most swamis were fraudulent. The agent, a woman, was a devotee. Bannister had been intrigued to learn that there is no charge for staying at the ashram. Only the wealthy are allowed to pay. The average person is told to go home and help the poor in his or her own country. Swami is perhaps the wealthiest guru in India. Or would be, if he did not spend all the money to build schools and hospitals and orphanages.

At dinner, Zizi announces that she is not going to Mysore. "I'll wait for you here at the Ashreya."

"I thought you said we'd all be killed," Bannister says. He's beginning to feel contentious. Greta has told him that Swami advises going on pilgrimage. Living at such close quarters, she says, grinds away the social veneer. We begin to see who we really are.

At the last minute Zizi realizes that with her three roommates gone, she'll have to pay the full price of a room. She decides to go to Mysore after all.

While the porters load the bus, Bannister establishes himself in the left front window seat, where he will have a flow of air and a clear view of the road ahead. He deposits his day pack on the seat next to him to save the space for Pascal. For a moment he'd thought of getting a seat where he could see Angeline and maybe hear her voice. There's an ache in his chest whenever he remembers what Greta has told him. The ache he carries for his wife is enough — why was he seeking more? He let common sense prevail, and decided to choose a good seat for himself regardless of where Angeline might sit.

As he settles himself, his hand recoils from a skin of grime on the chromium bar separating his seat from the stairwell. The upholstery of his seat has some of the same patina. The green vinyl is torn. In places it is patched with a different material. There is a cracked window. Though the floor is swept, the rubber mat is ripped away along the aisle. Bannister wonders about the condition of the engine, the brakes, the tires. Perhaps as insurance, somebody has taped a picture of Swami on the bulkhead separating the driver from the passengers.

Outside the bus, small, skinny porters are slinging baggage up to waiting hands on the roof. Two suitcases in a row do not reach high enough, and crash to the ground. Bannister leans out the window and yells at the porter to be more careful. The dark-faced porter tips his head from side to side. Bannister has been told that this sideways wobble serves the same function as the nod among Americans and Europeans. To Bannister it has the ambivalent feel of the word *maybe*. He yells a second time to make sure. Another sideways wobble. A large object thuds into the seat beside him. He turns to confront Greta's gleaming smile.

"Me again!" she says brightly.

Bannister's day pack now rests on Greta's lap alongside her purse.

"I was saving that seat for Pascal."

"I know," Greta says. "I thought I'd give you a guided tour through South India."

Bannister reminds himself that Greta spent her first two days and nights in India nursing Angeline and some of the other pilgrims through attacks of flu and dysentery. He holds his tongue. He's not sure he appreciates having his social veneer ground away. Maybe it will help if he gets out and throws a few suitcases onto the roof of the bus.

"I'll save your seat!" Greta warbles after him.

He picks up a suitcase and carries it to the bus. There's a commotion among the porters. Pearl yells at him from the hotel steps. He's taking their work away, she says. They get paid for it. He puts the suitcase down and apologizes. More sideways wobbling of heads. One head does not wobble. The eyes crackle with something that looks like murderous lust. Bannister has seen these burning, fanatical eyes in news photographs from blood-feud countries. Hindustan. Kurdistan. Baluchistan. He's seen them a few times in Bangalore. He'd like to think it's genetic, the way some people are born with a down-turned mouth. Bannister watches thin brown arms struggle with baggage he could have tossed like basketballs.

It seems to take forever to get started. Somebody is missing, or has lost a bag. Zizi goes back into the hotel on a mysterious mission. Myrtle, one of the older women, has to pee. Fred, a pilgrim who has frequent mishaps, discovers that the Hershey bars in his knapsack have melted all over his film containers. The bus waits while he mops up the mess and disposes of gooey Kleenex. Finally the engine rumbles and they move out into the street. It is Bannister's first experience in an Indian bus. It seems tame enough at first, with the traffic limited to the speed of a plodding ox or donkey. For a block or so, Bannister finds himself looking into the eye of an elephant lumbering alongside the bus. A red *kumkum* dot has been painted in the middle of the elephant's forehead.

Thick black exhaust pours from every tailpipe. Some of the pilgrims hold handkerchiefs to their mouths and noses. It is too hot to close the windows. The blast of horns is deafening. On the back of every truck and bus is a sign: PLEASE SOUND HORN. They mean it, Don tells Bannister, leaning forward from the seat behind. Besides telepathy, that's all they have. Side mirrors get knocked off by other vehicles passing too close.

After a while the bus is rocking along at near-suicidal speed with its nose four feet from the rear end of a truck. The truck swerves out into the oncoming lane. As if coupled to the truck, the bus follows, nose to tail, with completely blind forward vision. Greta leans against Bannister. "Watch this," she says. The truck passes three cars, then swings back into its own lane, leaving the bus facing a solid wall of oncoming traffic. Bannister is bracing for the impact when the oncoming vehicles veer off onto the shoulder, leaving the lane ahead clear so the bus can pass the cars and pull back in behind the truck. Greta does not seem bothered by their narrow escape. Don is leaning forward between Bannister and Greta. "By the time you've seen this ten or twenty times, you'll be a true believer."

The traffic thins, the outskirts of the city give way to farmland, fields, coconut and banana plantations. Soon the country begins to look like high desert, with granite hills so worn and rounded that they might be the oldest rocks on earth. Bannister is reminded of the tortured rock formations near Monterey in California where the bandit Murietta lay in wait to rob stagecoaches. He opens his knapsack and removes a map of South India. "A map!" one of the women cries. "What a splendid idea!" Bannister is the only one who has thought to bring a map. He has also brought a Boy Scout compass. Bannister likes to know where he is. At the moment they are a few miles north of the Melagiri Hills. Even the pilgrims who believe most firmly that Swami protects them grow quiet, watching the worn and pitted rocks and the exhausted desert.

After his wife left him, Bannister had merely wanted to get away from home for a while — a change of scene. It would not have occurred to him to travel so far. The dark-skinned travel agent was patient, almost motherly. She seemed to understand his disdain of cruises, tropical resorts, guided tours to foreign museums and architectural ruins. He was not sure what he wanted. "Perhaps it is not a good time for you to travel alone," she said. "There is a group leaving next week for India. It is the country of my birth." Bannister found himself trusting this thoughtful, dark-faced woman. She turned a silver frame on her desk to show him the person the group was going to visit.

Bannister had expected his traveling companions to be somewhat more peculiar than the people he meets on business trips, and he was not disappointed. There is Alvin, who locks himself in the bathroom with his harmonium to chant half the night. Darleen, a tall, pale woman who holds one arm over her head for hours at a time to strengthen her will. A husband and wife who teach firewalking. Everett, who belongs to an international organization of people who drink their own urine for health reasons.

Bannister had not been prepared for their credulity. They tell him that Swami materializes jewels, necklaces, statuettes, and perfumed sacred ash. One of the women shows him a large ruby ring. They say Swami understands all languages, that he alters the weather and delays trains and airplanes for the convenience of his devotees, that he can be in two places at once, appearing, for example, in a room in a foreign country to give counsel or save a life while he sits in plain view of a thousand people in his courtyard in India. Pearl tells Bannister in all seriousness how, before hundreds of people, Swami had resurrected a baby dead two days, how he'd brought back to life a devotee named William who had died while waiting for a new heart. William had lived another seven years with his old heart. He used to say that he saw Swami more often in his room at home in Vermont than he did at the ashram in India. William, Pearl said, had been King Solomon in another life.

The pilgrims grow familiar to each other quickly. One confides in another and soon the whole group knows. Bannister learns that

Angeline is not the only one who is dying. Another woman has cancer, six months to live. Her teenage daughter is with her, looking as if she carried her own death sentence. Bannister is not the only one who has lost a wife. One of the men, Carmody, is newly divorced. He is a small, cadaverous man who says little and eats almost nothing. Pascal, Bannister hears, is going through bankruptcy and his wife and children have left him. Two of the women have recently lost their husbands, one to cancer and one to a mental breakdown. Another of the men, Tim, was nearly killed in an auto accident. He died five times in the hospital, he says. Swami appeared and held his hand and brought him back each time. Tim has come to India to thank Swami in person.

Except for Tim, all the pilgrims have come to ask for help of some kind. What has Bannister come for? He feels as if he's with these people almost by accident. Many of their beliefs seem silly, their quest a waste of time. He wonders if he should leave the group and travel alone. But he holds off. He's learned so much about them that they're beginning to seem like family. When he meets Angeline's gaze he is sure there could have been something between them. The ache grows leaden in his chest. He tries to imagine what it must be like for her with three months to live. Sometimes he tries to avoid her eyes, tune out her voice. He's confided in Pascal. When you come to visit Swami, Pascal says, he ups the ante on you.

They do more shopping, visit museums, old palaces, the jungle game preserve in the mountains to the south. In Mysore there is no garbage on the streets. At every corner a trash fire burns all day. The smoke from the fires combines with automotive exhaust so it is impossible to see more than a block in any direction. Here too there is a thick flow and mingling of traffic. Bannister sees a hen and a dozen half-grown chicks scratching dirt in a traffic divider, a goat and two horses trotting along a busy boulevard as if they were their own masters. As in Bangalore, telepathy doesn't appear to work for everybody. Bannister also sees a dead donkey, and bleeding people sitting on the sidewalk near a taxi that has been half demolished by a truck.

Swami seems to be known everywhere. Greta draws attention to his picture in a taxicab, on a cash register, the front desk of a hotel, a travel agent's wall. She's even seen one, she says, in the cockpit of a Boeing 737. People in stores, hearing of the pilgrims' destination, place their palms together in front of their chests. The old deities too are everywhere, at least in name. Over the entrance of business enterprises from the grandest to the most humble, Bannister reads the names of Hindu gods and goddesses. In a closet-sized hole in the wall, two men squat on the dirt under a sign reading SHIVA BATTERY WORKS. The boulevards and streets are lined with such signs as VISHNU ENTERPRISES, GANESH TOURS, SRI VIJAY-ANA LAKSHMI RICE MILLS, SHAKTI CONSTRUCTION. There is HANUMAN MOPEDS, and a gas station called YIN-YANG PET-ROL. It's as if in the United States we encountered on every commercial street, signs reading JESUS AND MARY INVESTMENTS, JOHN THE BAPTIST CEMENT WORKS, SAINT JOSEPH MENS-WEAR, HOLY GHOST BUSINESS MACHINES, MARY MAG-DALENE KWIK-STOP GROCERY.

The morning the pilgrims set off on their return to Bangalore, Bannister is sitting in the hotel lobby watching Angeline at the checkout window. Greta plunks down in the chair next to him.

"She'll break your heart like your wife did," Greta says. "Only it will be more final."

Bannister has done his best to hide his feelings from Greta. It makes him angry that he's had so little success.

"What do you know about my wife?" he says. "I haven't told you anything."

"You don't have to. You're an open book."

He refuses to answer.

"It's all right," Greta says. "I understand."

"Understand what?"

"There's no guarantee that Swami will heal her, you know. He often tells people he can't help. He tells them their bank account has run out."

Greta's words affect him more than he would like. He hates to admit it, but he's been holding a secret hope that Swami can heal Angeline. He doesn't believe such things are possible. As annoying as Greta is, sometimes she hits the mark. Maybe it's time to get himself under control.

The pilgrims retrace their course across the dry, blown plateau of Karnataka toward Bangalore. It is a different bus, as grimy and rattletrap as the one that took them to Mysore. There is no picture of Swami on the bulkhead in front. The driver is less of a kamikaze, for which Bannister is grateful. The front seat has been left for Bannister, perhaps in honor of his map and compass. Pascal sits beside him. In restaurants and taxis, through sometimes complicated maneuvering, Bannister has managed to keep Greta at a distance, but in the bus he finds her near again, sitting behind him, next to Don.

On the plateau, traffic is light. The bus is stuck for a while behind a herd of sheep traveling at two or three miles per hour, stopped by a flock of ducks that do not want to get off the road, stopped again by a haywagon overturned on the pavement. As a bent, ancient man in a dhoti works to free the ox from the wagon, Greta leans forward. "He's probably no more than forty years old," she says. Greta has a way of making Bannister feel personally responsible for all the misery, disease, and death in India.

With the bus stopped, no air flows through the open windows. The heat becomes unbearable, and the pilgrims get out to find the nearest shade. It takes time to round them up again. In a parched village they stop for cold drinks at a store roofed with palm leaves. Near the entrance is a group of wiry dark men in short-sleeved shirts. Their conversation stops while the pilgrims file through the door. In one face Bannister sees the burning, ferocious eyes he's seen a few times in the cities. As he pays for his drink, he finds Greta at his elbow. "That bottle of soda," she says, "would cost one of these villagers a day's wages. Providing they had employment in the first place."

Bannister shrugs. He's fed up with her meddlesome, moralizing come-ons.

"You've been avoiding me," she says.

"You've been chasing me."

"Have I?"

Their eyes lock. He sees her anger, and feels his own rising to meet it.

"Well, never mind," she says. "We'll soon be separated at the ashram. Swami will protect you."

When they leave the store, the group of men has disappeared, along with their driver. Bannister looks at his watch and observes that at this rate it will be dark before they get to Bangalore. "No problem," Don says. "The Ashreya will hold our rooms."

The sun is dropping below the horizon when the bus stops at a crossroad. The driver leans out and talks to a man in torn cotton pants standing by a tree. The driver waves, and turns the bus to the right. Bannister studies his map. He does not find this cross-road or remember the turn. They are headed south. They should be headed northeast. Bannister talks to Pearl, who makes her way heavily to the driver's compartment. Pearl returns and explains that they've taken a detour. The highway ahead is closed for repairs. The new road is rough, the bus travels even more slowly. Bannister and Pascal try to talk to the driver themselves, in English, pointing to the map. The driver answers all their questions with a sideways head wobble. Either he does not understand, or he understands too well.

"Relax," Greta says when Bannister returns to his seat. "You don't see anybody else worrying. Even Zizi is sound asleep."

"I don't like it," Bannister says.

"I don't either," Pascal says. "There was nothing wrong with the highway four days ago."

"Where did we get this driver?" Bannister says.

"Pearl's travel agent in Mysore, supposedly."

Once again Bannister crouches in the aisle next to Pearl. Her travel agent had not been there when they loaded the bus. Usually, in every city an agent introduces the driver.

"What do you think?" she says.

"I don't know. I'll talk to Don and Pascal."

Bannister grabs the grimy metal bars on the seatbacks one by one as he makes his way forward on the rocking, jolting floor. Don and Pascal appear thoughtful after Bannister makes his report.

"It doesn't sound good," Don says.

"I'd feel better if we had a weapon of some kind," Pascal says.

"If we had a screwdriver," Don says, "maybe we could pull the bars off these seats."

"There's a screwdriver in my Swiss army knife," Bannister says.

"O ye of little faith," Greta says, shaking her head. "It's only a detour."

"Just in case it's not," Bannister says, reaching under the seat for his day pack. At this moment the bus turns sharply, rolling like a ship about to capsize. Bannister nearly tumbles into the stairwell. The bus lurches to a stop. There are voices outside. The door opens and a man stands in the dim light, yelling. Behind him, Bannister sees a man holding a rifle. He sees other men running toward the bus with lanterns; their shadows flicker hugely across the wall of a building.

Zizi wakes up.

"What is it?" she cries. "What's happening?"

The man at the door steps up into the stairwell and shines a flashlight inside the bus.

"Keep calm, everybody," Pearl calls. "Let me find out what they want." She says something in Tamil, to which the man with the flashlight responds with more yelling. Pearl's voice trembles.

"He says get out of the bus and leave our belongings here. Purses, wallets, jewelry, everything. Anybody who disobeys will be shot."

Zizi screams.

"Oh, my God, dacoits! I knew it!"

The man with the flashlight steps all the way into the bus. In his other hand he waves a pistol. Bannister sees more weapons outside. With Zizi screaming, Pearl probably can't hear what the man with the pistol is trying to tell them. Greta knows a little Tamil. "What is he saying?" Bannister says.

"I think he's asking who is the leader."

Bannister looks back as the flashlight catches Pearl's frightened eyes.

"I'm the leader," he says.

The flashlight beam and the pistol both point at him.

"Out!" the pistol yells. The flashlight sweeps the bus again. The pistol points everywhere, then back at Bannister. "Out!"

It sounds as if somebody in the rear is muffling Zizi, trying to reason with her.

"All right, everybody, keep calm," Bannister says. "Let's get out. When they tell you to do something, do it. Don't aggravate them." He wonders at himself. He's never taken charge of anything more significant than a committee to organize a party in high school. Why now, at the risk of his life?

Outside, the pilgrims huddle in the hot night, surrounded by eight dacoits. Bannister counts four lanterns and five rifles, plus the leader's automatic pistol. He briefly considers how he and Don and Pascal might gain control of the situation. Television thrillers are his only background in such heroics. He and Don and Pascal would almost surely be killed, and get some of the other pilgrims shot also.

The women are whimpering or stifling sobs. The man with the pistol begins yelling again, waving the pilgrims toward a crumbling stone building. The dacoits herd the pilgrims through a doorway onto a dirt floor. Stars shine overhead in the absence of a roof. The leader gives orders and soon there is a lantern hanging above the door, casting a dim light over the whole room. Bannister makes a quick scan: there are two doorways, the one they came through and one at the rear. No windows, walls too high to climb.

The leader is yelling again. Bannister has stayed close to Pearl. She translates. They are to sit on the floor. Make no attempt to leave the building or they'll be shot. Bannister turns and relays the message to the pilgrims, then sits down with them. A dacoit stands in each doorway with a rifle crooked over his forearm, ready for action. In the rear doorway Bannister recognizes the lunatic eyes of a terrorist. Don and Pascal and one of the other men have sat down near Pearl and Bannister. Furtively, Bannister motions them closer, to confer. The madman at the rear door points his gun and begins screaming.

"He says no talking," Pearl says. Bannister does not have to repeat the message as silence falls over the huddled group.

Bannister thinks they'll probably be killed. Two or three of the dacoits look as if they can hardly wait to start shooting. With the pilgrims dead, there will be nobody to identify them. If they're caught, though, the dacoits are probably dead men even if they don't kill the pilgrims. Why have they waited this long? Bannister wonders. Maybe they're waiting until they've raided the suitcases. Maybe they'll come in and search the pilgrims to make sure they've found everything of value, and then shoot them. Maybe the dacoits don't want to alarm the whole countryside with shooting until they're about to leave. On the other hand, maybe this building is so remote that nobody will hear the shooting. The dacoits will murder them and then search. What else might they do? Bannister has heard of them cutting off fingers to get rings.

Bannister looks at the pilgrims around him. From their faces he can easily imagine similar thoughts running through their minds. Carmody sits with his frail shoulders hunched, staring at the floor and cracking his knuckles. Pascal meets Bannister's eyes, as if ready to fight if given the signal. Some of the women are weeping. The lips of others seem to be moving in silent prayer. Pearl appears calm, as if reconciled to whatever lies ahead. Greta sits with her heavy arms shielding Zizi and another shivering woman. Bannister thinks again about fighting back. It is maddening to surrender without a struggle, yet it seems wiser to wait. The dacoits don't always slaughter everybody.

Just in case it is the end, Bannister thinks, shouldn't he be looking back, taking stock, composing himself? What has he accomplished? What has his life amounted to? Is anyone happier or better off for having met him? All those important questions. Nothing comes. His world has shrunk to the size of this room, his life to his remaining minutes in the company of these people he's known for less than a week.

Outside there are voices, thudding and crashing, sounds of objects being dragged across the ground. Bannister imagines suitcases being thrown off the bus. A woman at the outer edge of the group passes a whispered message. She can see through the doorway. The dacoits are opening baggage with a hatchet. Bannister wonders if the dacoits will use the hatchet to kill them, to avoid the noise of gunshots. After a minute or two the voices outside rise in pitch. It sounds like an argument. The voices subside, then rise again, several at once, agitated. Another message reaches Bannister: the dacoits seem to be arguing over something they've found in the luggage. At this moment a woman screams. Bannister turns to see the dacoit with the insane eyes dragging Angeline toward the rear door. She screams again, struggling. Bannister shouts and jumps to his feet. The dacoit drops Angeline's arm and brings his rifle to his shoulder. Bannister hears the click of the safety lever. At the same instant he sees a flicker in the corner of his eye, an object flying through the air. Greta's boot hits the dacoit in the leg, but it is enough to spoil his aim. The explosion is deafening. Some of the women scream. With his ears ringing, Bannister realizes he is not hit, the gun had jerked upward, the bullet had gone over his head, he thinks none of the pilgrims were hit either. The dacoit is levering another shell into the chamber and Bannister is in motion toward the dacoit when there is another explosion in the room. The leader of the dacoits is standing just inside the doorway with his pistol pointed skyward. He is waving what appears to be a sheaf of Swami's pictures, yelling. The lunatic dacoit snarls and levels his rifle at Bannister. The leader yells even louder and aims his pistol at the lunatic. For a second or two everybody is frozen; then there are several rapid shots in the distance, shouting outside the building. The leader throws the photographs down and both dacoits run to the door. The lunatic stops, turns, and aims at Bannister again. The leader grabs the rifle and drags the lunatic outside, cursing. There are more shots in the distance, running footsteps, voices fading. The pilgrims sit and listen. After a few moments, Pearl speaks.

"Swami's pictures stopped them. One of the dacoits said there would be terrible karma. A thousand lifetimes in the lower hells."

"But what were the shots out there?" one of the women says. "That's why they ran away."

"Maybe we should get out of here in case they come back," Pascal says.

"I don't think they're coming back," Pearl says.

"I'll have a look outside anyway," Bannister says, but as he gets to his feet there are motor sounds, running footsteps, flashlight beams sweeping the room, army uniforms crowding inside, rifles, a voice in passable English: "If you please not to be afraid. You are rescued now. Is any person being injured?"

As Bannister leaves the building, Angeline stands in his way. She opens her mouth, but no words come, as if she's not yet recovered enough for speech. He touches her shoulder, and she reaches up to wrap her fingers around his own. Her hand feels exactly as he'd imagined it.

Now that they're safe, the woman who is dying of cancer has become hysterical. Greta is holding her. Bannister meets Greta's eyes briefly over the woman's shoulder. Something about Greta is different, changed. He finds her later, outside, when the pilgrims are rescuing their belongings from the dirt and repacking damaged suitcases in the glow of army headlights. He kneels beside her. Her frizzy hair has fallen forward to half hide her face. He feels an odd rush of affection. "You saved my life," he says. "You could have been killed."

"Think nothing of it," she says, popping a bucket-sized brassiere into her suitcase without looking up. "Thank Swami."

Except for Angeline, who is too ill to come downstairs, the pilgrims gather in the dining room of the Ashreya Hotel to talk about their adventure. The miraculous timing of events. A farmer had seen the bus and alerted the army. Swami's pictures had delayed the dacoits just enough for the soldiers to get there. Greta's boot had delayed them a split second longer. One of the older women says she saw Swami sitting in the back of the bus when they turned off the highway. Fred of the melted Hershey bars says the officer in charge of the soldiers had a halo over his head. Zizi says it was more like a large, glowing umbrella. Don and Pascal nod as if they'd seen it too.

Pearl tells them she knew everything would be all right the minute they sat down in the roofless building. Swami had stepped out of a corner and had thrown little grains of light over all the pilgrims. They were like rice grains with tiny points sparkling at each end. "Didn't you see them?" Pearl says. "It was beautiful." She looks at Bannister. "When you stood up to protect Angeline, I felt no fear. I knew you could not be hurt."

Bannister is silent. Who is he to question their hallucinations? During the second or two when he was about to die, he thought he'd seen something himself. He understands it no better than he understands what the others thought they'd experienced. Once when she'd trapped him in a taxi, Greta had said that according to Swami we exist in a dream, a hypnotic state. As we awaken, we begin to see the reality behind appearances. There have been times when Greta made good sense. He does feel as if in some way he's been asleep. He searches for Greta's large, ruddy face, but she's taken a seat where he can't see her, on his side of the table at the other end, near Pearl.

SAMRAT UPADHYAY

The Good Shopkeeper

FROM MANOA

RADHIKA WAS MAKING the evening meal when Pramod gave her the news. The steam rising off the rotis she was making on the pan burned his nostrils, so he backed off into the narrow hallway next to the kitchen. She turned off the gas and joined him. He put his arms behind his back and leaned against the wall.

"What should we do?" she whispered, although there was no one nearby except the baby, who was asleep in the bedroom.

"I don't know," he said. "Who could have foreseen that this would happen?"

"Hare Shiva," she said, and opened the bedroom door to check on the baby. "How are we going to give the next month's rent to the landlady?" Her eyes turned watery.

"What is the use of crying now? That's why I don't like to tell you anything. Instead of thinking with a cool mind, you start crying."

"What should I do other than cry? You worked there for three years, and they let you go just like that? These people don't have any heart."

"It is not their fault." He tried to sound reasonable. "The company doesn't have money."

"So only you should suffer? Why couldn't it be one of the new accountants? What about Madan?"

"He knows computers," Pramod said.

"He also knows many influential people."

"All right, don't cry now. We will think of something. I will go and see Shambhuda tomorrow. Something or other is bound to happen. We will find a solution."

Despite the assurances he had given his wife, Pramod couldn't sleep well that night.

The next morning while it was still dark, he went to the Pashupatinath temple. He made a slow round of the temple complex, and even stood in line to obtain *tika* from the priest in the main shrine. By the time he had finished, the sky was tinged with a gray light. He became aware that he would not need to go home to eat and change and then go to work.

Yesterday afternoon, the director had called him into his office and said, "Pramodji, what can I say? Not everything is in my power." Power, thought Pramod. Of course he had the power! But he was a coward and didn't want to stand up for a man who had worked hard for his company.

Walking away from the temple, Pramod saw pilgrims on their way to pay homage to Lord Shiva. The beggars who slept around the temple complex were lined up on the side of the street, clanking their tin containers. When people threw money and food in their direction, the beggars eyed each other to see who had got the better deal. Monkeys that roamed the area were also alert now, ready to snatch bags and packets from timid people they could take advantage of. The smell of deep-fried jalebie, vegetable curry, and hot tea wafted out from stalls.

Pramod saw Ram Mohan slowly walking toward the temple, his cane hanging from his arm. A few years ago Pramod had worked with Ram Mohan in the accounts department of the Education Ministry.

Pramod looked away from him, but Ram Mohan had sharp eyes. "Pramodji, I didn't know you were such a religious man!" he shouted. Then, coming closer, he added, "What is the matter, Pramodji? Is everything well?"

Pramod hesitated, then remembered that Ram Mohan was a kind man and told him about the loss of his job.

"Tch, tch," said Ram Mohan, slowly shaking his head. "I had heard that the profits of your finance company were not so good these days, but I didn't imagine it would come to this — letting go of a diligent worker like you."

The ringing of the temple bells sounded in the background as they stood in the middle of the street, contemplating this strange twist of fate. Then Pramod remembered that he had to catch Shambhuda before he left for his office, so he excused himself.

At Shambhuda's house, there were two other people waiting in the living room. The old servant told Pramod that Shambhuda was still in *puja* and would be out in the next half-hour. Pramod sat down on the sofa and gazed at the pictures of the religious figures on the wall. The other two men eyed him suspiciously. He ignored them and stared at the framed picture of Lord Shiva with the snake god, Nag, around his blue neck. After a few minutes, one of the men asked him, "Aren't you Prakashji?"

Pramod gave him an irritated look and said, "No, my name is Pramod."

"Oh, yes, yes, Pramod. Why did I say Prakash? I know you, you are Shambhuda's brother-in-law, aren't you?" He was a small, ill-dressed man with a pointed nose and a small mouth.

Pramod nodded.

"I met you here a year ago — don't you remember me?" the man asked. Pramod shook his head.

"Kamalkanth, that's my name," said the man and looked at him expectantly. The other man, who had a broad, dull face, nodded.

"So what brings you here this morning?" the ill-dressed man asked.

"Oh, nothing," Pramod said. He wanted to slap the man.

"You work for Better Finance, don't you?" the man asked.

Pramod was about to say something when the servant came in with three glasses of tea and announced that Shambhuda was coming out. The other men forgot about Pramod and concentrated on the door, from which Shambhuda emerged shortly.

Shambhuda was wearing only a dhoti around his waist, unashamed of his hairy, bulging stomach and his ample breasts. He was singing a hymn from the *puja* he performed every morning. He unsmilingly distributed the *prasad* to his guests and asked the servant to bring him his juice, which the old man promptly did.

"What brings you here today, brother-in-law?" Shambhuda asked Pramod.

"Oh, it had been quite a few days, so I just came to inquire about your health. Radhika sends her regards."

Shambhuda nodded. He turned toward the other men.

The ill-dressed man extracted a sheaf of papers from his briefcase and said, "I have arranged everything here in order, Shambhuda. All the figures are accurate — I checked them again and again myself."

"All right," said Shambhuda. "Why don't you two come back again after a week? Then we can sit down and talk about your commission." Shambhuda was involved in construction contracts throughout the city, which entailed numerous under-the-table handouts.

The two men left, smiling obsequiously. Shambhuda turned his attention again to Pramod.

"Everything is finished, Shambhuda," Pramod said. "I am finished."

Shambhuda took a sip of his juice.

"I have lost my job."

"Why?" Shambhuda didn't look the least bit perturbed.

"They say the company doesn't have any money."

"Do they have other accountants?"

"Yes, a young man who knows computers."

"Ah, yes, computers. They are very fashionable these days, aren't they?" Shambhuda smiled, then became serious again. "This is not good. Not good. Hmmm. How is my sister taking all of this? How is the new baby?" Shambhuda was fond of Radhika, even though she was a distant sister.

They talked for a little while, and then Shambhuda said, "I will see what I can do. Not to worry." He asked Pramod about the director of his former company and jotted the name down. Then he stretched and yawned. The telephone rang, and he became engrossed in a conversation that brought forth only "hmmm" and "eh" from his mouth. Pramod looked at all the religious figures adorning the living room and wondered if they had anything to do with Shambhuda's prosperity and quiet confidence in life. When he saw that the telephone conversation was not going to end soon, Pramod got up to leave. Shambhuda covered the mouthpiece with his palm and said, "I will see what I can do."

Everyone came to know about Pramod's loss of his job, and everywhere he went, friends and relatives gave him sympathetic looks. He was sure some of them — those who saw his work at the finance company as having been lucrative and prestigious — sneered inwardly, gloating over his misery. He tried to maintain a cheerful attitude, telling his friends and relatives that these things happened to everyone and that he would ultimately find a job that was even better than the one he had lost. After all, his years of experience as an accountant had to count for something.

But he hated his voice when he said this. He hated his smile, which seemed to stretch the skin around his mouth painfully, he hated having to explain to everyone why he had lost his job, he hated their commiseration, and he hated the forlorn look on Radhika's face, especially when they were around her relatives, who were better off than his side of the family.

He took walks to the Pashupatinath temple every morning before sunrise. The fresh early-morning air cleared his mind, and he found solace in the temple lights, which stayed lit until dawn. A couple of times he came across Ram Mohan, who always asked anxiously, "Anything yet?" Eventually Pramod timed the walks so that he would not run into Ram Mohan again.

After his morning walk to the temple, he made his rounds to people of influence, people who could maneuver him into a job without the rigors of an examination or an interview. He tried to keep his faith that something would turn up, that one day he would find himself in a room of his own, seated behind a desk and served tea by a peon every couple of hours. He missed the ritual of going to the office in the morning, greeting his colleagues, and then settling down for the day's work, even though he had been doing the same kind of work for a number of years. He delighted in working with numbers, juggling them, working out percentages, making entries in his neat handwriting. He loved doing mental calculations, and saw it as a challenge to refrain from using calculators till the last moment, or only as a means of verification. He loved the midday lull, when everyone in the office ordered snacks and tea and a general feeling of camaraderie came over the workplace: people laughing and eating, talking about mundane things that had happened at home, teasing each other, commenting on politics.

Pramod maintained a frequent attendance at Shambhuda's residence, showing his face every week or so, asking if anything had come up, reminding Shambhuda of his predicament, reinforcing Shambhuda's sense of family by reminding him that Radhika was his favorite sister. On every visit, Shambhuda sounded positive, assuring Pramod that a job prospect appeared really good and that it would be finalized in a few days. But even though Shambhuda nodded his head gravely when Pramod told him about his strained financial situation, it took him longer and longer to give Pramod an audience. The ill-dressed man snickered whenever they happened to be in Shambhuda's house together. Sometimes, when he and his companion would look at Pramod and start murmuring, Pramod felt like getting up and leaving Shambhuda's house once and for all.

When a month passed with no job in sight, Pramod started to feel a burning in his stomach. He and Radhika managed to pay the month's rent from their savings, but the problem of next month's rent loomed in his mind. Radhika borrowed some money from her parents, but Pramod did not like that at all: it made him appear small in their eyes. "Don't worry," Radhika said. "We will pay this back as soon as you get your first salary." She was still trying to maintain an optimistic attitude, he knew, but it was an optimism he no longer shared.

A few nights later she brought up the idea of selling their land in the south to finance some sort of shop of their own, perhaps a general store or a stationery outlet. Pramod killed the idea instantly. "I am not going to become a shopkeeper at this stage in my life," he said. "I am an accountant, do you understand? I have worked for many big people." Later, when she slept, he regretted having snapped at her. He doubted very much whether the land in the south would fetch much money, as it was getting swampier every year and was far from any major roads. He didn't want to go to the village now to try to get a real estate agent. Moreover, he could never imagine himself as a shopkeeper. How humiliated he would feel if he opened a shop and someone like Ram Mohan came in looking for something. What would he say? Or would he even be able to say anything? What if someone like the ill-dressed man came in? Could Pramod refuse to sell him goods and ask him never to enter his shop again? No! If he did, what kind of reputation would his shop gain?

Staying up late engrossed in such thoughts became a habit for Pramod. He slunk into bed, faced the wall, and let his imagination run wild. Radhika put the baby to sleep and got into bed beside him. He could feel her vibrations coming toward him, but he did not turn. After some time, she muttered something, turned off the light, and went to sleep.

Often Pramod imagined how it would be if he were a feudal landlord, like those who used to run the farmlands of the country only twenty years before. He imagined himself with a big royal mustache that curved at the ends and pointed toward the sky, the kind that he could oil and caress as a show of power. He saw himself walking through a small village, a servant shielding him from the incessant southern sun with a big black umbrella while all the villagers greeted him deferentially. He saw himself plump and well cared for. Then he would imagine himself as an executive officer in a multinational company where Shambhuda worked as an office boy. Shambhuda was knocking on the door of Pramod's spacious air-conditioned office, where he sat behind a large desk in a clean white shirt and tie, his glasses hanging from his neck, a cigarette smoldering in the ashtray. He saw Shambhuda walk in, his cheeks hollow, wearing clothes that were clearly secondhand. Shambhuda started pleading for an advance, which Pramod refused. Shambhuda started crying, and Pramod, irritated, told him that the company didn't have a place for such whiners.

Pramod giggled at this little scene. Then, when he realized what he was doing, a moan escaped his lips. Radhika woke up, turned on the light, and asked, "What is the matter? Having a bad dream?"

One morning Pramod was sitting on a bench in the city park and smoking a cigarette after having made his usual futile, humiliating morning round, when a young woman came and sat next to him. She started shelling peanuts that she had brought bundled at the end of her dhoti. The cracking of the peanut shells was beginning to get on Pramod's nerves, and he was thinking of leaving when the woman asked him, "Do you want some peanuts?"

Pramod shook his head.

"They are very good. Nicely roasted and salty," she said. She was a small, plump woman. She looked like a laborer of some sort, or perhaps a villager who was working as a servant in the city.

"I can't eat peanuts in the morning," said Pramod.

"Oh, really? I can eat peanuts all day long," she said. "Morning, day, night."

Pramod did not answer and watched a couple of men in suits and ties walk into an office across the street, carrying briefcases.

"The mornings here are so beautiful, no?" he heard the woman say. "I come here every day." She watched him as she popped more peanuts into her mouth. "Where do you work?" she asked.

The gall of this woman, who was clearly in a class much below his own! "In an office," he said.

"It's nearly ten o'clock. Don't you have to go to the office? It is not a holiday today, is it?"

"No, it's not a holiday."

"I just came back from work. Holiday or no holiday, I have to work."

"Where?" asked Pramod.

"In Putalisadak," she said. "I wash clothes, clean the house. But only in the mornings. They have another servant who goes to school in the morning. My mistress is very generous, you know, she works in a hotel."

"Where is your husband?" asked Pramod. He felt a wry smile appear on his face. Talking to a servant girl in the park was an indication, he thought, of how low he had fallen.

"He is back in the village, near Pokhara. He works as a carpenter, building this and that. But, you know, the money is never enough. That's why I had to come here."

"You don't have any children?"

She shook her head and blushed.

They sat in silence, but Pramod felt her eyes on him in between the cracking of her peanuts. "You know, my husband says one shouldn't think too much." There was a note of pity in her voice.

"Why does he say that? Does he say that to you?"

"Not me. I don't think that much. What is there to think about? For us poor people, life is what God gives us. My husband says that when one of our relatives becomes unhappy and comes to him for advice. In this city I see so many worried people. They walk around not looking at anyone, always thinking, always worrying. This problem, that problem. Sometimes I think if I stay here too long, I will become like them."

Pramod felt like laughing at her simple ways.

By now the streets were getting crowded. People were on their way to work. The park where they sat provided a good view of the surrounding office buildings, many of which were major government complexes.

The woman got up, stretched, and said, "Well, I should be going home now. Make some tea and cook some rice for myself." She looked at him sweetly. "I can make some tea for you in my room."

Pramod was startled by her suggestion.

"It is all right," she said. "You don't have to come if you don't want to. Here you are sitting, worrying, and thinking I don't know about what. So I thought you might want some tea. My house is not that far, right here in Asan." She pointed in the direction of the large marketplace.

Pramod stared at her. "All right," he said.

They walked out of the park with her leading the way. He felt embarrassed, walking along with this servant girl, and afraid that someone would see him. He also felt a slow excitement starting in his abdomen and moving up toward his chest. He walked a few steps behind her, and she seemed to understand his predicament, for she didn't turn around to engage him in a conversation.

When they entered the neighborhood of Asan, they were swept into the crowd, but he maintained his distance behind her, using the bright color of her dhoti to keep her in sight. A pleasant buzz started in his ears. He sensed that whatever was happening to him was unreal, but then so were the events of the last two months. His worrying appeared to vanish as a lightheadedness came into him. He floated behind her, and the office-going and vegetable-buying crowd in the marketplace helped him move forward. He didn't feel constricted, as he normally did in such places. In fact, his chest seemed to have expanded and his heart to have grown larger.

They reached an old house in a narrow alley, and she turned around at the doorway. "I have a room on the third floor, the other side," she said. She led him into a dirty courtyard where snotty children were playing marbles. They went through another door, and Pramod found himself in the dark. He could smell garlic and onions on her and hear the swish of her dhoti. "The stairs are here," he heard her say. "Be careful, they are quite narrow. Watch your head." He reached out for her, and she held his hand as she led him up the wooden stairs. Now Pramod could see the faint outline of a door. "One floor more," she said, and he thought she looked quite pretty in that semidarkness. On the next landing she unlocked the door, and they entered a small room.

In one corner were a stove and some pots and pans, and in the other corner a cot. A poster of Lord Krishna, his chubby blue face smiling at no one in particular, was above the bed. A grayish light filtering through the one small wooden window illuminated her face and objects in the room. She was smiling at him.

He was drawn to the window, where he was startled to find a partial view of the center of the marketplace. In the distance the vegetable sellers squatted languidly next to their baskets, smoking and laughing. A faint din from the market lifted itself up into the room, like the hum of bees, and he stood by the window and gazed at the rooftops and windows of other houses that crammed this part of the city.

"You can sit on the bed," she said.

He promptly obliged. She proceeded to boil water for tea. He wondered how she, with the meager income of a housemaid, could afford a place like this. Then a curious thought entered his head: he wondered if she was a prostitute, though he knew she wasn't. Without turning, she said, "The owner of this house is from our village. He knew my father, and he treats me like a daughter. Very kind man. Not many like him these days, you know."

He smiled to himself. He knew a lot more than she did, but he didn't say anything.

When she brought the tea, she sat down next to him. They sipped in silence. Later he felt drowsy and lay on the bed. She lay down with him, took his hand, and placed it on her breast. He turned toward her and ran his forefinger across her plump face. Her eyes were closed. He didn't know what he thought of her, except that there was an inevitability to all of this — something he had sensed the moment he first talked to her in the park.

When he made love to her, it was not with any hunger or passion. The act had an inevitability that he could not control. He was not the one who lifted her dhoti, fumbled with her petticoat, smelled the ooze of her privacy. She didn't demand anything; she just lay under his body, matching his moves only as far as the act made it necessary.

He stayed with her till the evening. They ate, and slept, and then he got up to watch the marketplace again. The crowd had swelled.

Strident voices of women haggling with vendors rose up to the window. He felt removed from all of this, a distant observer who had to do nothing, fulfill no obligations, meet no responsibilities, perform no tasks.

When he reached home that evening, he felt uncharacteristically talkative. He even played with the baby, cooing to her and swinging her in his arms. Radhika's face brightened, and she asked him if there was good news about a job. But he said, "What job? There are no jobs," and her face turned dark again.

During the afternoons, Pramod still pursued his acquaintances, thinking something might come along, but the late mornings he reserved for the housemaid. They often met in the park after she finished her work, and then walked to her house in Asan. On Saturdays and holidays he stayed at home, sometimes playing with the baby and sometimes listening to the radio.

Once while he and Radhika were preparing to sleep, she looked at the baby and said, "We have to think of her future."

Pramod caressed the baby's face and said, "I am sure something will happen," though he didn't know what he meant by that.

Putting her hand on his, Radhika said, "I know you are trying. But maybe you should see more people. I went to see Shambhuda yesterday. He says he will find something soon."

"Shambhuda," said Pramod, suppressing a laugh.

"He is the only one who can help us."

"I don't need any help," said Pramod.

"Don't say that. If you say that, then nothing will happen."

Pramod jumped out of the bed and said, trembling, "What do you mean nothing will happen? What is happening now, huh? Is anything happening now?" His hands were shaking.

One cloudy morning as Pramod and the housemaid left the park and entered the marketplace, Pramod saw Ram Mohan coming toward them, swinging an umbrella in the crook of his arm.

"Oh, Pramodji, have you come here to buy vegetables?" Ram Mohan asked, looking at the housemaid curiously. Pramod did not know what to say, so he swallowed and nodded. "Nothing yet, huh?" Ram Mohan asked. "My nephew is also not finding a job. But his situation is different from yours."

Pramod became very conscious of the housemaid by his side and wished she would move on. He put his hands in his pockets and said, "Looks like rain, so I will take my leave," and he walked away, leaving her standing with Ram Mohan. Later, when she caught up with him, she said, "Why were you afraid? What is there to be afraid of?"

Pramod kept walking with a grim face, and when they reached her room, he threw himself on her cot and turned his face away from her. His chest was so tight that he had to concentrate to breathe properly. She didn't say anything more. After setting the water to boil for tea, she came and sat down beside him.

Pramod stopped looking for jobs altogether and was absent from the house most of the time. One night he even stayed over at the housemaid's place. When he reached home in the morning, Radhika was in tears. "Where were you?" She brought her face close to his to see if he had been drinking. "What has happened to you? Don't you know that you are a father? A husband?"

Now when he went to family gatherings, he didn't feel surprised if relatives looked at him curiously. The bold ones even started mocking him, "Pramodji, a man should not give up so easily. Otherwise he is not a man." Some sought to counsel him. "Radhika is very worried about you. These things happen to everyone, but one shouldn't let everything go just like that." He didn't feel the need to respond to them. He sat silently, abstractedly nodding his head. His father-in-law stopped talking to him, and his mother-in-law's face became strained when she spoke to him.

At a family feast one bright afternoon, Pramod was sitting on a chair and watching a game of flush. The men sat on the floor in a circle and threw money at the center while the women hovered around their husbands. The children were barred from the room. Shambhuda was immaculately dressed in a safari suit, and his ruddy face glowed with pleasure as he took out carefully folded rupee notes from his pockets. Radhika was sitting beside Shambhuda, peering at his cards and making faces.

"Pramodji, aren't you going to play?" asked a relative.

Pramod shook his head and smiled.

"Why would Pramodji want to play?" said another relative, a bearded man who had been Pramod's childhood friend. "He has better things to do in life." This was followed by a loud guffaw from everyone. Radhika looked at Pramod.

"After all, we are the ones who are fools. Working at a job and then — *poof!* — everything gone in an afternoon of flush." The bearded relative threw some money at the jackpot in a dramatic gesture.

"No job, no worries. Every day is the same day," someone else said.

Radhika got up and left the room. Pramod sat with his chin resting on his palms, not looking up.

Shambhuda looked at the bearded man scornfully and said, "Who are you to talk, eh, Pitambar? A bull without horns can never call itself sharp. What about you, then, who drives a car bought by his in-laws and walks around as if he earned it?"

At this, some men nodded their heads and remarked, "Well said" and "That's the truth." The bearded relative gave Shambhuda an embarrassed smile and said, "I was only joking, Shambhuda. After all, it is a time of festivities."

"You don't joke about such matters," said Shambhuda with a sharpness that was not in his character. "Why should you be joking about this thing anyway, eh? What about the time when you embezzled five lakh rupees from your office? Who rescued you then?"

The room became quiet. Shambhuda himself looked surprised that he had said such a thing.

Pitambar threw his cards down on the floor and stood up. "What did I say, huh, what did I say? I didn't say anything to you. Just because you are older than me, does that mean you can say anything?" His right hand started gesticulating wildly while his left hand rapidly stroked his beard, and his voice got louder. "What about you? Everyone knows that you had that police inspector killed. We are not fools. How do you make all your money, donkey?"

The use of the word *donkey* prompted the other men to get up and try to restrain Pitambar, who seemed to be almost frothing at the mouth. "Enough, enough!" cried one woman. Radhika came back into the room, asking, "What happened?"

A shadow came over Shambhuda's face, and he got up. "What do you think, huh, what do you think? Say that again, you motherfucker, just say that again. I can buy people like you with my left hand."

Radhika came up to Pramod. "See what you have started," she said.

Bitterness rose inside his chest, and he could no longer stay in the room. "You are a fool," he told her as he walked out.

A feeling of numbness engulfed him, and things disappeared into a haze. Words and phrases floated through his mind, and he thought of suicide. He had heard stories of how people jumped into the Ranipokhari pond at the center of the city and were sucked under water to their death by a demon. Could he do it?

Pramod walked two miles to Asan, toward the end jostling with the marketplace crowd. He moved through the darkness of the stairwell to the housemaid's room, his body becoming heavier with each step.

She was pleased to see him.

"I want to lie down," he told her.

"Shall I make tea for you?"

He shook his head and lay down on her cot. Its smell was usually intimate to him, but today he felt like a patient, ready to be anesthetized so that his insides could be removed.

"Are you all right?" She put her palm on his forehead.

He nodded and fell asleep. It was a short sleep filled with jerky images that he couldn't remember clearly when his eyes opened.

The housemaid was cooking rice. "You'll eat here?" she asked.

He gazed at her for a while, not saying anything. "Aren't you afraid your husband will come here? Unannounced?"

She laughed, stirring the rice. "Then he'll catch us, won't he?"

"What will you do then?"

"I don't know," she said. "I never think about it."

"Why?"

"It's not in my nature," she said as she took off the rice pot and put on another pot, into which she poured ghee. She put some cut spinach in the burning oil. It made a *swoosh* sound, and smoke rose from it in a gust. Pramod pulled out a cigarette and put it between his lips without lighting it.

"You know," she said, "if this bothers you, you should go back to your wife."

"It doesn't bother me."

"Sometimes you look worried. As if someone is waiting to attack you."

"Really?" He leaned against the pillow. "My face?"

"Your face, your body," she said. She stirred the spinach and sprinkled on some salt. "What will you do?"

"I will never find a job," he said, sucking on the unlit cigarette. He made an *O* with his lips and blew imaginary circles of smoke to the ceiling.

"No, I mean if my husband comes here."

He waved away the imaginary smoke in the air above him. "I will kill him," he said, then laughed.

She also laughed. "My husband is a big man. With big hands."

"I will give him one karate kick," Pramod said, and stood up. He kicked his right leg vaguely in her direction. Then he struck some of the poses he had seen in kung-fu movies. "I will hit Pitambar on the chin like this." He jabbed his fist hard against his palm. "I will kick Shambhuda in the groin." He lifted his leg high and threw it in the air. His legs and arms moved about him, jabbing, punching, kicking, flailing. He kept it up until he became tired, then sat down next to her, breathing hard, an embarrassed smile on his face.

"What good will it do," she said, "to beat up the whole world?"

He raised a finger as if to say, *Wait.* But when his breathing became normal, he merely smiled at her. Then he leaned over and kissed her on the cheek. "I think I should go now."

"But I made dinner."

"Radhika will be waiting," he said.

It was already twilight when he left the housemaid's room. The air had a fresh, tangible quality to it. He took a deep breath and started walking through the marketplace, passing rows of meat shops and sweets vendors.

At the large temple complex of Hanuman Dhoka, he climbed the steps to the three-storied temple dedicated to Lord Shiva. There were a few foreigners taking pictures. He sat down and watched the courtyard, which was emptying as the sky grew dark.

When he reached home, Radhika didn't say anything to him. She silently placed rice, dal, and vegetables in front of him. He ate with gusto, his fingers darting from one dish to another. When he asked for more, she said, "How come you have an appetite like this?" His mouth bulging with food, he couldn't respond. After dinner he went to get the baby, who stared at him as if he were a stranger. He picked her up by the feet and raised his arms to the ceiling, so that her tiny, bald head was upside down above his face. The baby smiled. Rocking her, Pramod sang a song popular on the radio: *The only thing I know how to do is chase after young girls, / then put them in a wedding doli and take them home.*

When Radhika finished in the kitchen, she came into the room and stood in the doorway, watching him sing to the baby. Without turning, he said, "Maybe we should start a shop, eh, what do you think?"

Radhika looked at him suspiciously at first, then realized he meant what he was saying. She became excited as they made plans. Later, when they were in bed and he was about to turn off the lights, he said, "Can you imagine me as a shopkeeper? Who would have thought of it?"

"I think you will make a very good shopkeeper," Radhika assured him.

"I will have to grow a mustache."

In the darkness, he started to think. Perhaps he would become such a good shopkeeper that even if the ill-dressed man came in to buy something, he would be very polite and say, "Thank you" and "Please." Pramod smiled inwardly. If Shambhuda came in, he would talk loudly with other customers and pretend Shambhuda was not there. And if the housemaid came in, he would invite her to sit on a stool and perhaps Radhika would make tea for her.

This last thought appealed to him tremendously.

STEVE YARBROUGH

The Rest of Her Life

FROM THE MISSOURI REVIEW

THE DOG WAS A MIXTURE of God knows how many breeds, but the vet had told them he had at least some rottweiler blood. You could see it in his shoulders, you could hear it when he barked, which he was doing that night when they pulled up at the gate and Chuckie cut the engine.

"Butch is out," Dee Ann said. "That's kind of strange."

Chuckie didn't say anything. He'd looked across the yard and seen her momma's car in the driveway, and he was disappointed. Dee Ann's momma had told her earlier that she was going to buy some garden supplies at Western Auto and then eat something at the Sonic, and she'd said if she got back home and unloaded her purchases in time, she might run over to Greenville with one of her friends and watch a movie. Dee Ann had relayed the news to Chuckie tonight when he picked her up from work. That had gotten his hopes up.

The last two Saturday nights her momma had gone to Greenville, and they'd made love on the couch. They'd done it before in the car, but Chuckie said it was a lot nicer when you did it in the house. As far as she was concerned, the major difference was that they stood a much greater chance of getting caught. If her momma had walked in on them, she would not have gone crazy and ordered Chuckie away, she would have stayed calm and sat down and warned them not to do something that could hurt them later on. "There're things y'all can do now," she would have said, "that can mess y'all's lives up bad."

Dee Ann leaned across the seat and kissed Chuckie. "You don't smell *too* much like a Budweiser brewery," she said. "Want to come in with me?"

"Sure."

Butch was waiting at the gate, whimpering, his front paws up on the railing. Dee Ann released the latch, and they went in and walked across the yard, the dog trotting along behind them.

The front door was locked — a fact that Chuckie corroborated the next day. She knocked, but even though both the living room and the kitchen were lit up, her momma didn't come. Dee Ann waited a few seconds, then rummaged through her purse and found the key. It didn't occur to her that somebody might have come home with her momma, that they might be back in the bedroom together, doing what she and Chuckie had done. Her momma still believed that if she could tough it out a few more months, Dee Ann's daddy would recover his senses and come back. Most of his belongings were still here.

Dee Ann unlocked the door and pushed it open. Crossing the threshold, she looked back over her shoulder at Chuckie. His eyes were shut. They didn't stay shut for long, he was probably just blinking, but that instant in which she saw them closed was enough to frighten her. She quickly looked into the living room. Everything was as it should be: the black leather couch stood against the far wall, the glass coffee table in front of it, two armchairs pulled up to the table at forty-five-degree angles. The paper lay on the mantelpiece, right where her momma always left it.

"Momma?" she called. "It's me and Chuckie."

As she waited for a reply, the dog rushed past her. He darted into the kitchen. Again they heard him whimper.

She made an effort to follow the dog, but Chuckie laid his hand on her shoulder. "Wait a minute," he said. Afterwards he could never explain to anyone's satisfaction, least of all his own, why he had restrained her.

Earlier that evening, as she stood behind the checkout counter at the grocery store where she was working that summer, she had seen her daddy. He was standing on the sidewalk, looking in through the thick plate glass window, grinning at her.

It was late, and as always on Saturday evening, downtown Loring was virtually deserted. If people wanted to shop or go someplace to eat, they'd be out on the highway, at the Sonic or the new Pizza Hut.

If they had enough money, they'd just head for Greenville. It had been a long time since anything much went on downtown after dark, which made her daddy's presence here that much more unusual. He waved, then walked over to the door.

The manager was in back, totaling the day's receipts. Except for him and Dee Ann and one stock boy, who was over in the dairy aisle sweeping up, the store was empty.

Her daddy wore a pair of khaki pants and a short-sleeved pullover with an alligator on the pocket. He had on his funny-looking leather cap that reminded her of the ones policemen wore. He liked to wear that cap when he was out driving the MG.

"Hey, sweets," he said.

Even with the counter between them, she could smell whiskey on his breath. He had that strange light in his eyes.

"Hi, Daddy."

"When'd you start working nights?"

"A couple of weeks back."

"Don't get in the way of you and Buckie, does it?"

She started to correct him, tell him her boyfriend's name was Chuckie, but then she thought, why bother? He'd always been the kind of father who couldn't remember how old she was or what grade she was in. Sometimes he had trouble remembering she existed: years ago he'd brought her to this same grocery store, and after buying some food for his hunting dog, he'd forgotten about her and left her sitting on the floor in front of the magazine rack. The store manager had carried her home.

"Working nights is okay," she said. "My boyfriend'll be picking me up in a few minutes."

"Got a big night planned?"

"We'll probably just ride around a little bit and then head on home."

Her daddy reached into his pocket and pulled out his wallet. He extracted a twenty and handed it to her. "Here," he said. "You kids do something fun. On me. See a movie or get yourselves a six-pack of Dr. Pepper."

He laughed, to show her he wasn't serious about the Dr. Pepper, and then he stepped around the end of the counter and kissed her cheek. "You're still the greatest little girl in the world," he said. "Even if you're not very little anymore."

He was holding her close. In addition to whiskey, she could smell aftershave and deodorant and something else — a faint trace of perfume. She hadn't seen the MG on the street, but it was probably parked in the lot outside, and she bet his girlfriend was in it. She was just three years older than Dee Ann, a junior up at Delta State, though people said she wasn't going to school anymore. She and Dee Ann's daddy were living together in an apartment near the flower shop he used to own and run. He'd sold the shop last fall, just before he left home.

He didn't work anymore, and Dee Ann's momma had said she didn't know how he aimed to live, once the money from his business was gone. The other thing she didn't know — because nobody had told her — was that folks said his girlfriend sold drugs. Folks said he might be involved in that too.

He pecked her on the cheek once more, told her to have a good time with her boyfriend and to tell her momma he said hello, and then he walked out the door. Just as he left, the manager hit the switch, and the aisle lights went off.

That last detail — the lights going off when he walked out of the store — must have been significant, because the next day, as Dee Ann sat on the couch at her grandmother's house, knee to knee with the Loring County sheriff, Jim Wheeler, it kept coming up.

"You're sure about that?" Wheeler said for the third or fourth time. "When your daddy left the Safeway, Mr. Lindsey was just turning out the lights?"

Her grandmother was in bed down the hall. The doctor and two women from the Methodist church were with her. She'd been having chest pains off and on all day.

The dining room table was covered with food people had brought: two hams, a roast, a fried chicken, dish upon dish of potato salad, cole slaw, baked beans, two or three pecan pies, a pound cake. By the time the sheriff came, Chuckie had been there twice already — once in the morning with his momma and again in the afternoon with his daddy — and both times he had eaten. While his mother sat on the couch with Dee Ann, sniffling and holding her hand, and his father admired the knickknacks on the mantelpiece, Chuckie had parked himself at the dining room table and begun devouring one slice of pie after another, occasionally glancing through the doorway at Dee Ann. The distance between where he was and where she was could not be measured by any known means. She knew it, and he did, but he apparently believed that if he kept his mouth full, they wouldn't have to acknowledge it yet.

"Yes, sir," she told the sheriff. "He'd just left when Mr. Lindsey turned off the lights."

A pocket-sized notebook lay open on Wheeler's knee. He held a ballpoint pen with his stubby fingers. He didn't know it yet, but he was going to get a lot of criticism for what he did in the next few days. Some people would say it cost him reelection. "And what time does Mr. Lindsey generally turn off the lights on a Saturday night?"

"Right around eight o'clock."

"And was that when he did it last night?"

"Yes, sir."

"You're sure about that?"

"Yes, sir."

"Well, that's what Mr. Lindsey says too," Wheeler said. He closed the notebook and put it in his shirt pocket. "Course, being as he was in the back of the store, he didn't actually see you talking with your daddy."

"No," she said. "You can't see the checkout stands from back there."

Wheeler stood, and she did too. To her surprise, he pulled her close to him. He was a compact man, not much taller than she was.

She felt his warm breath on her cheek. "I sure am sorry about all of this, honey," he said. "But don't you worry. I guarantee you I'll get to the bottom of it. Even if it kills me."

Even if it kills me.

She remembers that phrase in those rare instances when she sees Jim Wheeler on the street downtown. He's an old man now, in his early sixties, white-haired and potbellied. For years he's worked at the catfish plant, though nobody seems to know what he does. Most people can tell you what he doesn't do. He's not responsible for security — he doesn't carry a gun. He's not front office. He's not a foreman or a shift supervisor, and he has nothing to do with the live-haul trucks.

Chuckie works for Delta Electric, and once a month he goes to the plant to service the generators. He says Wheeler is always outside, wandering around, his head down, his feet scarcely rising off the pavement. Sometimes he talks to himself.

"I was out there last week," Chuckie told her not long ago, "and I'd just gone through the front gates, and there he was. He was off to my right, walking along the fence, carrying this bucket."

"What kind of bucket?"

"Looked like maybe it had some kind of caulking mix in it — there was this thick white stuff sticking to the sides. Anyway, he was shuffling along there, and he was talking to beat the band."

"What was he saying?"

They were at the breakfast table when they had this conversation. Their daughter, Cynthia, was finishing a bowl of cereal and staring into an algebra textbook. Chuckie glanced toward Cynthia, rolled his eyes at Dee Ann, then looked down at the table. He lifted his coffee cup, drained it, and left for work.

But that night, when he crawled into bed beside her and switched off the light, she brought it up again. "I want to know what Jim Wheeler was saying to himself," she said. "When you saw him last week."

They weren't touching — they always left plenty of space between them — but she could tell he'd gone rigid. He did his best to sound groggy. "Nothing much."

She was rigid now too, lying stiffly on her back, staring up into the dark. "Nothing much is not nothing. Nothing much is still something."

"Won't you ever let it go?"

"*You* brought his name up. You bring his name up, then you get this reaction from me, and then you're mad."

He rolled onto his side. He was looking at her, but she knew he couldn't make out her features. He wouldn't lay his palm on her cheek, wouldn't trace her jawbone like he used to. "Yeah, I brought his name up," he said. "I bring his name up, if you've noticed, about once a year. I bring his name up, and I bring up Lou Pierce's name, and I'd bring up Barry Lancaster's name too if he hadn't had the good fortune to move on to bigger things than being DA in a ten-cent town. I keep hoping I'll bring one of their names up, and after I say it, it'll be like I just said John Doe or Cecil Poe or Theodore J. Bilbo. I keep hoping I'll say it and you'll just let it go."

The ceiling fan, which was turned off, had begun to take shape. It looked like a big dark bird, frozen in mid-swoop. Three or four times she had woken up near dawn and seen that shape there, and it was all she could do to keep from screaming. One time she stuck her fist in her mouth and bit her knuckle.

"What was he saying?"

"He was talking to a quarterback."

"What?"

"He was talking to a quarterback. He was saying some kind of crap like 'Hit Jimmy over the middle.' He probably walks around all day thinking about when he was playing football in high school, going over games in his mind."

He rolled away from her then, got as close to the edge of the bed as he could. "He's just like you," he said. "He's stuck back there too."

She had seen her daddy several times in between that Saturday night — when Chuckie walked into the kitchen murmuring, "Mrs. Williams? Mrs. Williams?" — and the funeral, which was held the following Wednesday morning. He had come to her grandmother's house Sunday evening, had gone into her grandmother's room and sat by the bed, holding her hand and sobbing. Dee Ann remained in the living room, and she heard their voices, heard her daddy saying, "Remember how she had those big rings under her eyes after Dee Ann was born? How we all said she looked like a pretty little raccoon?" Her grandmother, whose chest pains had finally stopped, said, "Oh, Allen, I raised her from the cradle, and I know her well. She never would've stopped loving you." Then her daddy started crying again, and her grandmother joined in.

When he came out and walked down the hall to the living room, he had stopped crying, but his eyes were red-rimmed and his face looked puffy. He sat down in the armchair, which was still standing right where the sheriff had left it that afternoon. For a long time he said nothing. Then he rested his elbows on his knees, propped his chin on his fists, and said, "Were you the one that found her?"

"Chuckie did."

"Did you go in there?"

She nodded.

"He's an asshole for letting you do that."

She didn't bother to tell him how she'd torn herself out of Chuckie's grasp and bolted into the kitchen, or what had happened when she got in there. She was already starting to think what she would later know for certain: in the kitchen she had died. When she saw the pool of blood on the linoleum, saw the streaks that shot like flames up the wall, a thousand-volt jolt hit her heart. She lost her breath, and the room went dark, and when it relit itself she was somebody else.

Her momma's body lay in a lump on the floor, over by the door that led to the back porch. The shotgun that had killed her, her daddy's Remington Wingmaster, stood propped against the kitchen counter. Back in what had once been called the game room, the sheriff would find that somebody had pulled down all the guns — six rifles, the other shotgun, both of her daddy's thirty-eights — and thrown them on the floor. He'd broken the lock on the metal cabinet that stood nearby and he'd removed the box of shells and loaded the Remington.

It was hard to say what he'd been after, this man who for her was still a dark, faceless form. Her momma's purse had been ransacked, her wallet was missing, but there couldn't have been much money in it. She had some jewelry in the bedroom, but he hadn't messed with that. The most valuable things in the house were probably the guns themselves, but he hadn't taken them.

He'd come in through the back door — the lock was broken — and he'd left through the back door. Why Butch hadn't taken his leg off was anybody's guess. When the sheriff and his deputies showed up, it was all Chuckie could do to keep the dog from attacking.

"She wouldn't of wanted you to see her like that," her daddy said. "Nor me either." He spread his hands and looked at them, turning them over and scrutinizing his palms, as if he intended to read his own fortune. "I reckon I was lucky," he said, letting his gaze meet hers. "Anything you want to tell me about it?"

She shook her head no. The thought of telling him how she felt seemed somehow unreal. It had been years since she'd told him how she felt about anything that mattered.

"Life's too damn short," he said. "Our family's become one of those statistics you read about in the papers. You read those stories and you think it won't ever be you. Truth is, there's no way to insure against it."

At the time, the thing that struck her as odd was his use of the word *family*. They hadn't been a family for a long time, not as far as she was concerned.

She forgot about what he'd said until a few days later. What she remembered about that visit with him on Sunday night was that for the second time in twenty-four hours, he pulled her close and hugged her and gave her twenty dollars.

She saw him again Monday at the funeral home, and the day after that, and then the next day, at the funeral, she sat between him and her grandmother, and he held her hand while the preacher prayed. She had wondered if he would bring his girl-friend, but even he must have realized that would be inappropriate.

He apparently did not think it inappropriate, though, or unwise either, to present himself at the offices of an insurance company in Jackson on Friday morning, bringing with him her mother's death certificate and a copy of the coroner's report.

When she thinks of the morning — a Saturday — on which Wheeler came to see her for the second time, she always imagines her own daughter sitting there on the couch at her grandmother's place instead of her. She sees Cynthia looking at the silver badge on Wheeler's shirt pocket, sees her glancing at the small notebook that lies open in his lap, at the pen gripped so tightly between his fingers that his knuckles have turned white.

"Now the other night," she hears Wheeler say, "your boyfriend picked you up at what time?"

"Right around eight o'clock." Her voice is weak, close to break-ing. She just talked to her boyfriend an hour ago, and he was scared. His parents were pissed — pissed at Wheeler, pissed at him, but above all pissed at her. If she hadn't been dating their son, none of them would have been subjected to the awful experience they've just gone through this morning. They're devout Baptists, they don't drink or smoke, they've never seen the inside of a night-club, their names have never before been associated with unseemly acts. Now the sheriff has entered their home and questioned their son as if he were a common criminal. It will cost the sheriff their votes come November. She's already lost their votes. She lost them when her daddy left her momma and started running around with a young girl.

"The reason I'm kind of stuck on this eight o'clock business," Wheeler says, "is you say that along about that time's when your daddy was there to see you."

"Yes, sir."

"Now your boyfriend claims he didn't see your daddy leaving the store. Says he didn't even notice the MG on the street."

"Daddy'd been gone a few minutes already. Plus, I think he parked around back."

"Parked around back," the sheriff says.

"Yes, sir."

"In that lot over by the bayou."

Even more weakly: "Yes, sir."

"Where the delivery trucks come in — ain't that where they usually park?"

"I believe so. Yes, sir."

Wheeler's pen pauses. He lays it on his knee. He turns his hands over, studying them as her daddy did a few days before. He's looking at his hands when he asks the next question. "Any idea why your daddy'd park his car *behind* the Safeway — where there generally don't nothing but delivery trucks park — when Main Street was almost deserted and there was a whole row of empty spaces right in front of the store?"

The sheriff knows the answer as well as she does. When you're with a woman you're not married to, you don't park your car on Main Street on a Saturday night. Particularly if it's a little MG with no top on it, and your daughter's just a few feet away, with nothing but a pane of glass between her and a girl who's not much older than she is. That's how she explains it to herself, anyway. At least for today.

"I think maybe he had his girlfriend with him."

"Well, I don't aim to hurt your feelings, honey," Wheeler says, looking at her now, "but there's not too many people that don't know about his girlfriend."

"Yes, sir."

"You reckon he might've parked out back for any other reason?"

She can't answer that question, so she doesn't even try.

"There's not any chance, is there," he says, "that your boyfriend could've been confused about when he picked you up?"

"No, sir."

"You're sure about that?"

She knows that Wheeler has asked Chuckie where he was between seven-fifteen, when several people saw her mother eating a burger at the Sonic Drive-in, and eight-thirty, when the two of them found her body. Chuckie has told Wheeler he was at home watching TV between seven-fifteen and a few minutes till eight, when he got in the car and went to pick up Dee Ann. His parents were in Greenville eating supper at that time, so they can't confirm his story.

"Yes, sir," she says, "I'm sure about it."

"And you're certain your daddy was there just a few minutes before eight?"

"Yes, sir."

"Because your daddy," the sheriff says, "remembers things just a little bit different. The way your daddy remembers it, he came by the Safeway about seven-thirty and hung around there talking with you for half an hour. Course, Mr. Lindsey was in the back, so he can't say yea or nay, and the stock boy don't seem to have the sense God give a betsy bug. Your daddy was over at the VFW drinking beer at eight o'clock — stayed there till almost ten, according to any number of people, and his girlfriend wasn't with him. Fact is, his girlfriend left the country last Thursday morning. Took a flight from New Orleans to Mexico City, and from there it looks like she went on to Argentina."

Dee Ann, imagining this scene in which her daughter reprises the role she once played, sees Cynthia's face go slack as the full force of the information strikes her. She's still sitting there like that — hands useless in her lap, face drained of blood — when Jim Wheeler tells her that six months ago, her daddy took out a life insurance policy on her momma that includes double indemnity in the event of accidental death.

"I hate to be the one telling you this, honey," he says, "because you're a girl who's had enough bad news to last the rest of her life. But your daddy stands to collect half a million dollars because of your momma's death, and there's a number of folks — and I reckon I might as well admit I happen to be among them — who are starting to think that ought not to occur."

Chuckie gets off work at Delta Electric at six o'clock. A year or so ago she became aware that he'd started coming home late. The first time it happened, he told her he'd gone out with his friend Tim to have a beer. She saw Tim the next day buying a case of motor oil at Wal-Mart, and she almost referred to his and Chuckie's night out just to see if he looked surprised. But if he'd looked surprised, it would have worried her, and if he hadn't, it would have worried her even more: she would have seen it as a sign that Chuckie had talked to him beforehand. So in the end she nodded at Tim and kept her mouth shut.

It began happening more and more often. Chuckie ran over to Greenville to buy some parts for his truck, he ran down to Yazoo City for a meeting with his regional supervisor. He ran up into the north part of the county because a fellow there had placed an interesting ad in *National Rifleman* — he was selling a shotgun with fancy scrollwork on the stock.

On the evenings when Chuckie isn't home, she avoids latching on to Cynthia. She wants her daughter to have her own life, to be independent, even if independence, in a sixteen-year-old girl, manifests itself as distance from her mother. Cynthia is on the phone a lot, talking to her girlfriends, to boyfriends too. Through the bedroom door Dee Ann hears her laughter.

On the evenings when Chuckie isn't home, she sits on the couch alone, watching TV, reading, or listening to music. If it's a Friday or Saturday night and Cynthia is out with her friends, Dee Ann goes out herself. She doesn't go to movies, where her presence might make Cynthia feel crowded if she happened to be in the theater too, and she doesn't go out and eat at any of the handful of restaurants in town. Instead she takes long walks. Sometimes they last until ten or eleven o'clock.

Every now and then, when she's on one of these walks, passing one house after another where families sit parked before the TV set, she allows herself to wish she had a dog to keep her company. What she won't allow herself to do — has never allowed herself to do as an adult — is actually own one.

The arrest of her father is preserved in a newspaper photo.

He has just gotten out of Sheriff Wheeler's car. The car stands parked in the alleyway between the courthouse and the fire station. Sheriff Wheeler is in the picture too, standing just to the left of her father, and so is one of his deputies. The deputy has his hand on her father's right forearm, and he is staring straight into the camera, as is Sheriff Wheeler. Her daddy is the only one who appears not to notice that his picture is being taken. He is looking off to the left, in the direction of Loring Street, which you can't see in the photo, though she knows it's there.

When she takes the photo out and examines it, something she

does with increasing frequency these days, she wonders why her daddy is not looking at the camera. A reasonable conclusion, she knows, would be that since he's about to be arraigned on murder charges, he doesn't want his face in the paper. But she wonders if there isn't more to it. He doesn't look particularly worried. He's not exactly smiling, but there aren't a lot of lines around his mouth, like there would be if he felt especially tense. Were he not wearing handcuffs, were he not flanked on either side by officers of the law, you would probably have to say he looks relaxed.

Then there's the question of what he's looking at. Lou Pierce's office is on Loring Street, and Loring Street is what's off the page, out of the picture. Even if the photographer had wanted to capture it in this photo, he couldn't have, not as long as he was intent on capturing the images of these three men. By choosing to photograph them, he chose not to photograph something else, and sometimes what's outside the frame may be more important than what's actually in it.

After all, Loring Street is south of the alley. And so is Argentina.

"You think he'd do that?" Chuckie said. "You think he'd actually kill your momma?"

They were sitting in his pickup when he asked her that question. The pickup was parked on a turn row in somebody's cotton patch on a Saturday afternoon in August. By then her daddy had been in jail for the better part of two weeks. The judge had denied him bail, apparently believing that he aimed to leave the country. The judge couldn't have known that her daddy had no intention of leaving the country without the insurance money, which had been placed in an escrow account and wouldn't be released until he'd been cleared of the murder charges.

The cotton patch they were parked in was way up close to Cleveland. Chuckie's parents had forbidden him to go out with Dee Ann again, so she'd hiked out to the highway, and he'd picked her up on the side of the road. In later years she'll often wonder whether or not she and Chuckie would have stayed together and gotten married if his parents hadn't placed her off-limits.

"I don't know," she said. "He sure did lie about coming to see me. And then there's Butch. If somebody broke in, he'd tear them to pieces. But he wouldn't hurt Daddy."

"I don't believe it," Chuckie said. A can of Bud stood clamped between his thighs. He lifted it and took a swig. "Your daddy may have acted a little wacky, running off like he did and taking up with that girl, but to shoot your momma and then come in the grocery store and grin at you and hug you? You really think *anybody* could do a thing like that?"

What Dee Ann was beginning to think was that almost everybody could do a thing like that. She didn't know why this was so, but she believed it had something to do with being an adult and having ties. Having ties meant you were bound to certain things — certain people, certain places, certain ways of living. Breaking a tie was a violent act — even if all you did was walk out door number one and enter door number two — and one act of violence could lead to another. You didn't have to spill blood to take a life. But after taking a life, you still might spill blood, if spilling blood would get you something else you wanted.

"I don't know what he might have done," she said.

"Every time I was ever around him," Chuckie said, "he was in a nice mood. I remember going in the flower shop with Momma when I was a kid. Your daddy was always polite and friendly. Used to give me free lollipops."

"Yeah, well, he never gave me any lollipops. And besides, your momma used to be real pretty."

"What's that supposed to mean?"

"It's not supposed to mean anything. I'm just stating a fact."

"You saying she's not pretty now?"

His innocence startled her. If she handled him right, Dee Ann realized, she could make him do almost anything she wanted. For an instant she was tempted to put her hand inside his shirt, stroke his chest a couple of times, and tell him to climb out of the truck and stand on his head. She wouldn't always have such leverage, but she had it now, and a voice in her head urged her to exploit it.

"I'm not saying she's not pretty anymore," Dee Ann said. "I'm just saying that of course Daddy was nice to her. He was always nice to nice-looking women."

"Your momma was a nice-looking lady too."

"Yeah, but my momma was his wife."

Chuckie turned away and gazed out at the cotton patch for several seconds. When he looked back at her, he said, "You know what, Dee Ann? You're not making much sense." He took another sip of beer, then pitched the can out the window. "But with all you've been through," he said, starting the engine, "I don't wonder at it."

He laid his hand on her knee. It stayed there until twenty minutes later, when he let her out on the highway right where he'd picked her up.

Sometimes in her mind she has trouble separating all the men. It's as if they're revolving around her, her daddy and Chuckie and Jim Wheeler and Lou Pierce and Barry Lancaster, as if she's sitting motionless in a hard chair, in a small room, and they're orbiting her so fast that their faces blur into a single image which seems suspended just inches away. She smells them too: smells aftershave and cologne, male sweat and whiskey.

Lou Pierce was a man she'd been seeing around town for as long as she could remember. He had red hair and always wore a striped long-sleeved shirt and a wide tie that was usually loud-colored. You would see him crossing Loring Street, a coffee cup in one hand, his briefcase in the other. His office was directly across the street from the courthouse, where he spent much of his life — either visiting his clients in the jail, which was on the top floor, or defending those same clients downstairs in the courtroom itself.

Many years after he represented her father, Lou Pierce would find himself up on the top floor again, on the other side of the bars this time, accused of exposing himself to a twelve-year-old girl. After the story made the paper, several other women, most in their twenties or early thirties, would contact the local police and allege that he had also shown himself to them.

He showed himself to Dee Ann too, though not the same part of himself he showed to the twelve-year-old girl. He came to see her at her grandmother's on a weekday evening sometime after the beginning of the fall semester — she knows school was in session because she remembers that the morning after Lou Pierce visited her, she had to sit beside his son Raymond in senior English.

Lou sat in the same armchair that Jim Wheeler had pulled up near the coffee table. He didn't have his briefcase with him, but he was wearing another of those wide ties. This one, if she remembers correctly, had a pink background, with white fleurs-de-lis.

"How you making it, honey?" he said. "You been holding up all right?"

She shrugged. "Yes, sir. I guess so."

"Your daddy's awful worried about you." He picked up the cup of coffee her grandmother had brought him before leaving them alone. "I don't know if you knew that or not," he said, taking a sip of the coffee. He set the cup back down. "He mentioned you haven't been to see him."

He was gazing directly at her.

"No, sir," she said, "I haven't gotten by there."

"You know what that makes folks think, don't you?"

She dropped her head. "No, sir."

"Makes 'em think you believe your daddy did it."

That was the last thing he said for two or three minutes. He sat there sipping his coffee, looking around the room, almost as if he were a real estate agent sizing up the house. Just as she decided he'd said all he intended to, his voice came back at her.

"Daddies fail," he told her. "Lordy, how we fail. You could ask Raymond. I doubt he'd tell the truth, though, because sons tend to be protective of their daddies, just like a good daughter protects her momma. But the *truth*, if you wanted to dig into it, is that I've failed that boy nearly every day he's been alive. You notice he's in the band? Hell, he can't kick a football or hit a baseball, and that's nobody's fault but mine. I remember when he was this tall" — he held his hand, palm down, three feet from the floor — "he came to me dragging this little plastic bat and said, 'Daddy, teach me to hit a baseball.' And you know what I told him? I told him, 'Son, I'm defending a man that's facing life in prison, and I got to go before the judge tomorrow morning and plead his case. You can take that bat and you can hitch a kite to it and see if the contraption won't fly.' "

He reached across the table then and laid his hand on her knee. She tried to remember who else had done that recently, but for the moment she couldn't recall.

When he spoke again, he kept his voice low, as if he were afraid he'd be overheard. "Dee Ann, what I'm telling you," he said, "is I know there are a lot of things about your daddy that make you feel conflicted. There's a lot of things he's done that he shouldn't have, and there's things he should have done that he didn't. There's a bunch of shoulds and shouldn'ts bumping around in your head, so it's no surprise to me that you'd get confused on this question of time."

She'd heard people say that if they were ever guilty of a crime, they wanted Lou Pierce to defend them. Now she knew why.

But she wasn't guilty of a crime, and she said so: "I'm not confused about time. He came when I said he did."

As if she were a sworn witness, Lou Pierce began, gently, regretfully, to ask her a series of questions. Did she really think her daddy was stupid enough to take out a life insurance policy on her mother and then kill her? If he aimed to leave the country with his girlfriend, would he send the girl first and then kill Dee Ann's momma and try to claim the money? Did she know that her daddy intended to put the money in a savings account for her?

Did she know that her daddy and his girlfriend had broken up, that the girl had left the country chasing some young South American who, her daddy had admitted, probably sold her drugs?

When he saw that she wasn't going to answer any of the questions, Lou Pierce looked down at the floor. "Honey," he said softly, "did you ever ask yourself why your daddy left you and your momma?"

That was one question she was willing and able to answer. "He did it because he didn't love us."

When he looked at her again, his eyes were wet — and she hadn't learned yet that wet eyes tell the most effective lies. "He loved y'all," Lou Pierce said. "But your momma, who was a wonderful lady — angel, she wouldn't give your daddy a physical life. I guarantee you he wishes to God he hadn't needed one, but a man's not made that way . . . and even though it embarrasses me, I guess I ought to add that I'm speaking from personal experience."

At the age of thirty-eight, Dee Ann has acquired a wealth of experience, but the phrase *personal experience* is one she almost never uses. She's noticed men are a lot quicker to employ it than women are. Maybe it's because men think their experiences are somehow more personal than everybody else's. Or maybe it's because they take everything personally.

"My own personal experience," Chuckie told Cynthia the other day at the dinner table, after she'd finished ninth in the voting for one of eight positions on the cheerleading squad, "has been that getting elected cheerleader's nothing more than a popularity contest, and I wouldn't let not getting elected worry me for two seconds."

Dee Ann couldn't help it. "When in the world," she said, "did you have a *personal* experience with a cheerleader election?"

He laid his fork down. They stared at each other across a bowl of spaghetti. Cynthia, who can detect a developing storm front as well as any meteorologist, wiped her mouth on her napkin, stood up, and said, "Excuse me."

Chuckie kept his mouth shut until she'd left the room. "I *voted* in cheerleader elections."

"What was personal about that experience?"

"It was my own personal vote."

"Did you have any emotional investment in that vote?"

"You ran once. I voted for you. I was emotional about you then."

She didn't even question him about his use of the word *then* — she knew perfectly well why he used it. "And when I didn't win," she said, "you took it personally?"

"I felt bad for you."

"But not nearly as bad as you felt for yourself?"

"Why in the hell would I feel bad for myself?"

"Having a girlfriend who couldn't win a popularity contest — wasn't that hard on you? Didn't you take it personally?"

He didn't answer. He just sat there looking at her over the bowl of spaghetti, his eyes hard as sandstone and every bit as dry.

Cynthia walks home from school, and several times in the last couple of years, Dee Ann, driving through town on her way back from a shopping trip or a visit to the library, has come across her daughter. Cynthia hunches over as she walks, her canvas backpack slung over her right shoulder, her eyes studying the sidewalk as if she's trying to figure out the pavement's composition. She may be thinking about her boyfriend or some piece of idle gossip she heard that day at school, or she may be trying to remember if the fourth president was James Madison or James Monroe, but her posture and the concentrated way she gazes down suggest that she's a girl who believes she has a problem.

Whether or not this is so Dee Ann doesn't know, because if her daughter is worried about something, she's never mentioned it. What Dee Ann does know is that whenever she's out driving and she sees Cynthia walking home, she always stops the car, rolls her window down, and says, "Want a ride?" Cynthia always looks up and smiles, not the least bit startled, and she always says yes. She's never once said no, like Dee Ann did to three different people that day twenty years ago, when, instead of going to her grandmother's after school, she walked all the way from the highway to the courthouse and climbed the front steps and stood staring at the heavy oak door for several seconds before she pushed it open.

Her daddy has gained weight. His cheeks have grown round, the backs of his hands are plump. He's not getting any exercise to speak of. On Tuesday and Wednesday nights, he tells her, the prisoners who want to keep in shape are let out of their cells, one at a time, and allowed to jog up and down three flights of stairs for ten minutes each. He says an officer sits in a straight-backed chair down in the courthouse lobby with a rifle across his lap to make sure that the prisoners don't jog any farther.

Her daddy is sitting on the edge of his cot. He's wearing blue denim pants and a shirt to match, and a patch on the pocket of the shirt says *Loring County Jail.* The shoes he has on aren't really shoes. They look like bedroom slippers.

Downstairs, when she checked in with the jailer, Jim Wheeler heard her voice and came out of his office. While she waited for the jailer to get the right key, the sheriff asked her how she was doing.

"All right, I guess."

"You may think I'm lying, honey," he said, "but the day'll come when you'll look back on this time in your life and it won't seem like nothing but a real bad dream."

Sitting in a hard plastic chair, looking at her father, she already feels like she's in a bad dream. He's smiling at her, waiting for her to say something, but her tongue feels like it's fused to the roof of her mouth.

The jail is air-conditioned, but it's hot in the cell, and the place smells bad. The toilet over in the corner has no lid on it. She wonders how in the name of God a person can eat in a place like this. And what kind of person could actually eat enough to gain weight?

As if he knows what she's thinking, her father says, "You're probably wondering how I can stand it."

She doesn't answer.

"I can stand it," he says, "because I know I deserved to be locked up."

He sits there a moment longer, then gets up off the cot and

shuffles over to the window, which has three bars across it. He stands there looking out. "All my life," he finally says, "I've been going in and out of all those buildings down there and I never once asked myself what they looked like from above. Now I know. There's garbage on those roofs, and bird shit. One day I saw a man sitting up there, drinking from a paper bag. Right on top of the jewelry store."

He turns around then and walks over and lays his hand on her shoulder.

"When I was down there," he says, "scurrying around like a chicken with its head cut off, I never gave myself enough time to think. That's one thing I've had plenty of in here. And I can tell you, I've seen some things I was too blind to see then."

He keeps his hand on her shoulder the whole time he's talking. "In the last few weeks," he says, "I asked myself how you must have felt when I told you I was too busy to play with you, how you probably felt every time you had to go to the theater by yourself and you saw all those other little girls waiting in line with their daddies and holding their hands." He says he's seen all the ways in which he failed them both, her and her mother, and he knows they both saw them a long time ago. He just wishes to God *he* had.

He takes his hand off her shoulder, goes back over to the cot, and sits down. She watches, captivated, as his eyes begin to glisten. She realizes that she's in the presence of a man capable of anything, and for the first time she knows the answer to a question that has always baffled her: why would her momma put up with so much for so long?

The answer is that her daddy is a natural performer, and her momma was his natural audience. Her momma lived for these routines, she watched till watching killed her.

With watery eyes, Dee Ann's daddy looks at her, here in a stinking room in the county courthouse. "Sweetheart," he whispers, "you don't think I killed her, do you?"

When she speaks, her voice will be steady, it won't crack and break. She will display no more emotion than if she were responding to a question posed by her history teacher.

"No, sir," she tells her daddy. "I don't think you killed her. I *know* you did."

In that instant the weight of his life begins to crush her.

*

Ten-thirty on a Saturday night in 1997. She's standing alone in an alleyway outside the Loring County Courthouse. It's the same alley where her father and Jim Wheeler and the deputy had their pictures taken all those years ago. Loring is the same town it was then, except now there are gangs, and gunfire is something you hear all week long, not just on Saturday night. Now people kill folks they don't know.

Chuckie is supposedly at a deer camp with some men she's never met. He told her he knows them from a sporting goods store in Greenville. They all started talking about deer hunting, and one of the men told Chuckie he owned a cabin over behind the levee and suggested Chuckie go hunting with them this year.

Cynthia is out with her friends — she may be at a movie or she may be in somebody's back seat. Wherever she is, Dee Ann prays she's having fun. She prays that Cynthia's completely caught up in whatever she's doing and that she won't come along and find her momma here, standing alone in the alley beside the courthouse, gazing up through the darkness as though she hopes to read the stars.

The room reminds her of a Sunday school classroom.

It's on the second floor of the courthouse, overlooking the alley. There's a long wooden table in the middle of the room, and she's sitting at one end of it in a straight-backed chair. Along both sides, in similar chairs, sit fifteen men and women who make up the grand jury. She knows several faces, three or four names. It looks as if every one of them is drinking coffee. They've all got styrofoam cups.

Down at the far end of the table, with a big manila folder open in front of him, sits Barry Lancaster, the district attorney, a man whose name she's going to be seeing in newspaper articles a lot in the next twenty years. He's just turned thirty, and though it's still warm out, he's wearing a black suit, with a sparkling white shirt and a glossy black tie.

Barry Lancaster has the reputation of being tough on crime, and he's going to ride that reputation all the way to the Mississippi attorney general's office and then to a federal judgeship. When he came to see her a few days ago, it was his reputation that concerned him. After using a lot of phrases like *true bill* and *no bill* without bothering to explain precisely what they meant, he said, "My reputation's at stake here, Dee Ann. There's a whole lot riding on you."

She knows how much is riding on her, and it's a lot more than his reputation. She feels the great mass bearing down on her shoulders. Her neck is stiff and her legs are heavy. She didn't sleep last night. She never really sleeps anymore.

"Now, Dee Ann," Barry Lancaster says, "we all know you've gone through a lot recently, but I need to ask you some questions today so that these ladies and gentlemen can hear your answers. Will that be okay?"

She wants to say that it's not okay, that it will never again be okay for anyone to ask her anything, but she just nods.

He asks her how old she is.

"Eighteen."

What grade she's in.

"I'm a senior."

Whether or not she has a boyfriend named Chuckie Nelms.

"Yes, sir."

Whether or not, on Saturday evening, August second, she saw her boyfriend.

"Yes, sir."

Barry Lancaster looks up from the stack of papers and smiles at her. "If I was your boyfriend," he says, "I'd want to see you *every* night."

A few of the men on the grand jury grin, but the women keep straight faces. One of them, a small red-haired woman with lots of freckles, whose name she doesn't know and never will know, is going to wait on her in a convenience store over in Indianola many years later. After giving her change, the woman will touch Dee Ann's hand and say, "I hope the rest of your life's been easier, honey. It must have been awful, what you went through."

Barry Lancaster takes her through that Saturday evening, from the time Chuckie picked her up until the moment when she walked into the kitchen. Then he asks her, in a solemn voice, what she found there.

She keeps her eyes trained on his tie pin, a small amethyst, as she describes the scene in as much detail as she can muster. In a roundabout way, word will reach her that people on the grand jury were shocked, and even appalled, at her lack of emotion. Chuckie will try to downplay their reaction, telling her that they're probably just saying that because of what happened later on. "It's probably not you they're reacting to," he'll say. "It's probably just them having hindsight."

Hindsight is something she lacks, as she sits here in a hard chair, in a small room, her hands lying before her on a badly scarred table. She can't make a bit of sense out of what's already happened. She knows what her daddy was and she knows what he wasn't, knows what he did and didn't do. What she doesn't know is the whys and wherefores.

On the other hand, she can see into the future, she knows what's going to happen, and she also knows why. She knows, for instance, what question is coming, and she knows how she's going to answer it and why. She knows that shortly after she's given that answer, Barry Lancaster will excuse her, and she knows, because Lou Pierce has told her, that after she's been excused, Barry Lancaster will address the members of the grand jury.

He will tell them what they have and haven't heard. "Now she's a young girl," he'll say, "and she's been through a lot, and in the end this case has to rest on what she can tell us. And the truth, ladies and gentlemen, much as I might want it to be otherwise, is that the kid's gone shaky on us. She told the sheriff one version of what happened at the grocery store that Saturday night when her daddy came to see her, and she's sat here today and told y'all a different version. She's gotten all confused on this question of time. You can't blame her for that, she's young and her mind's troubled, but in all honesty a good defense attorney's apt to rip my case apart. Because when you lose this witness's testimony, all you've got left is that dog, and that dog, ladies and gentlemen, can't testify."

Even as she sits here, waiting for Barry Lancaster to bring up that night in the grocery store — that night which, for her, will always be the present — she knows the statement about the dog will be used to sentence Jim Wheeler to November defeat. The voters of this county will drape that sentence around the sheriff's neck. If Jim Wheeler had done his job and found some real evidence, they will say, that man would be on his way to Parchman.

They will tell one another, the voters of this county, how someone saw her daddy at the Jackson airport, as he boarded a plane that would take him to Dallas, where he would board yet another plane for a destination farther south. They will say that her daddy was actually carrying a briefcase filled with money, with lots of crisp green hundreds, one of which he extracted to pay for a beer.

They will say that her daddy must have paid her to lie, that she didn't give a damn about her mother. They will wonder if Chuckie has a brain in his head, to go and marry somebody like her, and they will ask themselves how she can ever bear the shame of what she's done. They will not believe, not even for a moment, that she's performed some careful calculations in her mind. All that shame, she's decided, will still weigh a lot less than her daddy's life. It will be a while before she and Chuckie and a girl who isn't born yet learn how much her faulty math has cost.

Barry Lancaster makes a show of rifling through his papers. He pulls a sheet out and studies it, lets his face wrinkle up as if he's seeing something on the page that he never saw before. Then he lays the sheet back down. He closes the manila folder, pushes his chair away from the table a few inches, and leans forward. She's glad he's too far away to lay his hand on her knee.

"Now," he says, "let's go backwards in time."

Contributors' Notes

100 Other Distinguished Stories of 1998

Editorial Addresses

Contributors' Notes

RICK BASS is the author of fifteen books of fiction and nonfiction, including the novel *Where the Sea Used to Be*. He lives in northwest Montana with his wife and daughters.

▪ One of the hazards of being a writer of both fiction and nonfiction — as well as of possessing a faulty, perhaps dysfunctional memory — is that sometimes after I write something I can't always remember whether it's true or not. Or rather, whether it really happened or not. Worse yet, I often read passages that I wrote, and I don't remember having written them. I don't know if it's this way for other writers, and they're afraid to admit it — I've never heard anyone admit to such forgetfulness — or if I'm in deeper trouble, memory-wise, than I have previously realized.

(It seems to me that forgetfulness is a natural side effect of storytelling: the pen moving always from left to right, and downstream, so that the model that's imprinted in your consciousness is for only that which lies ahead, even if it's the past, and the backstory — it lies just ahead of the pen's movement. That's one of the wonderful things that can happen, I think, that kind of almost reckless forgetfulness — as long as the pen is moving, unscrolling more tale, the story is still alive, breathing, pulsing, and choosing its own direction, making its way in the world . . .)

I don't mean to suggest that I can't remember how this story got written. I remember parts and fragments of it. I was at lunch with another writer a couple of Octobers ago, and a man from France sat down with us and got onto the subject of the Canadian writer Grey Owl, who evidently had once upon a time discovered a frozen lake with no water beneath it.

I remember my writer friend looking at me with a certain look that seemed to me to indicate that he was wondering if I was ever going to write about such an event. I must confess a certain failure in generosity of spirit, in that I did not dare ask my friend if he intended to write up that story, for fear that he might say yes.

At the time, as well, I had two young bird dogs that I was training, and I was having a rough time with them. It's a hundred times harder to train two young dogs than it is to train one. One dog will listen to you, but two will always be wanting to run off and play. I suppose that part of "The Hermit's Story," about the diligent, talented trainer, was wishfulness on my part that such a trainer existed: someone who could impose order upon the two hellion pups I was working with.

In an earlier draft of the story, which was much longer — a novella — I had a weightlifter living with that great dog trainer, living way back in the mountains, hiding out from what they perceived to be the excessive speed and clamor of the world and trying instead to live lives at a more tolerable pace, and in the almost submerged dreamtime of their lives in the hermitage, time still hurtled past, nearly as fast as if they had remained out in the center of the world, surrounded by noise and heat and speed.

I can't remember much else about writing this story, but I know that I wanted to write about a frozen lake without water in it, so I had the bird-dog trainer go up there with her dogs and fall down into it.

James Linville and George Plimpton at *The Paris Review* helped me cut out all the windy stuff about the weightlifter and focus instead on two things: the story and telling the story. To them, for this, I am grateful.

JUNOT DÍAZ is the author of *Drown* (1996). His stories have appeared in *Story, The New Yorker, The Paris Review, Time Out, Glimmer Train, African Voices, The Best American Short Stories 1996, The Best American Short Stories 1997,* and *Pushcart Prize XXII.* He has received a Eugene McDermott Award and a Guggenheim fellowship. He teaches creative writing at Syracuse University and is currently at work on his first novel.

▪ A couple of years back I went to Santo Domingo as an interpreter for a U.S.-sponsored dentistry mission. Ended up helping the dentists out, and we pulled like five thousand teeth on the trip and also rubbed shoulders with many of the country's elite, and I wanted to describe that time in a story. Hammered the story for over a year, and it always came out ass. The only thing that saved it was when, at the recommendation of a friend, I dumped the dentistry stuff and focused on the narrator's relationship meltdown. Once I got that insight, I finished the story in a single day, the culmination of sixteen months of work. I still remember that day. The first piece I'd finished since my book was published. My hands were shaking.

A native of India, CHITRA DIVAKARUNI teaches creative writing at the University of Houston and divides her time between San Francisco and Houston. She is the author of a book of short stories, *Arranged Marriage,* and two novels, *The Mistress of Spices* and *Sister of My Heart*, as well as of four books of poetry. Her awards include an American Book Award, two PEN/Syndicated Fiction Awards, and a PEN/Josephine Miles Award. Her work has appeared in *The New Yorker*, *The Atlantic Monthly*, and *Ms.*, among others. She is the founder of MAITRI, a hotline for South Asian women in the San Francisco Bay area, and a volunteer with DAYA, a similar organization in Houston.

▪ Some stories come to me easily, and others I struggle with for years. "Mrs. Dutta" was one of the latter. It had many false beginnings — in malls and amusement parks and public restrooms, and even a melodramatic one in a police station! Several times friends advised me to abandon it, but I couldn't. I had no choice. It had caught hold of me with its bulldog teeth, its Ancient Mariner eye.

I wanted to explore in this story a tragedy that I see as a major byproduct of diaspora: what happens to the parents we leave behind when we come to America? What happens to them back in the home country, and what happens to them if they follow us here? How do they — and we, their children, parents ourselves — deal with the failed notions of love and family that immigration sets in motion?

In its early incarnation, I wanted "Mrs. Dutta" to have a villain, someone I could blame for all the loss and sorrow. Only when I realized that blame was not the point did the story give itself to me.

STEPHEN DOBYNS has published ten volumes of poetry, twenty novels, and one book of literary essays. His most recent book of poems is *Pallbearers Envying the One Who Rides*, and his most recent novel is *Boy in the Water* (both 1999). His book of essays is *Best Words, Best Order* (1996). His first book of short stories, *Eating Naked and Other Stories*, will be published in 2000. He lives with his family near Boston.

▪ It is hard for me to say what is precisely true. Memory distorts. Psychology, emotion, good health or bad — all drag their feet across events. The details that I might remember one day are not those that I might remember on another day. And certainly my memory has its own agenda — to show me off this way or that. My subjectivity is the smudgy window through which I squint.

Given that, the bare skeleton of the first part of "Kansas" is as my father told it to me. He was hitchhiking through Kansas during the summer of 1930; a farmer in a pickup with a pistol gave him a ride to Lawrence, where my father was in summer school. The farmer was pursuing his wife and her lover. My father never knew whether the farmer caught them. This is something my father speculated about many times and I speculated about as well. As for the details of my father's life, they unwound themselves much as I describe.

My father died in October 1989. I present that time as I remember it. Such deaths seem larger than memory, too big for the head, yet they keep knocking at the skull, needing to be accommodated. I almost never write from direct experience, although all poetry and fiction seem autobiographical, even if indirectly so. However, I wrote two poems about my father's death that appeared in my books *Body Traffic* and *Velocities*. Then, in the winter of 1993, I spent a week teaching in the University of Idaho in Moscow. I was put up at a local Holiday Inn and arrived with a cold. The teaching load was light. I had a lot of time to stare out at the bare lentil fields. I again thought of my father's story, and my own short story began to evolve. Now it is part of my first book of short stories. It is the only (relatively) autobiographical story in the bunch.

Between 1995 and 1997, I submitted the story to five or six magazines, but editors kept rejecting it, saying it was too sketchy, too peculiar. I kept revising the story, still liking it. My revisions got down to taking out a comma and putting it back again, although I expect there will be changes before it appears in a book. In any case, in February 1998 I gave a series of poetry readings in Washington and Oregon, including one at Clackamas Community College, outside Portland. Tim Schell, a professor at the college and one of the editors of *The Clackamas Literary Review*, asked if he might have a story for his magazine. I gave him "Kansas."

Since the writing of the story, my mother has died. And friends have died, a lot of them. And there have been other hugenesses, not all of them bad. Translating these events into language is one of the ways in which I deal with them. The writing contains my grief, if the event concerns a loss, and my attempt to move on by turning the loss into language, by changing it to the metaphor, by being no longer the casualty of loss but its representative, its articulator for the reader, which, ideally, is one of the functions of art — to become a party to the reader's own experience, a shareholder to an emotion for which there is no easy language. And that lessens the grief, softens the memory — a whole series of memories, but especially the one that seemed to conclude them all: the movement of the body bag's silver zipper along my dead father's face and forehead, its glittering progression.

NATHAN ENGLANDER's first collection of stories, *For the Relief of Unbearable Urges*, was published in 1999. His fiction has appeared in *American Short Fiction, Story, The Atlantic Monthly,* and *The New Yorker,* and in *Pushcart Prize XXII*. Born and raised in New York, Englander has been living in Jerusalem since 1996.

• As a fourth-generation American who was raised with the Holocaust as a very large and looming part of my education, I'm interested in the act of remembering and what that means for generations born far away from and long after the event they are intended never to forget.

This story is partially about the size of that remembering. It's about a thing so large that it makes its way even to fabled Jewish towns — something so unforgiving that it invades literature itself.

TIM GAUTREAUX is the author of two collections of stories, *Same Place, Same Things* (1996) and *Welding with Children* (1999). His novel, *The Next Step in the Dance*, won the Southeastern Booksellers Award for best fiction of 1998. His stories have appeared in *The Atlantic Monthly, Harper's Magazine, GQ, Story, New Stories from the South,* and *The Best American Short Stories.* He has a doctorate in English from the University of South Carolina and teaches at Southeastern Louisiana University, where he is writer-in-residence.

▪ I like to write about service persons who visit our homes and get just a little entangled in our lives. I've written a few such stories and expect to write a few more. Pest control men, carpenters, and piano tuners might see us as we really are. They are not "company," and we don't greet them at the door with the polite façade we use for friends and relatives. We tend to be franker with them, though often we ignore them as we go about our own jobs. While they are taking apart our plumbing or air conditioners, we don't think they see us.

Many years ago I moonlighted as a rebuilder of player pianos and occasionally would get called out to repair a jammed bellows or mouse-eaten leather valve. People would talk to me while I was in their homes, and I could tell whether they were happy or sad. If I'd ask them a personal question, they would generally unload their histories on me. After all, whom could I tell? What did I care? Who was I, anyway?

I was in it for the money, but long after I'd left their houses, I still worried about some of the people whose pianos I'd serviced. Some of them were lonely, and some were a little odd. One woman had arranged dozens of antique baby dolls so that they were staring at her player grand, and it was a shock to reach out for a tool and find it in the lap of a hundred-year-old bisque child.

As far as the story in this volume is concerned, I decided to put a needy customer and a giving piano tuner together to see what would happen, maybe with the hope that he would do a better job than I could when I was in the business.

MELISSA HARDY was born and raised in Chapel Hill, North Carolina, and graduated from the University of North Carolina with a B.A. in English and honors in creative writing. She went on to do graduate work in postclassical history at the University of Toronto and has worked as an editor, a journalist, and a communications specialist. In 1994 she won the Journey Prize for the best piece of short fiction to appear in a Canadian literary journal in that year. She has published one novel, *A Cry of Bees* (1970), and one story cycle, *Constant Fire* (1995), and her short stories have been widely published as well as anthologized.

▪ For the past several years I have been writing a series of stories set in northern Ontario around the time of the Porcupine gold rush — between 1900 and 1922. Their backdrop is the cross-cultural nexus formed by the confluence into the area of fortune-seekers from all over the world — from Finland to China to Cornwall. The Porcupine's story is one first of traders, trappers, and prospectors, then of mines, railroads, surveys, and lumber camps. "The Uncharted Heart" focuses on one of the men who mapped this region. Its genesis lies in the true story of a native woman, Maggie Leclair, who lived on the shores of Kamiscotia Lake near Timmins — her trapper husband and children died of fever one night, and she buried them by herself the following day. However, I was also intrigued by the idea of mapping a hitherto uncharted region, and by the notion that unless a place was on the map, it did not exist in a real sense. I have also always been intrigued by the role that secrets play in our lives . . . and that, of course, is what "The Uncharted Heart" is about — a secret.

GEORGE HARRAR lives in Wayland, Massachusetts, with his wife, Linda, a documentary filmmaker, and teenage son, Tony, who also writes stories. Harrar's short fiction has appeared in *Story, New Press Literary Quarterly, Side Show Anthology, The Dickinson Review,* and *Quarter After Eight.* His first novel, *First Tiger,* is being published this fall.

▪ I ride the train from Lincoln, Massachusetts, to Cambridge several times each month, and I notice how people getting off rarely look at or acknowledge the people getting on. That prompted me to imagine two regular riders, a man and a woman, passing each other wordlessly every day until some small event — a gust of wind — inclines their parallel lives toward each other. My highly analytical male protagonist becomes consumed thinking about the woman, but not in a sexual or dangerously obsessive way. When she disappears, reason fails him, and the world suddenly appears fantastical. He loses his moorings as the familiarities of his life seem to turn against him.

A. HEMON was born in 1964 in Sarajevo, Bosnia-Herzegovina. He has lived in the United States since 1992. He began writing fiction in English in 1995. "Islands" is one of his first stories written in English. He has published stories in various magazines (*TriQuarterly, Chicago Review,* etc.), and he writes, in Bosnian, a regular column for the independent Sarajevo magazine *Dani*. He is working on his Ph.D. in English literature at Loyola University, Chicago. He is a soccer fanatic and plays soccer at least once a week.

- There are two main soccer teams in Sarajevo. The one I supported was traditionally, but respectfully, unsuccessful, and it was called Zeljeznicar, which means "the Railroad Worker." One of the pillars of the defense was a man named Josip Cilic. He was a hard worker, though he was not very skillful — he was a kind of player who had no glamour and no star quality, and no one particularly liked him, though everyone respected him. Toward the end of his career, which began and ended in Zeljeznicar, he scored a marvelous goal: he kicked the ball from forty meters out and it almost ripped the net in the upper right corner of the goal. Sports shows kept showing the goal, which was elected "the Goal of the Week." After the game, a reporter asked him to explain how he had scored the goal and to tell the fans where he had gotten the inspiration for such a brilliant goal. "Well," he said. "I got the ball, so I kicked it."

I got the ball from my father's uncle, a Ukrainian born in Bosnia, who in 1926 went to the USSR in pursuit of a utopian, just society. He was arrested as soon as he crossed the border from Poland and sentenced to three years for illegal border crossing. He lived in the Soviet Union for the next thirty-one years, twenty-five of which he spent in different prisons and camps and eventually in exile in Siberia. In the face of indescribable suffering, his faith in the socialist utopia just strengthened — not unlike Christian martyrs' faith. He believed that Stalin's crimes were due to his betrayal of the true socialist ideas. In 1990 I interviewed him in Zagreb, recording some fifteen hours of his reminiscences, which were all lost in the war in Sarajevo. Every day for a week I would visit him, we would have lunch at eleven o'clock, and then he would talk to me. At lunch — I was in my mid-twenties, so that was more of an early breakfast for me — I would deliberate over the plate, while he would wipe his plate clean in no time. "A camp habit," he said. "Otherwise, they snatch the food away from you." In 1987 he wrote a letter directly to Gorbachev, imploring him not to leave the path of socialism, for if he did so, all the suffering would have been in vain, he said. The wall had gone down, but he was still isolated in his forgotten suffering, locked within the faith that enabled him to withstand it, though it looked absurd to me. But I was young then, and it was easy to be right, since I didn't have to do anything for it.

PAM HOUSTON is the author of two collections of linked short stories, *Cowboys Are My Weakness*, which was the winner of the 1993 Western States Book Award and has been translated into nine languages, and *Waltzing the*

Cat, which was published in 1998. Her first collection of essays, *A Little More About Me,* is due out in early fall 1999. She lives in Colorado at nine thousand feet above sea level, near the headwaters of the Rio Grande.

• "The Best Girlfriend You Never Had" is the story of mine that I secretly love more than any other, because it so stretches its own structural limits. More than anything else I have written, this story is holding itself together by the skin of its teeth.

For me, writing is juggling, taking a bunch of moments, metaphors, story chunks, and throwing them into the air in a pattern. Sometimes these chunks of story are connected chronologically, thematically, or metaphorically, and sometimes they are connected by whatever bizarre little ganglions exist in my brain and produce connections even I don't understand. When I've got more balls, more chunks in the air than I think I can handle, and when the connections between them are tenuous at best and the whole thing seems apt to fly apart at any minute, but somehow all the pieces keep holding together as if by some forgotten law of physics, that's when I'm having the most fun I ever have as a writer.

The juggler in my imagination always has orange balls, and when I write, I think a lot about the moment when he gets so many balls in the air that the audience can't see the individual balls anymore, and what they see instead is a spinning orange hoop, the separation between the balls still existing but invisible to the eye. "The Best Girlfriend You Never Had" comes as close as I've ever come to creating that orange hoop. I wrote it at a time in my life when everything was spinning, and I think it captures that centrifugal force.

As for the juggling balls themselves, they came out of my first experience of the particular way a person can be alone when she is alone in the middle of a big city. I was alone, and it seemed everybody around me was alone, we were all so very much alone, all of us together, and it seemed needless and necessary all at the same time. When I tried to write about the aloneness, so many other things just stuck to it — the small and singular insanities that are taken for daily life in the big city, as well as the more obvious madnesses of childhood.

The fact that people would actually have hope enough to marry and begin lives together, the very hope contained in something as beautiful as a black Asian swan, seemed profound to me in the face of the continuous terror that seemed to define city life. I wrote this story in order to celebrate that isolated beauty, and to give my character Lucy a moment when she sees just the briefest shimmer of that hope.

HA JIN has recently published several books of fiction and poetry. His novel *In the Pond* was published in 1998, and his new novel, *Waiting,* is forthcoming. He teaches at Emory University.

▪ My wife and I often talk about our kindergarten experiences back in China. We have many painful memories, some of which became details in "In the Kindergarten." What's at stake here is the encounter with evil, which seems to be a part of human growth, especially in the given environment. At the beginning of the story, Shaona is quite innocent, but at the end she has learned how to deal with evil and also how to participate in it — she fights back and acts militantly, with pleasure and appetite. Is evil necessary for a child's development? I don't know the answer, but my story indirectly poses the question.

HEIDI JULAVITS is a native of Portland, Maine. She is a graduate of Dartmouth College and Columbia University, where in 1996 she received an M.F.A. in creative writing. Her short stories have appeared in *Writers Harvest 2: A Collection of New Fiction, Story, Esquire, Zoetrope,* and *McSweeney's Quarterly Concern.* Her first novel, *The Mineral Palace,* is forthcoming in 2000. She currently lives in Brooklyn.

▪ I got the structural idea for this story from a photo essay in *Doubletake.* The essay featured a wedding photographer's collection of unfortunate and irreverent images that hadn't, for obvious reasons, been included in the final wedding albums. As I was in the process of becoming married at the time and having a difficult time navigating the rigid nuptial expectations of relatives and caterers and, well, myself, I was all too familiar with the way many wedding albums (with their family portraits and cake cuttings and garter tossings) present an unvaryingly cheerful account of an event that is equal parts joy, ambivalence, and conflict. The idea of featuring the cutting-room-floor photos, however, allowed me the space to conjure the untold, imperfect, and wholly unique unfolding of events. In short, it provided me with both a story and a way to wrangle my own generic marital paranoia. The name Violet Sheidegger was a great inspiration for me, provided by a pregnant woman (Mrs. Sheidegger) I met in L.A. at a wedding. Though I gushed and gushed over the brash poetic potential of their runner-up choice, Violet, she admitted they probably weren't going to use the name. Violet Sheidegger seemed too splendid and suggestive and vital a moniker to go to waste. So I nicked it. Many thanks (and apologies, if needed) to the Sheideggers.

HESTER KAPLAN's story collection *The Edge of Marriage* won the 1998 Flannery O'Connor Award for Short Fiction and will be published this year. Her novel, *The Altruist,* is also forthcoming. "Would You Know It Wasn't Love" appeared in *The Best American Short Stories 1998.* She lives in Rhode Island with her husband, the writer Michael Stein, and their children.

▪ It's all too easy to be distracted while writing, especially when things

aren't going particularly well. During one of those moments, I was seized
by the urgent need to send away for a brochure from an island resort I'd
read about in a magazine. I never had the slightest intention of going to
the place, but the descriptions were too tempting to ignore, and the
pictures, when they arrived, weren't so bad to look at, either.

The brochure sat on my desk for weeks, and I began to wonder what it
would be like not so much to visit the island but to live there, and what
would happen if something were to come along and threaten paradise.
Henry Blaze was just such a visitor, bringing his hard realities about life
and love to the island-bound proprietor, who had closed himself off to
such things. I came to like Blaze very much, despite his manipulations and
small cruelties. Paradise is hard to come by, but it can be reached through
great acts of compassion, if only fleetingly.

SHEILA KOHLER grew up in South Africa, left for Europe at age seven-
teen, and now lives in New York City. She is the author of three novels, *The
Perfect Place* (1989), *The House on R Street* (1994), and the forthcoming
Cracks (1999), and of two books of short stories, *Miracles in America* (1990)
and *One Girl* (1999). Her work has been published abroad by Gallimard,
Klett-Cotta, Shinchosa, Distribuidora Rekord, Jonathan Cape, and Vintage
International. She has won three prizes: O'Henry, Open Voice, and Willa
Cather (the last, selected by William Gass, for her recent collection of
stories, which includes "Africans"). She teaches at the New School and at
the Writer's Voice, a program sponsored by the YMCA in New York City.

▪ No one can really explain how a story comes to be. Sometimes, something as unique as a thumbprint passes through one. Occasionally the
same story revisits in various avatars, like a recurring dream. This was one
of those. In my first novel, *The Perfect Place,* a girl is killed mysteriously, and
in the most recent, *Cracks,* a girl disappears on a walk with her classmates.
However, I have never been able to approach the seminal event as directly
— emotion not yet recollected with any tranquillity, perhaps — as I was
here, and I am very grateful to the many people who helped in the process: Dawn Raffel gave my name to Ann Hood and John Searles, and they
asked me to write a nonfiction piece about the death of a sibling for an
anthology. I showed the piece to Patty Dann, who teaches a nonfiction
course, and she explained very gently that what I had written had a few
extraneous elements, such as how my mother met her future mother-in-
law on a train in the Karoo. Why do we have the idea that nonfiction, being
the truth, does not require the structure that fiction does?

Eventually I turned back to story writing, which is more familiar to me,
and showed an early attempt to my husband. He expressed shock — always
a useful element — at a little paragraph about the role of the servants in

the house. This gave me the idea for the reversal at the heart of the story, but I continued to think, doggedly, of this as the beloved sister's story, and so I began with the paragraph which is now at the end. I shared various attempts with wonderful friends: Karen Satran, Victoria Rendel, and Therese Svoboda, who expressed interest in the Zulu's story, and so John, loosely based on a much-loved man in my life, to whom I dedicate this story, took his rightful place at the center. Finally, Lois Rosenthal, bless her heart, offered to publish it and polished it to a high shine.

JHUMPA LAHIRI was born in London and raised in Rhode Island. Her fiction has appeared in *The New Yorker, Agni, Epoch, The Louisville Review, Story Quarterly,* and elsewhere. She is the author of *Interpreter of Maladies,* a collection of short stories published in 1999. She lives in New York City.

▪ "Interpreter of Maladies" began as a title without a story. The title came to me after I bumped into an acquaintance who told me that his job was to interpret on behalf of Russian-speaking patients for a doctor in Brookline, Massachusetts. I wrote the phrase on a piece of paper at the back of my agenda, and for four years I tried to write a story to go with it. One day, on the same piece of paper, I wrote, "Monkeys stole the driver's clothes," which was what had happened when I was touring in the north of India with my family and our driver had set some laundry on the roof of his car. Eventually, these two phrases set the story in motion.

LORRIE MOORE is the author of five books of fiction. The most recent is the story collection *Birds of America,* which was nominated for the National Book Critics Circle Award. She lives in Madison, Wisconsin, with her husband and son.

▪ "Real Estate" is a story about the impossibility of possession. On the day the story first appeared in print, my house was suddenly invaded by late-summer bees that had built a six-foot hive in the wall of my dining room.

In constructing this tale, I set the main narrative and a secondary narrative running simultaneously toward a particular intersection; then I let them crash there. I'd never really done that before, and I found it ridiculously exciting. Such are the pitiful and vaguely immoral yet endlessly enticing pleasures of story writing.

A native of Ontario, ALICE MUNRO has twice received Canada's Governor's General Award and is the author of nine collections of short stories, including *Who Do You Think You Are?, The Moons of Jupiter, Open Secrets, Friend of My Youth, The Progress of Love,* and, most recently, *The Selected Stories of Alice Munro* and *The Love of a Good Woman,* which won the National Book

Critics Circle Award in 1998. Her story "Meneseteung" was selected by
John Updike to appear in *The Best American Short Stories of the Century.*

▪ In my part of the country there's been a big change in the last quarter
of a century. Most of the old barns are gone, the fences pulled out, the
farmhouses abandoned or renovated to suit the needs of people who don't
work on farms. There seems to be a lot more luxury and style around than
there used to be, as well as a lot more outright deterioration. Country
people aren't country people anymore, even if they do happen to be living
on the land they grew up on. And villages where housewives didn't dare
hang out a wash on Sundays are sprouting casinos and "love" shops.

When I wrote "Save the Reaper," this change was in my mind. So were
the changes in the lives of people like me, who are now in their sixties. The
choices mostly made and lived with by now, the shaky new patterns and
untrustworthy nostalgia for old patterns, the buffeting, surprising needs.
So I could say these came together in the story. But I always slightly
mistrust explanations like this, just because they are explanations, almost
excuses — as if you're saying to a doubtful reader, See, this story is okay,
it's almost like history or sociology, it's the study of something. When you
might just as easily say, It's about things you feel and don't quite know why
or things you pay attention to without being able to say why they are
important — the sun shining on the tight rolls of hay or the circles under
the young mother's eyes — and that would be just as true.

ANNIE PROULX lives and writes in Wyoming.

▪ "The Bunchgrass Edge of the World" was written as part of a collection
of short stories set in rural Wyoming. It is tied to my continuing interest in
rural ways and manners, the effects of climate, geography, and local tradition on isolated communities drifting on the edge of events.

JAMES SPENCER is a psychotherapist in private practice in Menlo Park,
California. His stories and poems have appeared in *The Virginia Quarterly
Review, The Gettysburg Review, Ontario Review, The Greensboro Review, Stanford
Short Stories,* and many other magazines and anthologies. His plays have
been produced by the Chelsea Theatre Center in New York City, the
American Conservatory Theatre in San Francisco, and other repertory
companies in this country. He is currently finishing his second novel.

▪ In 1993 I traveled to India in the company of eighteen pilgrims on
their way to visit a swami. Over the years, thousands of people had watched
this swami materialize some small, valuable object for them, and nobody
had ever caught him in any kind of trickery. Although I was curious about
this, I had heard other things that impressed me more than the miracles.
The swami himself says that he performs miracles only to draw people to

him and his true teaching, which is integrity, love, and compassion. With the money people give him he builds schools, orphanages, and hospitals. Visitors stay at his ashram free of charge. Meals cost a few cents a day. He accepts money only from the wealthy. He tells others to go home and help the poor in their own community. I decided that this was one swami I wanted to see for myself.

As Greta says, nothing in India behaves the way it's supposed to. By the time my Boeing 747 had set its wheels down at Tokyo Narita, I was beginning to feel a story coming on. In a group of pilgrims you soon know everybody's secrets. The disastrous marriages, the betrayals and abandonments, the bankruptcies, the death and incurable diseases. I took notes obsessively, in airplanes, on bumpy taxi and bus rides, at meals, in my bunk at the ashram. Back at home I had a novel and other work in progress, and it was several years before I had time to spread my notes out in front of me and go looking for the story.

The characters are composites or fictions to protect real people, but they are true to the spirit and intent of the journey. Although we never see the ashram or the swami, he is everywhere in the story, its reason for being. My protagonist is a skeptic with an open mind because it is the point of view most congenial to me. The events of the story opened Bannister's mind a bit, as they did my own. I had gone to India to study the swami and write about him. What emerged instead, I hope, was a tribute to the people I traveled with and the mysterious forces that tap us on the shoulder when we've gone to sleep.

SAMRAT UPADHYAY was born and raised in once-beautiful Katmandu, a city that finds its way into most of his work. He received his Ph.D. in English from the University of Hawaii and now lives with his wife, Babita, near Cleveland, where he teaches at Baldwin-Wallace College. His stories and poems have appeared in *Manoa, Indiana Review, Chelsea,* and other literary journals. A story also appeared in the 1999 *Best of Fiction Workshops,* edited by Sherman Alexie.

▪ The idea for "The Good Shopkeeper" came to me in 1992 when I went back to Katmandu for a visit after nearly four years. Since Nepal didn't open up to the outside world until the 1950s, I've found the rapid changes in the country, particularly Katmandu, stunning, and often disconcerting. That year I noticed that there were computers all over the city, which got me thinking — and the main character of the story was born. I never work with plot when I write a short story; I start with a strong image or a mood, then follow the impulse, letting language and characters dictate the story line. In "The Good Shopkeeper," the housemaid was not supposed to be a major figure: I just wanted Pramod to talk to someone in

the park because he had not had a good chat with anyone lately. But I like
how she cracked her peanuts, and thought she was kind of sexy. I can never
resist sex in a story.

A native of Mississippi, STEVE YARBROUGH lives in Fresno, California,
where he is a professor of English at California State University. He is the
author of the short story collections *Veneer, Mississippi History,* and *Family
Men.* His novel *The Oxygen Man* will be published in 1999. His stories and
essays have been published in many journals and magazines, and he has
won a Pushcart Prize and a fellowship from the National Endowment for
the Arts.

   ▪ In 1996, Kathleen Kennedy, who produced such movies as *The Color
Purple* and *E.T.*, read an essay of mine about southerners and guns and got
interested in my work. I went down to L.A. and had a meeting with her,
and before too long her production company had optioned an unpub-
lished novel of mine called *The Oxygen Man* and hired me to do the
screenplay for it.

   The novel has two time frames several years apart, and many of my
struggles with the screenplay involved either cutting out material from the
past or trying to find a way to work that material into the present action.
"The Rest of Her Life" is the first piece of fiction I wrote after finishing the
filmscript. The structure of the story, in which most of the action takes
place in the past, probably grew out of my impatience with the limitations
screenwriting placed on me.

100 Other Distinguished Stories of 1998

SELECTED BY KATRINA KENISON

LESLIE, PAUL
17 Reasons Why. *Ploughshares,* Vol.
24, Nos. 2 & 3.
LONG, DAVID
Morphine. *The New Yorker,* July 20.
LYCHACK, WILLIAM
The Old Woman and Her Thief.
Ploughshares, Vol. 24, No. 1.

MARTIN, VALERIE
The Change. *Ploughshares,* Vol. 24,
No. 1.
MASON, BOBBIE ANN
Charger. *The Atlantic Monthly,*
January.
McCANN, COLUM
Hunger Strike. *GQ,* November.
McCORKLE, JILL
Your Husband Is Cheating on Us.
The Oxford American, No. 20.
McCRACKEN, ELIZABETH
Juliet. *Esquire,* January.
McNAMER, DEIRDRE
Virgin Everything. *Double Take,*
Vol. 4, No. 2.
MILLHAUSER, STEVEN
Flying Carpets. *The Paris Review,*
No. 145.
MOORE, LORRIE
Lucky Ducks. *Harper's Magazine,*
March.
MUNRO, ALICE
Cortes Island. *The New Yorker,*
October 12.

NELSON, ANTONYA
Incognito. *American Short Fiction,*
No. 31.
NELSON, KENT
Rituals of Sleep. *Witness,* Vol. 12,
No. 2.

O'BRIEN, TIM
The Streak. *The New Yorker,*
September 28.
OFFUTT, CHRIS
Two-Eleven All Around. *Glimmer
Train,* No. 26.

OLMSTEAD, ROBERT
The Air Above the Ground. *The
Idaho Review,* Vol. 1, No. 1.
ORRINGER, JULIE
What We Save. *The Yale Review,* Vol.
36, No. 1.
OWENS, BRADLEY J.
A Circle of Stones. *Ploughshares,* Vol.
24, Nos. 2 & 3.
OZICK, CYNTHIA
Actors. *The New Yorker,* October 5.

PAINE, TOM
Unapproved Minutes. *Harper's
Magazine,* April.
PEARLMAN, EDITH
Deliverance. *Ascent,* Vol. 23, No. 1.
Home Schooling. *Alaska Quarterly
Review,* Fall and Winter.
PNEUMAN, ANGELA
Home Remedies. *The New England
Review,* Vol. 19, No. 1.
PRITCHARD, MELISSA
Port de Bras. *The Southern Review,*
Vol. 34, No. 2.
PROSE, FRANCINE
The Lunatic, the Lover, and the
Poet. *The Atlantic Monthly,* March.
PROULX, ANNIE
The Mud Below. *The New Yorker,*
June 22 & 28.

RUSSO, RICHARD
The Whore's Child. *Harper's
Magazine,* February.

SANDOR, MARJORIE
Orphan of Love. *The Georgia Review,*
Vol. 52, No. 1.
SCHLAKS, MAXIMILIAN
The Invitaton. *Manoa,* Vol. 10,
No. 2.
SCHUTT, CHRISTINE
Winterreise. *The American Voice,*
No. 45.
SCHWARTZ, SHEILA
Afterbirth. *Ploughshares,* Vol. 24,
Nos. 2 & 3.

Editorial Addresses of American and Canadian Magazines Publishing Short Stories

When available, the annual subscription rate and the name of the editor follow the address.

African American Review
Stalker Hall 212
Indiana State University
Terre Haute, IN 47809
web.indstate.edu/artsci/AAR
$24, Joe Weixlmann

Agni Review
Creative Writing Department
Boston University
236 Bay State Road
Boston, MA 02115
webdelsol.com/AGNI
$18, Askold Melnyczuk

Alabama Literary Review
Troy State University
Smith 253
Troy, AL 36082
$10, Theron E. Montgomery

Alaska Quarterly Review
Department of English
University of Alaska
3211 Providence Drive

Anchorage, AK 99508
$8, Ronald Spatz

Alfred Hitchcock's Mystery Magazine
1540 Broadway
New York, NY 10036
$34.97, Cathleen Jordan

Amelia
329 E Street
Bakersfield, CA 93304
$30, Frederick A. Raborg, Jr.

American Letters and Commentary
850 Park Avenue, Suite 5B
New York, NY 10021
$5, Jeanne Beaumont, Anna Rabinowitz

American Literary Review
University of North Texas
P.O. Box 13615
Denton, TX 76203
$15, Lee Martin

American Short Fiction
Parlin 108
Department of English

University of Texas at Austin
Austin, TX 78712-1164
$24, Joseph Krupa (has ceased
   publication)

American Voice
332 West Broadway
Louisville, KY 40202
*$15, Sallie Bingham, Frederick
   Smock*

Analog Science Fiction/Science Fact
1540 Broadway
New York, NY 10036
$34.95, Stanley Schmidt

Another Chicago Magazine
Left Field Press
3709 North Kenmore
Chicago, IL 60613
$8, Barry Silesky

Antietam Review
41 South Potomac Street
Hagerstown, MD 21740-3764
$5, Suzanne Kass

Antioch Review
P.O. Box 148
Yellow Springs, OH 45387
$35, Robert S. Fogarty

Apalachee Quarterly
P.O. Box 20106
Tallahassee, FL 32316
$15, Barbara Hamby

Appalachian Heritage
Berea College
Berea, KY 40404
Sydney_Farr@Berea.edu
$18, Sidney Saylor Farr

Arkansas Review
Dept. of English and Philosophy
P.O. Box 1890
Arkansas State University
Stae University, AR 72467
$20, William Clements

Ascent
English Dept.

901 8th St.
Moorehead, MN 56562
ascent@cord.edu
$9, W. Scott Olsen

Atlantic Monthly
77 N. Washington Street
Boston, MA 02114
www.theatlantic.com
$15.94, C. Michael Curtis

Baffler
P.O. Box 378293
Chicago, IL 60637
$20, Thomas Frank, Keith White

Baltimore Review
P.O. Box 410
Riderwood, MD 21139
Barbara Westwood Diehl

Bananafish
P.O. Box 381332
Cambridge, MA 02238-1332
Robin Lippincott

Baybury Review
P.O. Box 462
Ephraim, WI 54211
$7.25, Janet St. John

Belletrist Review
P.O. Box 596
Plainville, CT 06062
$14.99, Marc Saegaert

Bellingham Review
MS 9053
Western Washington University
Bellingham, WA 98225
$10, Robin Hemly

Bellowing Ark
P.O. Box 45637
Seattle, WA 98145
$15, Robert R. Ward

Beloit Fiction Journal
Beloit College
P.O. Box 11
Beloit, WI 53511
$9, Fred Burwell

Big Sky Journal
P.O. Box 1069
Bozeman, MT 59771-1069
bsj@mcn.net
$22, Allen Jones, Brian Baise

Black Dirt
Midwest Farmer's Market
Elgin Community College
1700 Spartan Drive
Elgin, IL 60123-7193
$10, Rachel Tecza

Black Warrior Review
P.O. Box 2936
Tuscaloosa, AL 35487-2936
www.sa.ua.edu/osm/bwr
$14, Christopher Chambers

Blood & Aphorisms
P.O. Box 702
Toronto, Ontario
M5S ZY4 Canada
www.interlog.com/-fiction
$18, Michelle Alfano, Dennis Black

BOMB
New Art Publications
10th floor
594 Broadway
New York, NY 10012
www.bombsite.com
$18, Betsy Sussler

Border Crossings
Y300-393 Portage Avenue
Winnipeg, Manitoba
R3B 3H6 Canada
$23, Meeka Walsh

Boston Book Review
30 Brattle Street, 4th floor
Cambridge, MA 02138
www.BostonBookReview.com
$24, Constantine Theoharis

Boston Review
Building E53
Room 407
Cambridge, MA 02139
$15, editorial board

Bottomfish
DeAnza College
21250 Stevens Creek Blvd.
Cupertino, CA 95014
$5, David Denny

Boulevard
4579 Laclede Avenue #332
St. Louis, MO 63108
$12, Richard Burgin

Briar Cliff Review
3303 Rebecca Street
P.O. Box 2100
Sioux City, IA 51104-2100
$4, Phil Hey

Bridges
P.O. Box 24839
Eugene, OR 97402
$15, Clare Kinberg

The Bridge
14050 Vernon Street
Oak Park, MI 48237
$8, Jack Zucker

Button
Box 26
Lunenberg, MA 01462
Sally Cragin

BUZZ
11835 West Olympic Blvd.
Suite 450
Los Angeles, CA 90064
$14.95, Renee Vogel

Callaloo
Dept. of English
Wilson Hall
University of Virginia
Charlottesville, VA 22903
www.press.jhu.edu/journals/cal
$35, Charles H. Rowell

Calyx
P.O. Box B
Corvallis, OR 97339
www.proaxis.com/-calyx
$18, Margarita Donnelly

Canadian Fiction
Box 946, Station F
Toronto, Ontario
M4Y 2N9 Canada
$34.24, Geoffrey Hancock

Capilano Review
Capilano College
2055 Purcell Way
North Vancouver,
British Columbia
V7J 3H5 Canada
$25, Robert Sherrin

Carolina Quarterly
Greenlaw Hall 066A
University of North Carolina
Chapel Hill, NC 27514
www.unc.edu/student/orgs/cquarter
$10, rotating

Chariton Review
Division of Language & Literature
Northeast Missouri State University
Kirksville, MO 63501
$9, Jim Barnes

Chattahoochee Review
DeKalb Community College
2101 Womack Road
Dunwoody, GA 30338-4497
$16, Lawrence Hetrick

Chelsea
P.O. Box 773
Cooper Station
New York, NY 10276
$13, Richard Foerster

Chicago Quarterly Review
517 Sherman Avenue
Evanston, IL 60202
*$10, S. Afzal Haider, Jane Lawrence,
   Brian Skinner*

Chicago Review
5801 South Kenwood
University of Chicago
Chicago, IL 60637
humanities.uchicago.edu/

humanities/review
$18, Andrew Rathman

Cimarron Review
205 Morrill Hall
Oklahoma State University
Stillwater, OK 74078-0135
$12, E.P. Walkiewicz

Clackamas Literary Review
196 South Molalla Ave.
Oregon City, OR 97045
www.clakamas.cc.or.us/clr
$10, Jeff Knorr and Tim Schell

Colorado Review
Department of English
Colorado State University
Fort Collins, CO 80523
creview@vines.colostate.edu
$18, David Milofsky

Columbia
415 Dodge
Columbia University
New York, NY 10027
$15, Ellen Umanksy and Neil Azevedo

Commentary
165 East 56th Street
New York, NY 10022
103115.2375@compuserve.com
$39, Neal Kozodoy

Confrontation
English Department
C. W. Post College of Long Island
   University
Greenvale, NY 11548
$8, Martin Tucker

Conjunctions
21 East 10th St.
#3E
New York, NY 10003
www.conjunctions.com
$18, Bradford Morrow

Cottonwood
Box J, Kansas Union
University of Kansas

Lawrence, KS 66045
$10, Tom Lorenz

Crab Creek Review
4462 Whitman Ave. N.
Seattle, WA 98103
$8, Kimberly Allison, Harris Levinson,
Laura Sinai, Terri Stone

Crab Orchard Review
Dept. of English
Southern Illinois University at
Carbondale
Carbondale, IL 62901
www.siu.edu/-orchard
$10, Jon Tribble

Cream City Review
University of Wisconsin, Milwaukee
P.O. Box 413
Milwaukee, WI 53201
www.uwm.edu/Dept/English/ccr/
tccrhome.htm
$12, rotating

Crescent Review
P.O. Box 15069
Chevy Chase, MD 20825-5069
$21, J. Timothy Holland

Crucible
Barton College
College Station
Wilson, NC 27893
Terence Grimes

Cut Bank
Department of English
University of Montana
Missoula, MT 59812
$12, Cat Haglund, Pamela Kennedy

Denver Quarterly
University of Denver
Denver, CO 80208
$25, Bin Ramke

Descant
P.O. Box 314, Station P
Toronto, Ontario

M5S 2S8 Canada
$25, Karen Mulhallen

Descant
Department of English
Texas Christian University
Box 32872
Fort Worth, TX 76129
$12, Neal Easterbrook

DoubleTake
Center for Documentary Studies
55 Davis Square
Somerville, MA 02144
www.duke.edu/doubletake
$32, Robert Coles, Alex Harris

Eagle's Flight
P.O. Box 832
Granite, OK 73547
$5, Rekha Kulkarni

Elle
1633 Broadway
New York, NY 10019
$24, Patricia Towers

Epoch
251 Goldwin Smith Hall
Cornell University
Ithaca, NY 14853-3201
$11, Michael Koch

Esquire
250 West 55th Street
New York, NY 10019
$17.94, Rust Hills,
Adrienne Miller

Eureka Literary Magazine
Eureka College
P.O. Box 280
Eureka, IL 61530
$10, Loren Logsdon

event
c/o Douglas College
P.O. Box 2503
New Westminster, British Columbia
V3L 5B2 Canada
$15, Calvin Wharton

Fiction
Fiction, Inc.
Department of English
The City College of New York
New York, NY
www.ccny.cuny.edu/fiction/fiction.htm
$7, Mark Mirsky

Fiddlehead
UNB Box 4400
University of New Brunswick
Fredericton, New Brunswick
E3B 5A3 Canada
$16, Norman Ravvin

Fish Stories Literary Annual
5412 N. Clark, South Suite
Chicago, IL 60640
$10.95, Amy G. Davis

Five Points
Department of English
Georgia State University
University Plaza
Atlanta, GA 30303-3083
$15, Pam Durban

Florida Review
Department of English
University of Central Florida
P.O. Box 25000
Orlando, FL 32816
$7, Russell Kesler

Flyway
206 Ross Hall
Dept. of English
Iowa State University
Ames, IA 50011
$24, Debra Marquart

Forty-nine Words
School of Visual Arts
209 East 23rd St.
New York, NY 10010-3994
www.schoolofvisualarts.edu

Folio
Department of Literature
The American University

Washington, D.C. 20016
$10, Carolyn Parkhurst

Fourteen Hills
Department of Creative Writing
San Francisco State University
1600 Holloway Avenue
San Francisco, CA 94132
www.sfsu.edu/-cwriting/14hills.html
$12, rotating

Gargoyle
Paycock Press
c/o Atticus Books and Music
1508 U Street, NW
Washington, DC 20009
www.atticusbooks.com/gargoyle.html
$20, Richard Peabody and Lucinda
    Ebersole

Geist
1062 Homer Street #100
Vancouver, Canada
V6B 2W9
geist@geist.com
$20, Stephen Osborne

Georgetown Review
400 East College Street, Box 227
Georgetown, KY 40324
$10, John Fulmer

Georgia Review
University of Georgia
Athens, GA 30602
www.uga.edu/garev
$18, Stephen Corey (acting editor)

Gettysburg Review
Gettysburg College
Gettysburg, PA 17325
$24, Peter Stitt

Glimmer Train Stories
812 SW Washington Street
Suite 1205
Portland, OR 97205
www.glimmertrain.com
$29, Susan Burmeister, Linda Davies

Good Housekeeping
959 Eighth Avenue
New York, NY 10019
$17.97, Arleen L. Quarfoot

GQ
350 Madison Avenue
New York, NY 10017
gqmag@aol.com
$19.97, Ilena Silverman

Grain
Box 1154
Regina, Saskatchewan
S4P 3B4 Canada
www.sasknet.com/corporate/skywriter
$26.95, Diane Warren

Grand Street
131 Varick Street
New York, NY 10013
www.voyagerco.com/gs
$40, Jean Stein

Granta
1755 Broadway, 5th floor
New York, NY
10019-3780
$32, Ian Jack

Great River Review
211 West 7th Street
Winona, MN 55987
$12, Pamela Davies

Green Hills Literary Lantern
North Central Missouri College
Box 375
Trenton, MO 64683
$5.95, Jack Smith

Green Mountains Review
Box A 58
Johnson State College
Johnson, VT 05656
$12, Tony Whedon

Greensboro Review
Department of English
University of North Carolina
Greensboro, NC 27412

www.uncg.edu/mfa/grhmpg.htm
$8, Jim Clark

Gulf Coast
Department of English
University of Houston
4800 Calhoun Road
Houston, TX 77204-3012
$22, Marsha Recknagel, Merrill Greene

Gulf Stream
English Department
Florida International University
North Miami Campus
North Miami, FL 33181
$4, Lynne Barrett, John Dufresne

G.W. Review
Box 20B, The Marvin Center
800 21st Street
Washington, DC 20052
$9, Julie Will

Habersham Review
Piedmont College
Demorest, GA 30535-0010
*$12, David L. Greene, Lisa Hodgens
   Lumpkin*

Harper's Magazine
666 Broadway
New York, NY 10012
$18, Lewis H. Lapham

Harvard Review
Poetry Room
Harvard College Library
Cambridge, MA 02138
haviaris@fas.harvard.edu
$12, Stratis Haviaris

Hawaii Review
University of Hawaii
Department of English
1733 Donagho Road
Honolulu, HI 96822
$20, Jason Minani

Hayden's Ferry Review
Box 871502
Arizona State University

Tempe, AZ 85287-1502
HFR@asuvm.inre.asu.edu
*$10, Christopher Melka, Kathleen
Sullivan Porter*

High Plains Literary Review
180 Adams Street, Suite 250
Denver, CO 80206
$20, Robert O. Greer, Jr.

Hudson Review
684 Park Avenue
New York, NY 10021
$24, Paula Deitz, Frederick Morgan

Idaho Review
Boise State University
Dept. of English
1910 University Dr.
Boise, ID 83725
$8.95, Mitch Weiland

Image
323 S. Broad Street
P.O. Box 674
Kendall Square, PA 19348
www.imagejournal.org
$30, Gregory Wolfe

India Currents
P.O. Box 21285
San Jose, CA 95151
info@indicur.com
$19.95, Arviund Kumar

Indiana Review
Ballantine Hall 465
Bloomington, IN 47405
$12, Laura McCoid

Ink
P.O. Box 52558
St. George Postal Outlet
264 Bloor Street
Toronto, Ontario
M5S 1V0 Canada
$8, John Degan

Iowa Review
Department of English
University of Iowa
308 EPB

Iowa City, IA 52242
$18, David Hamilton, Mary Hussmann

Iris
Box 323 HSC
University of Virginia
Charlottesville, VA 22908
$9, Susan K. Brady

Italian Americana
University of Rhode Island
College of Continuing Education
199 Promenade Street
Providence, RI 02908
$15, Carol Bonomo Albright

Jewish Currents
22 East 17th Street, Suite 601
New York, NY 10003-3272
$20, editorial board

Journal
Department of English
Ohio State University
164 West 17th Avenue
Columbus, OH 43210
$8, Kathy Fagan, Michelle Herman

Kairos
Dundurn P.O. Box 33553
Hamilton, Ontario
L8P 4X4
Canada
$12.95, R.W. Megens

Kalliope
Florida Community College
3939 Roosevelt Blvd.
Jacksonville, FL 32205
$12.50, Mary Sue Koeppel

Karamu
English Department
Eastern Illinois University
Charleston, IL 61920
$6.50, Peggy L. Brayfield

Kenyon Review
Kenyon College
Gambier, OH 43022
$25, David H. Lynn

Laurel Review
Department of English
Northwest Missouri State University
Maryville, MO 64468
$8, David Slater, William Trowbridge,
  Beth Richards

Lilith
250 West 57th Street
New York, NY 10107
$16, Susan Weidman

Literal Latté
Suite 240
61 East 8th Street
New York, NY 10003
www.literal-latte.com
$25, Jenine Gordon Bockman

Literary Review
Fairleigh Dickinson University
285 Madison Avenue
Madison, NJ 07940
www.webdelsol.com/tlr
$18, Walter Cummins

Louisiana Literature
Box 792
Southeastern Louisiana University
Hammond, LA 70402
$12, Jack Bedell

Lynx Eye
1880 Hill Drive
Los Angeles, CA 90041
$20, Pam McCully, Kathryn Morrison

Madison Review
University of Wisconsin
Department of English
H. C. White Hall
600 North Park Street
Madison, WI 53706
$15, rotating

Malahat Review
University of Victoria
P.O. Box 1700
Victoria, British Columbia
V8W 2Y2 Canada

malahat@uvic.ca
$15, Derk Wynand

Manoa
English Department
University of Hawaii
Honolulu, HI 96822
wwwz.hawaii.edu/mjournal
$18, Frank Stewart

Many Mountains Moving
2525 Arapahoe Road
Suite E4-309
Boulder, CO 80302
$18, Naomi Horii, Marilyn Krysl

Massachusetts Review
South College, Box 37140
University of Massachusetts
Amherst, MA 01003-7140
$15, Jules Chametsky, Mary Heath, Paul
  Jenkins

Matrix
1455 de Paisonneuve Blvd. West
Suite LB-514-8
Montreal, Quebec
H3G IM8 Canada
$15, Terence Byrnes

Meridian
Dept. of English
University of Virginia
Charlottesville, VA 22903
$10, Ted Genoways

Michigan Quarterly Review
3032 Rackham Building
University of Michigan
Ann Arbor, MI 48109
$18, Laurence Goldstein

Mid-American Review
Department of English
Bowling Green State University
Bowling Green, OH 43403
$12, Michael Czyzniejewski

Midstream
110 East 59th Street
New York, NY 10022
$21, Joel Carmichael

Minnesota Review
Department of English
State University of New York
Stony Brook, NY 11794-5350
$12, Jeffrey Williams

Mississippi Mud
7119 Santa Fe Ave
Dallas, TX 75223
Joel Weinsten

Mississippi Review
University of Southern Mississippi
Southern Station, P.O. Box 5144
Hattiesburg, MS 39406-5144
sushi.st.usm.edu/mrw/index.html
$15, Frederick Barthelme

Missouri Review
1507 Hillcrest Hall
University of Missouri
Columbia, MO 65211
www.missourireview.org
$19, Speer Morgan

Ms.
230 Park Avenue
New York, NY 10169
ms@echonyc.com
$45, Marcia Ann Gillespie

Nassau Review
English Department
Nassau Community College
One Education Drive
Garden City, NY 11530-6793
Paul A. Doyle

Nebraska Review
Writer's Workshop, ASH 212
University of Nebraska
Omaha, NE 68182-0324
unomaha.edu/-jreed
$11, James Reed

New Delta Review
Creative Writing Program
English Department
Louisiana State University
Baton Rouge, LA 70803
$10, Andrew Spear

New England Review
Middlebury College
Middlebury, VT 05753
www.middlebury.edu/nerview
$23, Stephen Donadio

New Letters
University of Missouri
4216 Rockhill Road
Kansas City, MO 64110
$17, James McKinley

New Orleans Review
P.O. Box 195
Loyola University
New Orleans, LA 70118
$18, Ralph Adamo

New Orphic Review
1095 Victoria Drive
Vancouver, BC
Canada V5L 4G3
$25, Ernest Hekkanen

New Quarterly
English Language Proficiency
   Programme
University of Waterloo
Waterloo, Ontario
N2L 3G1 Canada
$11.50, Peter Hinchcliffe,
   Kim Jernigan, Mary Merikle,
   Linda Kenyon

New Renaissance
26 Heath Road #11
Arlington, MA 02174
wmichaud@gwi.net
$11.50, Louise T. Reynolds

New Yorker
25 West 43rd Street
New York, NY 10036
www.enews.com/magazines/
   new_yorker
$32, David Remnick

New York Stories
English Dept.
La Guardia Community College
31-10 Thomson Ave

Long Island City, NY 11101
wdsblaine@aol.com
$15, Michael Blaine

Nimrod
Arts and Humanities Council
    of Tulsa
2210 South Main Street
Tulsa, OK 74114
www.utulsa.edu/Nimrod
$15, Francine Ringold

North American Review
University of Northern Iowa
1222 West 27th Street
Cedar Falls, IA 50614
webdelsol.com/NorthAmReview/NAR
$18, Robley Wilson, Jr.

North Dakota Quarterly
University of North Dakota
P.O. Box 8237
Grand Forks, ND 58202
ndq@sage.und.nodak.edu
$25, Robert Lewis

Northwest Review
369 PLC
University of Oregon
Eugene, OR 97403
$20, John Witte

Notre Dame Review
Department of English
University of Notre Dame
Notre Dame, IN 46556
$15, Valerie Sayers

Oasis
P.O. Box 626
Largo, FL 34649-0626
oasislit@aol.com
$22, Neal Storrs

Ohio Review
Ellis Hall
Ohio University
Athens, OH 45701-2979
$16, Wayne Dodd

Ontario Review
9 Honey Brook Drive

Princeton, NJ 08540
www.ontarioreviewpress.com
$12, Raymond J. Smith

Open City
225 Lafayette Street
Suite 1114
New York, NY 10012
$24, Thomas Beller, Daniel Pinchbeck

Other Voices
University of Illinois at Chicago
Department of English
(M/C 162) 601 South Morgan Street
Chicago, IL 60680
$20, Lois Hauselman

Oxford American
115½ South Lamar
Oxford, MS 38655
$16, Marc Smirnoff

Oxford Magazine
Bachelor Hall
Oxford, OH 45056
$8, David Mitchell Goldberg

Oxygen
535 Geary Street
San Fransisco, CA 94102
$14, Richard Hack

Oyster Boy Review
103B Hanna Street
Carrboro, NC 27510
$12, Chad Driscoll, Damon Suave

Paris Review
541 East 72nd Street
New York, NY 10021
www.voyagerco.com/PR
$34, George Plimpton

Parting Gifts
3413 Wilshire Dr.
Greensboro, NC 27408-2923
Robert Bixby

Partisan Review
236 Bay State Road
Boston, MA 02215
$22, William Phillips

Playboy
Playboy Building
919 North Michigan Avenue
Chicago, IL 60611
www.playboy.com
$24, Alice K. Turner

Pleiades
Department of English
Central Missouri State University
P.O. Box 800
Warrensburg, MO 64093
$10, R. M. Kinder

Ploughshares
Emerson College
100 Beacon Street
Boston, MA 02116
www.emerson.edu/ploughshares
$21, Don Lee

Porcupine
P.O. Box 259
Cedarburg, WI 53012
$13.95, group editorship

Potpourri
P.O. Box 8278
Prairie Village, KS 66208
Potporpub@aol.com
$12, Polly W. Swafford

Pottersfield Portfolio
The Gatsby Press
5280 Green Street, P.O. Box 27094
Halifax, Nova Scotia
B3H 4M8 Canada
www.chebucto.ns.ca/culture/WFNS/
    pottersfield/potters.html
$18, Ian Colford

Prairie Fire
423-100 Arthur Street
Winnipeg, Manitoba
R3B 1H3 Canada
$24, Andris Taskans

Prairie Schooner
201 Andrews Hall
University of Nebraska

Lincoln, NE 68588-0334
$22, Hilda Raz

Press
125 West 72nd Street
Suite 3-M
New York, NY 10023
www.paradasia.com/press
$24, Daniel Roberts

Prism International
Department of Creative Writing
University of British Columbia
Vancouver, British Columbia
V6T 1W5 Canada
www.arts.ubc.ca/prism
$16, rotating

Provincetown Arts
650 Commercial Street
Provincetown MA 02657
$10, Christopher Busa

Puerto del Sol
P.O. Box 3E
Department of English
New Mexico State University
Las Cruces, NM 88003
$10, Kevin McIlvoy

Quarry Magazine
P.O. Box 1061
Kingston, Ontario
K7L 4Y5 Canada
$22, Mary Cameron

Quarterly West
312 Olpin Union
University of Utah
Salt Lake City, UT 84112
$12, Margot Schilpp

RE:AL
School of Liberal Arts
Stephen F. Austin State University
P.O. Box 13007
SFA Station
Nacogdoches, TX 75962
$15, Dale Hearell

Red Rock Review
English Dept. J2A

Community College of Southern
Nevada
3200 East Cheyanne Ave
North Las Vegas, NV 89030
$9.50, H. Lee Barnes

Redbook
959 Eighth Avenue
New York, NY 10017
$11.97, Dawn Raffel

Riversedge
Dept. of English
University of Texas, Pan-American
1201 West University Drive, CAS 266
Edinburg, TX 78539-2999
$12, Dorey Schmidt

River Styx
Big River Association
14 South Euclid
St. Louis, MO 63108
$20, Richard Newman

Room of One's Own
P.O. Box 46160
Station D
Vancouver, British Columbia
V6J 5G5 Canada
$22, collective

Rosebud
P.O. Box 459
Cambridge, WI 53523
$18, Roderick Clark

Salamander
48 Ackers Avenue
Brookline, MA 02146
$12, Jennifer Barber

Salmagundi
Skidmore College
Saratoga Springs, NY 12866
$18, Robert Boyers

Salt Hill
Syracuse University
English Dept.
Syracuse, NY 13244
$7, Caryb Koplik

San Jose Studies
c/o English Department
San Jose State University
One Washington Square
San Jose, CA 95192
$12, John Engell, D. Mesher

Santa Monica Review
Center for the Humanities
Santa Monica College
1900 Pico Boulevard
Santa Monica, CA 90405
$12, Lee Montgomery

Seattle Review
Padelford Hall, GN-30
University of Washington
Seattle, WA 98195
$9, Colleen McElroy

Seventeen
850 Third Avenue
New York, NY 10022
$14.95, Susan Brenna

Sewanee Review
University of the South
Sewanee, TN 37375-4009
www.sewanee.edu/sreview/home.html
$18, George Core

Shenandoah
Washington and Lee University
P.O. Box 722
Lexington, VA 24450
www.wlu.edu/-shenando
$15, R. T. Smith

The Slate
Box 58119
Minneapolis, MN 55458
$15, Chris Dall, Rachel Fulkerson,
   Jessica Morris

Sonora Review
Department of English
University of Arizona
Tucson, AZ 85721
sonora@u.arizona.edu
$12, rotating

So to Speak
4400 University Drive
George Mason University
Fairfax, VA 22030-444
$10, Anne Bloomsburg

South Carolina Review
Department of English
Clemson University
Clemson, SC 29634-1503
$10, Wayne Chapman, Donna Hasty
  Winchell

South Dakota Review
University of South Dakota
P.O. Box 111 University Exchange
Vermillion, SD 57069
$15, Brian Bedard

Southern Exposure
P.O. Box 531
Durham, NC 27702
southern_exposure@14south.org
$24, Jordan Green

Southern Humanities Review
9088 Haley Center
Auburn University
Auburn, AL 36849
$15, Dan R. Latimer, Virginia M.
  Kouidis

Southern Review
43 Allen Hall
Louisiana State University
Baton Rouge, LA 70803
$20, James Olney, Dave Smith

Southwest Review
Southern Methodist University
P.O. Box 4374
Dallas, TX 75275
$20, Willard Spiegelman

Spindrift
1507 East 53rd St. #649
Chicago, IL 60615
$10, Mark Anderson-Wilk

Story
1507 Dana Avenue

Cincinnati, OH 45207
$22, Lois Rosenthal

Story Quarterly
P.O. Box 1416
Northbrook, IL 60065
$12, Anne Brashler, M.M. Hayes

Sun
107 North Roberson Street
Chapel Hill, NC 27516
$30, Sy Safransky

Sun Dog
The Southeast Review
406 Williams Building
Florida State University
Tallahassee, FL 32306-1036
$8, Russ Franklin

Sycamore Review
Department of English
Heavilon Hall
Purdue University
West Lafayette, IN 47907
www.sla.purdue.edu/academic/engl/
  sycamore
$10, rotating

Talking River Review
Division of Literature
Lewis-Clark State College
500 8th Avenue
Lewiston, ID 83501
$10, group editorship

Tampa Review
University of Tampa
401 Kennedy Blvd.
Tampa, FL 33606-1490
$10, Richard Matthews

Thema
Box 74109
Metairie, LA 70053-4109
$16, Virginia Howard

Thin Air
P.O. Box 23549
Flagstaff, AZ 86002
$9, Jeff Huebner,
  Rob Morrill

Third Coast
Dept. of English
Western Michigan University
Kalamazoo, MI 49008-5092
www.wmich.edu/thirdcoast
$11, Theresa Coty O'Neill

13th Moon
Department of English
SUNY at Albany
Albany, NY 12222
$18, Judith Emlyn Johnson

32 Pages
Rain Crow Publishing
101-308 Andrew Place
West Lafayette, IN 47906-3932
$10, Michael S. Manley

Threepenny Review
P.O. Box 9131
Berkeley, CA 94709
$16, Wendy Lesser

Tikkun
5100 Leona Street
Oakland, CA 94619
www.tikkun.org
$36, Michael Lerner

Timber Creek Review
3283 UNCG Station
Greensboro, NC 27413
timber_creek_review@hoopsmail.com
$15, John Freiemuth

Trafika
P.O. Box 250822
New York, NY 10025-1536
$35, Scott Lewis, Krister Swartz, Jeffrey
Young

TriQuarterly
2020 Ridge Avenue
Northwestern University
Evanston, IL 60208
$24, Susan Firestone Hahn

University of Windsor Review
Department of English
University of Windsor

Windsor, Ontario
N9B 3P4 Canada
$19.95, Alistair MacLeod

Virginia Quarterly Review
One West Range
Charlottesville, VA 22903
$18, Staige D. Blackford

Wascana Review
English Department
University of Regina
Regina, Saskatchewan
S4S 0A2 Canada
$10, Kathleen Wall

Weber Studies
Weber State College
Ogden, UT 84408
$20, Sherwin Howard

Wellspring
770 Tonkawa Road
Long Lake, MN 55356
$8, Meg Miller

West Branch
Department of English
Bucknell University
Lewisburg, PA 17837
$7, Robert Love Taylor,
Karl Patten

Western Humanities Review
University of Utah
Salt Lake City, UT 84112
$20, Barry Weller

Whetstone
Barrington Area Arts Council
P.O. Box 1266
Barrington, IL 60011
$7.25, Sandra Berris, Marsha Portnoy,
Jean Tolle

Wind
RFD Route 1
P.O. Box 809K
Pikeville, KY 41501
lit-arts.com/wind/magazine.htm
$10, Charlie Hughes, Leatha Kendrick

Witness
Oakland Community College
Orchard Ridge Campus
27055 Orchard Lake Road
Farmington Hills, MI 48334
$12, Peter Stine

Worcester Review
6 Chatham Street
Worcester, MA 01690
$10, Rodger Martin

Xavier Review
Xavier University
Box 110C
New Orleans, LA 70125
$10, Thomas Bonner, Jr.

Yale Review
1902A Yale Station
New Haven, CT 06520
$27, J. D. McClatchy

Yalobusha Review
P.O. Box 186
University, MS 38677-0186
$6, rotating

Yankee
Yankee Publishing, Inc.
Dublin, NH 03444
$22, Judson D. Hale, Sr.

Zoetrope; All-Story
AZX Publications
126 Fifth Avenue, Suite 300
New York, NY 10011
www.zoetrope-stories.com
Adrienne Brodeur

ZYZZYVA
41 Sutter Street, Suite 1400
San Francisco, CA 94104
www.webdelsol.com/ZYZZYVA
$28, Howard Junker